Daniels Bros

Illustrated Guide for Amateur Gardeners

Spring 1914

Daniels Bros

Illustrated Guide for Amateur Gardeners
Spring 1914

ISBN/EAN: 9783741198410

Manufactured in Europe, USA, Canada, Australia, Japa

Cover: Foto ©Andreas Hilbeck / pixelio.de

Manufactured and distributed by brebook publishing software
(www.brebook.com)

Daniels Bros

Illustrated Guide for Amateur Gardeners

Price 1/-

DANIELS BROS
· LIMITED ·
ILLUSTRATED GUIDE
FOR
Amateur Gardeners
· SPRING · 1914 ·

DANIELS BROS LTD. SEED GROWERS & NURSERYMEN. NORWICH

THE ROYAL NORFOLK SEED ESTABLISHMENT,

NORWICH, ENGLAND.

Head Office and Retail Establishment.
ROYAL ARCADE.
Telephone — No. 32

Seed Warehouses.
BEDFORD STREET.
Private Telephone.

Seed Grounds.
IPSWICH ROAD AND EATON
Private Telephone

Nurseries.
THE TOWN CLOSE NURSERIES.
NEWMARKET ROAD.
Telephone — No. 38

GOLD MEDAL AWARDED BY THE
ROYAL AGRICULTURAL SOCIETY
JUNE, 1911

TERMS OF BUSINESS, &c.

☛ All orders from unknown Correspondents must be accompanied by a sufficient Remittance or Bankers' or other satisfactory References. To save cost and trouble of Booking, a Remittance should in all cases be sent with Orders under 10s. in value.

ACCOUNTS—DISCOUNTS.—All accounts are due net in three months; we however allow a discount of 5 %, i.e., 1s. in the pound, on all orders of 20s. and upwards, when accompanied by a remittance, or when paid within fourteen days of date of invoice.

ADDRESSES.—Full Name and Address should be sent with every communication, and nearest Railway Station should be stated with every order, as much time is thereby saved, especially in our busiest season, when we often receive from 1000 to 1500 letters daily. In consequence of this large correspondence, we suggest that, at all seasons, Cut Flower Orders and other Urgent Letters should be so marked on the envelope.

CARRIAGE ON GOODS.—We pay carriage on the following Articles to any address in the British Isles :—
All KITCHEN GARDEN and FLOWER SEEDS offered in this Catalogue.
SEED POTATOES, CULINARY ROOTS, and HORTICULTURAL REQUISITES, if included in a general Garden Seed order of the value of 20s. in all.
DWARF and BUSH ROSES of the value of 7s. 6d. and upwards.
STANDARD ROSES   "   "   10s. 0d.   "
ROSES IN POTS   "   "   15s. 0d.   "
We also pay carriage to any Station on the G.E.R. or Mid. & G.N. Joint Line on :—
SEED POTATOES, CULINARY ROOTS, &c., to the value of 10s. and upwards
Owing to their heavy weight, in proportion to their value, we regret that we cannot pay carriage on the following :—
ROSES of less value than the amounts mentioned above.
TREES AND SHRUBS } But we continue to enclose extra plants, free of charge, to partially meet the cost of carriage.
PLANTS IN POTS
HORTICULTURAL SUNDRIES, such as Silver Sand, Mats, Tools, &c., when ordered alone, and of less value than 20s
MUSHROOM SPAWN

CHANGE OF RESIDENCE.—We shall esteem it a favour if our customers, on changing their residences, will kindly favour us with their new addresses, so that we may be able to send them our Catalogues as usual.

CHEQUES, MONEY ORDERS, AND POSTAL ORDERS.—Should be made payable to DANIELS BROS. LIMITED, and crossed "BARCLAY & CO., LIMITED," Bankers, Norwich. Letters containing coin must be registered according to Post Office regulations.

CO-OPERATION IN SENDING ORDERS.—Allotment holders, Cottagers, and members of Cottagers' Garden Societies, requiring individually but small quantities of Seeds and Seed Potatoes, if they join together in sending their orders, will be allowed a special discount of ten per cent., to be taken in seeds, besides the usual discount of five per cent. for cash, thus :— for every 20s. remitted, 23s. worth of seeds may be ordered. No order can be recognised under these terms unless over the net value of One Pound, and accompanied by prepayment in full. Each order will be packed separately and all can be consigned in one package, but full name and address of each customer ordering under this arrangement should be sent.

CORRESPONDENCE. Most Important.—Our customers having occasion to write to us respecting any order previously sent by them, will much facilitate attention to their letters if they will kindly state the date on which the order was sent, and if remittance was enclosed name the amount; this will enable us more readily to identify their orders on reference to our Registers.

ORDER EARLY.—All orders are executed in the rotation in which they are received, and we would ask our customers to send us their orders as soon as possible after receiving this Catalogue. If every one waits for favourable weather, or until seeds are actually needed for sowing, it involves such a rush that an excessive strain is put upon our large staff of executants, and sometimes delay is as a consequence unavoidable.

PACKAGES.—All packages are charged at the lowest cost price, and are not returnable, unless sent back in good condition, and Carriage Paid, within fourteen days of receipt of goods. Customers are particularly requested to put their name and address on each package, and to advise us by post when returned, or they cannot be credited.
All Fruit Trees, Roses, and Shrubs, will be so packed as to stand a journey of a week or ten days without injury. Should the packages arrive at their destination during a severe frost, it will be advisable not to unpack them, but to keep them cool and moist out of the reach of frost.

PACKETS.—Will our customers kindly note that, in all cases where Seeds are quoted by the "Packet," this is the minimum quantity that we can supply; smaller quantities or half-packets are not sold by us.

RECOMMENDATIONS.—The many kind recommendations to new customers with which we have been favored in the past have been very gratifying. Should any of our customers have friends requiring Seeds, Plants, &c., to whom a copy of our *Illustrated Guide* would be acceptable, we shall feel much obliged by an intimation of the fact.

WARRANTY.—We believe that all Seeds, Bulbs and Roots sold by us are of the description and kind specified by us at the time of sale, but owing to the practical impossibility in many cases of being certain of this, we give no undertaking that such Seeds, Bulbs, or Roots will correspond with the description under which they are sold, and we make all sales subject to this condition. We further give no warranty, express or implied, as to their growth, description, quality or productiveness, and will not be in any way responsible for the crop. If the Purchaser does not accept the goods sold to him, on these terms, they are at once to be returned to us

TELEGRAPHIC ADDRESS:—DANIELS NORWICH

January 1st, 1914

SEEDSMEN
BY APPOINTMENT
TO HIS MAJESTY
KING GEORGE V.

NURSERYMEN
BY APPOINTMENT
TO HER MAJESTY
QUEEN ALEXANDRA.

To·our·Customers

In once again issuing a new edition of our ILLUSTRATED GUIDE FOR AMATEUR GARDENERS, we take the opportunity of sincerely thanking our numerous customers for their continued patronage during the past year, and we beg to assure them we will continue to do our utmost to merit a continuance of their support.

We highly appreciate the many recommendations given by our customers to their friends, and are always pleased to forward Catalogues, free of charge, on receipt of the names and addresses of anyone to whom they may be of interest.

THE SEED HARVEST OF 1913. Although many of the growing seed crops were said to be suffering from the very dry weather in early Summer, we are pleased to state that the yield of most kinds of Peas and other Garden Seeds has been, on the whole, decidedly better than in 1912, whilst the germinating powers of all are excellent. Runner Beans were however a short crop, though of very good growth. We have secured an ample supply of the finest stocks of seed for our very large retail trade, and have pleasure in stating that in many instances we are able to quote lower prices than those of last year.

SEED POTATOES. Owing to the excessively dry weather of June and early July, all the early varieties are again scarce, and we strongly advise our customers to place orders promptly for these. All the later varieties however, yielded an excellent crop, and are reasonable in price. We would draw attention to the fine new varieties we offer this season, which we can highly recommend as worthy of a trial.

FLOWER SEEDS. These have been for many years a special feature in our large seed business, our very fine strains of Asters, Stocks, and other Choice Annuals and Florists' Flower Seeds having secured for us a widely extended reputation. Our list has again been thoroughly revised, and many fine novelties for the coming Season have been added.

OUR NURSERIES. We have an unusually well-grown stock of the Choicest Fruit Trees, Roses, Clematises, and other Hardy Climbers, Ornamental Trees and Shrubs, Hardy Herbaceous Plants, Florists' Flowers, &c. Our trade during the Autumn has been exceptionally brisk, and although we have good stocks on hand, we anticipate heavy demands during the coming Spring, and would therefore advise our customers to provide for the filling up of gaps or for starting new planting schemes as early as possible.

We have made every possible preparation for the prompt execution of orders, but as we are invariably very much pressed at the height of the sowing season, we venture to ask our regular customers to favour us with their orders as early as possible in the New Year, whatever may be the state of the weather.

January 1st, 1914. **DANIELS BROS., Ltd.**

KITCHEN GARDEN SEEDS.

☞ Our large experience in this department has enabled us to select the finest possible stocks, the same being grown on our own grounds or under our personal supervision. The growth of all seeds is carefully tested before sending out, and customers ordering from us may thoroughly rely on being supplied with the best and newest varieties, all of good growing quality.

DANIELS' COMPLETE COLLECTIONS OF CHOICE VEGETABLE SEEDS.

All Package and Carriage Free.

These Collections, of which we annually sell immense quantities, are carefully made up with seeds of finest quality in best varieties from each class with a view of furnishing an ample supply of Choice Vegetables throughout the year, and will be found extremely valuable for those who have not sufficient time or experience for making their own selection.

As our Collections are made up on a most liberal scale, intending purchasers will kindly bear in mind that it is only by having Seeds specially grown, and by preparing the packets beforehand in large numbers, that we can be so liberal in the quantity of the Seeds supplied for the amount charged, and that by ordering our selections, instead of making their own, will reap an advantage of at least 25 per cent. below the general Catalogue prices. We therefore wish it to be understood that no reduction, alteration, or substitution can be allowed in any of the collections. When ordering please quote Number and Price of the Collection required.

No. 1.	Contains 26 quarts of Choice Peas	And all	£5	5	0
No. 2.	Contains 20 quarts of Choice Peas	other	£4	4	0
No. 3.	Contains 16 quarts of Choice Peas	Seeds in	£3	3	0
No. 4.	Contains 12 quarts of Choice Peas	proportion	£2	2	0

No. 5. Daniels' Complete Collection, £1 11 6

Package and Carriage Free. All the best kinds for succession.

18 pints	Peas, Early, Medium, and Late	2 pkts.	Cauliflower, Autumn Giant, &c.	5 ozs.	Onion, Bedfordshire Champion, &c.
4 pints	Broad Beans				
2 pints	French Beans	2 pkts.	Celery, Giant Red and White	1 oz.	Parsley, Fine Curled
2 pints	Runner Beans	1 pkt.	Couve Tronchuda	3 ozs.	Parsnip, Hollow-crowned
2 pkts.	Beet, Crimson Perfection, &c.	1 pint	Cress, Plain	6 ozs.	Radish, Long and Turnip
1 pkt.	Borecole, Curled	2 pkts.	Cucumber, Frame and Ridge	5 ozs.	Spinach, Summer and Winter
2 pkts.	Brussels Sprouts, Colossal and Defiance	½ oz.	Endive, Curled	1 pkt.	Salsafy
		2 pkts.	Gourd or Pumpkin	3 ozs.	Turnip, Snowball, &c.
4 pkts.	Broccoli, Choice Sorts	½ oz.	Leek, Giant	2 pkts.	Vegetable Marrow
4 pkts.	Cabbage, Choice Sorts	4 pkts.	Lettuce, Cos and Cabbage	5 pkts.	Herbs
2 pkts.	Savoy, Drumhead, &c.	1 pint	Mustard, White	3 pkts.	Tomato, Choice Sorts
4 ozs.	Carrot, Scarlet Horn, &c.	1 pkt.	Melon, Choice	2 pkts.	Capsicum

No. 6. Daniels' Complete Collection, £1 1s.

Package and Carriage Free. All the best kinds for succession.

12 pints	Peas, Early, Medium, and Late	2 pkts.	Cauliflower, Autumn Giant, &c.	4 ozs.	Onion, White Spanish, &c.
3 pints	Broad Beans			2 ozs.	Parsnip, Hollow-crowned
1½ pint	French Beans	2 pkts.	Celery, Giant Red and White	4 ozs.	Radish, Long and Turnip
1 pint	Runner Beans	1 pkt.	Couve Tronchuda	4 ozs.	Spinach, Summer and Winter
1 pkt.	Beet, Crimson Perfection	8 ozs.	Cress, Plain and Curled	2 ozs.	Turnip, Snowball and Golden Ball
1 pkt.	Borecole, Curled	2 pkts.	Cucumber, Frame and Ridge		
2 pkts.	Brussels Sprouts, Colossal and Defiance	1 pkt.	Endive, Curled	1 pkt.	Vegetable Marrow, Large Cream
		2 pkts.	Gourd or Pumpkin		
3 pkts.	Broccoli, Early and Late	1 pkt.	Leek, Giant	4 pkts.	Herbs, Sweet and Pot
3 pkts.	Cabbage, Defiance, &c.	3 pkts.	Lettuce, Cos and Cabbage	2 pkts.	Tomato, Scarlet Perfection and Open Air
½ oz.	Savoy, Drumhead	6 ozs.	Mustard, White		
3 ozs.	Carrot, Intermediate and Scarlet Horn	1 pkt.	Melon, Choice	1 pkt.	Capsicum, Long Red
		1 oz.	Parsley, Fine Curled		

A Prize Collection
Grown from Daniels' Pedigree Seeds

DANIELS' SPECIAL COLLECTION
🢜 FOR EXHIBITORS. 🢜

The following Special Collection of our Choice Stocks of Vegetable Seeds has been carefully selected and arranged, and will be found especially useful to growers for competition, and at the same time for a good succession of Vegetables for general use. Customers ordering this Collection will effect a saving of quite 33% below our usual Catalogue prices.

OUR SPECIAL COLLECTION FOR EXHIBITORS.
Price 10s. 6d. Post Free.

CONTAINS THE FOLLOWING LIBERAL ASSORTMENT.

4 pkts.	Peas, Choice	1 pkt.	Cabbage, Intermediate Red	1 pkt.	Onion, Golden Globe
1 pkt.	Broad Beans, Daniels' Selected Long-pod	1 pkt.	Cauliflower, Daniels' King	1 oz.	Parsnip, Daniels' Improved
		2 pkts.	Carrot, Telegraph and Scarlet Perfection	1 pkt.	Parsley, Daniels' Queen
1 pkt.	Runner Beans			1 oz.	Radish, New Scarlet Turnip
1 pkt.	Dwart Beans	1 pkt.	Celery, Exhibition Pink	1 oz.	„ Best of All
1 pkt.	Beet, Crimson Perfection	1 pkt.	Cucumber, Improved Telegraph	1 pkt.	Tomato, King George V.
1 pkt.	Brussels Sprouts, Colossal	1 pkt.	Leek, Champion	1 oz.	Turnip, Improved Snowball
1 pkt.	Broccoli, Norfolk Giant	2 pkts.	Lettuce, Giant White Cos and Queen of Summer	1 pkt.	„ Golden Gem
2 pkts.	Cabbage, Defiance and Little Queen			1 pkt.	Vegetable Marrow, Large Cream

No. 7. Daniels' Complete Collection, 12s. 6d.

Package and Carriage Free. All the best kinds for succession.

6	pints	Peas, Early, Medium, and Late	1	pkt.	Cauliflower, Choice	
1	pint	Broad Beans	1	pkt.	Celery	
1	pint	French Beans	4	ozs.	Cress, Plain and Curled	
1	pint	Runner Beans	2	pkts.	Cucumber, Ridge and Frame	
1	pkt.	Beet, Dark-leaved	1	pkt.	Endive, Curled	
1	pkt.	Borecole, Curled	1	pkt.	Gourd or Pumpkin	
1	pkt.	Brussels Sprouts	1	pkt.	Leek, Giant	
2	pkts.	Broccoli, Choice Sorts	2	pkts.	Lettuce, Cos and Cabbage	
2	pkts.	Cabbage, Choice Sorts	3	ozs.	Mustard, White	
1	pkt.	Savoy, Drumhead	2	ozs.	Onion, White Spanish, &c.	
2	pkts.	Carrot, Intermediate, &c.				

1	pkt.	Melon, Choice
1	pkt.	Parsley, Fine Curled
1	oz.	Parsnip, Hollow-crowned
2	ozs.	Radish, Long and Turnip
2	ozs.	Spinach, Round and Prickly
1½	oz.	Turnip, Snowball and Orange Jelly
1	pkt.	Vegetable Marrow
3	pkts.	Herbs, Sweet and Pot
2	pkts.	Tomato

" The 12s. 6d. Collection of Vegetable Seeds gave magnificent results. I have had things from you for over twenty years, and in no instance have I been disappointed."—Mr. A. WILLIAMS, Llandudno.

" I took First Prize for a Collection of Vegetables grown from your Seeds, and that is two years in succession."—W. BISHOP, Esq., Stoke D'Abernon.

" I won First Prize at our Show for a Collection of Vegetables grown from your Seeds."—Mr. H. DINALL, Hordham.

No. 8. Daniels' Complete Collection, 7s. 6d.

Package and Carriage Free. All the best kinds for succession.

4	pints	Peas, Early, Medium, and Late	1	oz.	Carrot, Intermediate	
1	pint	Broad Beans	1	pkt.	Cauliflower, Autumn Giant	
1	pint	French Beans	1	pkt.	Celery, Red and White	
½	pint	Runner Beans	2	ozs.	Cress, Plain	
1	pkt.	Beet, Dark-leaved	1	pkt.	Cucumber, Ridge	
1	pkt.	Borecole, Curled	2	pkts.	Lettuce, Cos and Cabbage	
1	pkt.	Brussels Sprouts	1	pkt.	Leek, Musselburgh	
1	pkt.	Broccoli	1	oz.	Mustard, White	
1	pkt.	Savoy, Drumhead	1	oz.	Onion, White Spanish	
1	pkt.	Cabbage				

1	pkt.	Parsley, Fine Curled
1	oz.	Parsnip, Hollow-crowned
1	pkt.	Pumpkin
2	ozs.	Radish, Long and Turnip
1	oz.	Spinach, Summer
1	oz.	Turnip, Snowball
1	pkt.	Vegetable Marrow
2	pkts.	Herbs
1	pkt.	Tomato

" I had a 7s. 6d. Collection of Vegetable Seeds from you last year which did very well and gave great satisfaction."—Mr. R. B. BEAUCHAMP, Langfield.

" Your 7s. 6d. Collection of Vegetable Seeds has always given me great satisfaction."—Mr. W. BRISTON, Culhook.

" I am pleased to say that I took First Prize for the best collection of Vegetables at our Show."—Capt. MYRTLE, Holyhead.

No. 9. Daniels' Cottager's Collection, 5s. 0d.

Package and Carriage Free. This collection is of exceptional value.

3	pkts.	Peas, for succession	1	pkt.	Savoy, Drumhead	
1	pkt.	Broad Beans	1	oz.	Carrot, Intermediate	
1	pkt.	Runner Beans	1	pkt.	Cauliflower	
1	pkt.	French Beans	1	pkt.	Celery, Mixed	
1	pkt.	Beet, Dark-leaved	1	oz.	Cress	
1	pkt.	Borecole, Curled	1	pkt.	Cucumber, Ridge	
1	pkt.	Brussels Sprouts	1	pkt.	Leek	
1	pkt.	Broccoli	1	pkt.	Lettuce, Cos and Cabbage, Mixed	
1	pkt.	Cabbage, Nonpareil				

1	oz.	Onion, White Spanish
1	pkt.	Parsley, Fine Curled
1	oz.	Parsnip, Hollow-crowned
1	pkt.	Gourd or Pumpkin
1	oz.	Radish, Mixed Turnip
1	oz.	Spinach, Round
1	pkt.	Tomato
1	oz.	Turnip
1	pkt.	Vegetable Marrow

" Your 5s. Collection of Vegetable Seeds turned out grand last year, so please forward another similar collection to my brother."—Mrs. J. BLACKIE, Southland.

" I am pleased to tell you that I had splendid crops of Vegetables from your 5s. Collection of Seeds."— Mr. W. B. VENUS, Barham.

" The 5s. Collection of Vegetable Seeds gave every satisfaction last year."—Mr. W. NEWSON, Birmingham.

No. 10. The Cottager's Packet, 2s. 9d. Post free.

Containing sixteen varieties of choice Vegetable Seeds, including fair quantities of
Peas, Runner Beans, Broccoli, Cabbage, Carrot, Lettuce, Onion, Radish, Turnip, &c.
This is a very cheap collection which can be highly recommended.

" I have had good results from your 2s. 9d. Collection of Vegetable Seeds."—Mr. A. W. HAGREN, Folkestone.

" Your 2s. 9d. Collection of Vegetable Seeds turned out excellent."—Mr. G. GRIMSDELL, High Wycombe.

" The Cottagers' Collection of Vegetable Seeds I had last year did remarkably well."—Mr. W. LANGDALE, Wold Newton.

DANIELS' SEEDS FOR EXPORT.

For many years past we have given special attention to this department, and we take the greatest care that only seeds of the finest stocks, and of the highest germinating quality, are supplied to our clients residing abroad. We have had great experience in packing, and the care we exercise in this respect and in the selection of the best varieties, invariably gives the highest satisfaction.

We have a large number of customers in India, Australia, New Zealand, China, Africa, United States, South America and other parts, to whom we shall at all times be pleased to refer with respect to the fine results obtained from the seeds we supply to our clients abroad.

From G. H. ORAM, Esq., Southgate.

"I had great success with your Seeds last year, in fact they were on view at Gull Lake, Saskatchewan. I speak more particularly of Beet and Turnip which were very fine; some of the Turnips weighed over six lbs., and not a bit stringy."

From The Rev. C. WOOD, White Bay, Newfoundland.

"I should very much liked you to have seen two crops we dug this year. The Potatoes were your Sensation. It was a sensation reminding me of your plate showing a crop dug at Windsor. The other was a crop of James' Scarlet Intermediate Carrot."

From Mr. S. BELCHER, Elgin, Canada.

"The Seeds I had from you did remarkably well, especially the Peas and Lettuces. I shall be surprised if you do not get some orders from this part next year."

From F. E. BUSH, Esq., Ootacamund, India.

"I would like you to know that the Seed Potatoes which you sent to me have arrived in good condition; also the three packages of Seeds you sent per Parcel Post arrived in most excellent condition."

From C. KENELIN GRANT, Esq., Sierra Leone.

"I received your last lot of Seeds and they are coming out first-rate."

A GARDEN CORNER. From F. FAIREY, Esq., Adelaide, showing Daniels' Flower Seeds growing in S. Australia.

From Capt. G. KENDALL CHANNER, Almora, India.

"The Seeds you sent me out last year were as usual excellent. I had the best Vegetable and Flower Garden in the Station."

From A. DOUGLAS SUTHERLAND, Esq., Adelaide, Australia.

"You may be glad to know that your reputation, good though it has always been in Adelaide, is of a much wider magnitude than ever before; and the courtesy and promptitude with which your clients are treated is greatly appreciated."

From Mr. H. KENNETT KADINA, Australia.

"The Seeds reached me safely last season, and I had very good luck with them. I took several Prizes at different Shows."

From Mr. C. OFFORD, Estcourt, Natal.

"I had some Seeds from you about five years ago through a gentleman in this country, and they were so successful I should like to send you another order."

From Mr. W. LINCOLN, Toowoomba, Queensland.

"I took Twelve First Prizes at our Royal Agricultural Society's Show. I also took First Prize for your Telegraph Carrot. The King Edward VII. Tomato gave the best results, out of eighteen different sorts, both for quality and quantity. Everybody said they were A1."

VEGETABLE AND FLOWER SEEDS.

Special Collections of Vegetable and Flower Seeds for Export are offered, Carriage Free, as below. Where our customers, however, prefer to make their own selection of varieties from the body of the Catalogue an extra amount should be added to their remittance towards the cost of packing and postage. In the case of heavy seeds, such as Peas and Beans, the postage is an important item. All Vegetable and Flower Seeds can be supplied at any time or season.

DANIELS' PARCEL POST COLLECTIONS.

VEGETABLE SEEDS.

These Collections, which are made up from the most reliable and suitable varieties for Foreign and Colonial climates, are composed of the sorts mentioned below, in boxes containing proportionate quantities.

Price 10s. 6d., 15s., £1 1s., £2 2s., £3 3s., and £5 5s.

Post or Carriage Free to all countries included in the Parcel Post Union.

Peas, Choice Sorts	Cucumber	Onion
Beans, Dwarf French	Kohl-rabi	Parsley
Beans, Runner	Capsicum	Radish
Beet, Garden	Cress	Herbs
Brussels Sprouts	Leek	Marrow, Vegetable
Cabbages	Lettuce, Cos	Turnip
Cauliflower	Lettuce, Cabbage	Spinach
Carrot	Mustard	Tomato
Celery	Melon	

FLOWER SEEDS.

We offer liberal Collections from the list given below, and other choice sorts, at the following rates.

Price 5s., 7s. 6d., 10s. 6d., 15s., £1 1s., £1 11s. 6d., £2 2s.

Post or Carriage Free to all countries included in the Parcel Post Union.

Asters	Dianthuses	Pansy
Antirrhinums	Gaillardias	Poppies
Balsams	Godetias	Portulaca
Begonias	Larkspur	Salpiglossis
Calliopsis	Marigolds	Stocks
Candytuft	Mignonette	Sweet Peas
Canary Creeper	Nasturtiums	Sweet Williams
Carnations	Nemesias	Verbena
Celosias	Petunias	Wallflower
Chrysanthemums	Phloxes	Zinnias, &c., &c.

☞ *All orders from unknown correspondents must be accompanied by a sufficient remittance.*

PRESENTS OF SEEDS TO FRIENDS ABROAD. We suggest that the above make most useful and acceptable presents from friends at home, serving as they do, to remind absentees of the old country.

PEAS.

Cultivation.—Peas form one of the most valuable of garden crops, and when once started into growth, require, under favourable conditions, little attention beyond the staking of such varieties as need support, and mulching and watering in dry weather. Peas require a good rich soil, which should be well trenched, and should receive a liberal supply of well-decomposed manure early in the season. They are essentially a moisture loving plant, and only when the ground is well prepared can really satisfactory results be assured. Given these conditions, it is possible by a succession of sowings to have a continuous supply of Peas for the table from June till October, or even later.

First early varieties should be sown from the middle of January onwards, and the best sorts in this class are **Daniels' Gem of the Season, Earliest of All,** and **The Pilot** ; if the seed is sown in boxes under glass in January, hardened off in a frame and planted out at the latter end of March or early in April, an advantage of ten days or a fortnight may be gained. Second early and main crop kinds should be sown in March and April, and for late use a succession of sowings at intervals from the beginning of May until the end of June should be made. For these sowings the tall varieties will be found more productive, and not so liable to mildew during hot weather. It should be borne in mind that although most of the **Wrinkled seeded** varieties may be sown in March, we do not recommend this unless the season is exceptionally favourable. We find from a careful record extending over ten years, that little if any advantage is gained by too early sowings, and that Peas sown at the beginning of April take less time to come to maturity than the earlier sown ones. If this rule was more generally followed, we should hear less about bad germination amongst this class of Peas especially in cold wet seasons. The seed should be sown in drills and covered about two inches deep ; allow four or five feet between each row unless it is desired to grow some other crop between, when the rows may be 12 to 15 feet apart. Let the rows run from north to south, thus allowing the plants to receive a maximum of light and air.

Peas suffer greatly from the depredations of all kinds of vermin, and it will always be found of advantage to give protection either by wire pea guards or some other means while the plants are growing. The rows should be earthed up before they are staked, and this should be done when the plants are about four inches high. If the tops of the sticks are cut evenly, and the pieces which are cut off placed between the large sticks at the base, they will prevent the plants from falling about, and give them an upward tendency from the start.

A good mulching of manure placed on each side of the row will help to retain the moisture in dry weather. Where this is not possible they must be regularly watered during dry periods, and liquid manure given once a week ; a mixture containing four ounces of Nitrate of Soda to one gallon of water will be found very useful for this purpose.

When it is desired to grow Peas for exhibition purposes the following points should be observed :—Sow the seed very thinly on ground that has been especially deeply trenched for the purpose, and which has been dressed with old farmyard manure or the remains of an old mushroom bed. If they are needed for early Summer Shows it may be desirable to raise the seed on turves in a greenhouse and transfer them bodily to the border when about four inches high, but, generally speaking, if the seed is sown in rows in March and April it will be found early enough. When the plants have shown about four blooms, pinch out the leader or top of the haulm. As soon as the pods have formed, choose the best shaped, and remove the others, leaving only two or three on each plant. Always select the strongest and healthiest plants for this purpose. When ready to gather, do not handle the pods, but cut off with scissors so as to retain their bloom.

NEW PEA, DANIELS' EXPRESS.

A grand new first early Marrowfat variety, growing to the height of about 18 inches, and of great productiveness, bearing a profusion of handsome dark green pods, 4½ to 5 inches in length, well filled with peas of the most delicious marrow flavour. In habit of growth it somewhat resembles Competitor, but the pods are much darker in colour and better filled. We can strongly recommend this as one of the finest first early varieties yet introduced. Per pint 1s. 6d. ; per quart 2s. 6d.

NEW PEA, HUNDREDFOLD.

A new early marrow of great productiveness ; it grows about 2 feet high, bearing a heavy crop of fine, handsome dark green pods 5 inches in length, well filled with fine peas of excellent flavour. This variety is well worthy of a trial, as it is sure to give satisfaction. Per pint 1s. 6d. ; per quart 2s. 6d.

THE PILOT.

This valuable introduction has taken a leading place amongst the most useful varieties, both for market and private garden purposes. It is a first early cropper producing deep green pods of the well-known Gradus type, and on account of its hardy constitution and the seed being round it may be sown early with the certainty of a crop. It is a vigorous branching plant, growing three feet in height, bearing a large proportion of the pods in pairs, which contain fine deep green peas of excellent marrow flavour. Per quart 2s.

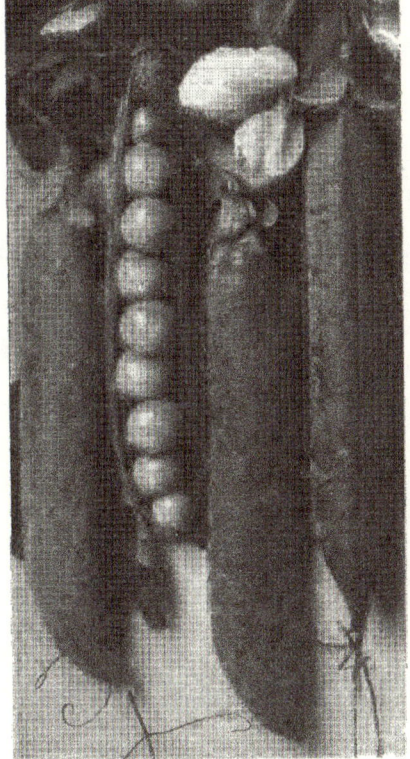

DANIELS' EXPRESS. *Reduced from a Photograph.*

PEAS.

Section I.—Earliest Varieties.

☞ DANIELS' SELECTED GRADUS.

This large-podded early wrinkled variety, is without doubt the finest and most distinct early Pea yet introduced. The haulm which grows to the height of three to four feet is well covered with large dark green pods, averaging five inches in length, and well filled with eight to ten fine Peas of the most exquisite flavour ; indeed, amongst the early varieties it has no rival in this respect. It is an excellent cropper, this combined with its earliness and grand flavour, has made it a favourite with all growers.

Per quart 2s.

DANIELS' SELECTED GRADUS   *Reduced from a Photograph.*

per quart.

☞ **DANIELS' COMPETITOR.** This grand Dwarf Pea s. d. is of the true Marrowfat type, and as early as English Wonder, the haulm does not grow more than about eighteen inches in height. It is exceedingly prolific, the numerous handsome pods are of large size, four to five inches in length, and well filled with large peas of excellent marrow flavour   per pint 1s. 6d.   2 6

☞ **DANIELS' BEST OF ALL.** A very fine dwarf Early Marrowfat variety, growing only about eighteen inches in height. It is an abundant cropper, bearing quite a profusion of handsome pods of 3½ to 4 inches in length, each with seven or eight large finely-flavoured peas. It is as early as English Wonder, and will prove a splendid and profitable Pea for the market or private grower   ..   .. per pint 1s. 6d.   2 6

DANIELS' GEM OF THE SEASON. The earliest Pea in cultivation, and very prolific. Is always the earliest, whether sown in Autumn, Winter, or Spring. Is also the hardiest, resisting frost better than any other kind, and is not affected by mildew. Being very prolific and of a most delicious flavour, will be found a most desirable variety for early work. Height 3 ft. 2 0

EARLIEST OF ALL. A round blue-seeded Pea of excellent and rich flavour ; very prolific, can be sown early. Height 2½ ft.   .. 1 0

EARLY BOUNTIFUL. A grand first early round Pea. Pods nearly twice the size of Earliest of All, and comes in only a few days later, very hardy, useful for early sowings. Height 3½ ft.   .. 1 4

ENGLISH WONDER. One of the most useful of the dwarf varieties, of good constitution and very prolific, may be sown earlier than some of the wrinkled sorts. Height 1 ft. 1 3

KING EDWARD VII. A new early dwarf variety of great productiveness, bearing a profusion of dark green pods, well filled with peas of fine quality. It is a wrinkled marrow, and a great acquisition to our early dwarf varieties. Height 1½ ft.   .. 1 0

LAXTONIAN. A fine early variety of dwarf habit and vigorous constitution, bearing a profusion of long dark green pods four to five inches in length, well filled with large peas of the finest flavour. Height 1½ ft. 2 0

LITTLE MARVEL. A fine dwarf early variety of compact growth, and an exceptionally heavy cropper. The pods are of medium size and well filled with fine peas of excellent flavour; a great acquisition to our first early sorts. Height 1 ft. 2 0

THE SHERWOOD. A remarkably productive early variety, and is one of the best Dwarf Peas ever offered. It is an enormous cropper, the haulm being literally covered with pods containing eight to ten large peas of rich deep colour, and of exquisite flavour. Height 1 ft. 1 6

THOMAS LAXTON. Award of Merit, Royal Horticultural Society. A large-podded first early Pea, coming in with Earliest of All but with pods of double the size, and rich dark green colour. It is a true wrinkled Marrow, a grand cropper, and the flavour is of the best. Height 3 ft.   ..   ..   —   — 2 0

WILLIAM HURST. An early blue wrinkled variety of good hardy constitution, very prolific and of fine table quality. Height 1 ft.   1 3

PEAS.

Section II.—Second Early.

☞ DANIELS' DWARF PROLIFIC.

A grand second early dwarf wrinkled Marrow, of strong constitution and sturdy habit, growing about 1½ feet high; it is enormously prolific, bearing a profusion of dark green, slightly curved pods, four inches long, well filled with eight to nine peas of excellent flavour, at the same time it is an excellent variety for forcing, being quite as prolific under glass as in the open. It is a very compact grower, and will be an acquisition to all gardens where space is limited, on account of the little room it occupies as compared with its heavy cropping qualities.

per quart 2s.

DANIELS' DWARF PROLIFIC.

		s.	d.
☞ **DANIELS' MIDSUMMER MARROW.** A grand early Marrowfat Pea of a good hardy constitution. It is an abundant bearer; the pods, which somewhat resemble Gradus in shape, are 4½ to 5 inches in length and well filled with nine or ten fine peas of excellent flavour. We can thoroughly recommend this as a first-class variety for all purposes. Height 3 to 4 ft.		2	0
☞ **DANIELS NORWICH WONDER.** A grand Second Early variety, bearing an abundance of fine shaped pods five inches in length, well filled with nine to ten peas of excellent flavour; a fine addition to our exhibition varieties, whilst its prolificness and excellent table quality make it a most desirable acquisition. Height 4 ft.		2	0
DUKE OF YORK. A fine wrinkled Marrow, of robust habit, pods five inches in length; a very profitable bearer, coming in a few days earlier than Duke of Albany, and like that variety, A 1 for exhibition. Height 3½ to 4 ft.		2	0
LYE'S FAVOURITE. Improved Stock. A new selection of this fine second early variety, of hardy constitution and enormous productiveness, bearing a profusion of long, handsome, slightly curved pods, well filled with peas of excellent marrow flavour. Very useful for early sowing on account of its extreme hardiness. Height 3 to 4 ft.		1	6
THE DAISY. A dwarf second early wrinkled Marrow of great merit. The haulm, which is very robust, is well hung with handsome pods four to five inches in length, well filled with large peas of excellent flavour. On account of its numerous good qualities it has been awarded a First Class Certificate by the Royal Horticultural Society. Height 1½ ft.		1	6
SENATOR. A very prolific variety, bearing the pods mostly in pairs; these are from four to five inches in length and well filled with peas of a fine marrow flavour. Height 3 ft.		2	0
WILLIAM THE FIRST. Selected stock. One of the finest early green Marrows, combining flavour and earliness, and produces a very heavy crop of slightly curved dark green pods, well filled with peas of excellent colour and flavour, and is one of the best varieties for market purposes. Height 4 ft.		1	6

•

PEAS.
Section III.—Main Crop.
☞ DANIELS' SELECTED DUKE OF ALBANY.

A fine selected stock of this useful Main Crop Pea. It grows between 4 and 5 feet in height. The haulm being covered with a very heavy crop of long handsome dark green pods, averaging five inches in length, which are well filled with 10 to 12 large peas of the true marrow flavour. A splendid variety for exhibition, whilst its fine cropping qualities combined with its excellent flavour will recommend it alike to the private grower and the market gardener. Per quart 2s.

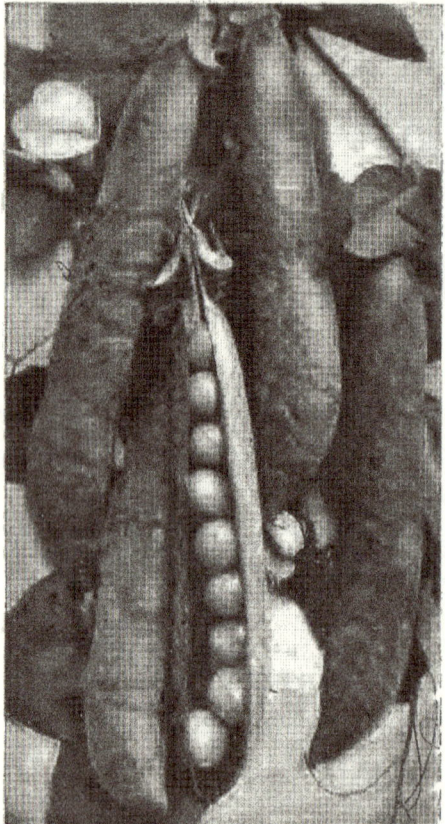

DANIELS' SELECTED DUKE OF ALBANY.

per quart.
s. d.

☞ **THE DANIELS'.** An extra large podded Main Crop variety of great merit. It is of robust constitution, the pods are long and handsome, averaging five to six inches in length, and well filled with ten to twelve large peas of the finest marrow flavour. It is a very heavy and reliable cropper, and a most useful sort for exhibition; strongly recommended for general crop. Height 4 ft. .. per pint 1s. 6d. 2 0

ALDERMAN. Received the highest award from the Royal Horticultural Society after trial at Chiswick. In habit it is strong and branching, producing, a few days later than Duke of Albany, very large handsome, straight, deep green and well-filled pods, which contain peas of the richest Ne Plus Ultra flavour and quality. Height 5 ft. 2 0

CAPTAIN CUTTLE. A fine wrinkled main crop variety of strong constitution and robust habit, producing a heavy crop of long dark green pods containing 9 to 10 large peas of the finest marrow flavour. The pods are of the same shape as the well-known "Ne Plus Ultra," but are much larger. Very useful for exhibition purposes .. .. Height 4 ft. 1 9

DR. MACLEAN. A fine wrinkled Marrow, of vigorous growth, wonderfully productive, flavour of the first quality .. .. .. Height 3½ ft. 1 0

FILLBASKET. Very prolific .. Height 3 ft. 1 3

GLADIATOR. The plant is very robust and vigorous, stem branched, growing about three feet in height, exceedingly productive, bearing in pairs an abundance of long, curved handsome pods, which are very closely filled with medium-sized peas of excellent quality. First Class Certificate, R.H.S. .. Height 3 ft. 1 0

MACLEAN'S WONDERFUL, or PRINCE OF WALES. Excellent cropping variety of superior flavour Height 3 ft. 1 0

MAGNUM BONUM. This grand Pea is of a fine robust constitution, and resists mildew in dry seasons. The pods are of a deep rich green colour, measuring about 5 inches in length, and contain 10 to 11 peas of excellent marrow flavour. A very heavy cropper Height 3 to 4 ft. 1 9

PEERLESS MARROWFAT. A grand large-podded main crop variety, which may be described as a dwarf Duke of Albany, the pods being equal in size to that variety, whilst it is quite as prolific, and has the decided advantage of growing only three feet in height Height 3 ft. 2 0

"I won First Prize in open class of twenty-three entries for a dish of your Matchless Marrow Pea."—Mr. T. WELLS, Cuckfield.

"I have won First Prize for three years in succession with your Matchless Marrow Pea. I got Eleven Prizes out of thirteen entries."—Mr. E. BAKER, Sidmouth.

"I have had your Matchless Marrow Peas for years, and always found them to do well."—Mr. C. NIBLETT, Wroxall.

"From the pint of Matchless Marrow Peas I purchased from you I gathered over fifteen pecks of fine pods like enclosed, and there are quite ten or eleven pecks more. All who have seen and tasted them think they are the finest they have ever seen."—Mrs. J. J. CORLETT, Michael.

"I took First Prize with your Matchless Marrow Pea, out of seventeen competitors."—Mr. E. LEWIS, Cardiff.

"I took Five First Prizes with your Matchless Marrow Pea."—Mr. W. DUDLEY, Beaufort.

Maincrop Pea.

Daniels'
Matchless
Marrow.

This splendid maincrop variety continues to hold its position as first favourite for all purposes, on account of its heavy cropping qualities and excellent flavour. It grows to the height of 4 to 5 feet, the haulm being well covered with fine dark-green pods 5 to 6 inches in length and of splendid appearance, each containing 10 to 12 large Peas of the most delicious marrow flavour. It is the leading variety for exhibition purposes, having obtained numerous First Prizes in all parts of the country.

Per pint 1s. 6d.
Per quart 2s. 6d.

Maincrop Pea.
Daniels' Recorder.

A grand long-podded maincrop variety, growing about 3 feet high. The haulm, which is very robust, is well hung with large pods, which are of a deep green colour, averaging from 5 to 6 inches in length, and contain 10 to 11 fine Peas of excellent colour and of the finest marrow flavour. Its great prolificness, combined with the large size of the pods, make it one of the most useful varieties, both for table and exhibition purposes. We can strongly recommend this fine variety to our customers.

Per pint 1s. 6d. ; Per quart 2s. 6d.

PEAS.

Section III.—Main Crop.

☞ QUITE CONTENT.

This is undoubtedly the largest-podded pea yet introduced. It somewhat resembles Alderman, but with stronger growth and longer pods. It is exceedingly prolific, and the pods hang mostly in pairs. Grand exhibition variety. Height 5 to 6 ft.

Per pint 1s. 6d. ; per quart 2s. 6d.

☞ DANIELS' COMMANDER. A fine dwarf Marrowfat of robust constitution, bearing a heavy crop of rich dark green pods, well filled with large peas of the finest flavour. Height 1½ to 2 ft.

Per pint 1s. 6d. ; per quart 2s. 6d.

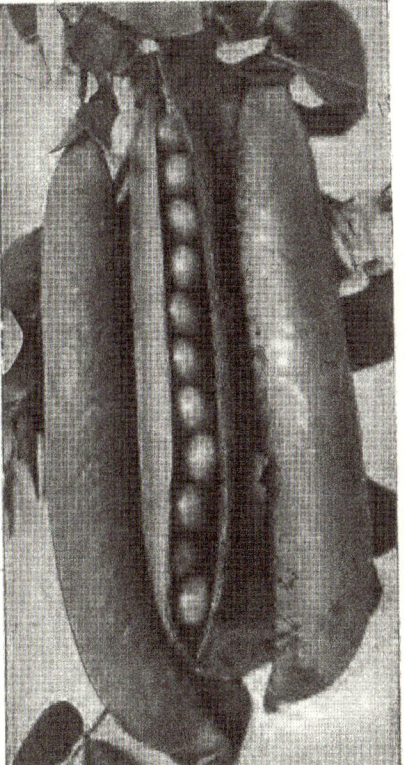

QUITE CONTENT. Reduced from a Photograph.

Per quart.
s. d.

☞ DANIELS' MAIN CROP MARROW. One of the finest Marrow Peas in cultivation, and of the same flavour as the old Ne Plus Ultra ; but the pods are longer. It is very prolific, bearing a profusion of dark green, well-filled pods, each containing eight to nine large peas of exquisite flavour ; as a Main Crop variety it should be in great demand on account of its numerous good qualities .. .. per pint 1s. 6d. 2 6

DANIELS' IMPROVED CHAMPION OF ENGLAND. A great improvement on the well-known variety. It is very prolific, bearing a profusion of well-filled pods, twice the size of the old variety, at the same time retaining the fine rich marrow flavour for which this pea is celebrated. Height 5 to 6 ft. 1 9

SATISFACTION. A remarkably heavy cropping maincrop variety, bearing a fine lot of long, square ended pods, well filled with nine to ten peas of large size and of the finest marrow flavour Height 3 ft. 2 0

STRATAGEM. This is a splendid variety, with pods five to six inches in length, containing eight to ten large fine flavoured peas. First Class Certificate, R.H.S. Our own selected and improved stock. Height 2 ft. 2 0

TELEGRAPH. A hardy variety of first-class quality and strong constitution, pods large and well-filled ; also fine for exhibition. Height 4 ft. 1 4

TELEPHONE. First Class Certificate, Royal Horticultural Society. This fine variety is good either for exhibition or market purposes. Height 4½ ft. 1 9

TRIUMPH. A blue wrinkled Marrow, of exquisite flavour ; the pods are long and well filled, each containing nine to eleven large peas. In constitution it is robust and hardy. Height 2 to 3 ft. 1 4

YORKSHIRE HERO. A fine dwarf Marrow Pea, of the Veitch's Perfection type, is very prolific, bearing a profusion of well-filled pods, containing six to eight large peas each ; flavour first-class. Height 3 ft. 1 0

" I took First Prize at Ealing show with your Quite Content Pea." - Mr. H. LURRING, South Ealing.

" I am glad to inform you that I am quite content with your Quite Content Pea."—Mr. D. R. JONES, Glanamman.

" I took three First Prizes with your Distinction Pea at our Show last year."—Mr. S. L. SPENCER, Harwell.

" I exhibited your Distinction Pea this year at our show. I am pleased to tell you that I got First Prize. I have gained three Firsts in four years."—Mr. E. SIMNETT, Burton-on-Trent.

" I won First Prize for your Distinction Pea, two Firsts for Onions, one First for Potatoes, one First for Beet and second for Melon."—Mr. E. MACE, West Malling.

" The Recorder Peas I have had from you lately have done splendidly."—Mr. J. BAUNER, Summerville.

" The Recorder Peas did splendidly this season and were admired by all."—Mr. P. TODD, Dalton-in-Furness.

" Your Matchless Marrow Peas took two First Prizes at Gt. Chart Show."—Mr. W. J. BAKER, Ashford.

" I gained First Prize for your well-known Matchless Marrow Pea, and the other Vegetables also gave every satisfaction."— Mr. G. GRAINGER, Ponders End.

PEAS.

Section IV.—Late Varieties.

☞ DANIELS' DISTINCTION.

A very fine late variety which comes in about the same time as "Ne Plus Ultra," and which it rivals in its culinary qualities. The plants are of strong robust growth, attaining a height of about 3½ feet, and producing an abundance of handsome dark green, slightly-curved pods, five to six inches in length, filled with large peas of the finest and most delicate flavour. We can highly recommend this as one of the very best for exhibition ; for a late crop it is unrivalled. Per pint 1s. 6d. ; per quart 2s. 6d.

GLORY OF DEVON. Award of Merit, Royal Horticultural Society. A fine addition to our late varieties of Peas. It is of hardy constitution and a robust grower, the foliage being of a rich dark green. The haulm, which grows about four feet in height, is well laden with fine handsome pods, each containing eight to ten large peas of delicious flavour. For exhibition it is first-class.
per quart 2s.

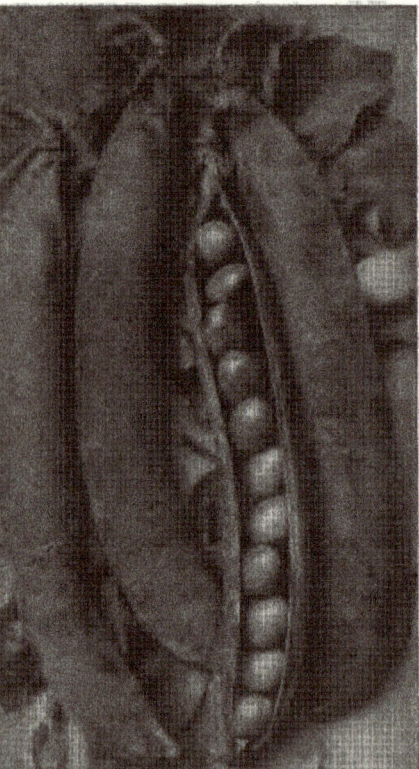

DANIELS' DISTINCTION. *Reduced from a Photograph.*

	per quart
	s. d.
AUTOCRAT. First Class Certificate, Royal Horticultural Society. Is of exceedingly robust habit, much branched, foliage of a dark lustrous green. Owing to its strong constitution it is perfectly free from mildew, and is the best late Pea in cultivation. Height 4 ft.	1 6
NE PLUS ULTRA. Extra select stock. Height 6 ft.	1 6
NE PLUS ULTRA. Delicious Marrow Pea, very prolific, quality first-class, fine for general crop. Height 6 ft. ..	1 3
QUEEN. A blue wrinkled Marrow Pea of sturdy branching habit. The pods are large, dark green, slightly curved, and well filled ; the peas are of delicious flavour. Height 2 to 2½ ft. ..	1 6
THE BELL. A grand late variety, with strong haulm, dark green foliage, long straight pods produced in pairs, containing ten to twelve peas of large size and exquisite flavour ; a heavy cropper, and one of the best for exhibition purposes. Award of Merit, Royal Horticultural Society. Height 3½ ft.	2 0
VEITCH'S PERFECTION MARROW. Extra select stock. One of the best-flavoured of our Marrow Peas. Height 3 ft. ..	1 6

DANIELS' SPECIAL COLLECTIONS OF CHOICE PEAS FOR SUCCESSION.

We highly recommend these Collections to the notice of the Amateur. By successional sowings, in accordance with instructions, an excellent supply of fresh green Peas may be secured throughout the season.

	per quart
	s. d.
DANIELS' BEST OF ALL. Fit to gather in about 12 weeks from time of sowing .. .. per pint 1s. 6d.	2 6
DANIELS' MATCHLESS MARROW. Fit to gather in about 13 weeks from time of sowing .. .. per pint 1s. 6d.	2 6
DANIELS' RECORDER. Fit to gather in about 15 to 16 weeks from time of sowing .. .. .. per pint 1s. 6d.	2 6
DANIELS' DISTINCTION. Fit to gather in about 17 weeks from time of sowing .. .. .. per pint 1s. 6d.	2 6

One pint each of the above, 5s.

One quart each of the above, 9s.

OTHER COLLECTIONS OF PEAS.

				s. d.
12 quarts for succession, our selection	..	..	..	18 0
6 " " "	..	..	..	9 0
4 " " "	..	..	..	6 0
12 pints for succession, our selection ..	..	..	..	9 6
6 " " "	..	..	..	5 0
4 " " "	..	..	..	3 6

SPECIAL COTTAGER'S COLLECTION.

4 varieties. One pint each for succession, our selection, 3s.

4 varieties. Half-pint each for succession, our selection, 1s 9d.

BEANS—Broad.

Cultivation.—This highly nutritious vegetable grows well in any good garden soil, but responds readily to liberal treatment and should, therefore, when possible, be grown in well-prepared ground which has received a good supply of manure. The cultivation is of the easiest and everybody should be able to grow them successfully.

The earliest sowing should be made in February with our "**Selected Long Pod,**" this being one of the earliest and best sorts. For the main crop, sow in March and for a succession in April.

The seed should be sown in double rows 6 inches apart, with an intervening space of 3 feet between the pairs of rows; place the seed 6 inches apart in the rows, earth up the plants by drawing the soil around them, when they are about 6 inches high, give a good covering of ashes to keep off the slugs.

When the plants have made a good growth and set a nice quantity of bloom, the centres should be nipped out, thereby throwing more vigour into the pods.

A liberal supply of liquid manure given at intervals during the bearing season will add much to the size of the pods, as also will a mulching of decayed manure, if put on before the hot weather comes.

The Windsor varieties whilst not giving such long pods are of excellent flavour; the best varieties for exhibition purposes are **Daniels' Norfolk Giant Long-pod,** which produces the finest pods of any of the long-podded section, and **Daniels' Mammoth Windsor,** which is by far the best of its class.

WHITE-SEEDED VARIETIES.

per quart—s. d.

☞ **DANIELS' NORFOLK GIANT LONG-POD.** The longest-podded Bean known, has been grown up to 18 inches in length. The pods are of very handsome shape and excellent quality. First-class for exhibition, having obtained numerous First Prizes per pint 1s. 3d. — 2 0

☞ **DANIELS' MAMMOTH WINDSOR.** The largest Broad Bean in cultivation. Very prolific, bearing a large quantity of fine broad pods, containing beans of exceptional size. These are of fine quality, and of flavour equal to the old Broad Windsor per pint 1s. 3d. — 2 0

DANIELS' SELECTED LONG-POD. A grand selection of the Early Long-pod. Very prolific; pods larger and finer than the old variety; useful for exhibition .. .. — 1 2

BROAD WINDSOR. Fine selected stock — .. .. — 0 9

HARLINGTON WINDSOR. Larger and finer pods than the old Windsor; very prolific .. .. — 1 0

JOHNSON'S WONDERFUL (Mackie's Monarch) .. .. — 0 9

MAZAGAN. Small, early, and hardy — .. — — 0 7

GREEN-SEEDED VARIETIES.

per quart—s. d.

☞ **DANIELS' IMPROVED GREEN WINDSOR.** An abundant bearer, pods large; a great improvement on the old variety .. 1 2

☞ **DANIELS' MAMMOTH GREEN LONG-POD.** A very fine selection of this type, the pods being longer and much better filled than those of the old variety; and of excellent flavour 1 4

BECK'S GREEN GEM. Excellent for small gardens — .. 1 6

"Your Seeds did very well last year, especially the Norfolk Giant Long pod Bean."— Mr. J. W. NEW, Isleworth.

"I am very pleased with the Long-pod Beans, having six to eight beans in each pod."—Mr. G. A. WEBB, Bletchley.

"I won First Prize with your Norfolk Giant Long-pod Beans and First Prize for a Collection of Vegetables."—Mr. R. SEELY, Camberley.

"I took First Prize at a local Show with your Selected Long-pod Bean, and was equally successful with your Sensation Potatoes."—Mr. J. E. HASTED, Woodbridge.

"I succeeded in taking First Prize with your Norfolk Giant Long-pod Bean and First Prize with Carrots."—Mr. J. BASKERVILLE, Gailinga.

"I took First Prize for your Beans, Parsnips and Turnips; also Second Prize for Carrots."—Mr. T. WILLIAMS, Llanfihangel.

"I am pleased with your Cabbage and Broad Beans, I have taken several Prizes with them."—Mr. J. CLARKE, Rotherham.

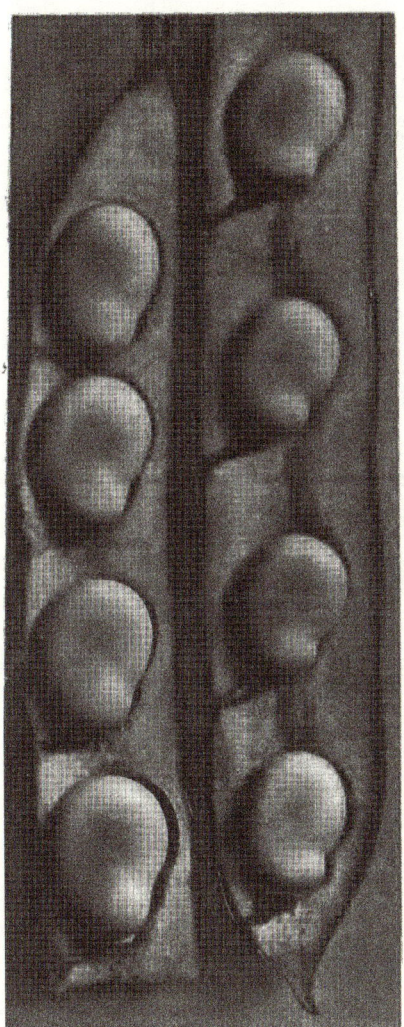

DANIELS' NORFOLK GIANT LONG-POD *From a Photograph.*

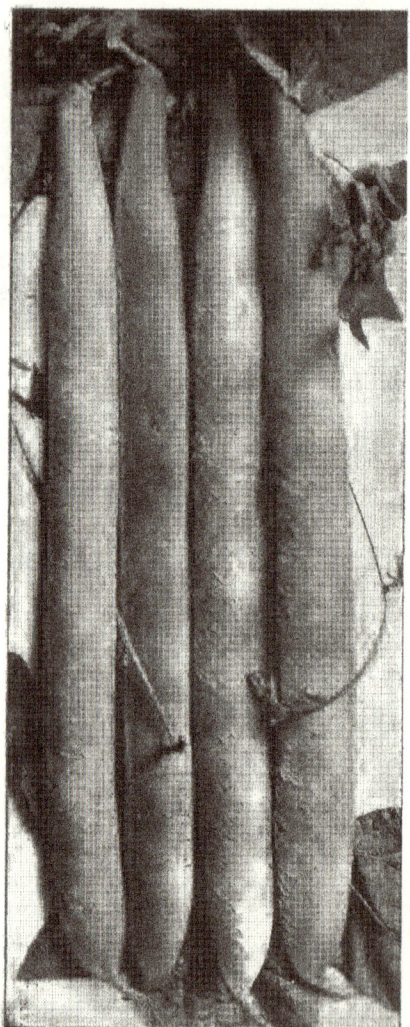

DANIELS' GIANT SCARLET. *Reduced from a Photograph.*

BEANS—Runner.

Cultivation.—Runner Beans form one of the most important and profitable of all garden crops grown for Summer and Autumn use, and yield a liberal supply of vegetables available for use after the main crop Peas are over.

They are easy of culture and may be grown as screens in small gardens, thus serving the double purpose of covering a trellis or wall and at the same time yielding a crop of delicious vegetables.

The ground should be prepared in the same manner as for other Beans, but Runners being somewhat tender the seed should not be sown until early in May.

Sow the seed in double rows 9 inches apart and, if possible, allow a space of 12 feet between each double row, cropping the intervening space with other vegetables.

For a succession make further sowings in June and July.

When the plants are about 9 inches high, draw the earth round them, and place tall, strong stakes to the rows, taking care to make them very firm and able to withstand the wind. A good mulching of rotted manure during the cropping season will lengthen the period of bearing and give quality to the beans.

Where it is impossible to procure tall stakes, it is the practice to take out the leading growths when the plants are about a foot high, thus encouraging a spreading habit and in this way good crops may be grown and space economised.

The best varieties both for exhibition and general purposes are Daniels' Giant White and Daniels' Giant Scarlet.

	per quart. s. d.
☞ **DANIELS' GIANT SCARLET.** A grand variety both for exhibition and the table, and is at the same time one of the most prolific varieties with which we are acquainted. The pods are long, straight, and of excellent quality. Our own selected stock pint 1s. 6d.	2 6
☞ **DANIELS' GIANT WHITE.** This is without doubt the finest type of Runner Bean extant, bearing in profusion long, green, thick, fleshy pods, upwards of twelve inches in length and nearly two inches in breadth. This variety, besides the best for culinary purposes, will also be found a grand exhibition kind .. pint 1s. 6d.	2 6
☞ **SCARLET EMPEROR.** A giant amongst Scarlet Runner Beans, producing fine straight pods fifteen inches in length, and is enormously productive. A grand sort for exhibition .. .. pint 1s. 6d.	2 6
☞ **WHITE EMPEROR** (new). A fine white seeded variety bearing a heavy crop of long straight pods quite equal to the Scarlet Emperor. It will make a most valuable variety for Exhibition, at the same time it is enormously prolific .. .. .. pint 1s. 6d.	2 6
BEST OF ALL. One of the longest-podded of the Scarlet Runners, very prolific. The pods, which are long, straight, and very handsome, are produced in large clusters. It is of excellent table quality, and one of the best for exhibition pint 1s. 3d.	2 0
NE PLUS ULTRA. A fine variety for exhibition and main crop, producing a large quantity of fine pods of splendid form, from ten to fourteen inches long, and quite straight. To grow it to perfection each bean should be planted one foot apart in the row .. .. per pint 1s.	1 9
OLD SCARLET RUNNER. For general crop .. per pint 8d.	1 2
VEITCH'S CLIMBING KIDNEY BEAN. First Class Certificate, Royal Horticultural Society. This Bean combines the best features of the two types, Dwarf French and Scarlet Runner. It crops earlier than the Runners and has all the delicate flavour and quality of the Dwarfs, height six to seven feet ..	2 0

" I am delighted with your Runner Beans. I have a grand crop ; the finest I have ever seen."—Mr. G. THORNE, Cardiff.

" Your White Emperor Runner Beans won First Prize at our Show."—Mr. W. SOWDEN, Torpoint.

BEANS—Dwarf French.

Cultivation. This useful vegetable may be grown by almost any one, as sufficient space for a row may be found in even the smallest garden. With attention to the preparation and manuring of the ground, there should be no difficulty in having a continuous supply of French Beans for a considerable portion of the Summer and Autumn.

The culture is of the simplest; the ground having been thoroughly dug and manured in early Spring, the Beans should be planted about the end of April; the rows should be 2½ feet apart and the Beans placed about 4 inches apart in the row, any gaps in the row may be filled up by transplanting the seedlings when just past the seed leaf.

The soil should be drawn round the plants to protect them from cold winds in Spring, and during the time of bearing occasional waterings with weak liquid manure will add much to the size of the produce and lengthen the period of bearing. Daniels' "Incomparable" can be highly recommended on account of its great prolificness and excellent quality.

Where greenhouses are available the earliest sowing may be made at the beginning of April and the young plants transferred to the outside border when large enough to handle. A crop may also be grown in the early months of the year in heated frames or greenhouses, the seed being sown in 8-inch pots half filled with good rich soil, and the pots gradually filled up with soil as the plants grow. It is most important that French Beans should be gathered as soon as ready, otherwise the plants will gradually give up blooming and the crop be much reduced.

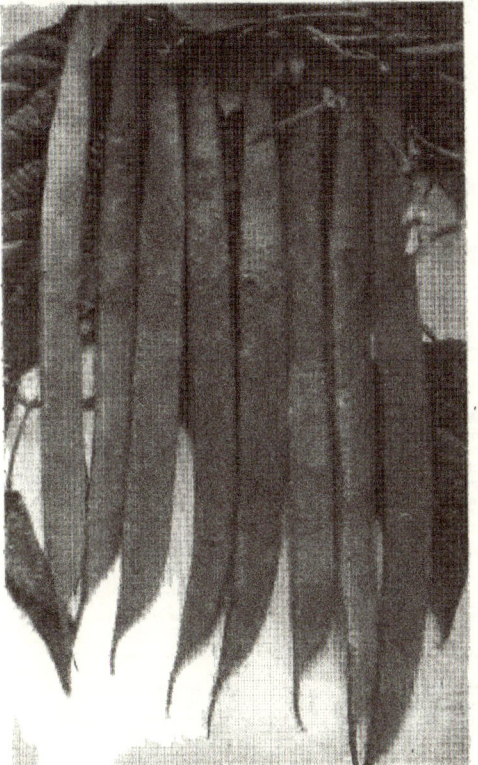

(DANIELS' INCOMPARABLE. *From a Photograph.*

per quart. s. d.

DANIELS' INCOMPARABLE (new). This splendid dwarf Kidney Bean since its introduction has fully justified our high opinion of it, both as regards quality and prolificness. The pods are of great length, straight, and of a rich clear green colour, very tender, and of the best culinary quality. It is of strong constitution, sturdy habit, and wonderfully prolific. It is quite distinct in the seed and has proved a decided acquisition .. per pint 1s. 6d. 2 6

DANIELS' EARLY BLACK WONDER. We can highly recommend this splendid variety as one of the hardiest and most prolific French Beans in cultivation. The pods are long, of a light rich green colour, tender, and of fine flavour 1 6

CANADIAN WONDER. Abundant bearer, very fleshy and tender. The pods are long and of excellent shape and quality; one of the best for general crop 1 0

EARLY GOLDEN BUTTER. Pods thick and fleshy, nearly transparent, and of a bright yellow colour, which is retained when boiled; excellent flavour 2 0

EARLY WARWICK. A distinct early variety of great productiveness; quality first-class; most useful 1 6

NEGRO LONG-POD. Useful variety, heavy cropper 1 0

NE PLUS ULTRA. The finest Kidney Bean in cultivation for all purposes. First Class Certificate, R.H.S. 1 4

NEWINGTON WONDER (or NONSUCH). Early .. 1 4

PALE DUN OR BUFF. Very early; one of the most useful 1 2

ALL KINDS MIXED 1 0

BEET.

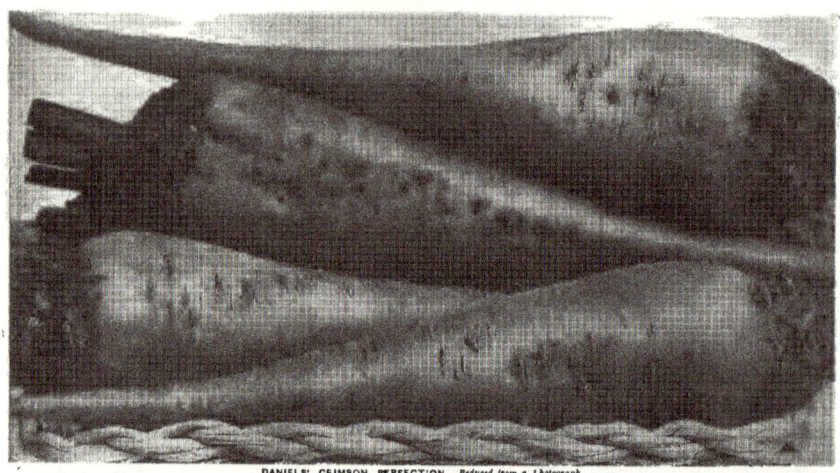

DANIELS' CRIMSON PERFECTION. *Reduced from a Photograph.*

Cultivation.—To ensure a crop of good Beetroot, it is of the highest importance that the seed should be of the very best strain procurable such as offered by ourselves. Another very important point to observe is that the ground must not be specially manured for this crop, a good plan being to select a plot that has been cropped during the previous season with French Beans, Potatoes, or Celery. The soil should be a good light loam where possible, and in an open part of the garden; the ground should be deeply trenched (the deeper the better) quite early in the season. Before sowing, the ground should be made firm and level.

Sow the seed any time from the middle of April to the end of May. For an early crop New Red Globe is one of the best. Daniels' Crimson Perfection and Green Top will be found the most useful for a general crop. The seed should be sown in drills one inch deep and about 18 inches from row to row. A liberal quantity of seed should be used to ensure a good plant, and when the seedlings are nicely up, they should be thinned out, leaving them about 9 inches apart. As a rule those sown at the end of May produce roots of better quality. Keep the beds regularly hoed and weeded so that the soil may be free about the plants.

When specimen roots are wanted for Exhibition, it is the usual practice to make holes about 2 feet deep in the bed with a crowbar, and fill them with fine soil. The seeds are sown in these and thinned out, one plant being left to each hole. In this way splendidly shaped roots are grown. The crop should be lifted in October and stored in dry sand in a shed or cellar for Winter use. Care should be taken that the roots are not injured in any way, or they will bleed and lose quality; also the leaves should not be cut but twisted off with the hand. In this way the roots may be kept until the following Summer.

	per qt.—s. d.
☞ **DANIELS' CRIMSON PERFECTION SALAD.** A grand dark-leaved variety of medium size and very symmetrical. The flesh, which is of the finest texture, is deep crimson in colour and of excellent quality. A first-class sort for exhibition. Owing to the fine deep colour of its foliage it is very valuable for ornamental purposes .. .. per pkt. 6d.	1 6
DANIELS' BLACK QUEEN. Fine dark-leaved variety, roots medium in size, and of good shape and colour .. per pkt. 3d.	0 9
CHELTENHAM GREEN-TOP. Roots very dark, of excellent quality; one of the best for pickling .. .. per pkt. 3d.	0 9
DARK RED SALAD. A very useful variety, roots of a good deep colour	0 6
DRACÆNA-LEAVED. A highly ornamental variety for the Flower Garden. The leaves are fine, long, and of a deep rich crimson. The root is of fine quality and excellent colour per pkt. 4d.	1 0

	per qt.—s. d.
☞ **DANIELS' GREEN-TOP.** This splendid Green-top Beet is chiefly remarkable for the fine deep colour of the roots, which are of excellent shape and of first-class quality and flavour .. .. per pkt. 4d.	1 0
DELL'S BLACK. A fine dark-foliaged variety, roots small, but of exceptionally fine shape and colour .. per pkt. 3d.	0 9
EGYPTIAN DARK RED TURNIP-ROOTED. One of the best for Summer Salads, as it comes to maturity very early	0 9
NEW RED GLOBE. A valuable variety for early use. The roots are of fine globular shape, of rich colour and excellent flavour. It should be used early, if allowed to stand too long it loses as to quality. Useful for exhibition .. .. per pkt. 4d.	1 0
NUTTING'S DWARF RED. Fine dark foliage .. .. 3d.	0 10
PRAGNELL'S EXHIBITION. A fine dark-leaved variety, roots very handsome and of good colour .. .. per pkt. 4d.	1 0
SILVER SEA KALE. The leaves make an excellent substitute for Spinach	0 9

"Your Vegetable Seeds last year were wonderful; not one failed."—Mr. J. DUTTON, Runcorn.

"All your Vegetable Seeds were the finest I have ever grown."—Mrs. WORTHINGTON, Templemore.

"The Seeds I had from you last year proved excellent. I took five First Prizes."—Mr. T. BARBER, Beeding.

"I took First Prize with your Red Globe Beet last year."—Mr. T. MORTIMER, Llanharran.

"I might say that I have never grown any better vegetables than those from your Seeds."—Mr. R. LEGG, Swindon.

"I was very successful in exhibiting the produce from your Seeds, of which I cannot speak too highly."—Mr. J. DEWIS, Nuneaton.

BRUSSELS SPROUTS.

Cultivation.—To grow Brussels Sprouts successfully the seed should be sown at the latter end of February or early in March on a sheltered border or in a frame. Prick out the seedlings about four inches apart into seed beds as soon as they have made the first leaves, and directly the weather allows plant out permanently into well prepared ground, such as is used for general garden crops. For a later crop, a sowing should be made at the end of March, or early in April, and the seedlings planted as soon as possible; they cannot very well be planted out too early. Brussels Sprouts require plenty of room to develop, and therefore they should never be planted thickly. About 2½ feet apart in the row and 3 feet between the rows would be a suitable distance. Give a good supply of water when they are first planted, and keep the ground loose by frequent use of the hoe.

Brussels Sprouts thrive much better by themselves than when planted amongst other crops. In dry weather liberal supplies of liquid manure will be found of great advantage. Daniels' Colossal and Defiance are first-class stocks, and will be found the best for exhibition purposes and for general use.

DANIELS' COLOSSAL. *Reduced from a Photograph.*

per oz.—s. d.

DANIELS' COLOSSAL. One of the finest and best in cultivation, of very vigorous growth, bearing sprouts of a large, compact, globular shape all the way up the stem; these will be found of a more delicate and finer flavour than any other of the Cabbage tribe .. .. .. per pkt. 6d. 1 6

DANIELS' DEFIANCE. A finely selected stock of medium height, is exceedingly productive, the stem being well covered with large compact sprouts of the most excellent flavour. A very useful variety for exhibition purposes, and one of the best for general use .. per pkt. 6d. 1 6

AIGBURTH. A tall growing variety, of fine quality. The sprouts are of good size and very firm 0 8

DALKEITH. A fine selected stock of medium height, the stems being well covered with solid sprouts of fine flavour .. per pkt. 3d. 0 9

SCRYMGER'S GIANT. An excellent tall variety; stems well covered with fine sprouts, of first-class flavour .. per pkt. 3d. 0 9

SOLIDITY. A fine dwarf variety, the stems being well covered with extra hard solid sprouts of medium size and of the finest quality per pkt. 4d. 1 0

"I have had splendid results from your Colossal Brussels Sprouts this year. Your Golden Rocca Onion has also done well."—Mr. G. WEST, Rochford.

"I took numerous Prizes last year. Out of twelve entries I took twelve Prizes. Your Colossal Brussels Sprouts were the finest I have ever grown."—Mr. E. PARKER, Stamford.

"I am quite satisfied with all your Seeds. I obtained several Prizes."—Mr. G. HILLS, Bury St. Edmunds.

"I took several Prizes last year with Vegetables grown from your Seeds."—Mr. W. HICKS, Malvern.

BORECOLE or KALE.

Cultivation.—Borecole is of great value for providing a supply of tender green heads from Christmas onwards, during the very severe weather when Cabbages and Broccoli are not available. Many varieties of Borecole are also quite ornamental and present most attractive objects in the kitchen garden. Sow the seed in April in seed beds, and when the plants are large enough transplant them into their permanent quarters about three feet apart. As an alternative they may be planted between Potato rows.

Borecole likes good soil, but does not require liberal treatment with liquid manure, etc., as many plants of the same family do. Give a thorough watering at the time of planting out. If there is any tendency to "clubbing" noticed in the garden, a dressing of lime applied in the Spring previous to planting will be found of great advantage. Daniels' Improved Drumhead can be highly recommended on account of its excellent flavour. It is much milder than some varieties. Daniels' Moss Curled Exhibition will be found invaluable for general purposes.

per oz.—s. d.

DANIELS' MOSS CURLED EXHIBITION. The finest strain of curled Kale in cultivation. It is of medium height, foliage dark green, and beautifully curled, is very hardy, and may be relied upon to stand the severest Winters. For exhibition it is unsurpassed .. .. per pkt. 6d. 1 6

DANIELS' IMPROVED DRUMHEAD. A valuable variety for Winter use. Hearts up like a Drumhead Cabbage with broad leaves; very mild and tender when cooked, and of the true Kale flavour per pkt. 4d. 1 0

COTTAGER'S. Exceedingly hardy .. .. " 3d. 0 8

DWARF GREEN CURLED. A hardy dwarf-stemmed variety, of mild flavour, one of the best for general crop 0 4

TALL GREEN CURLED. The Tall Scotch Kale 0 6

VARIEGATED or GARNISHING. A fine curled-leaved variety, beautifully variegated, very useful and ornamental for garnishing, also valuable for Winter gardening .. .. — per pkt. 4d. 1 0

ASPARAGUS KALE. Fine for winter use 0 8

BROCCOLI.

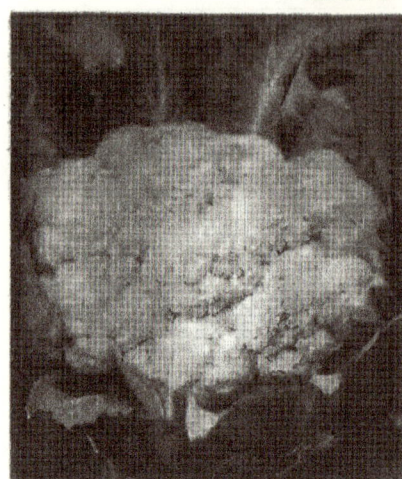

MICHAELMAS WHITE.

SECOND DIVISION.

Sow in April, May, and June, for cutting in January and February the following Spring.

	per pkt. s. d.	per oz. s. d.
DANIELS' NEW YEAR. A vigorous, compact, dwarf-growing variety, with self-protecting foliage over-lapping snow-white heads, of excellent quality and flavour; a most valuable variety	0 0	2 0
DANIELS' QUEEN OF SPRING. This splendid variety comes in for cutting during February, is of dwarf compact habit, producing large snow-white heads of the finest quality. Its earliness, combined with its excellent quality, makes it a valuable addition to our Spring Broccoli	0 0	2 0
DANIELS' SELECTED SNOW'S WHITE. A fine selected stock of this well-known Winter Broccoli. The heads are large, firm and beautifully white, one of the most useful of the Winter varieties	0 6	1 6
ADAMS' EARLY WHITE. A strong growing variety of hardy constitution. Heads large pure white	0 3	0 9
MAMMOTH WINTER WHITE. Large pure white heads of the finest quality, coming into use in mid-winter, well protected with long over-lapping leaves	0 6	1 6
PENZANCE EARLY WHITE. A useful early variety, producing fine large heads of excellent quality	0 4	1 0
ST. HILARY. A splendid Broccoli of hardy, vigorous constitution. Dwarf, compact growth, and large white heads, coming into use in January	0 6	1 6
WHITE SPROUTING. Produces a large crop of tender white sprouts of the most excellent flavour	0 6	1 6

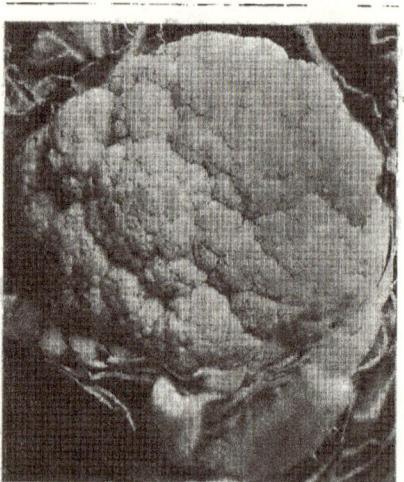

DANIELS' QUEEN OF SPRING.

BROCCOLI.

DANIELS' NORFOLK GIANT,

THIRD DIVISION.

Sow end of March and beginning of April for cutting in March and April the following season.

	per pkt. s. d.	per oz. s. d.
☞ **DANIELS' NORFOLK GIANT.** A magnificent variety of robust and compact habit, stem short, the flower heads are exceedingly large, beautifully white, and of the finest quality, being well protected by luxuriant, over-lapping foliage. The best and hardiest variety for general Spring use	0 9	2 0
EASTER DAY or SPRINGTIDE. A fine hardy variety of dwarf compact habit and vigorous growth, producing large, firm, white heads of excellent quality, which are well protected. One of the best kinds for maincrop in Spring	0 6	1 6
KNIGHTS' PROTECTING. One of the hardiest of our Spring Broccoli. The heads are well protected, large, and of fine quality	0 4	1 0
LEAMINGTON. Well-known hardy variety. Heads large and solid	0 4	1 0
PURPLE SPROUTING. Very hardy Winter variety, producing an abundant crop of Sprouts of excellent flavour	0 3	0 9

" Your **King of the Broccoli** are proving simply grand ; one head measured over one foot in diameter."- -Mr. **A. T. MARKS**, Farnham.

" The **Broccoli Seed** I had from you last year turned out splendidly."—Mr. **J. McLAREN**, Longniddry.

" Your **Knights' Protecting Broccoli** turned out well."- Mr. **H. COAD**, Crampound Road.

" Your **Broccoli** have done very well this year. I am sending for more Seed."—Mr. **T. WEBBER**, Bristol.

" I took five First and Two Second Prizes at our Show with produce grown from your Seeds."- Mr. **E. G. BELCHER**, Devonport.

FOURTH DIVISION.

Sow in May and June for cutting in May and June the following season.

	per pkt. s. d.	per oz. s. d.
☞ **DANIELS' KING OF THE BROCCOLI.** This splendid variety comes in for cutting from the beginning of May to the first week in June, and as a late kind cannot be surpassed. It is of a fine dwarf habit, and being well protected is exceedingly hardy. The heads are remarkably fine	0 6	1 6
DANIELS' LATEST WHITE. One of the best kinds for filling up the gap or period that occurs between Broccoli and Cauliflower	0 4	1 0
METHVEN'S JUNE. One of the latest Broccoli in cultivation, producing fine pure white heads till nearly the end of June	0 6	1 6
QUEEN. Very fine, heads well protected	0 4	1 0

Cultivation.—This excellent vegetable is of the greatest value during the Winter and early Spring, when Cauliflowers are not obtainable and vegetables generally are scarce. They like a good rich firm soil, which has during the previous Autumn been thoroughly trenched and liberally manured. If possible, choose a piece of land on which Celery has been grown.

The earliest sowing of seed should be made at the latter end of March, and the principal sowings during April, whilst May will be soon enough for the late varieties. Sow the seed either in a warm sheltered border or in a frame, in drills eight or nine inches apart and one inch deep. When the plants are large enough to handle, lose no time in pricking them out, as they quickly suffer if allowed to remain too long in the seed bed, becoming drawn and weak. The final plantings should be commenced in May, and followed on as opportunity occurs until the end of July, and as land becomes available. Choose the strongest plants first, as by this means a much better succession will be obtained.

The most important point in planting out Broccoli is to be quite sure that the ground is very firm ; the harder it is the better it will be for the plants, as they will thereby be able to withstand the Winter, therefore if the land was trenched and manured during the past Winter, do not have it dug again just previous to planting out. Make the rows about 2½ feet apart and place the plants about two feet apart in the rows. Water the plants thoroughly after planting and keep the weeds down.

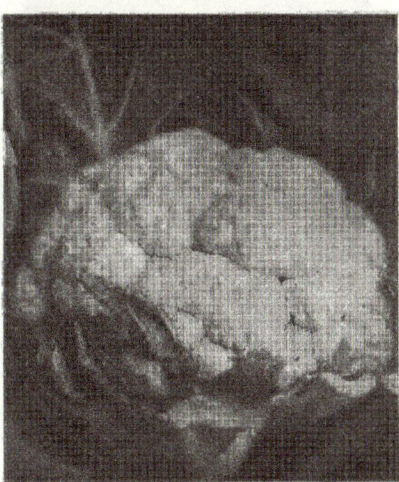

DANIELS' KING OF THE BROCCOLI.

☞ DANIELS' DEFIANCE. ☜
THE FINEST CABBAGE IN THE WORLD.

We highly recommend this magnificent Cabbage, which we claim to be the finest in the world. It is medium early, short-legged, and compact, and grows to a great size, at the same time retaining all the tenderness and delicacy of flavour of the smaller varieties. First-class for the private grower or market gardener. The seed we offer, which is our own true and original stock, has been carefully grown at our Seed Grounds from the stalks of fully developed and first-class Cabbages only, and owing to the many years of careful selection will be found of an unequalled and thoroughly reliable quality. Per packet 6d. ; per oz. 1s. 6d.

DANIELS' DEFIANCE. *Reduced from a Photograph.*

EVIDENCE OF QUALITY.

"The Defiance Cabbages, grown from your seed, are looking splendid and doing grandly on our soil."—Mr. W. HENRY, Colraine, Ireland.

"Your Defiance Cabbage Seeds were very successful, the people around here say the Cabbages are wonderful."—Mr. M. BINGRAM, Crookes.

"Your Defiance Cabbage is the finest in cultivation. I took First and Second Prizes at our show this year."—Mr. W. STAFFORD, Atherstone.

"I have had a grand crop of your Defiance Cabbage. It has been admired by everybody."—Mr. F. LEARY, Sheffield.

CABBAGES.

per oz.—s. d.

DANIELS' LITTLE QUEEN. The earliest Cabbage in cultivation. It is distinct in appearance and of dwarf compact habit, with very firm heads. A most useful variety both for Spring and Autumn sowing. Our own selected stock .. .. per pkt. 6d. 1 6

ELLAM'S EARLY DWARF. A first-class Early Cabbage in all respects. Being very compact, they can be planted close together, thus growing double the quantity of plants on the same space than most kinds. A fine early market kind, and one of the best for Autumn sowing .. per pkt. 3d. 0 9

DANIELS' IMPROVED ENFIELD MARKET. A first-class stock, earlier and larger than the ordinary variety per pkt. 4d. 1 0

EARLY DWARF YORK. Dwarf and compact.. .. .. 0 4

LARGE YORK. Very useful variety for late crop 0 4

ENFIELD MARKET. Excellent main crop variety 0 4

EWING'S No. 1. A very fine, early, dwarf Cabbage 0 6

FLOWER OF SPRING. An early variety of compact habit, heads solid and very tender. Very useful for Autumn sowing .. 0 6

NONPAREIL IMPROVED DWARF. Early variety, dwarf and compact ; very useful for market growers 0 6

OFFENHAM. A fine early variety of dwarf and compact habit, very useful ; one of the best for Autumn sowing 0 8

ROSETTE COLEWORT. Very hardy 0 8

ST. JOHN'S DAY. A fine, dwarf, very early variety of the Drumhead type, but much smaller than that variety and of fine quality 0 6

WHEELER'S IMPERIAL. A fine variety of the Nonpareil type, heads very firm and of fine quality 0 8

WINNINGSTADT. A most useful late variety, with pointed heads, which are exceedingly firm and keep sound a long time .. 0 6

DANIELS' EARLY DRUMHEAD. This variety does not grow quite so large as the ordinary field varieties, is of dwarf compact habit, with solid heads, and of mild flavour 0 4

CHRISTMAS DRUMHEAD. A fine, dwarf, compact Cabbage of excellent flavour, of a dark green colour. A splendid variety for culinary purposes .. .. .. per pkt. 3d. 0 9

"I have a nice show of your Defiance and Little Queen Cabbages, they both look well."—Mr. F. G. TOVEY, Aberbeeg.

"I am writing to say that the Ellam's Early Cabbage Seed I bought from you last Summer turned out a big success."—Mr. G. PRATT, Southampton.

"The Offenham Cabbage I had from you has done splendidly ; in fact everything has turned out well."—Mr. E. CONSTABLE, Romford.

"Your Defiance Cabbage has grown to a large size and of perfect shape."—Mr. G. SNELL, St. Mellion.

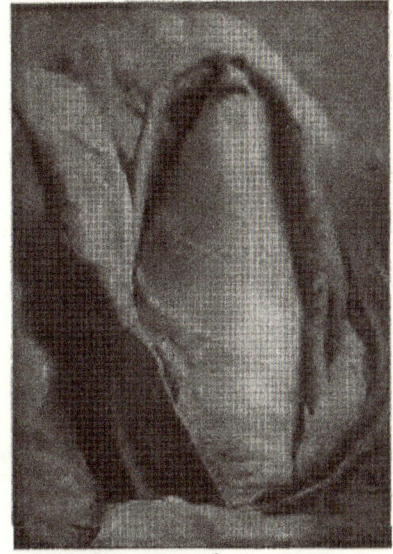

DANIELS' LITTLE QUEEN. *Reduced from a Photograph.*

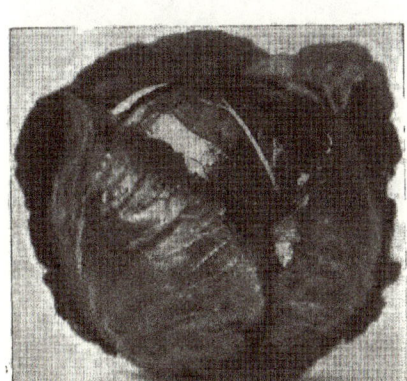

DANIELS' DWARF BLOOD RED. *Reduced from a Photograph.*

RED OR PICKLING CABBAGES.

per oz.—s. d

DANIELS' DWARF BLOOD RED. A dwarf, compact-growing variety, coming early into use ; heads of a fine deep blood red colour, and very firm ; can be planted much closer than the other sorts .. .. per pkt. 4d. 1 0

DANIELS' INTERMEDIATE RED. A fine type of Red Cabbage with medium sized heads, which are very firm and of a good deep colour. It is of medium height and very compact in growth ; fine for exhibition .. .. per pkt. 3d. 0 9

DANIELS' GIANT RED DRUMHEAD. A fine variety, grows to a large size, very firm, and of fine deep colour, and is undoubtedly the finest Red Cabbage known, excellent sort for Autumn sowing.. .. .. per pkt. 4d. 1 0

COUVE TRONCHUDA, OR PORTUGAL CABBAGE.

Per packet 4d., per ounce 1s.

"Extensive trials of Autumn sown Spring Cabbages were made by the National Vegetable Society in 1909-10, from samples sent by nineteen leading Seed Firms. Three varieties only, including Daniels' Little Queen, were selected as excellent in every way, good hearts and even stocks, equal to the best of other varieties sown on the same date, August 11th."—From "The Garden," June 25th, 1910.

"The last lot of Little Queen Cabbage did very well."—Mr. G. PARKER, Spalding.

"I have much pleasure in telling you that your Little Queen Cabbage has done well."—Mr. W. SMITH, Maybury.

"I am well satisfied with your Little Queen Cabbage." Mr. G. N. GOUDE, Whittlesea.

"Your Little Queen Cabbage took First Prize at our Show."- Mr. W. SMITH.

SAVOY CABBAGES.

SAVOY CABBAGE—DANIELS' SELECTED DRUMHEAD.

per oz.—s. d.

DANIELS' SELECTED DRUMHEAD. A fine variety for general use, producing large firm heads of exceptionally good quality ; very hardy 0 4

DANIELS' NONPAREIL. Splendid variety for early use, quite distinct ; the most delicately flavoured Savoy grown .. .. per pkt. 3d. 0 0

DANIELS' EXTRA EARLY. Fortnight earlier than Drawf Ulm, very dwarf and compact .. .. per pkt. 4d. 1 0

DWARF GREEN CURLED. Heads of fair size and very solid ; one of the best for general use 0 4

DWARF ULM. Early, very dwarf 0 6

GOLDEN AUTUMN. A distinct and beautiful variety per pkt. 3d. 0 0

GREEN GLOBE. A good hardy variety 0 6

NORWEGIAN. Excellent variety for late use, and well suited for northern and cold climates. The heads are very firm and of fine quality, keep sound a long time per pkt. 4d. 1 0

ORMSKIRK. A fine hardy variety, heads very compact, and of excellent quality 0 6

TOM THUMB. Very early, dwarf and compact 0 6

VICTORIA. Large and of fine quality .. per pkt. 3d. 0 0

" I took First Prize at our Show with your **Defiance Cabbage.** I also took a Prize with Autumn Sown Onions."—Mr. T. HAMBLING, Laxfield.

" I took two **Defiance Cabbages** to our Show at Thoresby and got First Prize for them."—Mr. C. HYDE, Fulstow.

" Your **Defiance Cabbage** has done splendidly. I cut one cabbage, and when trimmed it weighed 20½ lbs. Every one has admired it."—Mr. C. H. CATON, Waterbeach.

" I took First Prize at our Show with your **Defiance Cabbage.** Mr. W. MURBY, Markfield.

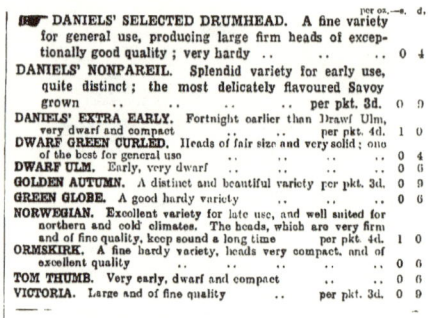

Cultivation.—Excellent Cabbages can be grown, without much outlay, by everyone possessing a garden. They prefer a good rich loamy soil, a liberal supply of manure, and as open a position as possible. The hoe should be kept going every week on the beds, and an occasional application of Nitrate of Soda or Sulphate of Ammonia (at the rate of one ounce to the square yard) is recommended before the hearts form, when good succulent Cabbages are assured. For Summer and Autumn use, sow the seed in March, and a succession in April and May if required, and when the plants are large enough, prick out into seed beds, and finally plant out in rows two feet apart for the stronger growing varieties, such as **Daniels' Defiance** and **Enfield Market**, with two feet between each plant. For the smaller varieties such as **Little Queen, Ellam's Early, Nonpareil, &c.,** rows 18 inches apart, and 15 inches from plant to plant fulfil requirements. Cabbages are highly appreciated in early Spring. For this crop the seed should be sown in the Northern districts in July, and in the Midland and Southern districts during August.

RED CABBAGES.—Seed may be sown either in Spring or Autumn ; if sown in the middle of August and planted out later, splendid heads will be produced the following Autumn.

" I have had great success with your **Defiance Cabbage.** I have had some very large ones and of beautiful flavour."—Mr. T. CLAY, Skewen.

" I have some splendid **Cabbages** grown from the Seed supplied by you."—Mr. E. THORNTON, Banbury.

" The Cabbage Seed I had from you has produced some splendid heads."—Mr. G. TOWNING, Horsfield.

" I obtained First Prize with your **Defiance Cabbage** last year."—Mr. J. W. REED, Broxholme.

" The Vegetable Seed you supplied this year have turned out most satisfactory."—Mrs. M. GIVIN, Cosmelina.

SAVOY CABBAGE DANIELS' NONPAREIL.

CARROTS.

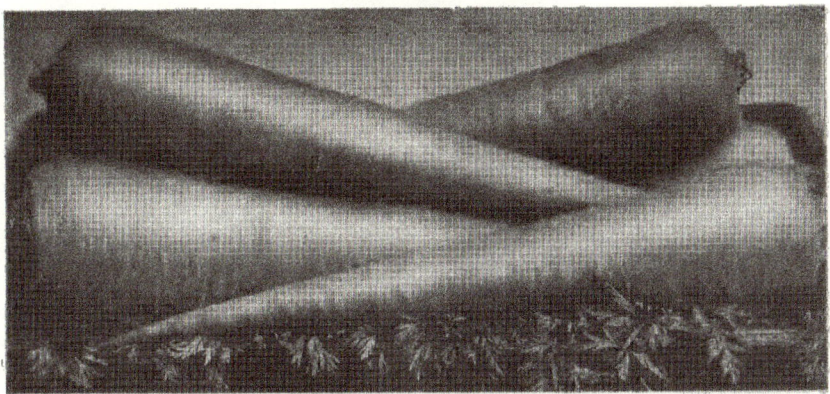

DANIELS' TELEGRAPH. *Reduced from a Photograph.*

Stump-rooted Varieties.

per oz. s. d.

☞ **DANIELS' SCARLET PERFECTION.** A grand main crop variety of the intermediate type, and being stump-rooted, it is well adapted for growing on soils where deep culture is not possible. The roots are of a bright orange colour, very handsome and uniform in shape, with a fine clear skin, which makes it a most desirable sort for exhibition. It is one of the best flavoured and heaviest cropping varieties for general use, and one we can highly recommend .. .. per pkt. 4d. 1 0

DANIELS' NEW EARLY FORCING HORN. One of the earliest Carrots yet introduced. In shape it is nearly round. They can be left thickly in the row, and drawn for use as required per pkt. 4d. 1 0

DANIELS' HARBINGER. A fine Carrot for early exhibition ; the roots are of good shape and excellent quality, averaging four to five inches in length, and three inches in diameter. It is a distinct and useful Carrot .. .. per pkt. 4d. 1 0

DANIELS' LONG RED WITHOUT HEART. Flesh bright red, without the core usually found in the carrot 0 8

EARLY FRENCH NANTES. A medium-sized, stump-rooted variety of very fine quality 0 8

EARLY SCARLET HORN. A stump-rooted variety. Very useful for first early crops 0 6

Long Varieties.

per oz. s. d.

☞ **DANIELS' TELEGRAPH.** This grand Carrot is one of the best forms of intermediate yet introduced, being far in advance of the old James' Scarlet. It produces a heavy crop of roots, which are of uniform shape, attractive colour, and very clear in the skin. Where sufficient depth of soil exists it will prove one of the most profitable sorts to grow. It is unequalled for exhibition purposes, having obtained more First Prizes than any Carrot with which we are acquainted

.. .. per pkt. 4d. 1 0

ALTRINCHAM IMPROVED LONG RED. Fine stock, and stores well 0 6

DANIELS' GIANT WHITE. Much larger and of finer quality than Belgian White. Highly recommended 0 6

JAMES' SCARLET (Intermediate). Excellent for shallow soils. One of the heaviest cropping and most useful for general use 0 6

LONG RED ST. VALERY. A very choice stock, producing clean handsome roots and a great improvement on the Long Surrey. Fine for exhibition 0 8

LONG RED SURREY or LONG ORANGE. Roots long, of good shape, and fine quality ; on a deep soil it will produce a very heavy crop 0 4

Cultivation.—By attention to a few points of importance, splendid clean straight Carrots can be cultivated without great delay. It is not necessary to manure the land for a Carrot crop, in fact, freshly manured land is a drawback ; the soil should be (where possible) of a deep light nature, and the land should, the Autumn previously, be deeply trenched two to three feet, and a quite light dressing of manure given at the same time ; land which has been recently used for Celery is excellent, and will not need specially manuring.

For the earliest crop, make a sowing on the hotbed in frames between the rows of early Potatoes, and pull the Carrots quite small. The first sowing of the outdoor crop should be made early in April on a warm border, Daniels' "Harbinger" or "Forcing Horn" being excellent kinds ; make other sowings in succession through the Summer until August, when the best kind to sow is "Scarlet Horn." For main crop, "Daniels' Scarlet Perfection" and "Telegraph" can be highly recommended.

Carrot seed should be sown on borders of finely worked soil, in drills about a foot apart. When the plants are nicely up, thin out gradually, leaving the smaller growing kinds such as "Forcing Horn," to be pulled as required, and the larger kinds seven to nine inches apart. Keep the hoe going between the sows to ensure cleanliness, and nothing more is needed until the end of October, when the crop should be lifted, the tops carefully twisted off, and the roots stored in dry sand in a cellar, for use as needed during the Winter.

When specimen roots are wanted for exhibition, it is the practice to make holes with a crowbar, and fill with fine soil, sowing the seeds on the top and thinning out to one plant in each hole, as advised for Parsnips.

CAULIFLOWERS.

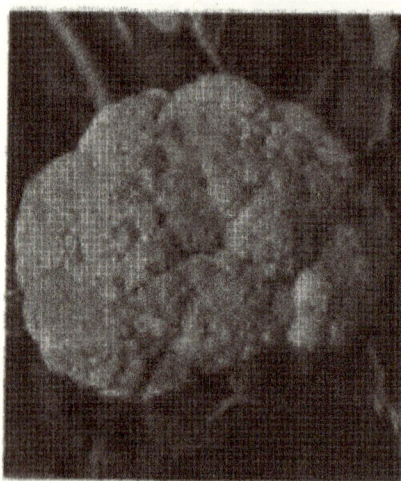

DANIELS' KING OF CAULIFLOWERS.

"I did very well last year with the **Cauliflowers** and **Onions** grown from your Seeds."
—Mr. T. HARPER, Newport.

The **Cauliflower** I had from you turned out very fine and I was pleased with it."—Mr. E. WOOD, Buckley.

"I am pleased with all the **Seeds** I had from you. I took eight First, two Second, four Third, and three Special Prizes at Woodchurch Show."—Mrs. MARSON, Woodchurch.

"I took several Prizes at our Show with **Vegetables** grown from your Seeds."—Mr. T. KNIGHT, Chorley Wood.

Cultivation.—The Cauliflower is one of the choicest of our vegetables, and requires much care and very liberal treatment. Cauliflowers are very liable to bolt if any check occurs in their growth, and therefore every care should be taken that they grow on from start to finish without a break. It does not much matter whether the soil on which Cauliflowers are grown is light or heavy, so long as it is thoroughly trenched, and a very liberal quantity of farmyard manure applied. To get the earliest Cauliflowers, the seed should be sown in September in the open, and transferred when big enough to cold frames for the Winter months. Early in March select a warm border and plant them out when a very early crop will be secured.

The earliest Spring sowing should be made in February in boxes on a hot bed, and the plants moved to frames and gradually hardened so as to be ready to plant out in May. A succession of sowings should be made in March in frames and in the open during April, May, and June, so as to secure an unbroken supply. Cauliflowers are most highly prized in Autumn when the Summer crops are over, and it is as well to have more than one batch. When planting and also during dry weather, great care should be given to watering. Frequent applications of liquid manure will give size to the heads for exhibition purposes.

Cauliflowers are particularly subject to white fly which causes the plant to become blind, and any suspicion of this should be met with a dressing of soot upon the leaves in the early morning. The beds should be regularly gone over to ensure the heads being cut before they get too old as they soon get past their best. For early work, **Daniels' King** is undoubtedly the best, followed by **Dwarf Mammoth** and **Autumn Queen.** For general crop, **Autumn Giant** will be found the most useful.

☞ **DANIELS' KING OF CAULIFLOWERS. The** earliest variety in cultivation, of very dwarf and compact habit, the heads beautifully white and of the finest texture. Seed raised in frames in February, and planted out as soon as the weather permits, will produce some fine heads in June. One of the best to sow for succession through the summer .. per pkt. 1s. 6d. and 2s. 6d.

DANIELS' SNOWBALL. An invaluable early variety of dwarf compact habit, producing fine white heads of excellent quality. Ready to cut in four months from time of sowing
per pkt. 1s. 6d. and 2s. 6d. —

DANIELS' DWARF MAMMOTH. A very superior dwarf early variety, grows to a larger size than Daniels' King, and forms a good succession to that variety, heads large, white, and compact. Also useful for forcing .. .. per pkt. 1s.   2 6

ECLIPSE. This is an excellent large Autumn variety, and very useful for Market purposes. By successional sowings it can be had from August to Christmas .. .. per pkt. 6d.   1 6

EARLY LONDON WHITE. Useful variety, growing to a large size, heads very white and firm .. .. per pkt. 4d.   1 0

SELF-PROTECTING AUTUMN GIANT. A fine late variety coming into use directly after Veitch's Autumn Giant. The heads are well-protected by luxuriant over-lapping foliage. May be had in good condition up to Christmas .. per pkt. 6d.   1 6

VEITCH'S AUTUMN GIANT. The most useful of our Autumn Cauliflowers and most valuable for general crop. It is very distinct in appearance, producing splendid large heads, beautifully white and firm, and of the finest texture   per pkt. 6d.   1 0

WALCHEREN. Sow under glass in February, to succeed the Spring Broccoli, and fit in beds from May to July for succession
per pkt. 4d.   1 0

☞ **DANIELS' AUTUMN QUEEN.** A grand variety, coming in fit for use three weeks earlier than Veitch's Autumn Giant, is very short-legged and compact; the heads are beautifully white and of the finest quality.
per pkt. 1s.   3 0

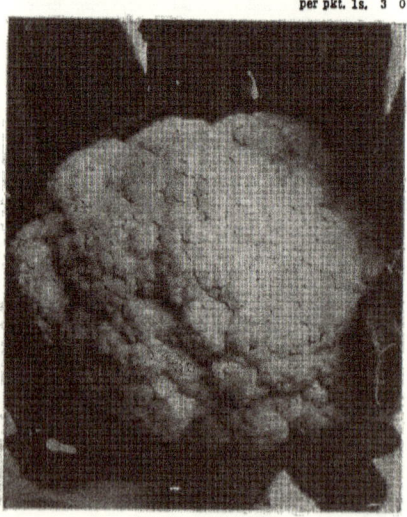

VEITCH'S AUTUMN GIANT.

CELERY.

Cultivation.—This very important vegetable is one that fully repays a liberal outlay both of labour and manure. Being a moisture loving plant and a gross feeder, it should, if possible, be raised in soil where, during the growing period, copious supplies of water can be applied. For the earliest crop sow the seed about the middle of February, giving some heat, and when the plants have made their seed leaves, have them pricked off into boxes or frames, giving if possible a gentle bottom heat to keep them growing. Make a further sowing in March in a similar way, and, if necessary, another in April in an open border; these later sowings will give some useful Celery for cooking. It is an excellent plan to get the Celery trenches ready quite early in the season, so that advantage may be taken of the first favourable showery day to put out the plants when large enough.

In making the trenches throw out the soil 12 or 14 inches deep and 18 inches wide, and be careful to retain the top soil so that it may be placed in the bottom of the trench; mix with it a good dressing of farmyard manure and in this mixture the young plants should be placed; the rest of the soil taken out of the trench should be piled up on the sides and used, when the time comes, for earthing up the Celery; allow a space of three or four feet between the trenches.

In planting out the Celery in the trenches, place the seedlings about nine inches apart, in a single row for the earliest crop; for the main crop they are often planted in double rows. In dry weather give liberal supplies of water or liquid manure to keep the plants growing, as if they get a check they are liable to bolt.

It is a good plan to give a sprinkling of soot over the foliage, while damp with the early morning dew, in order to keep away the Celery fly and snails.

The greatest care should be taken in earthing up Celery. As soon as the plants are about nine inches high, go over them and thoroughly clean off all side shoots, and tie the growth loosely with Raffia. Choose a fine day, and gradually work down some of the finest soil round the bases of the plants, being most careful not to allow any of the soil to get between the leaves; do not make the soil too hard, or it will stop the growth. Continue to earth up as the plants grow. The final earthing should form a ridge as a protection. In very severe weather it will be found an advantage to give a slight covering of straw or bracken over the top of the row.

WHITE VARIETIES.

per pkt.—s. d.

☞ **DANIELS' EARLIEST WHITE.** This fine white Celery has now firmly established its reputation as one of the very best for early work, and has become highly popular. Sown at the same time, it is ready for use quite six weeks earlier than any other variety. The heads which grow to a large size, are very firm and solid, and of a sweet nutty flavour ... 1 0

☞ **DANIELS' GIANT WHITE.** This grand Celery is undoubtedly one of the largest and best white varieties in cultivation. The heads are very solid and of excellent flavour. Very fine for exhibition 1 0

SANDRINGHAM DWARF WHITE. Useful early variety .. 3d. and 0 6
SEYMOUR'S SUPERB WHITE. Heads very solid, fine flavour. 3d. and 0 6
SILVER PLUME. A fine, white-leaved variety. It blanches well by simply tying up the plants with matting .. ... 6d. and 1 0

RED VARIETIES.

per pkt.—s. d.

☞ **DANIELS' EARLIEST PINK (new).** This grand new Celery is a useful companion to our Earliest White, and like that variety comes into use quite six weeks earlier than the old varieties. It grows to a large size, the heads being very solid and of excellent flavour. A most valuable variety for early shows 1 0

☞ **DANIELS' GIANT RED.** The largest red variety grown. The heads are of splendid colour, very solid, and of fine nutty flavour, one of the very best for exhibition purposes. The seed offered is saved from carefully selected heads only .. 1 0

☞ **DANIELS' EXHIBITION PINK.** A very fine Celery, producing large solid heads of a delicate rosy pink colour. A fine variety for exhibition, and of excellent flavour. 6d. and 1 0

CLAYWORTH PRIZE PINK. Heads very large, solid, and of a beautiful rosy pink colour. A most useful variety for general crop 6d. and 1 0
MANCHESTER FINE RED. Large, solid heads .. .. 3d. and 0 6
STANDARD BEARER. Heads firm, solid, and of an attractive nutty flavour; fine exhibition variety .. .. 6d. and 1 0
MIXED RED AND WHITE. Useful for Cottagers .. .. 3d. and 0 6
CELERIAC, or TURNIP-ROOTED CELERY. Very useful for flavouring soups, &c. 0 6

"I have taken over forty Prizes, mostly Firsts. I won First Prize with your **Giant Red Celery** in open competition."—Mr. G. SCOURFIELD, Neath.

"I have taken two First Prizes with your Celery at Swindon Show. It has been record year."—Mr. W. GRIFFIN, Swindon.

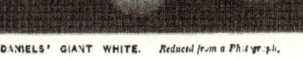

DANIELS' GIANT WHITE. *Reduced from a Photograph.*

CRESS.

CRESS, GROWING IN BOX.

	per oz.—s. d.
PLAIN. The best for early salads　　per qt. 1s. 6d., per pint 10d.	0 2
CURLED. For salads in the second leaf „ 1s. 8d., „ „ 1s.	0 2
AUSTRALIAN or GOLDEN. This valuable Cress is a most desirable addition to all salads	0 4
DANIELS' GARNISHING or PARSLEY-LEAVED. Useful alike for salads and garnishing	0 6
AMERICAN or LAND. Eaten as Water Cress in Winter	0 . 4
SORREL-LEAVED. The largest-leaved of all, dark green colour, and good flavour. A most useful salad	0 6
WATER. Sow in a moist shady place　　per pkt. 6d. and 1s.	—

Cultivation.—Cress is one of the most useful salads grown, and it is quite easy to keep up a continual supply, as no expensive appliances are needed. If a greenhouse is available, fill boxes with good soil to within about half inch of the top, pressing the soil firmly, then sow the seeds thickly and evenly but do not cover them with soil. Put the boxes in a dark place and give a good watering; in about a fortnight the cress will be ready to eat. By repeating this process a succession can be maintained throughout the early Spring.

During Summer a shady border should be selected, and the soil raked fine and pressed firm. Sow the seeds and press down with a board, giving good waterings and protection with mats until the seed has germinated. To keep up a constant supply a sowing should be made every week.

American or Land Cress is most useful for mixed salads, and is quite easy to grow; sow the seeds from March onwards on a north border and thin out to allow about four inches between each plant, using the outside leaves only.

Water-cress can be grown in ordinary garden soil provided a shady border is chosen and copious waterings given. The seed should be sown in April, and the plants thinned out, leaving about six inches between each. Keep the plants plucked to prevent them from flowering. In Autumn fill pans half full of soil and place some of the plants therein. Put them in a greenhouse and keep thoroughly watered, and a supply of good tender Water-cress will be available all the Winter.

MUSTARD.

	per oz.—s. d.		per oz.—s. d.
WHITE For early salads　　per quart 1s. 9d., per pint 1s.	0 2	**CHINESE.** Fine salad variety　　per quart 3s., pint 1s.	0 4

Cultivation.—The Common or White Mustard is much used for saladings, and is generally used with Cress. Out of doors, any cool, moist place is suitable for sowings, which should be made at frequent intervals during Spring and Summer. When sown under glass in Winter and early Spring, no better way exists than that recommended for Cress.

CAPSICUM.

Very valuable as decorative plants for the conservatory, besides being exceedingly useful for stews, pickles, &c.

	per pkt.—s. d.					per pkt.—s. d.
RUBY KING	1 0	**LONG YELLOW**				0 4
CELESTIAL	6d. and 1 0	**FROOOPF'S GIANT**				0 6
CHILI or BIRD	6d. and 1 0	**MONSTREUSE**				0 6
ELEPHANT'S TRUNK	0 3	**SWEET GOLDEN DAWN**				0 6
LONG RED	6d. and 1 0	**MIXED, all kinds**				0 4
	0 4					

CHICORY.

	per pkt.—s. d.
IMPROVED LARGE-LEAVED. Excellent for blanching	0 6
LARGE-ROOTED or COFFEE	0 6
WHITLOEF. Equally good as a salad or boiled. Sow in June	0 6

CORN SALAD (Lamb's Lettuce).

	per oz.—s. d.
GREEN CABBAGING. A fine variety, rosette-shaped　　per pkt. 4d.	0 6
LETTUCE-LEAVED	4d. 0 9
LARGE ROUND-LEAVED DUTCH	4d. 0 9

ENDIVE.

	per oz.—s. d.
☞ **DANIELS' SUPERB CURLED.** The best of all the Curled Endives, it bleaches well, is of first-class quality　　per pkt. 6d.	1 6
DANIELS' PRIZE MOSS CURLED. A splendid variety for exhibition, leaves beautifully curled, is very hardy, and bleaches well　　per pkt. 4d.	1 0
GREEN CURLED. Extra	0 8
BATAVIAN GREEN. Broad-leaved, very hardy, and desirable for Winter cultivation, tie up for blanching	0 8
EXTRA BROAD-LEAVED. An excellent variety, highly recommended　　per pkt. 6d.	1 0
WHITE CURLED. Useful variety　　„ 3d.	0 9

GOURD or PUMPKIN.

Large Varieties.

	per pkt.—s. d.
☞ **DANIELS' YELLOW MAMMOTH.** Seed from large, handsomely netted fruit, weighing one hundredweight or more　　6d. and	1 0
POTIRON JAUNE or MAMMOTH. A giant variety　　6d. and	1 0
COMMON PUMPKIN. Very useful for pies and preserves in Winter	0 3
VARIEGATED TURK'S CAP. Striped orange, green, and white	0 6

Smaller Ornamental Varieties.

	per pkt.—s. d.
SMALL ORANGE. Strongly resembling an orange	0 4
PEAR-SHAPED. Green and yellow, pretty	0 4

Twelve varieties, one packet of each, 2s. 6d.

CUCUMBERS.

per pkt.—s. d.

☞ **LORD ROBERTS.** An exceedingly handsome variety raised by Mr. W. H. Apthorpe, Cambridge ; the result of a cross between Royal Osborne and Lockie's Perfection. The fruit which are longer than the last named variety, are of a rich dark green colour, of splendid shape, with no neck, and are borne in the greatest profusion. It is useful for Winter or Summer cultivation, and on account of its prolificness and beautiful appearance, will prove a most valuable variety for the private or market grower per pkt. 1s. 6d. and 2 6

☞ **DISEASE RESISTER.** A very prolific variety of similar type to the Amateur, but a stronger grower. The strong leathery leaves resisting all kinds of disease much better and it keeps in bearing for a long period .. 1s. 6d. and 2 6

☞ **THE AMATEUR.** This can perhaps be best described as a very finely selected stock of The Rochford or Covent Garden type. It is enormously productive, bearing 3 to 4 fruit at a joint. The fruit, which are of handsome shape, average about 20 to 24 inches in length, are slightly spined and of fine colour, whilst the neck is very short. As its name implies, it will prove one of the best for the amateur grower for all purposes .. .. per pkt. 1s. 6d. and 2 6

☞ **DANIELS' IMPROVED TELEGRAPH.** A great improvement on the old Telegraph, bearing clean, straight fruit twenty to twenty-four inches long, an abundant bearer. Our own selected stock, all saved from picked fruit per pkt. 1s. 6d. and 2 6

☞ **DANIELS' DEFIANCE** (early prolific). A variety of hardy, robust constitution, producing in great abundance very short-necked and elegant fruit of a rich dark green colour, from eighteen to twenty-four inches in length, straight and uniform .. .. 1s. and 2 0

DANIELS' DUKE OF ALBANY. This is the finest Cucumber ever introduced for exhibition, having obtained numerous First Prizes. The fruit are long, straight, and of a beautiful dark green colour, very handsome, and of the finest quality .. .. .. 1s. and 2 0

DANIELS' DUKE OF EDINBURGH. A beautiful, white-spined variety of fine, robust constitution and habit, its fruit growing rapidly to the length of thirty to thirty-six inches .. .. .. 1s. and 2 6

EVERY-DAY. This fine Cucumber is of medium size, the fruit being dark-skinned, very handsome in shape, most prolific, and of splendid flavour. First Class Certificate, R.H.S. 1 0

THE ROCHFORD. A most prolific bearer. The fruit are slightly spined, eighteen to twenty inches in length, of a beautiful fresh green colour, and of the most handsome form 1 0

LOCKIE'S PERFECTION. The fruit are produced in great abundance 1s. and 2 0

ROLLISSON'S TELEGRAPH .. .. .. 6d. and 1 0

TENDER AND TRUE. Superior quality and flavour 1 0

SPECIAL NOTICE.

One of the great causes of failure in raising Cucumber Seed is too much moisture at starting. To begin with, the soil should be warm and not over moist ; plant in small pots three or four Seeds in each ; place in heat of from 80° to 90°. Be sure and give no water until the Seeds are well up, and then water but sparingly for a day or two. We have adopted this plan for many years past with the greatest success.

RIDGE CUCUMBERS.

per pkt.—s. d.

☞ **DANIELS' PERFECTION RIDGE.** The longest and best out-door variety in cultivation, is very hardy and prolific, bearing a heavy crop of nice shaped fruit, averaging fifteen to twenty inches in length and of superior flavour 6d. and 1 0

JAPANESE CLIMBING. A most useful variety for growing on trellis work, &c., being very ornamental. It produces a good crop of fruit, averaging from ten to twelve inches in length .. .. 6d. and 1 0

LONG PRICKLY. A very useful variety of fine flavour 0 4

SHORT PRICKLY. Very hardy, fine for pickling 0 3

STOCKWOOD. Fine selected stock .. .. 3d. and 0 6

PROLIFIC PICKLING. The most prolific out-door variety ; very hardy .. 0 4

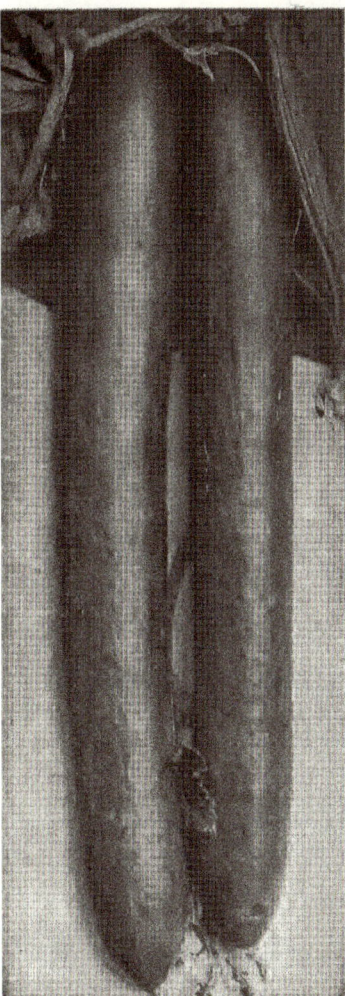

LORD ROBERTS. *Reduced from a Photograph.*

LEEKS.

Cultivation.—The Leek is one of the most nutritious vegetables cultivated, and although to produce exhibition specimens much care and attention is needed, still a thoroughly good crop for cooking purposes can be grown quite easily. Leeks are gross feeders and therefore require well tilled and liberally manured ground; the best plan is to give the land a thorough dressing of well-decayed manure in Autumn and trench it deeply, allowing it to remain rough for the Winter. The seed should be sown in drills in March for the main crop, and care must be taken to keep the ground thoroughly clean from the outset in order to give the seedlings a good start.

The easiest mode of culture is to dibble the young plants when about six inches high into holes made about twelve inches deep, giving occasional dressings of liquid manure. In September draw the earth round the plants. It is best to defer using Leeks till as late as possible in the Autumn, as the flavour improves.

When it is desired to grow Leeks for exhibition, a good plan is to grow them in trenches in the same way as Celery, allowing two feet between the trenches; for this purpose the seed should be sown on a gentle hotbed in February, and the seedlings pricked off into boxes when big enough; it is important that the young plants be thoroughly hardened, as they will not stand coddling, but cold draughts should be avoided. When the plants have made about six inches of growth, plant them into trenches, allowing about 15 inches between each plant; lift the plants out of the box with a trowel, to ensure getting a good lot of roots. As the plants grow, the soil must be carefully and firmly worked round the roots and this process continued all the Summer at intervals, giving frequent waterings of liquid manure. Some growers place collars of brown paper round the stems before commencing to earth up the plants as this excludes all light and is a great aid to blanching.

There is every encouragement to grow Leeks to a large size, as the flavour of the finest specimens is superior to the smaller ones. This is not so in most vegetables, but is certainly the case with Leeks.

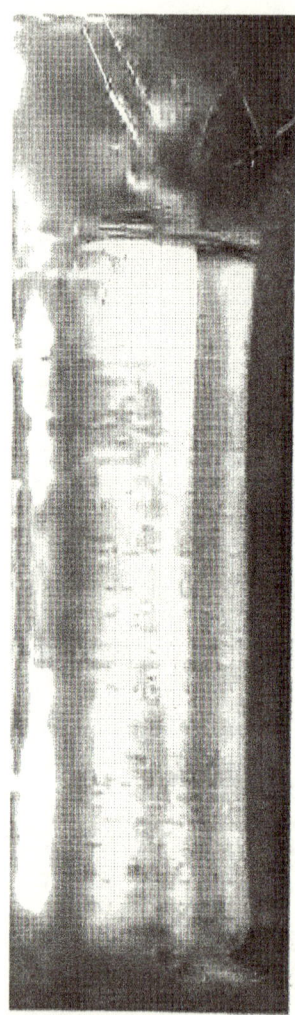

LEEK, DANIELS' CHAMPION.
Reduced from a Photograph.

	per oz.—s. d.
☞ **DANIELS' CHAMPION.** This is undoubtedly one of the finest Leeks in cultivation. It grows to a large size, and is unsurpassed for exhibition purposes, having produced specimens with 18 inches of blanched stem, and of perfect shape. It comes early into use, and is of exceptionally mild flavour. It has obtained First Prize at a great number of Shows on account of its extraordinary clearness of skin and handsome appearance. We strongly recommend this variety to intending exhibitors, as one likely to give the greatest satisfaction .. .. .. per pkt. 1s.	2 6
AYTON CASTLE GIANT. Remarkably large and good, may be grown ten to twelve inches in circumference, and with one foot of blanched stem per pkt. 4d.	1 0
CONQUEROR. First-class; very superior either for competition or culinary purposes. It is of large size and blanches for considerable distance up the stem; highly recommended .. .. per pkt. 1s.	2 6
HENRY'S PRIZE. Exceedingly large, blanches well, flavour mild, fine for exhibition .. .. .. per pkt. 4d.	1 0
LONDON FLAG. Large, broad-leaved. A good old variety possessing many excellent qualities	0 6
LYON. One of the largest kinds grown and excellent in every way. A kind much in demand for exhibition purposes .. .. per pkt. 6d.	1 6
MUSSELBURGH. Extra broad-leaved, blanches to a large size, flavour mild, highly esteemed for soups. A well-established kind of considerable merit and hardiness; grand stock .. .. .. per pkt. 3d.	0 9

MELONS.

Cultivation.—This delicious fruit is widely cultivated by all who can command sufficient heat. Melons are raised from seed in a similar way to Cucumbers, and their general treatment is much the same in the early stages of their growth.

Sow the seeds singly in a pot of fine loam and leaf mould, and place on a hot-bed; as soon as the plants are in the rough leaf, pot on into six-inch pots; keep at an even temperature to avoid checking the plants, meanwhile have the beds prepared by forming a mound of good rich turfy loam and well-decayed manure on the border of the greenhouse stage, or in the frame. When planting make the soil quite firm round the stem, and give liberal waterings of clear water.

When the fruits are set, they should be thinned out to about two or three fruits on each plant, and occasional waterings of weak liquid manure given. As they ripen keep the bed a little drier; the temperature for Melon growing should be about 75° to 80° in the day, and 65° to 70° at night.

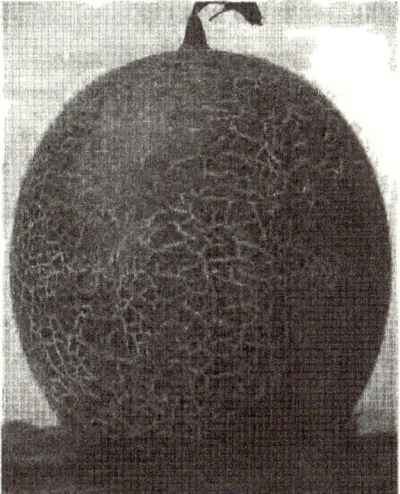

DANIELS' ROYAL NORFOLK. *Reduced from a Photograph.*

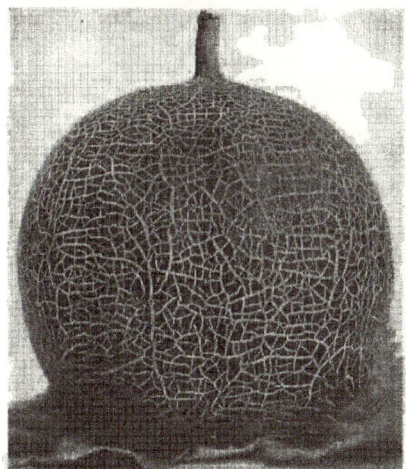

NEW MELON, EMINENCE. *Reduced from a Photograph.*

per pkt.—s. d.

☞ **NEW MELON, DANIELS' ROYAL NORFOLK.** This fine melon is the result of a cross between Hero of Lockinge and Read's Scarlet-Flesh. It is of strong habit of growth, a very free setter, bearing good useful sized fruit, oval in shape, of a dark green colour changing when ripe to a deep golden yellow, covered with a fine even net. The flesh is thick, of a lovely salmon colour, and of the most exquisite flavour, and without the green band next the skin so often met with in scarlet-fleshed melons .. .. 1s. 6d. and 2 0

☞ **NEW MELON, KING GEORGE.** A beautifully netted oval shaped variety. The fruit average three to four pounds in weight, and the flesh which is scarlet-orange in colour is exceedingly thick, juicy, and of excellent flavour. It is a free setter, and can be grown either with or without heat 1 0

☞ **NEW MELON, EMINENCE.** A fine variety, raised by Mr. A. McKellar, The Royal Gardens, Windsor. Received an Award of Merit from the Royal Horticultural Society. The fruit is rather large, roundish oval, skin bright yellow and beautifully netted, flesh white, thick. Very melting and of delicious flavour .. 1 6

IDEAL. This is undoubtedly a very valuable and desirable variety. It is the result of crossing Ingestre Hybrid and Royal Favourite. The flesh is thick and of a pale green colour, very luscious and of delicious flavour. The fruit is of medium size, rich yellow, and well netted. It is a free setter, and the fruit matures rapidly 1 6

GUNTON SCARLET (S.F.). A very superior scarlet-fleshed Melon of medium size, oval in shape, and finely netted. The flesh is very deep and the finest flavour of any Melon with which we are acquainted. Highly recommended .. 1s. and 2 0

*****BLENHEIM ORANGE** (S.F.). A grand scarlet-fleshed variety, very prolific and fine setter 1 0

DANIELS' IMPROVED GOLDEN PERFECTION. A splendid green-fleshed variety, regularly and beautifully netted; thin skin, flesh very thick, firm, of the most exquisite flavour .. 1s. and 2 0

DUCHESS OF YORK (W.F.). A cross between Best of All and Hero of Lockinge; fruit medium-sized, thick in the flesh, and of delicious flavour 1 6

HERO OF LOCKINGE (W.F.). Fine exhibition variety; very prolific 1 0

INGESTON HYBRID (S.F.). The fruit is large and handsome, and nicely netted. The flesh is thick, of rich salmon colour, juicy and melting, and of fine flavour 1 0

MUNRO'S LITTLE HEATH (S.F.). A well-known variety of excellent flavour 1 0

*****ROYAL SOVEREIGN** (W.F.). A grand variety. Raised at The Royal Gardens, Windsor; has received Award of Merit from the R.H.S. It has a robust constitution, and is a free setter. The skin is of a beautiful golden colour, slightly netted, flesh white 1 6

ROYALTY. A new variety of strong constitution, vigorous growth, and a free setter. The fruit is very handsome, round, yellow, and beautifully netted. The flesh pale green, melting, and juicy 1 6

*****READ'S SCARLET-FLESH.** One of the best red-fleshed varieties, a free setter; flesh thick, solid, and of excellent flavour 6d. and 1 0

CANTALOUP. This variety may be grown in a cool frame, and is very prolific. The fruit can be grown from four to six pounds in weight, and are delightfully refreshing during the hot weather 1 0

Abbreviations.—Those marked with an (*) have received a First Class Certificate from the Royal Horticultural Society. S.F. scarlet flesh, G.F. green flesh, W.F. white flesh.

LETTUCES—Cabbage Varieties.

DANIELS' CONTINUITY LETTUCE.

Daniels' Continuity.

The Longest Standing Cabbage Lettuce in the World.

This fine Cabbage Lettuce is remarkable from the fact that not even in the hottest and driest season does it ever run to seed, the heads remaining firm and crisp long after all others have bolted or decayed. A bed of these sown or planted will keep up a supply of good Lettuces for a long period, one sowing of these being equal to three or four sowings of other varieties Per pkt., 6d. ; oz., 1s. 6d.

	per pkt. s. d.	per oz. s. d.
DANIELS' EXHIBITION GIANT (new). One of the largest Cabbage Lettuces yet introduced, and grows to an enormous size without becoming coarse. The heads are very firm, crisp, and of excellent flavour. For exhibition purposes it is unrivalled, and is one of the best for Salads	0 6	1 6
DANIELS' MAGNUM BONUM. A splendid Cabbage Lettuce growing to a large size, the heads being very firm and crisp and of excellent flavour, stands well ; a useful variety for exhibition	0 6	1 6
DANIELS' GOLDEN BEAUTY. A grand Summer Lettuce of fine appearance ; the leaves are of a light golden colour, very crisp and solid, stands the drought well	0 1	1 0
DANIELS' MAMMOTH GREEN WINTER. A fine large Cabbage Lettuce. The heads although large are very firm and crisp ; an excellent variety for Autumn sowing	0 4	1 0

	per pkt. s. d.	per oz. s. d.
DANIELS' QUEEN OF SUMMER. This is one of the finest Summer Lettuces yet introduced. It is remarkable for its large size, splendid appearance, and for withstanding the drought. It produces fine, crisp, and tender Lettuces in the driest season ..	0 4	1 0
DANIELS' TENDER AND TRUE. A fresh, tender lettuce about the size of All the Year Round, with a slight tinge of red on edge of leaf, it is very delicate eating in the driest season	0 6	1 6
DANIELS' GIANT WHITE. An exceedingly large and fine variety, crisp and tender and of fine flavour, stands a long time without running to seed	0 4	1 0
DANIELS' BLACK-SEEDED TEXTER. Large, compact, and solid, one of the most splendid varieties in cultivation	0 4	1 0
ALL THE YEAR ROUND. One of the best for general use ; very hardy ..	0 4	1 0
DRUMHEAD or MALTA. Well known	0 3	0 8
LARGE WHITE WINTER. The best for Winter use ; heads large and solid	0 4	1 0
STANSTEAD PARK. A fine variety for sowing in Autumn to stand the Winter	0 4	1 0
NEW YORK. The heads attain a large size, and are very crisp and tender ; grand variety for exhibition ..	0 4	1 0
NEAPOLITAN. Leaves beautifully curled and tender, one of the finest Summer sorts	0 3	0 9
WHEELER'S TOM THUMB. The earliest variety grown, heads small, and very solid and tender	0 4	1 0
MIXED CABBAGE VARS. ..	0 2	0 6
MIXED. All kinds, Cos and Cabbage ..	0 2	0 6

"All the seeds I had from you did well, especially the Lettuces, which were grand."—Mr. W. MINERS, The Lizard.

"Your Large Winter White Cabbage Lettuce was a great success last year. I would like the same variety this year."—Mr. A. C. SMITH, Wigton.

"Your Dreadnought Lettuce turned out splendidly, each weighing 4 lbs."—Mr. J. RINGER, Farnborough.

DANIELS' QUEEN OF SUMMER.

LETTUCES—Cos Varieties.

DANIELS' GIANT WHITE COS LETTUCE. *Reduced from a Photograph.*

	per pkt. s. d.	per oz. s. d.
DANIELS' GIANT WHITE. The finest and largest Cos Lettuce in cultivation, very tender and crisp, with fine solid hearts, and will stand a long time without running to seed ; should be grown in all gardens ; unrivalled for exhibition purposes ..	1 0	2 6
DANIELS' DREADNOUGHT. One of the largest Cos Lettuces in cultivation, the heads being very solid, crisp, and of fine flavour. An invaluable variety for exhibition ..	1 0	2 6
DANIELS' ALL HEART. A fine Cos Lettuce growing to a large size, the leaves folding well over the hearts, which are very solid and of fine flavour ..	0 6	1 6
DANIELS' SELECTED PARIS WHITE. Self-blanching, tender, and mild flavour ; useful exhibition variety	0 4	1 0
DANIELS' BLACK-SEEDED BATH ..	0 4	1 0
DANIELS' GREEN WINTER. An excellent and hardy kind, valuable for Winter and early Spring ..	0 4	1 0
DANIELS' SOLID BROWN. A medium-sized Lettuce, outer leaves brown, hearts very solid and of a beautiful creamy yellow ; very crisp, requires no tying. An invaluable variety for Winter use ..	0 4	1 0
HICKS' HARDY WHITE. A superior variety both for Summer and Winter use ..	0 4	1 0
PARIS WHITE. Best for general use ..	0 3	0 10
MIXED COS VARS. All the best for succession	0 2	0 6
DANIELS' LITTLE GEM. A very early Cos Lettuce, coming into use at the same time as the Cabbage varieties. It is very dwarf and compact, the heads, which are self-folding, require no tying ..	0 6	1 6

"I have been very lucky with the Seeds I purchased from you. I won three Prizes with your Giant Cos Lettuce."—Mr. E. SPOONER.

DANIELS' LITTLE GEM.

Cultivation.—It is often necessary that a practically continuous supply of Lettuces should be maintained throughout the year, and by a succession of sowings this may be done. For the earliest crop the seed should be sown in boxes under glass during January, and when big enough to handle prick out the plants about three inches apart into frames, there to be hardened off ready for planting out in a south border when the weather permits. Early in March a sowing may be made out of doors, preferably on a south border. Sow the seeds in drills, cover lightly with soil and protect from the birds if possible ; when the plants are big enough prick them out six inches apart. By cutting some of the plants early space will be left which will allow the remainder to develop.

A succession of sowings may be made until the beginning of September, and the plants which are to stand the Winter should be finally pricked out in October, the most sheltered position in the garden being chosen. In a severe Winter it will be found necessary to give some protection to these plants ; a slight covering of straw or bracken being suitable. To secure crispness and succulence in Lettuces, liberal supplies of water should be given, and the hoe kept going regularly between the rows. For Spring and Summer use we recommend in the Cos varieties, "Daniels' Giant White" and "Daniels' All Heart" ; in the Cabbage varieties, "Daniels' Queen of Summer" and "Daniels' Continuity," the latter is a kind which very rarely runs to seed even in the hottest weather. For Autumn and Winter work "Daniels' Solid Brown" and "Daniels' Green Winter," both very hardy Cos Lettuces, and "All the Year Round" and "Large White Winter," and "Daniels' Mammoth Green" in Cabbage Lettuces, are to our mind the pick of the List.

ONIONS FOR SPRING SOWING.

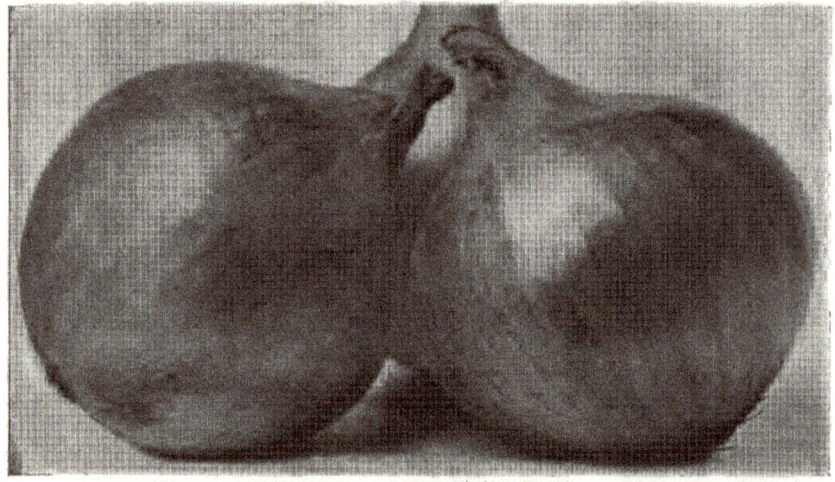

DANIELS' SELECTED AILSA CRAIG. *Reduced from a Photograph.*

DANIELS' SELECTED AILSA CRAIG. This grand Onion has now taken its place as one of the largest and most useful varieties for all purposes. It is very good sown either in Spring or Autumn, and produces a heavy crop of fine handsome bulbs, which are unrivalled for exhibition purposes. They have been grown to the enormous weight of 26, 28, 30, and 34 lbs. per dozen bulbs. Our own selected stock grown from picked bulbs. Per pkt. 9d. ; per oz. 2s.

per oz.—s. d.

ROUSHAM PARK HERO. A magnificent variety of the White Spanish type. The bulbs, which are very solid, grow to a large size, producing a heavy crop of excellent quality and fine appearance. It is a grand sort for exhibition purposes, and an extra good keeper .. .. .. per pkt. 4d. 1 0

CRANSTON'S EXCELSIOR. A superior variety of fine globular shape, very deep, with fine skin; has been grown two to three pounds in weight, is very mild in flavour; a good keeper and excellent exhibition variety .. per pkt. 9d. 2 0

per oz.—s. d.

DANIELS' NEW RED GLOBE. The finest Red Onion in cultivation. The bulbs are large, of a fine globular shape, and of a beautiful dark crimson. Besides being very attractive in appearance, it has the mild flavour and good keeping qualities of the very best of the White Spanish type .. .. per pkt. 4d. 1 0

UP-TO-DATE. A fine new variety of globular shape. It is very solid, and has a well developed shoulder, and will therefore produce a heavier crop than the older sorts. The skin is a bright straw colour. It is an excellent keeper, and will be found a useful variety for exhibition .. .. per pkt. 4d. 1 0

EVIDENCE OF QUALITY.

ONIONS FOR SPRING SOWING.

DANIELS' IMPROVED WHITE SPANISH. *Reduced from a Photograph.*

DANIELS' IMPROVED WHITE SPANISH. This grand stock of Onion has been carefully selected by us for a great many years, and we have no hesitation in recommending it to our customers as one of the very best of its type ; grows to a large size, very even, and it is unequalled for mildness of flavour. It is a very heavy cropper, a grand variety for Exhibition purposes, and is sure to give satisfaction.

Per pkt. 9d. ; per oz. 2s.

	per oz.—s.	d.
JAMES' KEEPING. An excellent keeper of fine globular shape, producing a very heavy crop of bulbs of the finest quality	0	9
NUNEHAM PARK. Much recommended, bulbs of fine globular shape and of good keeping quality	0	8
BEDFORDSHIRE CHAMPION. A well-known variety, producing a very heavy crop of good sized bulbs. Keeps well	0	9
BROWN GLOBE. Very useful, heavy cropper	0	9
DANIELS' BLOOD RED. Fine rich colour, very hardy	0	8

	per oz.—s.	d.
WHITE SPANISH. Ordinary stock. A heavy cropper, flesh very firm, and keeps well	0	4
WHITE SPANISH, Portugal or Reading. A finely selected stock, producing a very heavy crop of handsome bulbs, of first-class keeping quality	0	8
ZITTEAU GIANT YELLOW. A magnificent variety with fine yellow skin, and grows to a large size, the bulbs are of handsome appearance and excellent quality, remains sound till June. May also be sown with advantage in Autumn	0	6
STRASBURGH or DEPTFORD. Well known	0	4
MIXED, all sorts for Spring sowing	0	6

DANIELS' GOLDEN GLOBE. One of the finest types of Globe Onion in cultivation. The bulbs are of true globular shape with bright golden yellow skin ; the flesh is very solid and of mild flavour. It produces a very heavy crop of fine, handsome bulbs, and is one of the best keepers. A most useful variety for all purposes. **Per pkt. 6d. ; per oz. 1s. 6d.**

EVIDENCE OF QUALITY.

" I sowed half an ounce of your Golden Globe Onion Seed at springtime and I have taken up twenty stones of Onions."—Mr. J. RASPIN, Driffield.

" I had a fine crop of Onions this year from your Seed (Golden Globe); a packet produced five bushels on one rod of ground."—Mr. H. SIVIOUR, Mitcham.

" The Golden Globe Onion Seed I had last year was very good." Mr. H. CAUSTON, Mundford.

" I cannot speak too highly of your Golden Rocca Onion."—Mr. W. JONES, Poole.

" I am pleased to tell you that I have taken First Prize two years running with your Golden Rocca Onion."—Mr. J. WOOSTER, Southall.

" I took seven First and one Second Prize at Wymondham Show with Onions grown from your Seeds."—Mr. W. JOLLEY, Old Buckenham.

" We have been shown a photograph of your Onions grown by Mr. Davis Ibley, from one ounce of your Seed, and the total weight of Onions lifted out of the Seed was 1 cwt, 3 qrs. 14 lbs, most of which are four to five inches across. It is a remarkable crop in every respect."—THE STROUD JOURNAL.

I took the First Prize at our Show with your Golden Rocca Onion. I have not been beaten with this variety." Mr. H. BRIDGES, Stockton-on-Tees.

DANIELS' GOLDEN GLOBE.

ONION–Allan's Reliance.

ALLAN'S RELIANCE. *From a Photograph.*

☞ **ALLAN'S RELIANCE.** This fine Onion has been grown and selected by Mr. Allan, of Gunton Park Gardens, for many years past, and, as will be seen from our illustration, is now brought up to the very highest type of a White Spanish Onion ; besides being of splendid size and keeping quality, it is unsurpassed for exhibition.   Per pkt. 6d. ; per oz. 1s. 6d.

ALL THE YEAR ROUND. A new type of Onion growing to a large size, but having the advantage over many of the present exhibition varieties of being a grand keeper. The bulbs ripen off well, and from seed sown early in Spring have been grown to over 1¼ lb. each. Per pkt. 6d. ; oz. 1s. 6d.

COCOANUT. This fine Onion has been grown to the weight of three pounds each. The skin is a very delicate pale straw colour, flesh white and mild ; one of the best for exhibition.   Per pkt. 1s. ; per oz. 2s. 6d.

Silver Skinned or Pickling Varieties.

per oz.—s. d.

EARLY WHITE GEM. One of the earliest in cultivation, three weeks earlier than the Queen, and comes to maturity from eight to ten weeks from time of sowing. Very useful for pickling   ..   ..   ..   per pkt. 4d.   1 0

per oz.— s. d.

EARLY QUEEN. Remarkably quick-growing, may be sown in July and will ripen the same year 0 9

SILVER SKIN. Of very quick growth, best for pickling   ..   0 9

Cultivation.—There are few vegetable crops upon which so much care is expended as the Onion, and during recent years its culture has received much more attention than was formerly the case. When the seed can be raised in January in heat (thereby obtaining an early start) it is possible to grow bulbs of equal size to those grown from seed sown the previous Autumn ; about the last week in January is the time for the earliest sowing.

Sow the seed in boxes or pots in fine soil, a good mixture being two parts of good loam to one part of decomposed manure, or leaf soil. When the young plants are about three inches high prick them off into boxes, and give all the light possible, gradually admitting air, and hardening as the days lengthen, until the time arrives for planting out in the beds about the middle of April. The earliest sowing out of doors should be made in February, and the main sowing of all kinds in March.

The greatest care should be taken in preparing the Onion bed, the ground being thoroughly raked over, all the stones cleared off, and a perfectly fine surface obtained and the soil made quite firm. Sow the seeds very evenly in shallow drills about eighteen inches apart and carefully cover the seed by putting the soil from the side of the drills with the feet. The whole bed should then be well trodden down both down the bed and across as well, after this, again rake the soil level and little further work is necessary beyond keeping the hoe going and thinning out the plants when the time arrives. Unless specially fine bulbs are required it is not advisable to thin too much. To prevent an attack of Onion Maggot in a dry season, a good watering with lime water will be found to be of much service.

Great care is necessary in harvesting the Onion crop. It is a good plan to bend over the tops of the plants in August by going over the plants individually, this will assist the ripening of the bulbs. Onions require to be thoroughly ripened before being taken off the ground and should, therefore, be pulled about the middle of September and turned over on the ground every two or three days for a fortnight, when they should be gathered into an airy shed in readiness for roping together, this being the best method of storing them for Winter use.

ONIONS FOR AUTUMN SOWING.

DANIELS' GOLDEN ROCCA. *Reduced from a Photograph.*

☞ **DANIELS' GOLDEN ROCCA.** One of the largest and finest Onions ever introduced. Fine globular shape, golden yellow skin, mild flavour, and with careful cultivation comes equal to the imported Portugal Onions, and keeps sound till June. This variety is the best exhibition kind known, and has obtained more Prizes than any other Onion. If sown in Autumn, and kept under first-class cultivation, will grow bulbs two to three pounds each ; may also be sown in Spring, and will produce some fine bulbs.   **Per packet 6d. ; per ounce 1s. 6d.**

	per oz.—s. d.		per oz. s. d.
DANIELS' GIANT ROCCA. A splendid large globular variety of delicate flavour ; grows to a large size	0 9	**TRIPOLI ITALIAN RED.** Fine dark red skin ; a well-known and popular sort	0 8
DANIELS' WHITE ELEPHANT TRIPOLI. The largest and best of the Tripoli sorts .. .. .. per pkt. 4d.	1 0	**TRIPOLI ITALIAN WHITE.** Similar to the above, but milder ..	0 8
SILVER SKIN. Very early, excellent for Spring use	0 9	**LISBON WHITE.** Very useful for pulling green for salads early in Spring	0 4

PLANTS.

Strong Autumn sown, to plant out for show purposes, can be supplied in Spring of the following kinds only :—

White Elephant Tripoli, Golden Rocca, Giant Rocca
Ailsa Craig, and Zitteau Giant Yellow. All Carriage Paid } .. .. each sort 2s. per 100.

The Autumn sowing of these, which offers many advantages to the cultivator, has very much grown in favour of late years. When sown in Autumn, Onions grow to a much larger size, and are milder in flavour than those sown in Spring, especially when transplanted, and being much less liable to attack from fly, are rarely destroyed by maggot. They are besides exceedingly valuable for the supply of fresh green Onions in early Spring which can always be relied on.

Cultivation.—For securing specially fine Onions there is no doubt that it is much better to sow the seed in the Autumn. The ground should be prepared as for the Spring crop, except that the drills should be made a little deeper. Sow the seed any time from the middle of July to the end of August and treat in the same manner as advised for Spring sowing. Keep the ground clear of weeds, and give good soakings of water, if the Autumn is a dry one. If cooking size only is needed it will merely be found necessary to thin out the Onions and a good crop will be obtained, but if exhibition bulbs are required, the strongest must be selected in Spring, lifted carefully with a trowel, and transplanted nine inches apart on to a specially prepared bed of rich soil. Water thoroughly, at the same time making the soil firm round the bulbs. Keep the hoe going and excellent Show specimens should be produced without further trouble.

Potato Onions are a very useful crop and produce a heavy yield of underground bulbs ; they are grown from bulbs (see page 52) and should be planted out in February in rows about 1½ feet apart, allowing ten inches between each bulb in the row. Draw the earth round them as for Potatoes and gather the crop in June

PARSLEY.

DANIELS' QUEEN OF THE PARSLEYS GROWING AT OUR SEED GROUNDS. *From a Photograph.*

per oz. -z. 0.

DANIELS' QUEEN OF THE PARSLEYS.¶ An extra selected stock carefully grown on our own Seed Farm. The most useful for garnishing, and extremely valuable as an ornamental plant for the flower-border .. .. per pkt. 4d. 1 0

GIANT CURLED. A very handsome variety, leaves finely curled, grows to a large size, and is very ornamental ; this is the best sort to grow where Parsley is required in large quantities .. .. per pkt. 3d. 0 9

COVENT GARDEN GARNISHING. A splendid variety, beautifully curled 0 4

EXTRA-FINE CURLED, Fine for garnishing 0 4

Cultivation.—Parsley being a deep-rooting plant pays well for liberal cultivation ; it likes a good rich soil in a cool but not too shady position. Parsley is often grown as an edging to other kitchen garden crops and has a pleasing effect when thus used, and as it is in demand the whole year round it is an excellent plan to make a succession of sowings during the year to ensure a continuous supply. Make the first sowing in a box in February and when the plants have been gradually hardened off they should be planted out during April in the permanent border, allowing about twelve inches between each plant. Another sowing at the end of March will be of value for a succession.

For a Winter supply, a sowing should be made in June or July, choosing a sunny aspect on a south border. The plants should be thinned out to prevent over-crowding ; those taken out may be potted up and placed in a cold frame or greenhouse and will yield an excellent supply of leaves for Winter garnishing. In the event of severe weather it will be found advisable to cover the outside beds with mats or an old frame, and a sprinkling of soot in the early morning during the growing season will be found to have an excellent effect.

HERBS (Sweet and Pot).

Per packet 3d. Per dozen packets, 2s. 6d.

‡ **ANGELICA.** The mid-rib may be eaten as Celery, or when candied makes an excellent confection.

* **ANISE.** The seeds are much used for medicinal purposes ; the leaves for garnishing or seasoning.

* **BALM.** For making balm tea, which is invaluable in cases of fever ; makes also a fine-flavoured wine.

* **BASIL, Bush.** The leaves and tops impart the flavour of Cloves to soups, and are much used for seasoning.

* **BASIL, Sweet.** For flavouring salads and soups.

* **BORAGE.** The young leaves used as salad or pot herb.

‡ **BURNET.** The young leaves have the flavour of Cucumbers.

‡ **CARAWAY.** For flavouring soups.

* **CHERVIL, Green Curled.** Very fine for salads.

* **CORIANDER.** The tender leaves are used for soups or salads.

‡ **DILL.** The leaves are used in soups, sauces, and pickles.

‡ **FENNEL.** Used in sauces for fish and for garnishing.

‡ **HOREHOUND.** Makes an esteemed well-known beverage.

‡ **HYSSOP.** Young shoots used as pot herbs.

‡ **MARIGOLD, Pot.** The flowers impart a beautiful colour to broths and soups.

* **MARJORAM, Sweet or Knotted** ⎫ Aromatic and sweet flavour, used in
‡ **MARJORAM, Pot** ⎭ soups and stuffings.

‡ **LAVENDER.** Cultivated for its flowers, which are very aromatic.

* **PURSLANE, Green** ⎫ The shoots and succulent leaves are cooling when
* **PURSLANE, Golden** ⎭ used in Spring as salads.

‡ **RAMPION.** The leaves used as salads ; the roots, which have a pleasant nutty flavour, used as Radish.

‡ **ROSEMARY.** The leaves make a drink esteemed for relieving head-ache.

‡ **RUE, Broad-leaved.** Leaves used medicinally ; also used as a remedy for croup in fowls.

‡ **SAGE.** Used in stuffing and sauces.

* **SAVORY, Summer** ⎫ The tops being very aromatic are used in salads
* **SAVORY, Winter** ⎭ and soups ; they improve the flavour if boiled with Peas or Beans.

‡ **SKIRRET.** The tubers when boiled and served up with butter are most delicious.

‡ **SORREL, Broad-leaved** ⎫ The leaves are used in salads, soups, and
‡ **SORREL, Lettuce-leaved** ⎭ sauces.

‡ **TANSY.** Used for colouring and flavouring confections.

‡ **TARRAGON.** The leaves are excellent when pick'ed.

‡ **THYME.** Broad-leaved. Used in stuffings, soups, and sauces.

‡ **WORMWOOD.** Fine tonic when taken as tea ; and imparts bitterness to drinks.

Annuals marked thus (*).   *Biennials* (†).   *Perennials* (‡).   *For Plants of most of the Perennial sorts, see page 51.*

PARSNIPS.

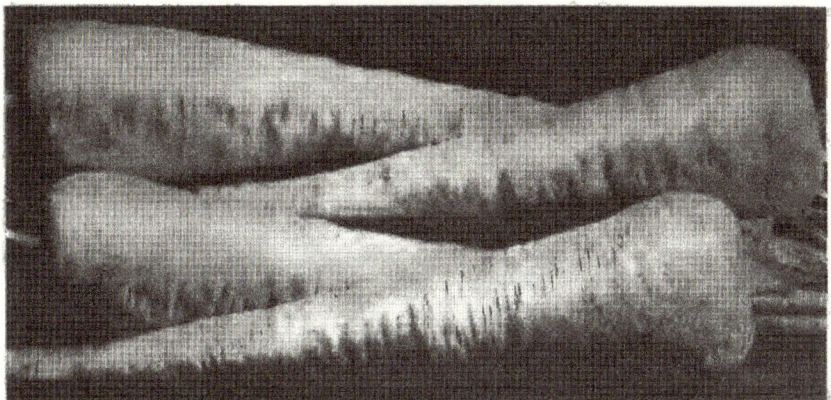

DANIELS' IMPROVED HOLLOW-CROWNED. *Reduced from a Photograph.*

per oz. s. d.

DANIELS' IMPROVED HOLLOW-CROWNED. A finely selected stock of the Hollow-crowned variety. It grows to a very large size without becoming coarse. The roots are of grand symmetrical shape and very clear in the skin. It produces a heavy crop of even-sized Parsnips, and is the best variety for exhibition purposes .. .. per lb. 6s. 0 8

ELCOMBE'S IMPROVED. Very choice stock, of fine flavour, much esteemed for exhibition .. .. per lb. 6s. 0 6
GUERNSEY or JERSEY MARROW. A fine, large, and heavy cropping variety 0 4
HOLLOW-CROWNED. Largest and best for general use ; a fine selected stock .. .. per lb. 3s. 0 3
THE STUDENT. A first-class variety, but requires a good depth of soil 0 6
TURNIP-ROOTED. Excellent for shallow soils 0 6

Cultivation.—Parsnips are amongst the most nutritious of vegetables, and are quite easy to grow ; a good loamy soil free from stones being the most suitable. Have the ground thoroughly trenched (at least two feet deep) in the Autumn, and give a good dressing of farmyard manure, leaving it rough for the Winter. Early in February the bed should be levelled, forked down, and the seeds sown in drills about 1½ feet apart ; thin the young plants out to about 12 inches apart as soon as it is possible to handle them, and be sure to keep the ground thoroughly clean between the rows by frequent hoeing.

When specimen roots are being grown for exhibition, holes should be bored three or four feet deep with a crowbar, and filled with specially mixed soil, leaf mould, and wood ashes ; sow four or five seeds in each hole and thin out the plants, leaving one to each ; weed the ground carefully and apply a sprinkling of soot to keep away pests.

Parsnips are always better when allowed to remain in the ground and lifted when required for use, but when it is necessary to lift and store them, they should be placed in dry sand in a dark shed or cellar.

SPINACH.

per oz. s. d.

LONG STANDING. A most valuable variety for Summer use, as it stands the dry weather and keeps longer fit for use than any other sort
per qt. 2s. ; per pt. 1s. 3d. 0 4
MONSTROUS ITALIAN or VIROFLAY. Large and superior ; leaves dark green, and extremely thick and fleshy ..per qt. 2s. ; per pt. 1s. 3d. 0 4
NEW ZEALAND. Large and succulent 0 6
PERPETUAL or SPINACH BEET. Produces an abundance of green leaves close to the ground, as soon as these are cut fresh leaves appear, producing a supply during the Autumn and Winter 0 6
PRICKLY, NEW GIANT-LEAVED. A great improvement on the ordinary winter spinach The leaves are much larger and of greater substance, and it remains fit for use for a much longer period .. .. .. per qt. 2s. ; per pt. 1s. 3d. 0 4
PRICKLY. Ordinary stock for winter use .. .. per qt. 1s. 9d. ; per pt. 1s. 0 3
ROUND. For Summer use ; best for general crop .. .. per qt. 1s. 9d. ; per pt. 1s. 0 3

Cultivation.—All kinds like a good rich soil ; for the Summer Spinach select a warm border and sow the seeds in rows, where a little shade can be given ; it is often grown between the rows of Peas and Beans. It is important that the plants should be thinned out so as to allow plenty of room for each to develop, and that the crop should be kept well gathered while young.

Winter Spinach should be sown in July or August in drills one inch deep, and twelve inches apart in a well-drained border, care being taken to thin out well, otherwise the leaves will decay, as they will also if grown on heavy water-logged soil. New Zealand Spinach is a useful vegetable for the Summer, but will not stand the frost. Sow it on a warm border in April, and thin out the plants to about two feet apart.

RADISHES.

WHITE TURNIP.   DANIELS' BEST OF ALL.   DANIELS' EARLY SCARLET TURNIP.
FRENCH BREAKFAST.

LONG VARIETIES.

per qt.—r. d.

☞ **DANIELS' BEST OF ALL.** A new and distinct long variety; colour, beautiful bright scarlet, flesh pure white, very tender and crisp. It comes into use very early; and will be found a most useful variety, its bright colour making it very attractive both for the table and market purposes .. per pint 2s. 6d.   0   0

☞ **DANIELS' LONG WHITE.** A new variety of excellent quality. It is the same shape as the Wood's Frame, and pure white in colour. The flesh is exceedingly firm and crisp, and it keeps solid and in good condition a long time   0   0

DANIELS' LONG SCARLET. A fine select Stock, beautiful colour, and very crisp, best for general crop per qt. 3s.; per pt. 1s. 9d.   0   4

WOOD'S EARLY FRAME. The best for early crop, forces well per qt. 3s.; per pt. 1s. 9d.   0   3

SCARLET SHORT-TOP. Best for general crop and market purposes per qt. 2s.; per pt. 1s. 3d.   0   2

OLIVE-SHAPED VARIETIES.

FRENCH BREAKFAST. Scarlet, tipped white, oval shaped, forces well, mild and crisp; useful market variety per pint 1s. 9d.   0   4

OLIVE-SHAPED SCARLET. Early, good forcer, very tender and mild .. .. per qt. 3s.; per pt. 1s. 9d.   0   4

OLIVE-SHAPED WHITE. Of quick growth, mild and crisp, handsome shape .. .. per qt. 3s.; per pt. 1s. 9d.   0   4

OLIVE-SHAPED MIXED .. per qt. 3s.; per pt. 1s. 9d.   0   3

"I took eleven Prizes last year at our Show for Vegetables, all grown from your Seeds."—Mr. C. F. FRANKLIN, Harrow-Weald.

TURNIP VARIETIES.

per qt.—s. d.

☞ **DANIELS' EARLY SCARLET TURNIP.** A very early variety, the roots are firm, solid, and of true globular shape. Colour, rich glowing crimson scarlet. This is unquestionably the earliest forcing Radish extant. It grows very rapidly, is of delicate flavour, and is fit to use in three weeks from time of sowing per pint 2s. 6d.   0   0

☞ **CRIMSON GIANT.** A new Radish of fine colour, and the same shape as our Early Scarlet Turnip, but attains more than twice the size in the same period of growth; it also remains quite firm and crisp for a much longer time   0   0

SPARKLER (new). A quite distinct variety, the upper half of the root is bright scarlet and the lower portion pure white. The two colours are sharply defined and do not merge into each other. Has a most dainty appearance on the table   0   6

TURNIP, Scarlet, White-tipped. Delicious and handsome per pint 1s. 9d.   0   4

TURNIP, Scarlet   { For Summer }   "   White   and   } qt. 2s. 6d.; pt. 1s. 6d.   0   3   "   Mixed   { Autumn use }

WINTER RADISHES.

CHINESE ROSE-COLOURED. Of oblong shape and mild flavour; for Winter use .. .. .. per pint 2s.   0   4

BLACK SPANISH. For Winter salads; sown in Autumn for Spring use .. .. per pint 2s. 6d.   0   6

Cultivation.—The Radish is one of the most popular of all salads, and to be crisp and mild in flavour should be quickly grown. It requires a good rich soil and liberal supplies of water during hot dry weather. Care should be taken in making the sowings to ensure a continuous succession rather than a great quantity at one time. The earliest sowing (for which our new variety, "Best of All," is most suitable) should be made between the rows of early Potatoes or other vegetables grown in frames on the hot-bed. Be sure to admit plenty of air as they will not bear excessive heat.

From February onwards sowings may be made about every fortnight in a warm sheltered bed out of doors, making provision for covering the beds with mats or straw on cold nights. This covering must always be removed in the day-time. It is most important, however, that protection from birds be made in the day-time, and fish netting is generally used for this purpose. In the middle of Summer a north-east border will be found a most suitable position for Radishes. Sow the seed broadcast and evenly, so that they are not too crowded. For Winter work the varieties "Chinese Rose" and "Black Spanish" are the best; they should be sown in August and the plants thinned out about four inches apart.

GARDEN TURNIPS.

DANIELS' IMPROVED SNOWBALL. *Reduced from a Photograph.*

WHITE-FLESHED VARIETIES.

per oz.—s. d.

DANIELS' IMPROVED SNOWBALL. An early and distinct variety of perfect shape, having only a single tap root. It is small, very solid, sweet and crisp, and of remarkably quick growth, flesh snow-white and juicy, one of the very best for exhibition purposes, having obtained numerous first prizes   per pint 2s.   0 6

DANIELS' GREEN TOP STONE. One of the most useful varieties for late sowing, being very hardy will stand well into the Winter. The roots are of splendid shape, and the flesh firm, crisp, and juicy per pint 1s. 6d.   0 4

EARLY WHITE MILAN. Of similar shape and quality to the Red-top Milan, quite as early, but pure white in colour 0 6

CHIRK CASTLE (Black Stone). Very hardy, one of the most useful varieties for Winter 0 6

EARLY MILAN RED-TOP. One of the earliest varieties in cultivation, roots flat, of medium size and quite smooth. First-class Certificate, Royal Horticultural Society 0 4

EARLY WHITE STRAP-LEAVED. One of the earliest grown ..   0 4

EARLY WHITE STONE, or DUTCH SIX WEEKS   per pint 1s.   0 2

SCARLET GEM. This is quite distinct; in shape, round and flat, the colour is a rich glowing scarlet; top small and neat; flesh white and of excellent flavour 0 6

VEITCH'S RED GLOBE. Useful variety 0 4

YELLOW-FLESHED VARIETIES.

per oz.—s. d.

DANIELS' GOLDEN GEM. A distinct variety. The top is small and neat; the roots are very handsome, with very fine tap-root. The skin and flesh are of a rich golden-yellow, and of excellent quality   ..   ..   per pint 3s.   0 6

GOLDEN BALL. Fine stock..   ..   per pint 1s. 6d.   0 4

ORANGE JELLY. Fine for late sowing   ..   per pint 1s. 6d.   0 4

Cultivation.—This most wholesome vegetable is a lover of moisture, and to be crisp and juicy (as it should be) must be grown quickly and not checked in its growth. Choose good rich soil which has been dug over some time previously, and if possible, in a slightly shady position, as during the Summer months Turnips become stringy and hard if exposed to the hot sun.

For the first crop sow Daniels' "Snowball" on a very warm border early in March, and a succession of varieties onwards until July. Thin out the plants when in the seed loaf, leaving the single roots twelve inches apart. Give occasional dustings with wood ash and soot in the early morning to ward off the deadly Turnip fly.

For Autumn and Winter use sow in August and September either broadcast or in rows. Keep the hoe going and all weeds cleared off to hasten the growth and ensure crisp tender roots.

" I took First Prize with your **Improved Snowball Turnip**, also First Prize with your **Ailsa Craig Onion.** I have been successful in winning several Prizes."—Mr. J. GODDARD, Resimelud.

DANIELS' GREEN TOP STONE.

SALSAFY.

per oz.—s. d.

SANDWICH ISLAND MAMMOTH. Splendid variety per pkt, 6d.   1 6

COMMON ..   ..   ,, 3d.   0 9

SCORZONERA.

per oz.—s. d.

RUSSIAN IMPROVED ..   ..   ..   per pkt, 4d.   1 0

COMMON ..   ..   ,, 3d.   0 9

Cultivation.—Salsafy is a vegetable which deserves to be more grown, as it has quite a rich and distinct flavour. Being a deep rooting plant, it must have well-worked land. The seed should be sown early in May in drills about fifteen inches apart, and the plants thinned out to about nine inches in the row. If specimen roots are desired for exhibition, they may be grown in holes made by a crowbar and filled with fine soil as recommended for Parsnips and Beetroot; a liberal supply of water should be given in dry weather and the soil kept loose between the rows by hoeing during the Summer. Salsafy should be lifted and stored in dry sand in a cellar for Winter use.

Scorzonera is a vegetable resembling Salsafy, being purple in colour. It requires similar treatment, but is somewhat hardier and requires a little more space in the drill.

TOMATOES.

TOMATO DANIELS' KING GEORGE V
Reduced from a Photograph

☞ **DANIELS' KING GEORGE V.** This grand variety introduced by us two years ago has proved itself one of the most useful sorts for all purposes. It is of strong constitution and a free setter. The fruit which are of a rich glowing scarlet colour, are of perfect shape and of excellent flavour. For exhibition purposes it will prove a great acquisition 1 6

☞ **DANIELS' KING EDWARD VII.** This fine Tomato is a decided advance on most existing varieties, and certainly one of the best yet sent out. It is a free setter, and an abundant bearer. The large, splendidly coloured fruits, which are produced in handsome clusters of eight to ten or twelve, are very deep, almost round in form, and very solid and heavy, whilst in flavour it is all that can be desired. This fine Tomato is admirably suited for growing in pots, and will be found a really first-class variety, alike for the market grower or amateur exhibitor 1 0

☞ **AILSA CRAIG.** A new variety of great excellence, bearing a heavy crop of fine shaped, grand coloured fruit, which are produced in great ropes and trusses. It is a very free setter, bearing up to eight and ten bunches on a plant. A good sort for pot culture and exhibition work 1 0

☞ **WISETON PROLIFIC** (new). A grand variety raised by Mr. Musk, The Gardens, Wiseton Hall. The fruit, which are of good size, are of grand colour, very firm, and of excellent flavour. It is enormously prolific and will be found first-class for exhibition 1 0

Cultivation.—One of the chief things which has contributed to the great popularity of the Tomato is the fact that it is so very easily grown. It is now generally recognised that Tomatoes can be quite successfully cultivated without such heavy dressings of manure as were used at one time, although there are certain periods when good liberal dressings of manure are necessary; but when the plants are young they do not need it.

For the earliest Spring crop the seed should be sown in January or early in February in pots or pans of light rich soil, and these should be placed on a shelf in the greenhouse; the vessel should be covered over with a sheet of glass to hold the moisture and kept at an even temperature until the seed has germinated. As soon as the plants have formed the seed leaf, have them potted off singly into three-inch pots and grow them on in a warm house, potting on into six-inch pots later, in which size they should remain until permanently planted out in the borders, or potted into the fruiting pots.

Many people prefer to grow their early crops in pots ten inches to twelve inches in diameter, claiming (we believe rightly) that they are better able to attend to the careful watering of the plants and thus avoid any injury to the roots. The treatment of young Tomato plants is pretty much the same as would be given to early Cucumbers, they should have a temperature of 60° during the day, and not less than 50°—55° at night. For a main crop sow the seed in February or March, then transfer into pots as before advised; it is of great importance that the plants be kept sturdy and therefore air should be given on all favourable occasions. The drainage of both the pots in which the young plants are grown or of the borders or boxes in which they are to fruit should be very carefully looked to, so as to allow of their receiving copious supplies of water, especially during the fruiting period. When planted out in the greenhouse border, the plants should be placed about 18 inches apart and supported either by means of a stake or tied up with soft string to the roof, all side growths should be cleared off as they appear, and only the main stem allowed to grow away, this being stopped when it reaches the glass, or when three or four trusses of fruit have been set.

The best soil for Tomatoes is a good rich loam to which has been added a light dressing of farmyard manure, say one-fifth of the bulk; many growers do not put any manure in the soil at the time of planting, leaving the feeding until the first truss of fruit has set, when they apply regular dressings of artificial manure, or give a mulching of well-decayed manure and water the same thoroughly in. In no case must the manure used be taken from a heap that is heated or the result will be disastrous.

TOMATOES—RED VARIETIES.

per pkt.— s. d.

THE DANIELS. The fruit are of good size, rather above the medium, smooth, brilliant scarlet in colour, of beautiful form, exquisite flavour, and remarkably solid. It is a robust grower, and a marvellously profuse and continuous bearer. A first-class variety for cultivation under glass 1 0

*SUNRISE.** This grand variety has received a First Class Certificate from the Royal Horticultural Society for its numerous good qualities. It is very early, a free setter, and enormously prolific, bearing ten to eleven even sized fruit in one bunch. Colour rich scarlet. It is equally prolific either in the open air or under glass .. .. 6d. and 1 0

*DANIELS' SCARLET PERFECTION.** Very handsome, perfectly round and smooth, firm and solid, flavour first-class and of a beautiful glossy scarlet colour; obtains first prize wherever exhibited 1 0

*DANIELS' HARBINGER.** This variety, being very early and a prolific bearer, will be found extremely valuable for growing in the open air. The fruit are round, smooth, solid, and of a bright red .. .. 6d. and 1 0

UP-TO-DATE. One of the heaviest cropping varieties, the smooth round fruit are of medium size and produced in clusters, bearing as many as twenty fruit at a joint; bright crimson.. 6d. and 1 0

DANIELS' SELECTED OPEN AIR. The heaviest cropping out-door variety with which we are acquainted. It is of hardy constitution, bearing large clusters of bright crimson fruit of medium size and good shape. Its distinct and delicate flavour will make it a favourite with all lovers of the Tomato 1 0

*FROGMORE SELECTED.** A very free setter 6d. 1 0
*KING HUMBERT or CHISWICK RED 0 4
*EARLY RUBY.** Very prolific, is of dwarf habit, good shape, colour bright scarlet, flesh solid, succeeds well in the open air .. 0 6
SUPREME. Awarded Highest Marks, R.H.S. The fruit are medium sized, round, very smooth, and of a beautiful scarlet 6d. and 1 0
*LAXTON'S OPEN-AIR.** Very early and hardy 0 6
*LARGE RED.** Very prolific and useful 0 3
MIXED. All sorts 0 2

YELLOW VARIETIES.

DANIELS' GOLDEN BEAUTY. A new and beautiful variety of splendid flavour. The fruit, which are freely produced in large clusters, are of good size, round, smooth, and of a rich bright golden yellow, occasionally flushed with a pale red 1 0
*GOLDEN EAGLE.** This is the most prolific variety that we know, and there is none to equal it in flavour .. .. 6d. and 1 0
*LARGE YELLOW IMPROVED.** A fine variety 0 4

Those marked thus * are the best for open-air cultivation.

" I have had the best crop of Tomatoes this year I ever had, and they were grown from your King George V. Seed."—Mr. J. ORCHARD, Nottingham.

" I have this year grown your King Edward VII. Tomato without heat. I planted 85 plants in a cold frame and they produced 832 lbs. of fruit of excellent size and quality."—Mr. A. GREEN, Gt. Wakering.

" Your King Edward VII. Tomato has grown splendidly. From 72 plants I have already picked 130 lbs. of fruit."—Mr. W. MILLARD, Cardiff.

" I am pleased to tell you that I won two First Prizes with your Tomatoes."—Mr. A. TAYLOR, Wednesford.

VEGETABLE MARROWS.

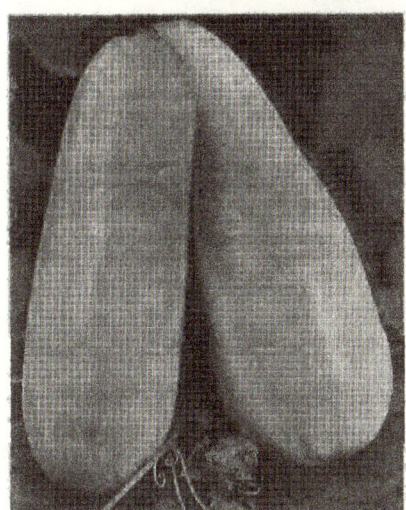

DANIELS' LARGE CREAM.

per pkt. s. d.

DANIELS' EARLY WHITE. A long white variety coming into use before any other of the long kinds. It is very prolific, bearing its fruit immediately it begins to run 0 6

DANIELS' LARGE CREAM. One of the best Marrows in cultivation, grows to a large size, very handsome, and is an immense cropper, unequalled for general crop .. 0 6

DANIELS' GOLDEN CREAM. A very prolific variety, fruits medium size, and of a beautiful pale cream colour, flavour first-class 0 6

PEN-Y-BYD (The best in the World). Awarded two First Class Certificates. This distinct variety is enormously prolific and a continuous bearer. The vine is extremely short-jointed, setting a fruit at every joint. The fruit is of handsome appearance, almost globular in form, sometimes very slightly ribbed, averaging about six inches in diameter 0 6
CUSTARD-SHAPED. Prolific, ornamental-shaped variety .. 0 4
GREEN BUSH. Very prolific; compact habit of growth .. 0 4
LONG GREEN. Good variety, forms a striking contrast with other kinds 0 4
LONG WHITE-RIBBED, or BUSH. Good; a prolific kind .. 0 4
MOORE'S CREAM. Very prolific, delicious flavour .. 0 3
VEGETABLE MARROW and SQUASH. Various sorts mixed .. 0 3

Cultivation.—Vegetable Marrows are easy to grow, and it is possible in every garden to find a corner in which to grow two or three plants; they are often planted on old heaps of refuse, etc. It is not, however, essential that they should be planted on manure heaps, as they will grow quite well in the open garden in a hole which has been well manured, and in fact, they continue to fruit longer when so grown.

Copious supplies of water are necessary for Vegetable Marrows, and the fruits should be cut when young, as otherwise they become tough, and the plants cease bearing sooner. Sow the seeds singly in small pots, and plant out when about a foot high, giving protection for the first few nights. Another plan is to sow the seeds in the mound, where they are to grow, and to cover the plants with a hand-light, or some similar covering until frost has disappeared. Frequent waterings with liquid manure at the time of fruiting will add much vigour to the plants and size to the fruits.

SEED POTATOES.

For many years past we have devoted great attention to the cultivation and selection of our choice stocks of Seed Potatoes, and have been fortunate in introducing to the public several fine varieties of our own raising that have attained to great popularity. By adopting this system, and by adding to our collection the finest varieties raised by other growers, we are enabled to offer a really first-class selection of the best kinds. The past season has been on the whole a favourable one for potatoes, the Main-crop and late varieties have especially yielded well ; on the other hand, owing to the dry weather in June and July some of the earlier kinds are rather scarce, and we strongly recommend early orders for these to prevent disappointment. Our leading varieties such as Duke of York, Sensation, Express, Early Puritan, Factor, and a few others have been grown in Scotland, and we are able to offer fine healthy stocks of these. We have also great pleasure in introducing several new varieties of great merit, which we can strongly recommend for their heavy cropping and fine cooking qualities, and will also be a valuable addition to the exhibition table.

NEW AND SELECT POTATOES FOR 1914.

DANIELS' NORFOLK BEAUTY. (See illustration opposite page.) A fine strong growing Maincrop variety of handsome appearance, producing a very heavy crop of even-sized oval-shaped tubers, with white skin and flesh. It is very clear in the skin with shallow eyes. The cooking quality is excellent. On account of its handsome appearance it will prove a great acquisition as an exhibition variety. Per lb. 6d. ; 7 lb. 3s. ; 14 lb. 5s.

DANIELS' SURPRISE. (See illustration opposite page.) This fine variety introduced by us last year has again proved itself a very heavy cropper. It is a handsome second early variety, with white skin and flesh. The haulm, which is strong and vigorous, grows about 2—2½ feet in height. The tubers, which are very handsome, are oval shaped, somewhat inclined to kidney, with finely netted skin. It is an extraordinary cropper, producing a heavy weight of fine shapely tubers of good size, with very few small. A grand sort for Exhibition, and of the finest table quality. Per lb. 6d. ; 7 lb. 3s. ; 14 lb. 5s.

DANIELS' DREADNOUGHT. A fine Maincrop Kidney of handsome appearance and great productiveness, and has proved itself up to the present a great disease resister. During the wet Summer of 1912 it produced fine crops where other sorts failed ; it is of robust constitution, and the tubers are of fine shape and of most excellent table quality ; a useful exhibition sort. Per 14 lb. 3s. ; 56 lb. 10s. 6d.

KING GEORGE V. A very useful Maincrop variety of recent introduction ; it is an enormous cropper and of fine table quality. The tubers, which are kidney-shaped with white skin and flesh, are very handsome, with a finely netted skin. A fine exhibition sort. Per 14 lb. 3s. ; 56 lb. 10s. 6d.

SUMMIT. A late White Kidney somewhat oblong in shape and of strong, robust constitution. The haulm is very strong and upright, with white bloom. It is a very heavy cropper, many roots producing twenty tubers of large size with very few small ones. It is without doubt one of the best late varieties of recent introduction. Per 14 lb. 3s. ; 56 lb. 10s. 6d.

ARRAN EARLY. A very handsome early White Kidney of great productiveness and fine table quality, the eyes are few and nearly even with the surface ; it will be a useful sort for exhibition purposes. Per 14 lb. 3s. ; 56 lb. 10s. 6d.

EVIDENCE OF QUALITY.

"Norfolk Beauty, in spite of the season here, turned up splendid, quite free from disease and a wonderful cropper, perfect in shape, very shallow eye, with all the good qualities of a Maincrop variety, likewise for exhibition and a table potato I consider it a grand introduction, and will not be long in making headway."—Mr. H. GANDY, Gardener to the Marquis of Bath.

"Daniels' Surprise is well-named. It is a wonderful cropper, perfect in shape, eyes flat on the surface, with a fine russety skin: a model potato for Exhibition purposes. I have tested it—roasted, steamed, and baked, and in each case it was excellent."—Mr. B. ASHTON, Lathom Gardens.

"Daniels' Surprise yielded a heavy crop of even-sized, shallow-eyed, shapely tubers of the finest cooking quality. I consider it a fine addition to the list of second early varieties."—Mr. WM. LOW, Euston Hall Gardens.

"Daniels' Surprise produced a heavy crop of fine tubers of excellent shape and finest table quality, and were free from disease."—Mr. WM. ALLAN, Cunton Park Gardens.

"I have shown your Surprise Potato and obtained two First Prizes ; they have done very well."—Mr. W. F. WILLIAMSON, Hucknall.

"The Seeds I had from you in the Spring did well. I took First Prize with your Surprise Potato, and three Prizes for other things."—Mr. J. MORGAN, Ferndale.

TWO·SPLENDID·NEW·POTATOES

DANIELS'
NORFOLK
BEAUTY.

DANIELS'
SURPRISE.

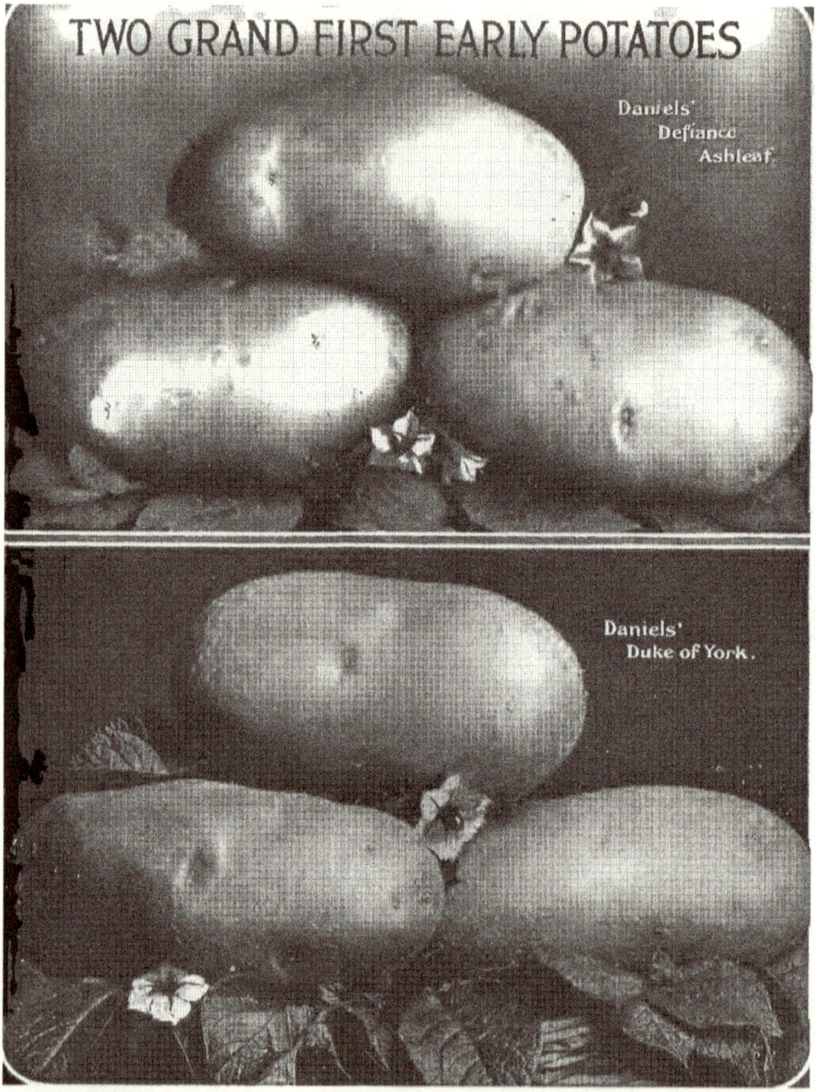

TWO GRAND FIRST EARLY POTATOES

Daniels'
Defiance
Ashleaf.

Daniels'
Duke of York.

POTATOES.

FIRST EARLY VARIETIES.

DANIELS' DUKE OF YORK. This grand variety still holds its own as one of the best heavy-cropping Earlies in cultivation. In habit of growth, it is very compact, the haulm being only a foot high. The leaves are smooth and of a rich glossy green colour, whilst the tubers cluster compactly round the stem, and are very easy to raise. The tubers are large, oval, smooth and handsome, and distinct in appearance, the eyes are few and quite even with the surface, ensuring a minimum of waste; the flesh is dry and mealy when cooked, and of the most excellent flavour. (See illustration, opposite page.) Scotch grown Seed.　　　　　　　　　　　　　　　　Per 14 lb. 2s. 6d.; 56 lb. 8s. 6d.; cwt. 15s.

DANIELS' DEFIANCE ASHLEAF. This variety has now been several years before the public and still holds its place as one of the best of the first earlies, and in most seasons it can be lifted before the disease makes its appearance. It is one of the heaviest cropping varieties of this class, producing a full crop of good sized tubers of first-class table quality, having the exceptional flavour found only in the best Ashleaf sorts. (See illustration, opposite page.)　　　　　　　　　　　　　　　　　　　　　　　Per 14 lb. 3s. 6d.; 56 lb. 12s.

MYATT'S ASHLEAF, IMPROVED. This will be found a heavier and more reliable cropper than the old variety, and of exceptionally good table quality.　　　　　　Per 14 lb. 3s.; 56 lb. 10s. 6d.

EARLY ASHLEAF KIDNEY. Useful variety.　　　　　　　　　Per 14 lb. 3s.; 56 lb. 10s. 6d.

EXPRESS. A fine early White Kidney of handsome appearance and excellent cooking quality, and is at the same time a very heavy and sure cropper; has proved one of the best during the past season. (Scotch grown Seed.)　　　　　　　　　　　　　　　　　　　　　　　　Per 14 lb. 3s.; 56 lb. 10s. 6d.; cwt. 18s.

EARLY PURITAN. A well-known variety of great excellence, which still maintains its reputation amongst the early varieties for its fine cropping and good cooking qualities. First-class Certificate, R.H.S. (Scotch grown Seed.)　　　　　　　　　　　　　　　　　　　　　　　Per 14 lb. 2s. 6d.; 56 lb. 8s. 6d.; cwt. 15s.

MAY QUEEN. A first early White Kidney of exceptional productiveness. The tubers are kidney shaped, with white skin and flesh, and of first-class table quality. This is one of the best of the early kidney varieties. (Scotch Seed.)　　　　　　　　　　　　　　　　　　　　　　　　Per 14 lb. 3s. 6d.; 56 lb. 12s.

	per 14 lb. s. d.	per 56 lb. s. d.
EARLY ECLIPSE. A handsome first early White Kidney of great productiveness, with white skin and flesh, it cooks well early and late, and during the past season it has again yielded a very heavy crop of nice clean tubers ... ... per cwt. 15s.	2 6	8 6
LADY LLEWELYN. A fine early potato, similar in appearance and growth to the well-known Sir J Llewelyn, but of stronger constitution and a much heavier cropper, and of first-rate cooking quality ... ... per cwt. 18s.	3 0	10 6
SIR JOHN LLEWELYN. This splendid White Kidney, in consideration of its earliness, heavy cropping, good quality, and disease resisting properties, has become highly popular.. The tubers are of good size and shape, and when cooked, white and floury. Award of Merit, R.H.S. This is a really first-class early Potato.. ... ... per cwt. 18s.	2 6	8 6
SHARPE'S VICTOR. A specially selected and improved stock of this well known early variety, of fine appearance, and producing twice the weight of the old sort ... ... per cwt. 18s.	3 0	12 0
SOUTHERN QUEEN. An early white kidney of handsome appearance, the tubers being of beautiful kidney shape; it is an abundant cropper of the best table quality	3 0	10 6

SECOND EARLY VARIETIES.

DANIELS' DUCHESS OF NORFOLK. A grand variety of handsome appearance and a heavy cropper. It is a second early, growing about 2 feet high, the foliage being quite distinct. The tubers, which are pebble-shaped or round, with shallow eyes, are of good size, producing a nice even crop of marketable tubers with a minimum of small. The skin and flesh are white and of the finest table quality; very useful for exhibition.　Per 14 lb. 3s.; 56 lb. 10s. 6d.; cwt. 18s.

DANIELS' PRINCE EDWARD. This grand new Potato is a seedling from our celebrated Duke of York, crossed with The Factor. It is a second early of enormous productiveness, having produced 32 times its own weight. It shows the character of both its parents, and is a nice upright grower (about 2 feet in height) with strong leathery dark green foliage and white flowers. The tubers, which are kidney-shaped, with clear white skin and flesh, are of the finest table quality.　　　　　　　　　　　　　　　　　Per 14 lb. 2s. 6d.; 56 lb. 8s. 6d.; cwt. 15s.

	per 14 lb. s. d.	per 56 lb. s. d.
EARLY ROSE. A well-known variety suitable for light sandy soils, of full table quality (scarce)	2 0	8 6
EARLY WHITE HEBRON. A well-known variety of fine cooking quality ... ... per cwt. 18s.	2 0	8 6
BRITISH QUEEN. A second early variety of great merit. The skin and flesh are white, and of extra fine table quality; this, combined with its great productiveness and good keeping qualities, make it a most desirable variety (Scotch Seed) ... per cwt. 18s.	2 6	8 6
BEAUTY OF HEBRON. A well-known variety of good table quality	2 6	8 0
SNOWBALL. The tubers are almost round in shape, with white flesh and a finely netted skin; it is of excellent cooking quality, and first-class for exhibition purposes	2 6	8 6
ROYAL KIDNEY. A handsome and sure cropping white kidney of good table quality and a capital disease resister ...	2 6	8 6

A GRAND NEW POTATO,
ARRAN CHIEF.

NEW POTATO, ARRAN CHIEF. *From a Photograph.*

ARRAN CHIEF. A distinct new Main Crop variety of Scotch origin. The tubers, which cluster compactly round the plant, are very numerous, of good size, nicely rounded, and have comparatively shallow eyes ; they are of the very best quality, and make a splendid table Potato. The majority of the tubers are of good marketable size, with very few small, whilst its handsome shape will make it a fine addition to the exhibition table. During the past season it has produced over 17 tons per acre under ordinary cultivation, with hardly any diseased tubers. Per lb. 6d. ; 7 lb. 3s. 6d. ; 14 lb. 5s.

MAIN CROP VARIETIES.

CLOSEBURN CASTLE (New). A most useful variety, of thick kidney shape, somewhat inclined to oval, with beautifully white flesh of fine cooking quality. It is a huge cropper, producing a fine lot of marketable tubers, with very few small. Per 14 lb. 2s. 6d. ; 56 lb. 8s 6d.

	per 14 lb.		per 56 lb.	
	s.	d.	s.	d.
KING EDWARD VII. A very fine Main Crop variety ; the haulm grows to the height of two feet and is fairly robust, producing a large crop of handsome tubers. The skin is white, with a blotch of pink about the eyes, which gives it a very pleasing appearance. It is a good cooker and free from disease ; for exhibition it is first class. Scotch seed .. .. .. per cwt. 14s.	2	6	8	6
RADIUM. The tubers are oval in shape, with beautifully netted skin, and of the finest table quality. The haulm which grows to about two feet in height is very robust, and of a fine dark green, and the flowers which are produced in abundance are white. As a cropper and cooker we consider it one of the best introductions of recent years .. .. per cwt. 15s.	2	6	8	6
SCOTTISH TRIUMPH. A large oval-shaped white skinned variety of finest table quality. It is one of the heaviest cropping varieties with which we are acquainted. The tubers are large and of fine shape	2	6	8	6
WARRIOR. A handsome white round variety. It is a strong growing variety, and a most excellent cropper, producing a fine crop of large handsome tubers of the best table quality	2	6	8	6

A GRAND NEW POTATO.
THE PREMIER.

NEW POTATO, THE PREMIER. *Reduced from a Photograph.*

THE PREMIER. A grand new Main Crop Kidney of exceptional qualities. The tubers are white, thick kidney shaped, very handsome in appearance, and of the finest cooking quality. It is of strong robust constitution, with dark foliage and mauve flower. It is an enormous cropper, and during the very dry season of 1911 produced at the rate of 16 tons per acre under ordinary cultivation; in the past season it has again produced an exceptionally heavy crop practically free from disease. Without doubt a fine addition to our exhibition varieties, and can be strongly recommended.

7 lb. 1s. 9d. ; 14 lb. 3s.

MAIN CROP AND LATE VARIETIES.

	per 14 lb. s. d.	per 56 lb. s. d.
THE FACTOR. A fine oval-shaped White-skinned Potato of robust habit, and a splendid cropper, the tubers being of good size and handsome appearance. It is one of the best keepers, and will cook splendidly quite into May. One of the very best Main Crop varieties of recent introduction. (Scotch grown seed) .. .. per cwt. 15s.	2 0	8 6
DUCHESS OF CORNWALL. A Main Crop variety of exceptional merit, the tubers are of good size and thick pebble-shaped with a white skin. The haulm is strong and vigorous It is a grand cropper, remarkably free from disease, and of excellent table quality. (Scotch grown seed) .. .. per cwt. 16s.	2 0	8 6
UP-TO-DATE. A large handsome Kidney of very heavy cropping qualities, skin roughly netted, flesh white, dry, and mealy when cooked. (Scotch grown seed).. .. .. per cwt. 12s.	2 0	7 6

COLOURED VARIETIES FOR EXHIBITION.

EDGCOTE PURPLE. A very handsome purple Kidney of exceptional table quality (scarce) .. .. .. per 7 lb. 2s.	3 6	—
PEERLESS ROSE. A flat, smooth, very handsome kidney-shaped Potato: skin of a delicate pink colour, eyes even with the surface; fine quality, and excellent for exhibition	3 0	10 6
THE SUTTON FLOURBALL. A red round variety of extra good cropping qualities, and good table quality; very useful for exhibition purposes, and a good disease resistor	3 0	10 6
VICAR OF LALEHAM. A handsome round variety, with rich dark purple skin, a good cropper, cooks well, and fine for exhibition ..	3 0	10 6
WONDERFUL RED KIDNEY. A heavy cropping and handsome red kidney, with clear smooth skin; fine for exhibition ..	2 0	8 6

DANIELS' SENSATION.

DANIELS' SENSATION. *From a Photograph.*

DANIELS' SENSATION. This grand Main Crop Potato is one of the heaviest-cropping and best varieties we have ever grown. It is of a good, robust constitution, the haulm growing about two feet high. The tubers are of good size, thick pebble-shape, with very shallow eyes, almost level with the surface ; the skin is white and slightly netted—a sure indication of good cooking qualities—the flesh being white, mealy, and of the finest texture. Its splendid cropping and good culinary qualities, combined with its very handsome appearance, have made this variety a great favourite alike with the cook and exhibitor. Seed direct from Scotland.   Per 14 lb. 2s. 6d. ; 56 lb. 8s. 6d. ; cwt. 15s.

HINTS ON POTATO CULTURE.

Cultivation.—The varieties quoted in our list are the best in cultivation. It is most important that frequent changes of seed should be made, as Potatoes deteriorate if repeatedly saved from the same soil and district. For those growing for exhibition it is necessary to select varieties which are not only handsome in appearance, but also of known good quality for cooking purposes, such as "Duke of York," "Arran Chief," "Sensation" and "The Premier." For early work, "Duke of York," the well-known variety introduced by ourselves is still pre-eminent, and the increasing demand for this kind proves its superiority over all others as a first early.

Much depends upon the selection and treatment of the "sets" ; it is therefore necessary to secure good moderate sized Potatoes which should be set up on end in shallow boxes or trays, and allowed to sprout before being planted, as when this is done much advantage is gained both in the development of the plants and in the weight of the crops. Potatoes like a good open position in the garden, and the most suitable soil is a medium to light one in a well-drained position ; the ground should be deeply dug and manured in the Autumn. Where stable manure is available a good dressing should be given at the time of planting, placing a layer on the bottom of the trenches ; well-decayed leaf-mould, or the remains of an old mushroom bed are also excellent for this purpose.

When planting it is important that an abundance of room be left between the rows and the sets in the row ; allow a distance of two feet between rows for the early, and three feet for the late strong-growing sorts, and twelve to eighteen inches between the sets in the rows. Where the land is naturally low and wet it is a capital plan to elevate the rows by forming ridges and so planting the sets on about a level with the natural soil ; it is also good to keep the surface soil constantly stirred with the hoe until the earthing up commences.

When the young growths begin to push through the soil care must be taken to protect them from the frost by continually earthing up the soil round them (neglect of this has often resulted in the loss of a complete crop of Early Potatoes), and when it is desired to grow exhibition specimens only, one haulm should be left to a plant, all the weakest ones being drawn out as they appear. Slight dressings of soot or of "Norwich Fertilizer" during the growing season will be of much advantage. Immediately the growth is completed, the crop should be lifted ; choose fine weather for the work and store them after having had a few hours' sun on them.

Where small quantities only are grown it is much better to store Potatoes in a cool dry place where they can be easily got at, as they are not so liable to develop disease as when stored in a pit or trench.

☞ **IMPORTANT NOTICE.**—Seed Potatoes procured during the Winter and early Spring, when not required for immediate planting, should be taken out of the bag or package in which they are received and laid out in a dry, airy place protected from frost, or they will begin to sprout and a weakly growth will be the result.

MISCELLANEOUS PLANTS & ROOTS

ASPARAGUS PLANTS.

An abundance of fine Asparagus may be grown with less than half the expense usually incurred in making costly " beds," and will succeed admirably on most soils when planted in lines or clumps on the Kitchen Garden borders, or amongst dwarf-growing Fruits where the space will admit, a liberal cultivation being all that is required to ensure the best results. The roots are liable to injury if removed during severe weather in Winter. They are best planted when growth has commenced in Spring, and when they can be carefully taken up and packed so as to travel a long journey, without injury. They should, however, in all cases be planted as quickly as possible after receiving them. We consider March and April the best months for planting.

CONNOVER'S COLOSSAL   Two and three years old   ..   .. per 100, 5s. and 7s. 6d.
TRUE GIANT.   Two and three years old   ..   ..   .. per 100, 3s. 6d. and 5s.

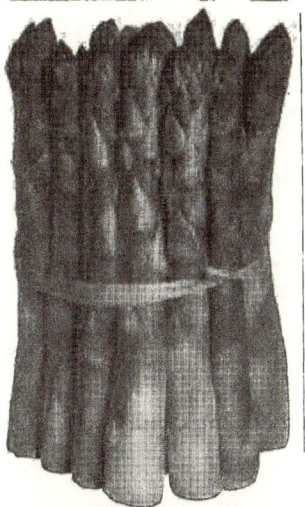

ASPARAGUS—CONNOVER'S COLOSSAL.

ASPARAGUS SEED.

		per os.—s. d.
TRUE GIANT. A fine variety, producing large heads of excellent quality per lb. 4s.		0 4
CONNOVER'S COLOSSAL. A very large variety, very prolific, and of fine flavour		
	per lb. 6s.	0 6
EARLY GIANT PURPLE (Argenteuil). As grown by the celebrated French growers for		
Paris Market ; robust variety of the most delicious flavour ..	per lb. 7s.	0 8

RHUBARB.

One of the most useful, wholesome, and profitable of garden plants. The ground for this should be well broken up and manured, and the plants should be 2½ to 3 feet apart. March is the best month for planting, but it is not advisable to pull any of the stalks the first season for fear of unduly weakening the growth. A top-dressing of well-decayed manure in Winter is very beneficial.

CHAMPAGNE.   Deep red stems, early, one of the very best for general use.
   each 1s. ; per doz. 10s. 6d.
DAWS' CHALLENGE.   A remarkable variety for forcing, growing up to 4 feet.   Very fine colour, First Class Certificate, R.H.S.   ..   ..   ..   each 1s. 6d.
DAWS' CHAMPION.   A fine new variety of great size and splendid colour.   Very productive
   each 1s. ; per doz. 12s.
EARLY RASPBERRY.   A splendid early variety, good colour and raspberry flavour, each 1s.
PARAGON.   The most prolific kind known   ..   ..   each 1s. ; per doz. 10s 6d
NEW CRIMSON QUEEN.   A fine new and very early Rhubarb.   The stalk is of a beautiful bright red quite through, whilst it is also of a very superior and delicate flavour.   each 9s.
STOTTS' MONARCH.   Green-skinned   ..   ..   ..   each 2s. ; per doz. 21s.

Two-year Seedlings, strong transplanted roots of the following, each 9d. ; per doz. 7s. 6d.
   MYATT'S LINNÆUS.   ROYAL ALBERT.   MYATT'S VICTORIA.

SEA KALE.

This valuable esculent is easily forced if care is taken only to apply heat gradually, as it will not succeed if placed in too high a temperature at starting. Place several crowns a few inches apart in large pots, and stand them in a temperature of about 45 degrees, with an inverted pot placed over each to exclude light and insure blanching ; a mushroom house, pit or cellar, will do well for this purpose. Sea Kale may also be easily forced in the open ground by covering it over with large specially made pots, and applying fermenting material. The heads should be cut when in about the condition shown in illustration, and taken off in the same way.

STRONG PLANTING ROOTS   ..   ..   .. per doz. 1s. ; per 100, 7s. 6d.
GOOD STRONG ROOTS, for forcing   .. per doz. 1s. 6d. ; per 100, 10s. 6d.
EXTRA STRONG ROOTS, for forcing, very fine   .. per doz. 2s. ; per 100, 15s.

SEA KALE.

SWEET AND POT HERBS.

We have a fine collection of these, including the following useful sorts :—

	per doz.—s. d.			per doz.—s. d.	
BALM ..	..	4 0	ROSEMARY ..	.. each 6d.	5 0
CHAMOMILE ..	..	4 0	RUE ..	..	4 0
CHIVES ..	.. each 5d.	4 0	SAGE, Common ..	.. each 5d.	4 0
HOREHOUND ..	..	4 0	SAVORY, WINTER ..	..	4 0
HYSSOP ..	..	4 0	SORREL, GIANT FRENCH .. each 5d.		4 0
LAVENDER ..	.. each 6d.	5 0	TARRAGON ..	.. each 5d.	4 0
MARJORAM, POT ..	..	4 0	THYME, LEMON ..	.. each 5d.	4 0
MINT, LAMB ..	..	4 6	„ COMMON ..	..	4 0
„ PEPPER ..	..	4 0	WORMWOOD ..	..	4 0
PENNYROYAL ..	.. each 5d.	4 0			

The most useful varieties assorted, our selection, per doz. 1s. ; per 100, 5s.

MISCELLANEOUS PLANTS, ROOTS, AND SEEDS.

ARTICHOKE DANIELS' WHITE MAMMOTH.

ARTICHOKES.

DANIELS' WHITE MAMMOTH. This is a pure white skin variety of the Jerusalem Artichoke The tubers, which are more regularly formed than those of the old variety, are somewhat globular in shape and of excellent quality.
Per 14 lb. 2s. 6d. ; 56 lb. 8s. 6d.

JERUSALEM. Good sound tubers
per peck (14 lbs.) 2s. ; bush (56 lbs.) 7s.

GLOBE. Strong plants .. .. .. per doz. 9s.

CARDOONS.

	per pkt.—s.	d.
SMOOTH SOLID. Cultivated for the mid-rib of the leaf ..	0	6
LARGE SPANISH	0	6

SEA KALE (Seed).

ORDINARY .. .. per pint 2s. ; per oz. 6d.
LILY WHITE (Special) .. per pint 3s. 6d ; per oz. 1s.

For Plants, see page 51.

FRUIT SEEDS.

CURRANT, GOOSEBERRY, GRAPE, STRAWBERRY, RASPBERRY, APPLE PIPS, PEAR PIPS .. each 6d. and 1s. per pkt.

RHUBARB (Seed).

	per pkt.—s.	d.		per pkt.—s.	d.
CHAMPAGNE	0	6	MYATT'S LINNÆUS ..	0	6
MONARCH. Excellent new sort	0	6	MYATT'S VICTORIA ..	0	6
ROYAL ALBERT ..	0	6	MIXED	0	4

CROSNES (Stachys tuberifera). First Class Certificate, Royal Horticultural Society. This is a tuberous vegetable introduced from Japan. It is a hardy plant, producing a large quantity of tubers in the same way as the Potato. Its culture is very easy, as it grows well in any good garden soil, and is readily propagated by means of its numerous tubers. They may be left in the ground until required for use, as the severest frost does not injure them in any way. The best and simplest way of cooking this vegetable is to boil in water with a pinch of salt, then fry them. They are of delicate flavour, somewhat resembling boiled chestnuts.

FINE ENGLISH GROWN TUBERS .. .. per lb. 1s. ; 7 lb. 6s.

DANDELION.

Very valuable for Winter Salads when blanched.

	per pkt.—s.	d.
IMPROVED LARGE-LEAVED	0	6
THICK-LEAVED CABBAGING	0	6

EGG PLANT OR AUBERGINE.

(Solanum Esculentum.)

Till comparatively recent times these handsome plants have only been grown for decorative purposes. They are now, however, coming into great favour as a delicious esculent, and when generally known will be in great demand, and we should advise all who have not yet grown these to give them a trial.

	per pkt.—s.	d.
DANIELS' IMPROVED LARGE PURPLE. Fine handsome fruit ; very prolific ..	6d. and 1	0
BLACK CHINESE. Very effective	6d. and 1	0
LARGE WHITE. A very useful variety ..	6d. and 1	0

"I won eight First and Second Prizes at our Show with Onions grown from your Seed."—Mr. R. GIBSON, Little Massingham.

CHIVES AND GARLIC.

CHIVES. Fine strong clumps .. .. each 5d. ; per doz. 4s.
GARLIC BULBS .. .. .. per lb. 1s.

POTATO ONIONS.

BULBS. Fine select stock .. .. per lb. 6d. ; 12 lb. 5s.

MERCURY (Good King Henry).

(Chenopodium Bonus Henricus.)

A hardy and useful vegetable, much grown in Lincolnshire ; it forms an excellent substitute for Spinach .. .. .. per pkt. 6d.

SHALLOTS.

(Sow and Cultivate as Onions.)

Far superior to Onions for pickling.

BULBS. Fine sound bulbs .. .. .. per lb. 1s. ; 7 lb. 6s.
SEED. From extra large bulbs .. .. 6d. and 1s. per pkt.

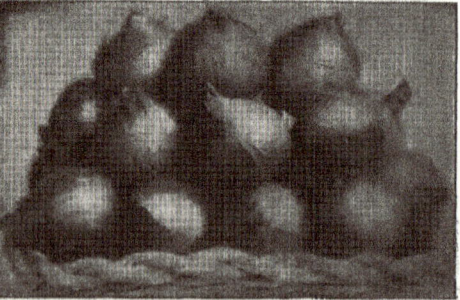

SHALLOT BULBS.

HOME-GROWN FARM SEEDS.

MANGELS.

Our stocks of these are all English grown, and can be fully relied on as really first-class. All growers of Mangels should give our Seeds a trial, as we feel sure the result would be most satisfactory.

	per lb.—s. d.
DANIELS' CORONATION GLOBE. A new variety carefully selected by ourselves. It is of large size, perfect form, very solid, and of a feeding quality rivalling the famous Golden Tankard ; a very heavy cropper	0 9
DANIELS' INTERMEDIATE or GATE-POST. A grand stock ; one of the finest Mangels ever introduced, grows to a great size, with a uniform crop of very heavy, handsome, and clean roots ..	0 9
DANIELS' RED INTERMEDIATE. Our stock is very fine, and can be highly recommended	1 0
DANIELS' GOLDEN TANKARD. Specially selected for its yellow or golden flesh, its richness in saccharine matter, and handsome shape	0 9
DANIELS' CHAMPION ORANGE GLOBE. Highly recommended for its neat top, fine clear skin, and tap root ; a heavy cropper..	0 9
YELLOW GLOBE. Good stock .. .. — —	0 8

Price per Cwt. on application.

CABBAGES.

		per lb.—s. d.
DANIELS' CHAMPION DRUMHEAD. Produces large solid heads	per oz. 4d.	4 0
DANIELS' EARLY DRUMHEAD. Comes into use some weeks before the larger varieties .. .. per oz. 4d.		4 0
ROBINSON'S DRUMHEAD .. .. .. „ 4d.		3 6
THOUSAND-HEADED KALE. Selected stock .. „ 3d.		2 0

KOHL RABI.

EARLY WHITE VIENNA. Best for garden pkt. 4d. ; per oz. 1s.		
DANIELS' SHORT-TOP GREEN. For field culture		2 6

SWEDE TURNIPS.

	per lb.—s. d.
DANIELS' NORFOLK GIANT PURPLE-TOP. The roots are somewhat oval, and of a deep rich purple. It is a heavy cropper and excellent keeper. All farmers should give it a trial —	0 10
DANIELS' IMPROVED PURPLE-TOP. Selected Stock .. —	0 9
DANIELS' DEFIANCE GREEN-TOP. A first-class keeper —	1 0

WHITE-FLESHED TURNIPS.

DANIELS' NORFOLK GREEN ROUND. Excellent for main crop, hardiest of the Globe varieties	0 8
DANIELS' PURPLE-TOP MAMMOTH. Early Turnip, very heavy cropper, large and handsome roots	0 10
BELL or DECANTER. Extra selected stock	0 10

YELLOW-FLESHED TURNIPS.

DANIELS' GREEN-TOP YELLOW SCOTCH. Grows a heavy crop, flesh solid and juicy, much relished by cattle ..	0 9
DANIELS' PURPLE-TOP YELLOW SCOTCH	0 10

Price per Bushel on application.

CARROTS.

		per lb.—s. d.
DANIELS' GIANT YELLOW INTERMEDIATE. Our own stock ; grown from selected roots, and the heaviest cropper we know of — — — —	All	3 0
GIANT WHITE BELGIAN. Very large and of fine quality		2 6
YELLOW BELGIAN. Best for general crop, roots large and of good shape	Clean	2 0
JAMES' SCARLET or INTERMEDIATE. A heavy cropper, one of the best for shallow soils	Seed	3 0
ALTRINCHAM. A fine long Red variety		3 6

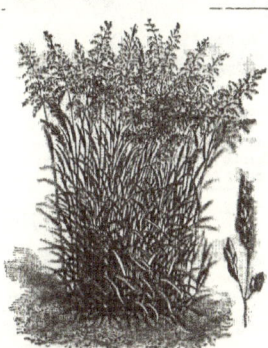

ROUGH-STALKED MEADOW GRASS.

CLEANED GRASS SEEDS & CLOVERS,

For all Soils and Situations, for Pasturage, Ensilage, &c.
Samples and Special Quotations on Application.

DANIELS' MIXTURES.

FOR ALTERNATE HUSBANDRY OR ROTATION CROPS.

DANIELS' SPECIAL PERMANENT PASTURE.

FOR LIGHT, MEDIUM, AND HEAVY SOILS

DANIELS' SPECIAL RENOVATING MIXTURES. RYE GRASSES AND CLOVERS OF THE FINEST QUALITIES.

Orders for Farm Seeds not less than 20s. Carriage paid to any Station in England and Wales. £2 and upwards free to any Railway Station in Scotland or Shipping port in Ireland.

OUR FARM SEED CATALOGUE FOR SPRING, 1914,

Will be published on March 2nd, and will be sent gratis and post free on application. If you are interested, let us register your name at once.

It contains a complete list of the choicest sorts of Mangels, Swedes, Turnips, and other Root Seeds, Clovers, Grasses, and other Forage Plants, besides many valuable hints on cultivation.

DANIELS' SUPERIOR GRASS SEEDS FOR LAWNS, &c.

☞ For many years we have given close attention to the selection of the most suitable Grasses for producing the best Lawns, Tennis Courts, Cricket Grounds, Golf Links, &c., and we have much pleasure in recommending the splendid mixtures we offer as the very best procurable for the purposes named. March and April are the best months for sowing in Spring. September and early October for Autumn sowing. For renovating existing lawns, lightly rake the worst places and bare patches, then sow our Peerless Mixtures (Nos. 5 or 6) at the rate of half-pound to the rod, or more thickly if the lawn is very bare ; apply a thin sprinkling of finely sifted soil, and roll with a light garden roller ; protect the newly sown parts from birds.

No. 1. DANIELS' SPECIAL MIXTURE FOR LAWNS.

This is a special mixture of the finest leaved dwarf evergreen Grasses, and will produce an extra fine close velvety turf. First-class for making new lawns or for renovating. Highly recommended. Per lb. 2s., per bushel 30s.

No. 2. DANIELS' FINE MIXTURE OF DWARF GRASSES.

A splendid mixture of fine Grasses, suitable for Tennis Courts, Croquet Grounds, &c., also a most useful mixture for renovating bare and weak patches.
Per lb. 1s. 6d., per bushel 25s.

No. 3. DANIELS' MIXTURE OF DWARF GRASSES.

A good cheap mixture for producing a fine close turf.
Per lb. 1s., per bushel 20s.

No. 4. DANIELS' MIXTURE FOR SHADY LAWNS AND UNDER TREES.

A useful mixture for producing a fine turf in enclosed and shady places. Per lb. 1s. 6d., per bushel 25s.

No. 5. DANIELS' PEERLESS MIXTURE
Without Perennial Rye Grass.
FOR GARDEN LAWNS.
This mixture is composed of the finest dwarf-growing Grasses for producing a fine velvety Turf of extra good quality.
Per lb. 1s. 6d. and 2s., per bushel 25s. and 30s.

No. 6. DANIELS' PEERLESS MIXTURE.
Without Perennial Rye Grass.
FOR TENNIS LAWNS.
A mixture of fine Grasses for producing a close, dwarf, springy Turf, most suitable for this purpose.
Per lb. 1s. 6d. and 2s., per bushel 25s. and 30s.

Where larger quantities than those mentioned are required we shall always be pleased to make special quotations.

N.B.—Where no definite instructions are given, we shall supply our Special Mixtures, containing Perennial Rye Grass.

DANIELS' SUPERIOR GRASS SEEDS FOR GOLF LINKS, &c.

A GOLF GREEN, SOWN WITH OUR SPECIAL MIXTURE.

No. 7. DANIELS' SPECIAL MIXTURES FOR GOLF LINKS.

For Putting Greens. A selection of the finest Grasses for producing a smooth even surface. Per bushel 30s.

Other mixtures for Golf Courses, 15s. to 25s. per bushel.

No. 8. DANIELS' SPECIAL MIXTURES FOR BOWLING GREENS.

A selection of fine Grasses, specially adapted for hard wear and at the same time producing a fine even turf.

Per lb. 1s. and 1s. 6d., per bushel 20s. to 25s.

No. 9. DANIELS' SPECIAL MIXTURE FOR CRICKET & FOOTBALL GROUNDS.

Per bushel 15s. to 20s.

No. 10. DANIELS' SPECIAL MIXTURES FOR PARKS, RECREATION GROUNDS, &c.

Per bushel 15s. and 18s.

Where larger quantities than those mentioned are required we shall always be pleased to make special quotations.

Hints on Lawns.—There is no part of a garden which requires such careful and regular attention as the lawn, and certainly there is nothing more delightful than a well-kept lawn in proximity to a residence. It is quite possible for even the smallest cottage to have its plot of grass, providing sufficient care is taken at the outset in forming it. The following hints will be found of help to those about to form or renovate a lawn.

Choose an open space as level as possible, and naturally well drained; if the ground is at all uneven it must be levelled by removing the higher to the lower parts. The whole of the ground should be well dug and pulverized to a depth of eighteen inches, giving a good dressing of manure at the same time, after digging rake the surface level and very carefully remove all stones, rolling it quite firm all over. Care must be taken not to allow any carting or wheeling upon the ground after being dug unless boards are laid down for the purpose.

The best time for sowing Grass Seeds is the Spring, during March and April, although satisfactory results are often obtained when sown in September. To ensure the securing of a good thick even turf, it is imperative that the seed be sown very thickly, in fact it is much better to sow a liberal quantity at first than to have to renovate at the end of the season. Four or six bushels per acre is not too much, generally speaking about one to two lb. to a rod of ground is a good dressing.

Remove all weeds as they appear and as soon as the grass is three or four inches high it should be mown with a scythe and well rolled. Frequent rolling and cutting must be done if a really fine turf is desired, and an occasional dressing of Daniels' Lawn "Manure," applying about two to three ounces to the square yard, will be found to promote a healthy growth of the young sward.

The renovating and improving of old lawns is most important work and may be done either in March or September. The seed should be sown evenly over all bare places and in all holes, using the finest lawn mixture; cover the seeds with a slight sprinkling of finely sifted soil and roll the whole surface down evenly and firmly. The sowing of Lawn Seeds should always be done in calm fine weather when there is no fear of either the seed being blown about or of the soil adhering to the roller. Small birds are very fond of grass seeds, and it is therefore most advisable to give some protection (when convenient) until the young grass gets hold.

HORTICULTURAL MANURES, &c.
DANIELS' NORWICH FERTILIZER.

Without doubt the finest Manure for Fruit, Chrysanthemums, and all ¦general Garden Crops ; the sales have again more than doubled those of any previous year, and we strongly recommend our customers to give it a trial.

NORWICH FERTILIZER

IS SENT

Carriage Paid on orders of 56 lbs. and upwards to any Railway Station in England and Wales, and to Edinburgh, Glasgow, and Irish Ports.

PRICES.

7 lbs.	...	1s. 9d.
14 lbs.	...	3s. 0d.
28 lbs.	...	5s. 6d.
56 lbs.	...	9s. 6d.
112 lbs.	...	17s. 6d.

Copies of a special article on "Manures for Vegetable Crops," by Mr. J. Gibson, F.R.H.S., Head Gardener to His Grace The Duke of Portland, Welbeck Abbey, may be had on application.

House containing 2nd bunches Black Hamuro Grapes, grown by Lady Mansel, Cotton House, fed with Norwich Fertilizer only.

SPECIAL LAWN MANURE

This will be found of great value on newly established Lawns and will also give vigour and strength to all Grasses, especially on poor soils.

Apply at the rate of two to three ounces to the square yard, mixed with an equal quantity of fine soil during showery weather.

In Packets 1/- each,
Post Free.

3½ lbs.	...	1s. 6d.
7 lbs.	...	2s. 6d.
14 lbs.	...	4s. 6d.
28 lbs.	...	7s. 0d.
56 lbs.	...	12s. 0d.
112 lbs.	...	20s. 0d.

All Carriage Paid.

DANIELS' DAISY DESTROYER.

This preparation has become an immediate success, having given great satisfaction in every instance.

We have made arrangements for an increased demand during the coming Spring, and all who value a velvety clean lawn should use it if troubled with Daisies or Plantains. We have every confidence that it will give entire satisfaction wherever used. It will be found to thoroughly eradicate all Daisies, and at the same time, as a fertilizer, give renewed vigour to the finer grasses.

A dressing of about 4 ounces to the square yard will be found sufficient, and the best time to apply it is in April, choosing dry weather for the work ; where the lawn is badly infested with Daisies it should be carefully applied to the plants individually.

Price—7 lb. 2s. 6d. ; 14 lb. 4s. 6d. ; 28 lb. 7s. 6d. ; 56 lb. 12s. 6d. ; 112 lb. 25s.   *Carriage Paid on 1 cwt. and ½ cwt. lots.*

OTHER GARDEN MANURES.

*CANARY GUANO. Tins, 6d. and 1s. ; 14 lb., 3s. 6d. ; 28 lb., 6s. ; 56 lb., 11s. ; 1 cwt., 20s.
CLAY'S FERTILIZER. In tins, 6d. and 1s. each. In bags, 7 lb., 2s. 6d. ; 14 lb., 4s. 6d. ; 28 lb., 7s. 6d. ; 56 lb., 12s. 6d. ; 1 cwt., 20s.
ICHTHEMIC GUANO. In tins, 6d. and 1s. ; 7 lb., 2s. 6d. In bags, 14 lb., 4s. 6d. ; 28 lb., 7s. 6d. ; 56 lb., 12s. 6d. ; 1 cwt., 20s.
*THOMSON'S VINE, PLANT, AND VEGETABLE MANURE. In tins, 1s. ; 7 lb., 2s. 6d. ; 14 lb., 3s. 6d. ; 28 lb., 6s. ; 56 lb., 10s. ; per cwt., 20s.
*THOMSON'S CHRYSANTHEMUM MANURE. Of great value in growing Chrysanthemums for exhibition. 7 lb., 3s. 6d. ; 14 lb., 6s. ; 28 lb., 11s. ; 56 lb., 20s.
WATSON'S LAWN SAND. In tins, 1s. and 2s. 6d. ; 14 lb., 5s. 6d. ; 28 lb., 9s. 6d. ; 56 lb., 18s. ; per cwt., 34s.
* Carriage paid on orders of 28 lbs. and upwards on the G.E.R. and Mid. & G.N.R.

POTTING MATERIALS.

CHARCOAL. In Lumps. Used very extensively for Orchids, &c. Per bushel, 2s. 6d.
COCOA-NUT FIBRE. 1s. 6d. per bushel ; 8s. per sack.
JADOO FIBRE. Peck bag, 1s. ; bushel bag, 3s. 6d.
LEAF SOIL. 1s. 6d. per bushel. LOAM. Fibrous, 1s. 6d. per bushel.
PEAT. Best Orchid, 5s. per bushel. Ordinary Potting, 2s. 6d. per bushel.
SILVER SAND. Fine and coarse, 4s. per bushel. SPHAGNUM MOSS. 2s. 6d. per bushel.

RAW MANURES.

BASIC SLAG. An excellent dressing for lawns. 14 lb., 1s. ; 28 lb., 1s. 9d. ; 56 lb., 3s. ; 112 lb., 6s. 6d.
BONES. ½-in., ¼-in., 10s. per cwt., 6s. ½ cwt., 3s. 6d. ¼ cwt. These should be used liberally when forming Vine borders.
BONE MEAL. 12s. per cwt., 6s. 6d. ½ cwt., 3s. 6d. ¼ cwt., 2s. per 14 lbs. Excellent for all crops, forms a splendid Manure for Lawns.
GUANO, Peruvian. Price, 18s. cwt. Highly concentrated. First-rate for Tomatoes and other quick-growing crops.
KAINIT. 14 lb., 1s. 6d. ; 28 lb., 2s. 6d. ; 56 lb., 4s. ; 112 lb., 6s. 6d
MURIATE OF POTASH. 4d. per lb., 2s. 6d. per 14 lb.
NITRATE OF SODA. A most powerful assistant in the Vegetable Garden. Per lb., 2d. ; per stone, 3s. 6d.
SULPHATE OF AMMONIA. Specially adapted for Chrysanthemum growing. Per lb., 2d. ; per stone, 3s. 6d.
SUPERPHOSPHATE. 14 lb., 1s. ; 28 lb., 1s. 9d. ; 56 lb., 3s. ; 112 lb., 6s. 6d.

STERILISED SOIL.

Per Bushel 2s. Special Quotations for large quantities.

It has been found that when the soil is sterilised and thus cleaned of all hurtful agencies the ammonia producing Bacteria increases rapidly, and there is a corresponding greater production of plant food from the soil, followed by an increase of crop of a more healthy character.

DANIELS' SWEET PEA FERTILIZER.

An excellent stimulant for applying to Sweet Peas. We have thoroughly tested it and can thoroughly recommend it. About 4 ounces to each plant about once a fortnight, or if applied as a liquid, about the same quantity to a gallon of water

3½ lb., 1s. 6d. ; 7 lb., 2s. 6d. ; 14 lb., 4s. 6d. ; 28 lb., 7s. ; 56 lb., 12s. ; 112 lb., 20s. Carriage Paid.

INSECTICIDES AND FUMIGATORS.

INSECTICIDES, &c.

TRADE MARK REG^d

"ABOL" INSECTICIDE.

XL ALL LIQUID INSECTICIDE

"**ABOL**" **INSECTICIDE.** Most effectual, and may be used by any amateur. Pints, 1s. 6d. ; quarts, 2s. 6d. ; half-gallons, 4s. ; one gallon, 7s. 6d.
BANDING GREASE FOR FRUIT TREES. 1s. and 2s. 6d. per tin.
"**CARMUM.**" A certain cure for rust in Carnations and Chrysanthemums. Price 1s. 6d., 3s., and 6s. per bottle.
EWING'S MILDEW COMPOSITION. 1s. 6d. per bottle
FIR TREE OIL. An excellent Insecticide. In bottles, 1s. 6d., 2s. 6d., and 4s. 6d. each.
FORMICACIDE. Ant destroyer. 1s. 6d. per bottle
FOWLER'S GARDENERS' INSECTICIDE. A preparation we recommend. In jars, 1s. 6d.
GISHURST COMPOUND. Especially useful for the winter cleansing of fruit trees. In boxes, 1s. and 3s. each.
GISHURSTINE. An excellent dressing for gardeners' boots. 6d. and 1s. per tin.
HELLEBORE POWDER. 8d., 1s., and 2s. per tin.
LETHORION VAPOUR CONE. 6d., 8d., and 1s. each.
McDOUGALL'S CARBOLIC SOFT SOAP. Tins, 1s. and 2s. 6d. each.
MEALY BUG DESTROYER. 1s. per jar.
QUASSIA CHIPS. 6d. lb. ; 7 lbs., 3s. ; 14 lbs., 5s. 6d
QUASSIA EXTRACT (THE BEST). Per gallon, 3s. 8d. ; half-gallon, 2s. 6d. ; and in 6d. and 1s. tins.
SLUGENE. A certain exterminator of Slugs. Tins, 6d. and 1s. each.
SULPHUR, YELLOW. 6d. per lb. Excellent remedy for Red Spider.
TOBACCO POWDER. 6d., 1s., and 2s. 6d. per tin.
V. I. FLUID. For winter spraying of fruit trees. Per quart, 2s. 6d. ; gallon, 7s. 6d.
V. II. FLUID. For summer spraying of fruit trees. Per quart, 3s. 6d. ; per gallon, 10s. 6d.
VAPORITE. For destroying Wireworms, &c., in soil. Tins, 9d. and 2s. ; 28 lbs., 4s. 6d. ; ½-cwt., 7s. 6d. ; 1 cwt., 11s. 6d.
WEED KILLER, McDOUGALL'S NON-POISONOUS. 1 gallon tin, 3s. ; 5 gallon drums, 2s. 6d. per gallon ; 40 gallon casks, 2s. gallon. *All packages free.*

NICOTICIDE

FUMIGATORS.

DANIELS' RELIABLE COMPOUND TOBACCO PAPER.

1-lb. and 2-lb. Packets, 1s. and 2s. *Every packet is accompanied with full instructions for use.*

CAMPBELL'S FUMIGATING INSECTICIDES—

	s. d.
No. 3 Roll, sufficient for 1,000 cubic feet .. .. each	0 8
No. 4 ,, ,, 2,000 ,, ... ,,	1 2

McDOUGALL'S INSECTICIDE FUMERS. Sufficient for 1,000 cubic ft., 8d. each ; per doz., 8s. ; for 2,000 ft., 1s. each ; 12s. per doz.

McDOUGALL'S SELF-ACTING INSECTICIDE SHEETS, each sufficient for 1000 cubic feet, 8d. each ; per doz., 8s.

NICOTICIDE VAPORISING COMPOUND. An excellent Compound for vaporising greenhouses, &c., for the destruction of insects

No. 1 bottle.—1 pint containing sufficient for 40,000 cubic ft., each 15s.	
No. 2 bottle.—½ ,, ,, ,, 20,000 cubic ft., each 7s. 6d.
No. 3 bottle.—6 oz. ,, ,, 12,000 cubic ft., each 4s. 6d.
No. 4 bottle.—4 ,, ,, ,, 8,000 cubic ft., each 3s
No. 5 bottle.—1 ,, ,, ,, 2,000 cubic ft., each 10d.

FUMIGATORS for above (will last for years). These are made in one size only, large enough for 5,000 cubic feet, each 1s.

XL ALL SPECIALITIES.

RICHARD'S PATENT FUMIGATOR.

XL ALL VAPORISING COMPOUND, in solid dry cake. This cake when used in the XL All Fumigator first melts, and then passes entirely away as vapour and is as effective and safe as XL All Liquid Vaporising Compound. These cakes, each of which is sufficient for 1000 cubic feet, are packed in boxes to correspond with the liquid contained in the various sizes of bottles, viz. :—Boxes for 40,000 feet, 20s. ; 20,000 feet, 10s. 6d. ; 10,000 feet, 5s. 6d. ; 5000 feet, 2s. 10d. ; 2000 feet, 1s. 2d. per box.

BOX OF 10 CAKES, EACH FOR 1000 CUBIC FT. OF SPACE

IN SOLID DRY CAKE.

XL ALL VAPORISING FUMIGATOR—

No. 4 bottle contains Liquid Compound for 5000 cubic feet of space	2s. 10d.
No. 3 bottle ,, ,, ,, 10,000 cubic feet ,, ...	5s. 6d
No. 2 bottle ,, ,, ,, 20,000 cubic feet ,, ...	10s. 6d.
No 1 bottle ,, ,, ,, 40,000 cubic feet ,, ...	20s. 0d.

Fumigators complete for above, each 1s. 9d. and 2s.

XL ALL WASH FOR MILDEW. A certain cure for mildew, killing insects at same time. Pints, 2s. 6d. ; quarts, 4s. ; half-galls, 6s. 6d. ; galls., 12s. 6d
AL ALL INSECTICIDE. The safest and most effectual Insecticide. Pints, 2s. ; quarts, 3s. 6d. ; half-gallons, 5s. ; gallons, 10s.
XL ALL WINTER WASH (non-poisonous). The most effectual wash for applying to all kinds of Fruit Trees and Bushes. Must be used in Winter when the trees are dormant. Price 1s. per tin ; 12 tins for 10s.

HORTICULTURAL SUNDRIES.

TOOLS AND IMPLEMENTS.

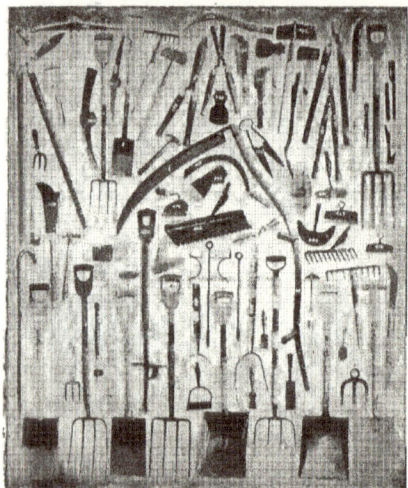

TURFING IRONS. Best solid blades, handled, 10s. 6d.
WATER CANS. Galvanized Iron. 1 gallon, 2s. 6d.; 2 gallon, 3s. 3d.; 3 gallon, 4s. 3d.
WATER CANS (HAWES' PATTERN). With two roses. 3 quarts, 4s. 3d.; 4 qts., 5s.; 6 qts., 6s.; 8 qts., 6s. 9d.; 10 qts., 7s. 0d.; 12 qts., 9s. each.
WHEELBARROWS. Ash frame, deal body, wrought-iron wheel, £1 17s. 6d. Fitted with leaf boards, 10s. extra.

KNIVES, &c.

ASPARAGUS KNIVES. 68, 3s. 6d. each.
BUDDING KNIVES. 204, 3s.; 204B, 3s. 0d.; 207, 3s. 6d.; 316, 3s.; 324, 3s.; 325½, 3s. 9d.; 329, 3s. 6d.
GOOSEBERRY PRUNERS. 60, Straight, 2s. 6d.
    ,,   60, With hook, 3s.
PRUNING KNIVES. 186½, 3s.; 189, 3s. 3d.; 190, 3s.; 191, 3s. 3d.; 191½, 3s. 6d.; 193, 3s. 6d.; 194, 3s.; 195, 3s. 6d.; 195½, 3s. 6d.; 196, 4s.; 197, 3s. 6d.; 312SB, 2s. 6d.; 313, 2s.; 038, 3s. 6d.
SCISSORS. FLOWER-GATHERING. 53, 6 in., 3s.; 7 in., 3s. 6d.; 8 in., 4s.
 ,,   **PRUNING.** 52, 6 in., 2s. 6d.; 7 in., 3s. 3d.
 ,,   **VINE.** 51, 6 in., 2s. 6d.; 7 in., 3s. 6d.; 8 in., 4s. per pair.
 ,,   **SHRED.** 50, 2s. 6d. per pair.
SECATEURS. 57, With Aubert's Spring. 6½ in., 3s. 6d.; 7½ in., 4s.; 8½ in., 4s. 6d.
 ,,   56, All bright, 7 in., 3s. 9d.; 8 in., 4s. 3d.
 ,,   56A, Not bright, 7 in., 3s.; 8 in., 3s. 9d.
 ,,   Hercules Patent. 55, Spiral Spring, 8 in., 4s.
 ,,   54, Nickel plated, for Ladies' use, 2s. 9d. per pair.
SCYTHE BLADES. 4s. and 4s. 6d. each.
STANDARD TREE PRUNER. 8 ft., 7s. 6d.; 10 ft., 8s. 6d.; 12 ft., 10s. 6d.

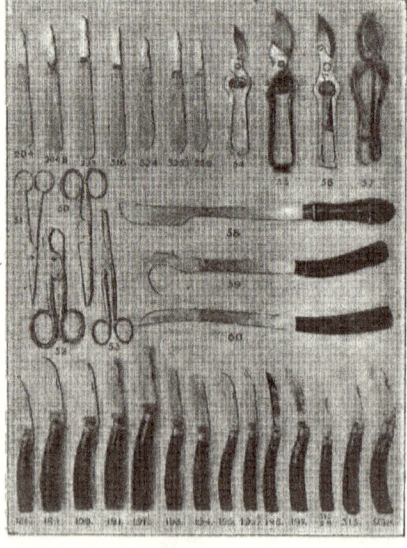

AVERUNCATORS, PATENT TREE PRUNERS. 5s. 6d., 7s. 6d., and 10s. 6d. each. Handles any length can be supplied extra.
BILL HOOKS. All bright, 4s. each.
BROOMS, BIRCH. 4d. each; 3s. 6d. per doz.
BUCO CULTIVATOR. For breaking up surface of soil in dry weather. 5s. each. Smaller sizes, 1s. 6d. and 3s. 9d. each.
DAISY GRUBS. 2s. 6d. each. Extra strong with long handles, 3s. 6d. each.
DIBBERS, GARDEN. 1s. 6d. each.
      Small size, 1s. 3d. each.
EDGING IRONS, CAST STEEL. 3s. 6d. each; with handle, 4s. 6d. each.
FORKS, GARDEN. Four or five prongs. 3s. 9d. and 4s. 6d. each.
 ,,   **HAND.** 1s. and 2s. 6d. each.
 ,,   **LADIES' DIGGING.** 2s. 6d. each
HAMMERS. No. 1, 2s.; No. 3, 2s. 6d.
HATCHETS. 2s. 6d. each.
HOES, DUTCH. 5 in., 1s. 3d.; 6 in., 1s. 6d.; 7 in., 1s. 8d.; 8 in., 1s. 9d.
 ,,   **DRAW.** 5 in., 1s.; 6 in., 1s. 3d.; 7 in., 1s. 4d.; 8 in., 1s. 6d.
 ,,   **BURY.** 5 in., 1s. 3d.; 6 in., 1s. 6d.; 7 in., 1s. 8d.; 8 in., 1s. 9d.
PLIERS. For Wire cutting. Extra good quality. 1s. 9d. and 2s. 6d.
RAKES, DAISY. 6s. and 7s. 6d. each.
 ,,   **IRON.** 8 teeth, 10d.; 10 teeth, 1s.; 12 teeth, 1s. 3d.
 ,,   **AMERICAN STEEL, WITH ASH HANDLES.** 8 teeth, 2s. 6d.; 10 teeth, 3s.; 12 teeth, 3s. 6d.; 14 teeth, 4s. each.
REELS, GARDEN. 2s. each; Lines (30 & 60 yds. long), 1s. 3d. & 2s. 6d. ea.
SAWS, PRUNING, WITH BILL HOOK. 6s. each.
 ,,   **PRUNING, CAST STEEL.** 3s. each.
SHEARS, GRASS. 4s. per pair.
 ,,   **EDGING.** 6s. 9d. per pair.
 ,,   **SHEEP.** 3s. per pair.
 ,,   **SLIDING PRUNING.** 6s. 6d., 8s. 6d., and 11s. per pair.
SHOVELS. Improved London, 3s. 3d. each.
SPADES, GARDEN. "The Sword," all bright, 4s. each.
 ,,   All bright, "The Norfolk," 4s. 6d. and 4s. 9d. each.
 ,,   **LADIES'.** 2s. 6d. each.
SPUDS, CAST STEEL. 1s. 3d. each; with walking stick handles, 2s. each.
TAPES, MEASURING. 7s. 6d. each.
TROWELS, BRIGHT STEEL. 6 in., 1s. 6d.; 7 in., 1s. 9d.; 8 in., 2s. 3d. each.

HORTICULTURAL SUNDRIES.

SYRINGES AND DISTRIBUTORS.

ABOL" NEW PATENT. For distributing Insecticides and for ordinary Syringing. Each, 8s. 6d., 10s. 6d. and 14s. 6d. Bonds for any size, 1s. 6d. extra. Postage 4d. extra.

THE "ABOL' SYRINGE.

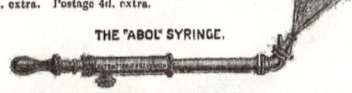

APHICIDES, OR SPRAY DIFFUSERS (Hughes'). Fitted with mouthpiece and cork attached for mouth of bottle. 1s. 6d. each.
THE FOUR OAKS SYRINGE. A great improvement on the old types. 10s. and 12s. each, including bend.
REID'S PATENT SYRINGE, with extra Rose. Superior make, 19s. each.
USEFUL GARDEN SYRINGE, with Rose, 5s. each.
ALPHA SPRAYING MACHINES. The most simple and efficient sprayer yet introduced. No constant pumping; once charged the machine empties automatically. Charged with compressed air by means of any ordinary bicycle foot-pump. Any tree-spraying solution may be used in these machines, and the spray can be maintained at will until the whole of the contents are discharged.
Knapsack Machine, 3½ gals., complete, with powerful foot-pump. 60s.
Hand Sprayer, 3 quarts. 17s. 6d. *See illustration.*

THERMOMETERS & BAROMETERS.

THERMOMETERS, BOXWOOD. 1s., 1s. 6d., and 2s. 6d. each.
    ,,   **WHITE JAPANNED SCALES**; especially adapted for the garden (Negretti and Zambra), 3s. 6d. each. *See illustration.*

THERMOMETERS, CONSERVATORY. Porcelain Index, Maximum and Minimum combined, 10s. 6d. and 15s. each.
    ,,   **MINIMUM AND MAXIMUM REGISTERING**; japanned case, 5s. 6d., 7s. 6d., and 7s. 6d. each.
PLUNGING THERMOMETERS, for hot-beds, 5s. and 7s. 6d. each.
BAROMETERS (Horticultural). In metal cases, 12s. 6d. each.
    ,,   Ornamental Oak Frames, 18s. 6d., 27s. 6d. and 35s. each.
MAGNIFYING GLASSES with three lenses, mounted in horn folding case, 5s.

GARDENING GLOVES.

GLOVES, Strong Norfolk Hedging. 1s. 9d. per pair, Postage extra
   ,,   Men's Drummonds'. 1s. 9d. per pair, machine sewn.
   ,,   2s. per pair, hand sewn.
   ,,   Best Oxfords. 2s. per pair
   ,,   Cape Oxfords. 2s. 6d. per pair.
   ,,   Ladies' Gardening. Dark Tan. 2s. per pair.
   ,,   Housemaid's. Strong, 1s. 6d. per pair.
   ,,   Gentleman's Best. 2s. 6d. and 3s. 6d. per pair.

SHADING MATERIALS.

SCRIM CANVAS, BROWN. 54 in. wide, 9d. per yard; 72 in. wide, 1s. per yard.
GREEN ROT-PROOF SHADING. 54 in. 1s. 7d. per yard.
WHITE ditto, 54 in. 1s. 2d. per yard.
TIFFANY. A thin material for shading. 20 yards long by 38 ins. wide, 5s. per piece.
SUMMER CLOUD, "ELLIOTT'S." For shading greenhouses. In ¼-lb. packets, 1s. each.
SUMMER SHADING, "THE PERFECT." 1 lb. tins, 1s.
TANNED NETTING (FOR PROTECTING FRUIT TREES, &c.). 2 and 4 yards wide. 3d. and 6d. per yard run. In pieces 50 by 4, or 100 by 2, 10s. per piece.

GENERAL SUNDRIES.

APHIS BRUSHES. 2s. each.
BASKETS (TRUCK). Made of strong wood, and are indispensable to every garden.
No. 2, 11½ in. by 6 in., 1s.; No. 3, 13½ in. by 7½ in., 1s. 3d.; No. 4, 15 in. by 8¼ in., 1s. 6d.; No. 5, 17½ in. by 9½ in., 1s. 9d.; No. 6, 20½ in. by 10½ in., 2s. 3d.; No. 7, 23 in. by 12 in., 2s. 6d.; No. 8, 26 in. by 14 in., 3s.; No. 9, 28 in. by 15 in., 3s. 6d.

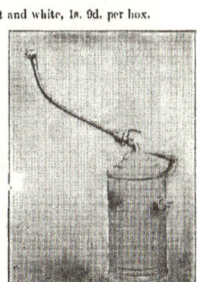

BOUQUET WIRE, 7 in. lengths. 1s. to 2s. per lb.
BOWLS. Suitable for growing bulbs in, a great variety. Price, each 9d., 1s., 1s. 3d., 6d., 2s., and upwards.
CLOTH SHREDS. Per lb., 6d.; per stone, 5s. 6d.
DEANS' MEDICATED SHREDS in Boxes of 100, 2 in., 6d.; 2½ in., 7½d. 3 in., 8d.; 3½ in., 9d. per box.
DRIED CAPE FLOWERS. Scarlet and white, 1s. 9d. per box.
FLORAL AID. A useful device for arranging flowers in bowls, &c. 1s., 1s. 6d. & 2s. 6d. each.
FLORAL CEMENT OR GUM. 1s. per bottle.
GARDENERS' APRONS. Sballoon, 4s. 6d., 4s. 9d., and 5s. each. Serge, 3s., 3s. 3d., and 3s. 9d. each.
GRAFTING WAX. 8d., 1s. 3d., and 2s. 6d. per tin.
LAYER PEGS (ZINC). In boxes of 100. 1s. each.
MARTIN FLOWER RACK. An ingenious and simple contrivance for the easy arranging of cut flowers. In bowls 6d., 9d., 1s., 1s. 3d., and 1s. 6d. each.
MELON NETS (STRING). Per doz., 3s. 6d.
NAIL BAGS. Leather, best quality. 5s. each.
PENCILS, WOLFF'S GARDEN. 3d. each.
SPRINGTHORPE CUPS AND TUBES, for exhibiting Roses and Chrysanthemums. 9s. per dozen.
STYPTIC. For preventing bleeding in vines, 1s. 6d. and 2s. 6d. per bottle.
"TAM O'SHANTER" HONES. The best, each 1s.; in case, 3s. each.
TOBACCO POWDER DISTRIBUTORS, INDIA-RUBBER WITH BRASS NOZZLE, 2s. 9d. each.
BELLOWS, 2s. per pair.
VERBENA PINS (GALVANIZED WIRE). For pegging down Verbenas, &c. Per box of 1 gross, 1s.
VIRGIN CORK. 3s. per stone. Quarter-cwt., 6s.; half-cwt., 11s.; cwt., 20s. Carriage Paid on 1 cwt. and upwards.
WALL NAILS. Square cast, 3d. per lb.; per stone, 2s. 6d.; French, 4d. per lb.; per stone.
WALL NAILS, CHANDLER'S PATENT. A useful invention. Shreds not required. Boxes of 100, 1¼ in., 1s. 9d.; 1½ in., 2s.
WATSON'S LAWN SAND DISTRIBUTOR. For applying the sand to individual weeds 10s. 6d. each.
WIKEHAM WEED ERADICATOR (PATENT). An excellent instrument for destroying Dandelions, Docks, &c., on Lawns. Fill with Weed Killer, stab the crown of the weed and it will soon perish. 9s. 6d. each.
WIRE ALUMINIUM. 1s. per coil of 40 foot.
WIRE FRAMES, for supporting Weeping Standard Roses. 2s. 9d. each.
WREATH AND CROSS TROUGHS, for holding Cut Flowers; the very best made. 1s. 6d., 2s., and 2s. 6d. each.

ALPHA SPRAYING MACHINE.
PRICE 17/6.

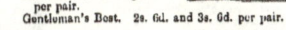

DANIELS' SUPERIOR MUSHROOM SPAWN.

This illustration (from a Photograph) represents a group of mushrooms in all stages of growth taken while growing at Ashwellthorpe Hall.

In Bricks, each 6d., 4 bricks 1s. 6d., one bushel of 16 bricks, 5s.

COMPLETE INSTRUCTIONS FOR CULTIVATION WILL BE SENT WITH EVERY ORDER.

From Mr. O. BEETON, Head Gardener to W. K. D'Arcy, Esq.,
The Gardens, Bylaugh Park.

"I am very pleased with the Mushroom Spawn you have supplied to us for several seasons; it is very productive; and the Mushrooms are of fine quality. This season it promises to be equally good, as Mushrooms were showing in five weeks from the time the bed was spawned."

From Mr. H. HOLLAND, New Barnet.

April 2nd.

"The Mushroom Spawn I had from you last year turned out very good indeed. The Mushrooms were showing within a month from the time the bed was spawned. The persons who saw them said they were a fine lot of Mushrooms. Some weighed about three-quarter pound each."

PACKING AND TYING MATERIALS, Etc.

BAMBOO CANES. 4 ft. Thin. Medium. Thick. 5 ft. 6 ft. 7 ft.
2s. 6d.   3s.   4s.   6s.   7s.   9s. per 100.
BAMBOO POLES. Suitable for forming arches, &c., 8 to 10 ft. long (tapering), 2s. per doz.; 16s. per 100.
BAMBOO TIPS. For supporting Carnations, 2s. 3d. per 100.
CARNATION COIL STAKES. Galvanized and painted green. 20 in., 1s. per doz., 7s. 6d. per 100; 25 in., 1s. 6d. per doz., 10s. 6d. per 100; 30 in., 2s. per doz., 13s. 6d. per 100; 30 in., 2s. 6d. per doz.; 17s. 6d. per 100.
DAHLIA STAKES.—Painted Green, with tarred ends.

per doz.	2 ft.	2¼ ft.	3 ft.	4 ft.	4½ ft.	5 ft.
	1s.	1s. 3d.	1s. 6d.	2s.	2s. 6d.	2s. 9d.

FLOWER STICKS.—Unpainted Deal.

	1 ft.	1½ ft.	2 ft.	2½ ft.	3 ft.	3½ ft.	per 100
	9d.	1s. 3d.	1s. 6d.	2s.	2s. 6d.	3s.	

FLOWER STICKS.—Painted Green. Per 100, 1 ft., 1s. 3d.; 1½ ft., 1s. 9d.; 2 ft., 2s.; 2¼ ft., 2s. 6d.; 3 ft., 3s.; 3½ ft., 3s. 9d.; 4 ft., 4s. 6d.; 5 ft., 5s. 6d.
LABELS, WOOD.—Painted, in boxes of 100.

4 in.	5 in.	6 in.	7 in.	8 in.	9 in.	12 in.
	7d.	9d.	10d.	1s.	1s. 3d.	1s. 6d.	2s 6d.

LABELS, WOOD.—Plain.

4 in.	5 in.	6 in.	7 in.	8 in.	9 in.	12 in
5d.	6d.	8d.	10d.	1s.	1s. 3d.	2s.

LABELS, ZINC, IMPERISHABLE, for Roses and Fruit Trees, 2s. and 3s. 6d. per 100
METALLIC INK, for writing on above, 6d. and 1s. per bottle
LABELS, ACME GARDEN. For Roses, 1s. 3d. per doz.; for Fruit Trees, 1s. 9d. per doz.
    Please give names of varieties wanted.
MATS. Archangel, large, new. 2s. each, 21s. doz.
MATS. St. Petersburg. 1s. to 1s. 6d. each; 10s. 6d. to 15s. doz.
PUNNETS. ¼ lb., 7d. per doz. ⎫ Either square or
PUNNETS. ½ lb., 9d. per doz. ⎬ round.
RAFFIA. Very best quality for tying. In bundles, 6d.; per lb., 1s. 6d.
RAFFIA.—GREEN. 2s. per lb.
RAFFIA TAPE. 1s. 6d. per reel.
TAR TWINE. In balls, thin, medium, and thick, ¼ lb., 9d.; 1 lb., 1s. 3d.
WADDING, BLEACHED. For packing, in sheets measuring about 36 in. by 18 in., 3s. 6d. per doz. sheets.
WHITE OR BLUE TISSUE PAPER. 3s. 6d. to 5s. per ream.
WOOD WOOL. Finest quality for fruit packing. 6d per lb.; 5s. 6d. per stone.

ACME LABEL.

FLOWER SEED DEPARTMENT

The careful attention we have given for so many years to the growth and selection of our fine strains of choice Florists' and other Flower Seeds, has secured for us a world-wide reputation for their excellence, and a very large and steadily increasing business in this Department.

We are especially famous for our splendid strains of Asters, Stocks, Begonias, Phloxes, Pansies, Primulas, Wallflowers, Godetias, Clarkias, Mignonettes, etc., most of which are especially grown for our retail trade, and may be relied on as the finest procurable.

We have again carefully revised our List of Flower Seeds, and several interesting and valuable additions have been made, whilst some fine Novelties in Sweet Peas, and other choice flowers, have been introduced, for which we anticipate a great demand.

As a consequence of the very unfavourable climatic conditions during last Summer and Autumn, we regret to say that seeds of many of the newer and choicer varieties of Sweet Peas are again exceedingly scarce. To prevent disappointment we strongly advise our customers, who wish to secure special sorts, to send us their orders as early as convenient after receiving this Catalogue.

ASTERS DANIELS' DWARF PERFECTION BEDDING growing at our Trial Grounds.

DANIELS' SUPERB PRIZE ASTERS.

☞ We have long been famous for our magnificent strains of Asters, which form an important branch of our Flower Seed business, and we would mention that our seeds of these having been grown especially for our retail trade may be relied on as the very finest procurable.

PLEASE NOTE.—We do not as a rule count the seeds contained in our packets, but customers may in all instances rely on liberal quantities of good seeds being given for the prices charged.

DANIELS' GIANT OSTRICH PLUME.

☞ We have much pleasure in recommending this grand new strain of beautiful varieties which we have every confidence in saying will give the highest satisfaction amongst our customers.

The plants are of a strong bushy habit of growth, and attain a height of 15 to 18 inches. The very large handsome flowers, which are borne on long wiry stems, are of the true Ostrich Plume type, and of immense size—when well grown, frequently measuring six inches and even seven inches in diameter, whilst the colours embrace the most beautiful and delicate shades known in Asters. These will prove a splendid class alike for garden decoration, as cut flowers or for exhibition.

				s.	d.				s.	d.
1	A COLLECTION OF 8 BEAUTIFUL VARS., DISTINCT	—		3	6	7	DANIELS' ROSY LILAC	.. per pkt.	0	6
2	DANIELS' BRILLIANT ROSE	per pkt.		0	6	8	DANIELS' BRILLIANT CRIMSON	.. ,,	0	6
3	DANIELS' LILAC BLUE			0	6	9	DANIELS' DARK BLUE	.. ,,	0	6
4	DANIELS' PURE WHITE	,,6d. & 1	0			10	DANIELS' CHOICEST MIXED	.. ,,	1	0
5	DANIELS' AZURE BLUE			0	6	11		.. smaller pkt.	0	6
6	DANIELS' DELICATE ROSE			0	6					

DANIELS' DWARF PERFECTION, BEDDING.

See Illustration (page 61)

These beautiful dwarf Asters, introduced by us a few years ago, have proved themselves by far the finest and best dwarf bedding varieties in existence. The plants grow only about 7 or 8 inches high, with stiff upright stems and branches, and form handsome circular bushy plants with the flowers well above the foliage. The blooms are of large size, perfectly double, beautifully imbricated and of the most perfect form. This is a superb class for bedding and general garden decoration, and planted in beds of the distinct and beautiful colours mentioned below, or used as an edging to large beds, they are splendidly effective and continue in bloom for quite a long time.

					s.	d.				s.	d.
12	AN ASSORTMENT OF SIX FINE VARIETIES	..			2	0	16	DANIELS' BRIGHT ROSE	per ¼ oz. 3 6 per packet	0	6
13	DANIELS' BRILLIANT SCARLET	per ¼ oz. 3 6	per packet 0	6	17	DANIELS' LIGHT BLUE	3 6 ,,	0	6
14	DANIELS' DARK BLUE	,, 3 6		0	6		18	DANIELS' CHOICEST MIXED	3 0 ,,	1	0
15	DANIELS' PURE WHITE	,, 3 6		0	6		19		smaller packet	0	6

ASTER—NEW TALL BRANCHING.

A splendid new class of beautiful late blooming varieties, growing about 2 ft. high, and branching almost from the base of the stem. The blooms, which are produced in the greatest profusion, are of medium size and are borne on very long wiry stems, rendering them of especial value for cut flowers.

			s.	d.				s.	d.
20	SIX VARIETIES AS FOLLOWS, one packet of each	—	1	9	24	LIGHT BLUE	.. per pkt.	0	4
21	PURE WHITE		0	4	25	SHELL PINK	.. ,,	0	4
22	SALMON ROSE	per pkt. 0	4	26	CRIMSON	.. ,,	0	4
23	DARK BLUE	,, 0	4	27	VERY CHOICE MIXED	.. 6d. and 1	0	

DWARF VICTORIA.

A beautiful, compact-growing class, with the same form of flower as Victoria, but growing only one foot in height. An excellent variety for bedding.

			s.	d.
28	SIX BEAUTIFUL VARIETIES	—	1	9
29	WHITE, Splendid	per pkt.	0	4
30	BRILLIANT CRIMSON ..	,,	0	4
31	INDIGO BLUE	,,	0	4
32	VERY CHOICE MIXED	,,	0	4

DANIELS' IMPROVED PRIZE QUILLED.

A fine strain of splendid varieties, producing beautifully formed perfectly double flowers of the most charming colours. Being on long wiry stems the flowers are very useful for cutting, but the plants are too straggly for bedding.

			s.	d.
33	AN ASSORTMENT OF 6 CHOICE VARIETIES	..	1	6
34	CHOICEST MIXED	per pkt.	0	6
35		smaller pkt.	0	3

DANIELS' IMPROVED PÆONY-FLOWERED PERFECTION.

These Asters are of the greatest perfection, producing large flowers of the most perfect Pæony form, and in a great variety of beautiful colours.

			s.	d.				s.	d.
36	AN ASSORTMENT OF 6 SPLENDID VARIETIES	—	1	9	42	DARK PURPLE VIOLET	.. per pkt.	0	4
37	BRILLIANT CRIMSON	per pkt.	0	4	43	PURE WHITE	.. ,,	0	4
38	SKY BLUE	,,	0	4	44	SPLENDID MIXED	.. ,,	1	0
39	DELICATE ROSE	,,	0	4	45		.. smaller pkt.	0	6
40	LIGHT BLUE AND WHITE	,,	0	4	46	,,	.. smallest pkt.	0	3
41	DARK SCARLET AND WHITE	,,	0	4					

RAY ASTER—New Giant White.

A fine new robust growing variety, attaining the height of eighteen inches or two feet. It is of a free branching habit, is a splendid drought resistor, and blooms freely in the hottest weather. The very large pure white flowers are composed of long, straight, needle-like petals which radiate from a yellow centre, giving the blooms a most handsome appearance. The flowers being produced on long wiry stems will be found of great value to cut for decorative purposes.

47 Per packet .. .. 6d. and 1s.

We beg to intimate that we cannot "break" packets quoted in this list.

DANIELS'
GIANT OSTRICH PLUME ASTERS.

Daniels' Superb Prize Asters

No. 1.
Daniels' Dwarf Bedding.
No. 2.
Daniels' Comet.
No. 3.
Daniels' Single Flowered.

DANIELS' SUPERB PRIZE ASTERS.

GIANT VICTORIA.

A very fine class of splendid flowers. The plants grow about fifteen inches high, and produce extra large double flowers of the most beautiful colours.

				s.	d.
48	SIX DISTINCT VARIETIES	..	..	2	0
49	CHOICEST MIXED	..	per pkt. 6d. and	1	0

ASTERS, "Ostrich Plume."
(ORDINARY CLASS.)

Charming varieties of exquisite beauty. The large flowers are borne on long stems, sixteen to eighteen inches in length, and the long petals are beautifully curled and twisted, giving them somewhat the appearance of Japanese Chrysanthemums. Very useful for bedding, besides being of great value for cut flowers or for exhibition.

					s.	d.
50	AN ASSORTMENT OF SIX BEAUTIFUL VARIETIES				1	9
51	PURE WHITE. Splendid for cutting	..	..	per pkt.	0	6
52	ROSE. Beautiful	..	..	,,	0	4
53	CRIMSON. Very fine	..	..	,,	0	4
54	DARK BLUE ..	..	..	,,	0	4
55	WHITE, CHANGING TO ROSE ..	..	..	,,	0	4
56	REDDISH LILAC	..	..	,,	0	4
57	CHOICEST MIXED	..	per pkt. 3d. and	0	4

SINGLE-FLOWERED ASTERS.

58 **SINGLE MAUVE (Sinensis)**—This is well described as the best and grandest of the Single-flowering Asters. The plants form elegant branching bushes about 18 inches high, well furnished with rich dark green foliage, and produce an abundance of large, handsome single flowers three to four inches across, having a single row of delicate pale mauve florets, with golden central disc. It is a plant of great beauty, quite distinct from the single German, and far away the most beautiful of all the Single Asters. First-class as border plant or for cut flowers .. .. 3d. 6d. and 1s.

GIANT SINGLE—A fine, showy class for garden decoration, and very effective when grown in large beds of separate colours. The flowers are produced on long wiry stems and are very useful to cut for decoration.

						s.	d.
60	BRIGHT ROSE	..	..	..	..	0	6
61	PURE WHITE	..	..	..	..	0	6
62	DARK BLUE ..	..	..	..	..	0	6
63	CHOICE MIXED	..	..	6d. and	1	0

DANIELS' IMPROVED VICTORIA.

A magnificent class, growing about fifteen inches high, and producing an abundance of large, perfectly double and beautifully imbricated flowers, four to five inches across. This is one of the most splendid Asters for garden decoration, and a first-class variety for exhibition.

					s.	d.
64	AN ASSORTMENT OF 12 BEAUTIFUL VARIETIES		..	3	6
65	,, ,, 9 ,, ,,			2	6
66	PURE WHITE	..	per pkt.	0	4
67	FINEST MIXED. In beautiful variety	..		1	0
68	,, ,, ...	..	smaller pkt.	0	6

DWARF CHRYSANTHEMUM-FLOWERED.

This fine class is a decided acquisition. It commences blooming when many other Asters are off, and is invaluable for a late display; its height is only nine inches, and in consequence of its fine dwarf habit of growth it is admirably suited for beds, edgings, pots, &c.

					s.	d.
69	AN ASSORTMENT OF SIX FINE VARIETIES	..	..	1	6
70	VERY CHOICE MIXED	..	per pkt.	1	0
71	,, ,, ,,	..	smaller pkt.	0	6

ASTER—Salmon Queen.

A new and beautiful variety growing about 18 inches high, and producing a profusion of large beautiful flowers on long wiry stems. The colour of the flower is a beautiful bright salmon-rose, quite a new colour amongst Asters. A splendid variety for cut flowers.

72 Per Packet .. .. 6d. and 1s.

ASTER—Hercules.

A grand new variety growing 15 to 18 inches high and of a robust branching habit of growth. The pure white blooms are of immense size and under good culture will attain as much as six or even seven inches diameter, the long curly petals giving them the appearance of well-grown Japanese Chrysanthemums. The plant is of vigorous growth, and the very handsome flowers are borne on long stout stems, useful for cutting.

73 Per Packet .. .. 1s.

DWARF COMET.

A charming strain of beautiful colours. The plants grow only about nine inches high, and the numerous double flowers have the elegant form and lovely colours of the larger growing varieties.

					s.	d.
74	PURE WHITE. Beautiful	..	..	6d. and	1	0
75	CHOICEST MIXED	..	..		1	0
76	,, ,,	..	smaller pkt.	0	6

COMET ASTERS,
New Large-flowered or Giant.

An elegant strain of highly improved and beautiful varieties, growing about fifteen inches high, the individual flowers resembling those of the Japanese Chrysanthemum, and are of great size. The blooms are very useful for cutting, the pure white and the delicately-striped flowers being extremely beautiful.

					s.	d.
77	SIX BEAUTIFUL VARIETIES				1	9
78	LIGHT BLUE AND WHITE	..	..	per pkt.	0	4
79	WHITE. Very fine variety	..		,,	0	4
80	THE BRIDE. White, shading to delicate rose; beautiful	..	,,	0	4
81	DARK BLUE, with white centre. Splendid variety	,,	0	4
82	RUBY. Rich scarlet; fine	..		,,	0	4
83	ROSE. Beautiful	..	..	,,	0	4
84	DARK VIOLET. Fine colour	..		,,	0	4
85	MAUVE or ROSY-LILAC	..	..	,,	0	4
86	CHOICEST MIXED	..	..	,,	0	6
87	,, ,,	..	smaller pkt.	0	3

CULTIVATION OF ASTERS.

Cultivation.—Asters form one of the chief attractions in all gardens in which annuals are grown. They are procurable in every colour from white to deep crimson, are very easy to raise from seed, and give a glorious display of bloom in Autumn after many other plants have ceased to flower.

Asters are alike useful for borders and as cut flowers, the single kinds being of especial value for the latter purpose. The seed should be sown in March or April in boxes of good rich soil, and treated in the same manner as other half-hardy annuals; give plenty of room between the plants, and place the boxes in a sunny position under glass, allowing abundance of air and water; after about three weeks remove the boxes to a frame where the lights can be lifted off during the day, and so gradually harden the plants in readiness for their removal to the borders. The greatest care should be exercised in transplanting from the boxes, so as to ensure the seedlings getting a good start. For a succession of flowers seed may be sown at the latter end of April in the open border where they are to bloom. Good sturdy plants may be raised by this method, and will give a supply of late flowers, until the frost cuts them off.

Asters respond readily to liberal treatment although they will thrive in any good garden soil. An excellent position for them is on beds or borders which have been well trenched and liberally manured early in the season. Occasional waterings with weak manure water will be found of great benefit when the plants are developing their blooms. Such treatment gives substance to the flowers and extends the period of blooming. Where the space is available, it is an excellent plan to grow beds in the kitchen garden of separate colours of Asters specially for cutting purposes. Such varieties as Giant Ostrich Plume, Improved Comet, and the Single Sinensis will be found admirable for this purpose, and a supply for the house will be at hand without spoiling the effect of the beds. When only one kind can be grown we should strongly recommend our customers to try our Giant Ostrich Plume as being in our opinion the most delightful of all the doubles. The flowers which are very large, are borne on tall graceful stems often 18 inches long, and the colours are most distinct and varied. Ostrich Plume are quite as easily grown as the ordinary sorts.

Our Large-flowered Comet, while not growing quite so tall as the former, gives large, beautiful flowers, and is of great value both for bedding and cutting purposes. The perfect type of Dwarf Bedding Aster is found in our Dwarf Perfection, which forms an ideal edging to a bed of taller kinds, or is equally effective in a bed by itself.

GIANT ENGLISH BROMPTON STOCKS.

An exceedingly fine and useful class of Spring flowering plants of the old cottage garden type, producing large, handsome spikes of beautifully coloured and deliciously scented flowers in April and May. The seeds should be sown in May or early in June; sow thinly, and soon as the young plants are large enough to handle, prick them out about six inches apart on nursery beds in a sheltered position where they can remain during Summer. In September or October they should be planted out where intended to bloom in Spring. For this purpose some sheltered spot, as on a sunny border or under a South wall, should always be selected, as the plants are liable to suffer from severe frosts in early Spring if too much exposed. The plants grow about two feet high and should be planted eighteen inches or more apart.

				s.	d.								s.	d.
88	SIX CHOICE VARIETIES. Separate		..	2	0	92	BRILLIANT ROSE. Splendid variety	..		.. per pkt			0	6
89	DARK BLOOD RED. Splendid colour	.. per pkt.	0	6	93	DARK PURPLE. Fine colour ..	..		.. "			0	6
90	SNOW WHITE. Very fine	..	.. "	0	6	94	CHOICEST MIXED ⎫					1	0
91	CARMINE. A beautiful colour	..	.. "	0	6	95	" " ⎭ In beautiful variety	..	smaller pkt.			0	6

Cultivation of Stocks.—These deliciously-scented half-hardy annuals are amongst the most popular of all Summer bedding plants and they are deservedly given a place in both large and small gardens.

Ten-Week Stocks are easily raised from seed, but require careful treatment when in the seedling stage, as they are liable to damp off if over-watered and kept close, but if they are given an abundance of air and kept moderately moist, nothing need be feared and sturdy plants are assured.

During recent years much care has been devoted to the improvement of Stocks, both with regard to increasing the size of the individual flowers as well as the spike, and to the introduction of much clearer colours. It is now possible to grow them in every shade of colour from pure white to deep crimson and purple.

When planted in clumps of distinct colours on borders or in separate beds, Ten-Week Stocks form most attractive subjects, and the perfume is so delicious that after a shower of rain a bed in full bloom will fill the garden with its delightful odour.

The seed may be sown at any time from February to June, according to the time the plants are required to bloom; they are best raised in a frame or greenhouse. Either shallow wooden seed boxes or pans may be used, and the seed can be sown either in drills lengthwise down the boxes or (in the case of pans) sprinkled lightly over the surface, the seed being spread as evenly as possible.

The soil used should be rich potting mould finely sifted, and after sowing, the seed should be thinly covered with the same, keep the frame close and shaded until the seeds have germinated, when a little air should be given and the amount gradually increased as the plants gain strength.

When the plants are large enough to handle with safety they should be transplanted into boxes, allowing nine inches between each plant.

They can then be gradually hardened off, but should be at first carefully protected at night from the frost.

Give abundance of air during the daytime, and after about three weeks or a month they should be ready for planting out in the positions in which they are to bloom in the border or beds.

When a succession of flowers is desired, a sowing of Stocks should be made in the open border when strong sturdy plants will be raised; these will follow on in succession after those raised inside.

Always be careful that the borders are thoroughly trenched and given a liberal supply of decomposed manure before the Stocks are planted.

If possible, select showery weather for planting out, and be sure that the plants are thoroughly watered into the ground and kept shaded during the middle of the day for the first few days.

In planting out seedling Ten-Week Stocks, with a view to securing the largest number of double flowers, preference should always be given to those with a good share of *fine fibrous* roots, even if the plants are somewhat weaker; we have found from long experience that those having coarse forked roots invariably produce the largest percentage of single blooms.

By sowing the seed in July and potting the seedlings in single pots and growing on in a frame, a good display of bloom may be had in the greenhouse during the Winter months.

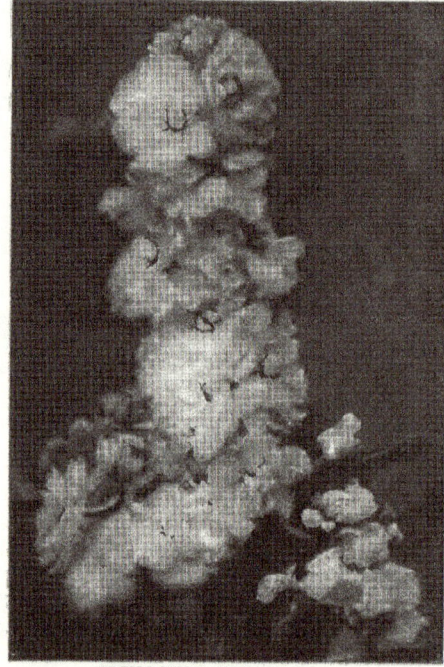

WINTER-FLOWERING STOCK—BEAUTY OF NICE.

WINTER-FLOWERING AND INTERMEDIATE STOCKS.—This is a very useful class for Winter blooming. The seed should be sown in July and the plants potted on into 5 inch pots, placing 3 plants in each pot; no artificial heat is needed, but the plants may be grown on, and placed in a greenhouse or conservatory, where they will provide a splendid show of bloom in the early part of the year.

DANIELS' SUPERB TEN-WEEK AND OTHER STOCKS.
PERPETUAL PERFECTION TEN-WEEK.

A new and exceedingly valuable class, growing to the height of about eighteen inches, and blooming profusely from July till late in Autumn. If sown in July or August and potted up may be wintered in a cool frame, and will bloom splendidly under glass in early Spring.

		per pkt.—s. d.					per pkt.—s. d.
96	SIX CHOICE VARIETIES	2 6	99	LIGHT BLUE			1 0
97	CRIMSON	1 0	100	CANARY YELLOW			1 0
98	PURE WHITE	1 0	101	CHOICEST MIXED	6d. and		1 0

INTERMEDIATE STOCKS.

EAST LOTHIAN AUTUMNAL—
Splendid for late blooming on the open border or for Winter decoration in the greenhouse.

		per pkt.—s. d.
102	AN ASSORTMENT OF 4 DISTINCT VARIETIES	1 0
103	SCARLET	0 6
104	CRIMSON	0 6
105	PURPLE	0 6
106	WHITE	0 6
107	CHOICEST MIXED	0 6
108	,, ,, smaller pkt.	0 3

LARGE-FLOWERED EMPEROR—
Remarkable for their large flowers and vigorous habit. If sown in March will produce a magnificent effect in Autumn.

109	AN ASSORTMENT OF 8 SPLENDID VARIETIES	2 0
110	FINEST MIXED	0 6

AUTUMN FLOWERING INTERMEDIATE—
A fine class for late flowering.

111	AN ASSORTMENT OF 6 SPLENDID VARIETIES	2 0
112	CHOICEST MIXED	0 6

IMPROVED WALLFLOWER-LEAVED TEN-WEEK.

A very distinct and beautiful class, growing about nine inches high, with rich glossy dark green foliage, which contrasts admirably with the bright colours of the flowers.

		per pkt.—s. d.
113	SIX CHOICE VARIETIES, DISTINCT	1 0
114	DARK BLOOD RED	0 4
115	PURE WHITE	0 4
116	DARK BLUE	0 4
117	CHOICEST MIXED	0 6
118	,, ,, smaller pkt.	0 3

DWARF GERMAN TEN-WEEK.

Useful compact growing class. Height nine inches.

				per pkt.—s. d.
119	SIX CHOICE VARIETIES, DISTINCT			1 6
120	SCARLET	per pkt.		0 3
121	PURPLE	,,		0 3
122	WHITE	,,		0 3
123	CHOICE MIXED	,,		0 3

From R. NOWELL, Dalton-in-Furness.

Oct. 16th.
"I won First with Stocks grown from your Seeds supplied by you last season."

From T. E. KIMPTON, Shortlands.

July 29th.
"The Ten-week Stocks are simply perfect, I am pleased to say, without any exaggeration I have at least 90 per cent. doubles; my friends are surprised with the fine shape and bloom."

ALMOND BLOSSOM.

WINTER-FLOWERING STOCKS

A splendid race of tall growing varieties, producing magnificent spikes of very large deliciously-scented double-flowers. Sown in July or August and potted up in Autumn, these will furnish some beautiful flowers under glass in Winter and early Spring, the long flower-stems making them of especial value for cutting. If sown in February or March and planted out in good soil, some grand spikes of bloom may be had during the summer and autumn.

		per pkt.—s. d.			per pkt.—s. d.
124	**ALMOND BLOSSOM.** Long central spikes and numerous side branches of lovely white flowers delicately shaded with carmine. Height 2 feet 6d. and	1 0	127	**NAVY BLUE.** Fine spikes of rich dark purplish blue, double flowers 6d. and	1 0
125	**BEAUTY OF NICE.** Large spikes with very large blooms of a delicate satiny flesh colour. Height 2 feet 6d. and	1 0	128	**MAUVE BEAUTY.** A superb variety with noble spikes of large double flowers of the most beautiful pale bluish mauve. Quite distinct. Height 2 feet 6d. and	1 0
126	**CRIMSON KING.** Brilliant fiery crimson, large blooms and spikes. Finely scented. Beautiful variety. 2 ft. 6d. and	1 0	129	**QUEEN ALEXANDRA.** Magnificent spikes of very large sweet-scented flowers of a lovely soft rosy-lilac colour. 2 ft. 6d. &	1 0

129A   Choice Mixed, from the above six varieties, 6d. and 1s.

DANIELS' SUPERB TEN-WEEK STOCKS

Our splendid strains of Ten-week and other Stocks are especially grown for our retail trade by one of the most famous growers, and may be thoroughly relied on to produce the largest percentage of fine double flowers procurable from seed.

DANIELS' LARGE-FLOWERED TEN-WEEK.

This is incomparably the finest strain of Ten-week Stocks in existence, and, where space is limited, should always be grown in preference to others. The plants which attain about one foot in height are of the same compact habit as the dwarfer varieties, but the flowers when well grown are nearly double the size of those of the old variety. The seeds of this always produce a high percentage of double flowers, whilst in substance of petal, brilliancy of colouring and richness of fragrance they are unrivalled.

			s.	d.
130	A COLLECTION OF 12 SUPERB VARIETIES. The most distinct and beautiful colours		3	6
131	" 6 " " " " " "		2	0

		per pkt.—s. d.			per pkt.—s. d.			per pkt.—s. d.
132	DANIELS' SPECIAL MIXTURE of the most brilliant varieties .. 1 6	137	PURE WHITE .. 0 6	143	BRIGHT ROSE .. 0 6
133	DARK BLOOD RED .. 0 6	138	LIGHT BLUE .. 0 6	144	DARK PURPLE .. 0 6
134	DARK VIOLET .. 0 6	139	FLESH COLOUR .. 0 6	145	ROSY LILAC .. 0 6
135	SULPHUR YELLOW .. 0 6	140	SALMON ROSE .. 0 6	146	CHOICEST MIXED .. 1 0
136	BRILLIANT ROSE .. 0 6	141	BRILLIANT CARMINE.. 0 6	147	" " smaller pkt. 0 6
		142	ASH GREY .. 0 6		

FINE NEW VARIETIES.

The following splendid new varieties of our superb strain of Large-flowered Ten-week Stocks bloomed magnificently at our Seed Grounds last Summer, and were greatly admired by our many visitors. The colours of these will be found distinct and beautiful, with exceptionally large spikes of fine double blooms, and a decided advance on most of the older sorts.

			per pkt.—s. d.
148	DANIELS' SPECIAL WHITE ..		6d. and 1 0
149	DANIELS' SPECIAL SCARLET ..	Producing very fine spikes of large perfectly double flowers of the most delicious fragrance	6d. and 1 0
150	DELICATE FLESH COLOUR ..		6d. and 1 0
151	NEW SALMON ROSE ..		6d. and 1 0
152	NEW LIGHT BLUE ..		6d. and 1 0

153 One packet of each above 5 Superb Varieties, 2s. and 4s.

DANIELS' GIANT PERFECTION TEN-WEEK.

A grand class of tall growing, beautiful varieties. The plants attain a height of from 15 to 18 inches, are of a handsome pyramidal form with branching habit, and throw up long central spikes of large, beautifully double flowers. This is an exceedingly fine strain that we can highly recommend.

		s. d.			per pkt. s. d.			s. d.
154	SIX CHOICE VARIETIES, distinct 1 6	157	LIGHT BLUE .. 0 6	160	ROSE .. per pkt. 1 0
155	CRIMSON .. per pkt. 0 6	158	DARK BLUE .. 0 6	161	CHOICEST MIXED 1 0
156	CANARY YELLOW .. " 0 6	159	PURE WHITE .. 0 6	162	" " smaller pkt. 0 6

DANIELS' MINIATURE TEN-WEEK.

A very beautiful class of dwarf-growing German Ten-week Stock, height about eight inches, and producing a large percentage of fine double flowers, which are carried well above the foliage.

		s. d.						s. d.
163	SIX CHOICE VARIETIES .. 1 6	165	PURE WHITE .. per pkt. 0 4	167	CHOICEST MIXED .. per pkt. 1 0
164	DARK BLOOD RED .. per pkt. 0 4	166	DARK PURPLE .. 0 4	168	" " smaller pkt. 0 6

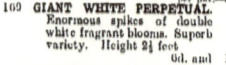 SUMMER FLOWERING STOCKS.

	per pkt.—s. d.
169	**GIANT WHITE PERPETUAL.** Enormous spikes of double white fragrant blooms. Superb variety. Height 2½ feet .. 6d. and 1 0
170	**PRINCESS ALICE.** Pure white, deliciously-scented double flowers. The plant is of a branching habit. Height 18 inches .. 6d. and 1 0
171	**PRINCESS MAY.** A beautiful early-flowering variety with double primrose yellow flowers. Wallflower leaved. Height only 8 inches .. 6d. and 1 0

STOCK—MAUVE QUEEN.

	per pkt. d
172	**SCARLET QUEEN, DWARF TEN-WEEK.** A charming variety, growing only 6 inches high and literally covered by its numerous spikes of deep blood crimson flowers. Splendid for beds, edgings, or pots .. 6d. and 1 0
173	**MAUVE QUEEN** (Heliotrope). A beautiful variety, growing about 1 foot high, with finely scented double flowers of a pale blush mauve colour, quite a distinct and novel shade of colour amongst Stocks 6d. and 1 0

DANIELS' SUPERB STRAIN OF

LARGE-FLOWERED TEN-WEEK STOCKS

NEW SWEET PEAS

Daniels Bros Ltd
NORWICH

No. 1
King White.

No. 2.
Lilian.

No. 3.
Nettie
Jenkins.

SWEET PEAS.

☞ We regret to state that owing to the unfavourable weather conditions of last Season, seeds of most of the new and choicer Spencer Varieties of Sweet Peas are again very scarce, the crops in some instances having been almost a total failure. We therefore strongly advise all who wish to secure special varieties to send us their orders as early as convenient after receiving this Catalogue.

SUPERB VARIETIES OF RECENT INTRODUCTION.

The following list includes the finest and most beautiful of the new varieties. Most of these have been grown and selected at our Nurseries during the past season, and can be highly recommended as really first-class for garden decoration or exhibition.

	per pkt.—s.	d.
174 **AGRICOLA.** Pale blush suffused rosy lilac. A distinct and charming flower. One of the prettiest. Award of Merit, 1912	1	0
175 **BARBARA.** A lovely salmony-orange self, with large, beautifully waved flowers of true Spencer type, mostly produced four on a stem. May be called an improved Earl Spencer, but withstands the sun better than that variety. F.C.C., N.S.P.S., 1911	1	0
176 **CRIMSON GIANT.** A true giant Spencer of the richest crimson colour. The flowers are larger than those of Maud Holmes, and the colour is deeper. A strong grower, many stems having four blooms .. .. .. 6d. and	1	0
177 **EMPRESS EUGENIE.** Large beautifully waved and crimped flowers. The colour is a delicate tone of light grey flaked with pale lavender. A vigorous grower and free bloomer, often producing four on a stem, and is charmingly effective	1	0
178 **ILLUMINATOR.** A very fine and exceedingly beautiful variety. The flowers are well placed on long stout stems and are of fine substance, the standards being bold, well expanded and waved. The colour is a glowing orange-scarlet and very attractive	1	0
179 **KING WHITE.** A magnificent pure white Spencer of immense size and frequently producing four blooms on a stem. The very large standards are splendidly formed and of great substance. A.M. National Sweet Pea Society, 1913 6d. and	1	0
180 **LILIAN.** A superb variety, pale cream-pink slightly flushed with buff. Flowers large, on long stems, mostly four on a stem	1	0

	per pkt.—s.	d.
181 **NETTIE JENKINS.** A lovely pale lavender mauve of immense size, frequently four on a stem. A first-class exhibition flower .. .. 6d. and	1	0
182 **"PRINCE GEORGE."** This is an extremely handsome and distinct flower, and has caused great excitement amongst lovers and admirers of the Sweet Pea. The standard is a warm lilac rose, base of standard solferino red, wings violet rose ; it is a strong grower with always an abundance of four bloom sprays, a gem for exhibition ; very scarce .. 6d. and	1	0
183 **PRINCESS MARY.** Lovely sky blue, a most beautiful flower, and one of the finest of its class	1	0
184 **RED CHIEF.** Large splendidly formed flowers, colour a lovely shade of bright mahogany red shaded orange. A strong grower and frequently produces four on a stem	1	0
185 **ROSABELLE.** Brilliant rose, lighter at the base of standard, a most beautiful variety producing four blooms on a stem. A first-class exhibition variety .. .. 6d. and	1	0
186 **THOMAS STEVENSON.** Brilliant orange-scarlet, almost a self, with large waved flowers. A superb variety. First-class for exhibition, garden decoration, or cut flowers. Highly recommended. F.C.C., 1911 .. .. 6d. and	1	0
187 **WEDGEWOOD.** A beautiful variety of finest Spencer form, the blooms are of great size, mostly produced four on a stem, and of a unique shade of Wedgewood blue as popular in china, and quite in advance of any other in its class 6d. and	1	0

188 **One packet of each above 14 Superb Varieties, 9/6**

DANIELS' SPECIAL COLLECTIONS OF SWEET PEAS FOR EXHIBITION.

We highly recommend these special collections to the notice of intending exhibitors. All the varieties included are first-class exhibition sorts, and have been carefully selected and arranged to give the best possible variety of colours.

* † Arthur Unwin, cream and rose
* † Asta Ohn Spencer, mauve
  † Charles Foster, rosy pink
  † Clara Curtis, primrose yellow
* † Constance Oliver, creamy rose
  † Earl Spencer, orange salmon

  Edna Unwin Improved, orange scarlet
* † Etta Dyke, pure white
  Frank Dolby, lavender blue
* † John Ingman, rosy carmine
  King Edward Spencer, crimson
  Mrs. C. Masters, rose and white

  Mrs. Hugh Dickson, pale rose
  Mrs. Townsend, white, edged blue
  † Picotee, white, edged rose
* † Sunproof Crimson, crimson scarlet
  † Thomas Stevenson, orange scarlet
  † Tom Bolton, maroon

189	**EIGHTEEN SUPERB VARIETIES**, one packet of each as above	..	..	..	**6s. 6d.**	
190	**TWELVE SPLENDID VARIETIES**, marked (†)	..	..	..	**5s. 0d.**	
191	**SIX FINE SELECTED SORTS**, marked (*) ..	..	..	..	**2s. 6d.**	

DANIELS' SPECIAL COLLECTIONS OF SWEET PEAS.

The following liberal collection include what we consider the best selection of varieties for garden decoration or for cut flowers :—

† * Countess Spencer, pink
† * Constance Oliver, rose and cream
† * Colleen, crimson and white
  * Dorothy Eckford, pure white
† * Florence Morse Spencer, blush
  Helen Lewis, rosy orange
  Helen Pierce, marbled blue
† * Hon. Mrs. Kenyon, primrose

  * John Ingman, brilliant rose
  * King Edward Spencer, crimson scarlet
† * King Edward VII., crimson
  * Lady Grisel Hamilton, lavender blue
  Lord Nelson, dark blue
† Marie Corelli, rosy carmine
  Miss Willmot, orange pink
  * Mrs. C. W. Breadmore

  * Mrs. Townsend, white, edged blue
  † Nora Unwin, pure white
  † Picotee, white, edged rose
  * Primrose Spencer, primrose
  Queen Alexandra, scarlet.
  * Tom Bolton, maroon
  * Winsome, rosy heliotrope
  * Zoe, bright blue

192	**TWENTY-FOUR SPLENDID VARIETIES**, one packet of each as above ..				**6s. 0d.**	
193	**EIGHTEEN SELECTED VARIETIES**, marked (*) ..	..	..	..	**4s. 6d.**	
194	**TWELVE SUPERB VARIETIES**, marked (†) ..	..	..	..	**3s. 0d.**	
195	**SIX FINE VARIETIES**, Dorothy Eckford, Constance Oliver, Evelyn Hemus, King Edward VII., Lady Grisel Hamilton, John Ingman				**1s. 9d.**	

From Mr. M. F. MURRAY, Rye.

July 16th.
"The Sweet Pea got from you are superb and they are a perfect sight."

From Mr. F. PLATT, Fernie,

March 16th.
"I grew the finest Sweet Peas in this town grown from your seeds."

SWEET PEAS—Select Varieties.

We no longer catalogue the older and inferior varieties of Sweet Peas, and the following list only includes those which we consider the most beautiful and distinct in each class. To assist our Customers in making their selection, we have classified the varieties in their prevailing shades of colour.

☞ All Flower Seeds quoted in 3d. packets may be had at 2s. 6d. per dozen.

MRS. HARDCASTLE SYKES. (No. 213.)

PURE WHITE.

per pkt.—s. d.
196 **DOROTHY ECKFORD.** One of the finest pure white Sweet Peas yet raised.   0 3
197 **ETTA DYKE.** Very large beautiful pure white flowers with bold wavy standards, on long wiry stems, undoubtedly the finest of all the pure whites. A splendid exhibition flower   0 6
198 **MONEYMAKER.** Pure white, beautifully waved flowers, claimed to be the finest pure white in existence   6d. and   1 0
199 **NORA UNWIN.** A magnificent pure white, which easily takes its place in the front rank. The flowers are of great size, with the same bold wavy standard as Gladys Unwin   .. 0 3

PICOTEE EDGED.

200 **DAINTY.** Large beautiful flowers of splendid form, a lovely white, delicately edged with pink ..   0 3
201 **EVELYN HEMUS** (syn. Mrs. C. W Breadmore) Rich cream shading to yellow with a picotee-edging of bright terra-cotta red. Very large flowers of Spencer form. Superb   ..   0 4
202 **MAID OF HONOUR.** White, edged with pale blue ; charming variety   0 3
203 **MRS. TOWNSEND.** Large white flowers edged and flushed with pale lilac blue. A most charming variety ..   0 4
204 **PICOTEE.** Large, splendidly waved flowers, three and four on a stem ; colour pearly white, distinctly edged bright carmine   ..   0 4

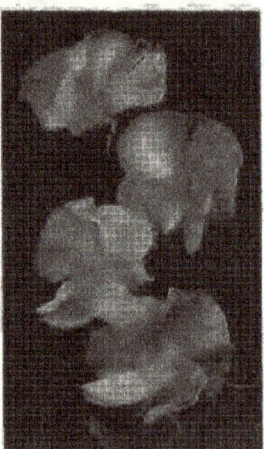

MIRIAM BEAVER. (No. 222.)

PALE ROSE AND PINK.

per pkt.—s. d.
205 **BOBBY K.** Large beautiful flowers, with bold wavy standards. The colour is a lovely pale apple-blossom blush   0 6
206 **BOLTON'S PINK.** A beautiful erect pink-self, with very large flowers. The standard shaded delicate rose   0 3
207 **COUNTESS SPENCER.** (True.) A lovely shade of pink, with large wavy standards The flowers are of splendid size   0 4
208 **ELFRIDA PEARSON.** A beautiful light rosy pink self. Flowers large waved and frequently four on a stem. 6d. and   1 0
209 **FLORENCE MORSE SPENCER.** Delicate blush with pink margin. A most beautiful variety of splendid size   0 4
210 **GLADYS UNWIN.** The flowers are large, bold, with a crinkled or wavy standard and broad wings. The colour is a lovely pale rosy pink   0 3
211 **HERCULES.** Beautifully waved flowers, The colour is a lovely clear rose shading off to deep rosy pink at the edges 6d. and   1 0
212 **MRS. ALFRED WATKINS.** Very large flowers, produced three and four on long stems ; the colour is a beautiful pale rose, with bold wavy standards..   0 3
213 **MRS. HARDCASTLE SYKES.** Rosy pink, with white at base of standards. A superb flower ..   0 4

STRIPED OR FLAKED VARIETIES.

214 **AMERICA SPENCER.** Deep blood-red striped ; handsome .. 0 3
215 **AURORA SPENCER.** Large beautiful waved flowers, white ground, striped with bright salmon-red ..   0 3
216 **ETHEL ROOSEVELT.** Large, beautiful flowers of the most perfect Spencer form. The colour is a soft primrose overlaid with dainty flakes and splashes of blush crimson 6d. and   1 0
217 **MRS. W. J. UNWIN.** A beautiful flower of splendid size, white ground flaked with orange scarlet   .. 6d. and   1 0
218 **PRINCE OLAF.** Blue striped and flaked ..   0 3
219 **SENATOR SPENCER.** Rosy heliotrope striped chocolate   0 6

CREAM-PINK.

per pkt.—s. d.
220 **CONSTANCE OLIVER.** Cream, suffused with delicate rose. Flowers large with waved standards ; one of the most beautiful varieties yet raised   ..   0 4
221 **DORIS USHER.** Cream heavily suffused with pink. Large beautiful wavy flowers. Magnificent variety   .. 6d. and   1 0
222 **MIRIAM BEAVER.** Large beautifully waved flowers, three and four on a stem. The colour is a bright soft pinkish salmon on a primrose ground. A variety of the most charming effect   0 6
223 **MRS. HENRY BELL.** Beautiful pale rosy-pink, suffused with apricot cream at base of standards. A most lovely flower..   0 3
224 **MRS. HUGH DICKSON.** A beautiful pale salmon pink self, one of the finest of recent introduction ..   0 4
225 **MRS. ROUTZAHN.** Very large beautiful flowers, with broad, deep, wavy standards. The colour is a rich apricot, shaded with salmon pink. A distinct and lovely variety   0 4
226 **W. T. HUTCHINS.** Apricot and lemon overlaid with blush. Flowers three and four on a stem. A true Spencer and one of the most superb varieties yet raised 0 6

MAROON, CLARET, CHOCOLATE.

227 **ANNA LUMLEY.** A very fine deep maroon Spencer ; large, richly coloured waved flowers, three and four on a stem   0 3
228 **BLACK KNIGHT.** Deep maroon self ; one of the very finest   0 3
229 **OTHELLO SPENCER.** Deep brown chocolate red, very large waved flowers ; fine   ..   0 4
230 **TOM BOLTON.** Very deep maroon, large waved flowers, the finest of its class   ..   0 6

BLUE AND LAVENDER.

per pkt.—s. d.

231 **AFTERGLOW.** Standard a bright violet blue, shading to glowing rosy amethyst; wings electric blue. The flowers are large, of true Spencer form   6d. and 1 0
232 **ASTA OHN SPENCER.** Lavender tinted mauve, a magnificent variety with large splendid flowers 0 6
233 **BERTRAND DEAL, IMPROVED.** Beautiful rosy lilac, finely waved. The flowers are of immense size, and borne three and four on a stem 1 0
234 **FLORENCE NIGHTINGALE.** The flowers are of great size, beautifully waved. Colour a charming soft, clear, lavender blue   .. 6d. and 1 0
235 **FLORA NORTON SPENCER.** Beautiful bright blue self, large waved flowers 0 4
236 **FRANK DOLBY.** A lovely pale blue, larger than Lady Grisel Hamilton .. 0 3
237 **HELEN PIERCE.** Pale blue front, with darker back, marbled mottled   .. 0 3
238 **IRISH BELLE.** Large, beautifully waved flowers, colour rich lilac suffused with pink   .. 6d. and 1 0
239 **LADY GRISEL HAMILTON.** Flowers of a beautiful shining pale lavender .. 0 3
240 **LORD NELSON.** (Brilliant Blue.) Deep bright blue self. Very fine .. 0 3
241 **MASTERPIECE.** Very large flowers of a beautiful lavender blue 0 6
242 **MAY FARQUHAR.** A deep, rich, bronzy-blue Spencer with large waved flowers. Distinct and striking 6d. and 1 0
243 **ZOE.** Clear blue self. Very fine   .. 0 3

"BARBARA." (No. 175.)

SCARLET MONARCH. (No. 208.)

SALMON & ORANGE-RED SHADES.

per pkt.—s. d.

244 **ANGLIAN ORANGE.** Large splendidly formed flowers, three and four on a stem ; colour a beautiful bright salmon pink.. 0 6
245 **EARL SPENCER.** Flowers of great size, waved, three and four on a stem ; colour a brilliant orange-rose, magnificent variety 0 6
246 **EDNA UNWIN IMPROVED.** A brilliant, deep orange-scarlet self. A fine exhibition flower. Selected stock   .. 6d. and 1 0
247 **EVELYN BYATT.** The richest orange-coloured Sweet Pea. The standard is rich bright salmon, and the falls a trifle deeper 0 3
248 **HELEN LEWIS (The Orange Countess) (true).** Flowers very large, standards wavy and of a rich orange colour, wings rosy. 0 4
249 **MISS WILLMOT.** Beautiful bright orange pink, shaded with rose ; one of the largest and most beautiful varieties   .. 0 3

CREAM AND YELLOW SHADES.

250 **CLARA CURTIS.** Beautiful primrose yellow, one of the best 0 4
251 **DORA BREADMORE.** Pale yellow delicately tinged with rosy pink. A very beautiful large-flowered variety   .. 0 3
252 **GIANT CREAM WAVED.** A superb variety, with very large beautifully waved flowers. The colour is a deep rich cream 0 6
253 **HON. MRS. KENYON.** Large beautiful flowers of a delicate primrose yellow 0 3
254 **MRS. A. MALCOLM.** Beautiful rich creamy yellow. Large splendid flowers borne three and four on a stem. Very free-flowering and first-class for exhibition 0 4
255 **PRIMROSE SPENCER.** Large flowers of a beautiful primrose or creamy yellow, with three and four blooms on a stem 0 3

MAGENTA, MAUVE, HELIOTROPE.

256 **A. J. COOK.** Deep bright mauve. A fine variety 0 3
257 **CHARLES FOSTER.** A peculiar and charming combination of lavender and rosy pink, very distinct and attractive .. 1 0
258 **DOROTHY.** A truly gigantic rosy-lilac self, beautifully waved and borne mostly four on a stem. One of the finest 6d. and 1 0
259 **MENIE CHRISTIE.** The standards are a beautiful bright purplish carmine, with rosy magenta wings, beautifully waved 0 6
260 **MRS. WALTER WRIGHT.** A beautiful shade of mauve .. 0 3
261 **THE MARQUIS.** Rosy heliotrope. A charming flower   .. 0 4
262 **WINSOME.** Bright heliotrope-rose with white at the base .. 0 4

SCARLET AND CRIMSON.

per pkt. s. d.

263 **CERISSIE UNWIN.** Light clear cherry scarlet, flowers of splendid form and substance, very beautiful and quite distinct .. 0 6
264 **DORIS BURT.** Brilliant glowing scarlet shaded cerise, a very fine variety, placed by the N.S.P.S. as first in the scarlet section 0 6
265 **KING EDWARD SPENCER.** Splendid flowers of a deep rich crimson scarlet, on long wiry stems. Blooms, three and four on a stem, of immense size, and borne on long robust stands 0 6
266 **KING EDWARD VII.** A grand variety. The blooms are large, of splendid form, and borne on long robust stems .. 0 3
267 **QUEEN ALEXANDRA.** Brilliant pure scarlet ; one of the best 0 3
268 **SCARLET MONARCH.** Deep, rich, scarlet Spencer, equal in colour to "Queen Alexandra," but much larger   6d. and 1 0
269 **SUNPROOF CRIMSON (Maude Holmes).** Flowers borne three and four on a stem. An improvement on King Edward Spencer 0 6
270 **VERMILION BRILLIANT.** Intense brilliant scarlet, quite distinct from Scarlet Monarch. Large flowers of splendid form 1 0

DEEP ROSE AND CARMINE.

271 **E. J. CASTLE.** Rosy carmine standard, bright rosy wings 0 3
272 **JOHN INGMAN (True.)** A grand flower, very large and of good substance. Colour a bright rich rosy carmine   .. 0 4
273 **LORD ROSEBERY.** A self-coloured rosy magenta   .. 0 3
274 **MARIE CORELLI.** Brilliant rosy carmine, showing a little white at the base. Beautiful for garden or exhibition   .. 0 4
275 **PRINCE EDWARD OF YORK.** Large flowers, standards scarlet, wings of a beautiful deep rose 0 3
276 **ROSE DU BARRI.** Deep rich carmine-rose and orange 0 4

BICOLORS.

277 **APPLE BLOSSOM SPENCER.** Standard rosy pink, wings blush rose. Large beautiful flowers on very long stems..   .. 0 4
278 **ARTHUR UNWIN.** A vigorous grower, with splendid large flowers. Standards rosy pink, wings creamy-blush 6d. and 1 0
279 **COLLEEN.** A magnificent new bicolor. The bold standard is of an intense deep carmine, and the wings a faint blush .. 0 4
280 **JEANNIE GORDON.** Standards bright rose, shaded cream, wings creamy suffused with rose ; most beautiful variety .. 0 3
281 **MRS. ANDREW IRELAND.** Rosy-pink and blush waved 0 4
282 **MRS. C. MASTERS.** Standard bright rosy pink, wings white ; beautiful flowers on long stems. The finest bicolor   6d. and 1 0
283 **MRS. CUTHBERTSON.** Bright rose standards with creamy white wings 1 0

All Flower Seeds quoted in 3d. packets may be had at 2s. 6d. per doz.

SWEET PEAS.

SPENCER SWEET PEAS IN VASE.

DANIELS' LARGE-FLOWERED.
In Selected Colours.

	per or.—s.	d.
284 DANIELS' BRILLIANT SCARLET	1	0
285 DANIELS' LIGHT BLUE —	1	0
286 DANIELS' BRIGHT ROSE ..	1	0
287 DANIELS' PURE WHITE ..	1	0
288 DANIELS' DARK BLUE ..	1	0
289 DANIELS' PRIMROSE YELLOW	1	0
290 DANIELS' DELICATE ROSE ..	1	0
291 DANIELS' ROSE AND WHITE ..	1	0

Beautiful large-flowered varieties, specially selected for cut flowers or garden decoration.

New Large-flowered Varieties in Collections.

The sorts given in these collections are carefully selected to ensure the best possible variety.

	s.	d.
292 12 CHOICE VARIETIES, 100 seeds of each	2	6
293 6 " " " "	1	6

DANIELS' SPECIAL MIXTURE OF GIANT-FLOWERED SPENCERS.

We highly recommend this splendid mixture which we feel sure will give great satisfaction. The varieties included are all of the true Giant-flowered Spencer type, and the colours include all the most brilliant and beautiful shades of scarlet, crimson, magenta, orange, salmon, pink, mauve, cream and primrose to the purest white. This will prove a first-class mixture where really good Sweet Peas are required for cut bloom.

294 Per pint, 7s. 6d.   295 Per half-pint, 4s.   296 Per oz., 9d.

Large-flowered in Mixture.

Splendid varieties in choicest mixture, including a good proportion of the light and delicately coloured sorts. Very highly recommended.

297 Per pint, 4s. 6d.   298 Per half-pint, 2s. 6d.   299 Per oz., 6d.

SWEET PEAS—Ordinary Class, Choice Mixed.

300 Per quart, 4s. 6d.   301 Per pint, 2s. 6d.   302 Per oz., 4d.

Cultivation.—To grow really fine Sweet Peas, the ground should be deeply dug or trenched and plenty of well-decayed manure, with some coarse bone meal worked well in and to the bottom of the trench. This should be done in Autumn if convenient, or as early as possible in Spring, so as to allow of the ground settling down firmly before planting out.

For early blooming, sow the seeds thinly in pots or pans in January or February, and place in a gentle heat; harden off as soon as the plants are well up, and plant out as soon as convenient in March. If intended to be grown for exhibition, we should recommend planting in clumps four feet apart, six or eight plants in a clump, or they may be planted in single or double rows six feet apart; but in any case the plants should be not less than six or eight inches apart in the row or clump. Stakes should be placed as soon as the plants are three or four inches high. The ground should be kept free of weeds, and water given if the weather is dry.

As growth advances some weak liquid manure should be given once or twice a week, and if the weather continues dry, a mulching of some short, well-decayed manure should be placed on the surface about the roots. This will be of great benefit in stimulating a healthy growth, and some splendid flowers will be produced.

An excellent liquid manure can be made by dissolving Daniels' Sweet Pea Fertilizer, about four ounces to the gallon of water, or guano, about two ounces to the gallon, with the addition of some soot. Either of these are splendid stimulants for promoting growth and improving the size and brilliancy of the flowers. Drainings from a cowshed or manure heap, mixed with five or six times its bulk of clear water, also forms a very good liquid manure.

For later successive blooming the seeds may be sown out of doors at intervals from early March to the middle of May, giving them a similar treatment to that recommended above. Excellent results may also be had by sowing in October or November in a sheltered position in the garden. These, with a slight protection, will survive a moderately severe Winter and furnish some nice blooms for cutting earlier than those sown in spring.

If the blooms are closely gathered and seed pods not allowed to develop, the plants will continue in bloom for a much longer period.

From Mr. R. T. KIRK, Oulton Broad.
"I have had a splendid show of Sweet Peas from your seed, and they are as large as ever. I only had 3 ozs. (No. 118). I think there is now 400 to 500 blooms."

From Mr. C. THOMAS, Byfleet.
March 11th.
"We took Second Prize for Coronation Sweet Peas, and Second for another bunch from seed we had off you."

GYPSOPHILA ELEGANS GRANDIFLORA ALBA (New).

This splendid hardy Annual is a great improvement on the old White Gypsophila, and should be freely grown wherever cut flowers are in demand. It grows about 2½ feet in height, and throws out numerous branches with light feathery sprays or panicles of numerous pure white flowers. These can be cut with long stems, and have a very graceful and pretty effect in association with Sweet Peas when used for table or other decorations.

303	GYPSOPHILA ELEGANS GRANDIFLORA ALBA	..	..	..	per oz. 1s. 6d.	per packet, 3d. and 6d.
304	" " "	ROSEA, rosy pink, very pretty,	..	1s. 6d.	" 3d. and 6d.	

ALPHABETICAL LIST OF FLOWER SEEDS.

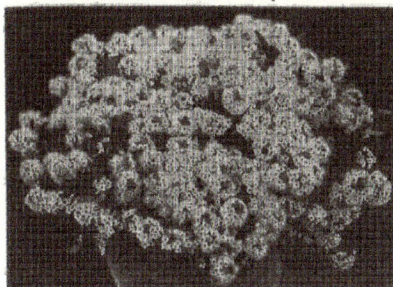

ALYSSUM COMPACTUM—LITTLE GEM.

ALYSSUM.

per pkt—s. d.

305	COMPACTUM "LITTLE GEM." A charming little dwarf-growing annual only 4 or 5 inches high, and bearing quite a profusion of pretty white flowers. A splendid little plant for edgings, beds, or rockwork, blooming throughout the Summer and well into Autumn	0 4
306	PROCUMBENS (White Carpet). A beautiful dwarf creeping variety, growing quite close to the ground and continuing in bloom for a long period. Splendid for edgings or rockeries..	0 6
307	MARITIMUM (Sweet Alyssum). A free-flowering hardy annual of great value as an edging to large beds, &c. Flowers white. Height about 9 inches ..	0 3
308	SAXATILE COMPACTUM. A fine hardy perennial, growing about 6 inches high and quite covered with bright yellow flowers in Spring. First-rate for rockwork or borders	0 4

AGERATUM.

Very useful and effective half-hardy annuals. Excellent for bedding out.

309	LITTLE BLUE STAR. A beautiful miniature variety, bearing a profusion of pretty pale blue flowers, a charming plant for edgings	0 6
310	IMPERIAL DWARF BLUE. Fine for bedding ..	0 3
311	IMPERIAL DWARF WHITE. Fine for bedding ..	0 3
312	PRINCESS VICTORIA LOUISE (new). Pale, with a white centre, very pretty	0 6

ANTIRRHINUMS.

These fine hardy perennials make a beautiful display during the Summer and Autumn, and are very attractive. The Tom Thumb varieties, which grow only about 6 inches high, are very useful and pretty for dry banks and rockeries, and form a splendid edging for large beds or borders, continuing in bloom for a long time. Sow the seeds in February or early in March in light, rich soil and place in a gentle heat, prick out in pans or boxes to strengthen and plant out where intended to flower as soon as large enough. These will bloom during the Summer and Autumn. The tall varieties grow 2 to 3 feet in height, the semi-dwarf, 12 or 18 inches.

per pkt.—s. d.

313	TALL VARIETIES, 6 brilliant sorts, with names		1 0
314	,,	VENUS, pale rose and white, very beautiful..	0 6
315	,,	CORAL PINK, bright rosy pink, beautiful ..	0 6
316	,,	BLACK PRINCE, dark maroon crimson	0 6
317	,,	PURE WHITE, beautiful variety ..	0 6
318	,,	NIOBE, dark crimson, white throat	0 4
319	,,	ROSEUM, delicate rose ..	0 6
320	,,	AURORA, cinnabar scarlet with white throat	0 4
321	,,	FIRE KING, scarlet and orange ..	0 6
322	,,	GOLDEN YELLOW, very fine	0 6
323	,,	ROSE DORE (new). Lovely salmon-rose shaded gold	0 6
324	,,	ORANGE KING, brilliant colour, most effective	0 4
324A	,,	CHOICEST MIXED, in beautiful variety .. 3d. and	0 4

SEMI-DWARF, OR INTERMEDIATE—

The following splendid varieties are highly recommended as the most desirable for garden decoration.

325	DAPHNE. Carmine rose and white			0 6
326	PURE WHITE. Beautiful ..			0 6
327	SCARLET KING. Brilliant scarlet			0 4
328	CRIMSON KING. Very fine			0 6
329	GOLDEN QUEEN. Rich yellow, splendid			0 6
330	AMBER QUEEN (new). Canary yellow overlaid with chamois, strikingly handsome, large flowers			0 6
331	THE BRIDE. Pure white, without any yellow on lip			0 4
332	APPLE BLOSSOM. Rose and white, very pretty ..			0 4
333	ROSEUM SUPERBUM. Beautiful rose pink			0 4
334	VESUVIUS (new). Deep vivid orange scarlet, very effective..			0 6
335	CHOICEST MIXED. In fine variety ..			1 6
336	TOM THUMB, 6 brilliant varieties, with names ..			0 6
337	,,	,,	Pure white	0 6
338	,,	,,	Scarlet	0 6
339	,,	,,	Yellow	0 6
340	,,	,,	Rose	0 6
341	,,	,,	Crimson	0 6
342	,,	,,	Choicest mixed .. 6d. and	1 0

Beautiful varieties, for edging large or small beds.

From Mr. J. A. DERRICK, Portsmouth.

March 1st.
"The Antirrhinum Seed was very good as you supplied me with this year."

From Mr. J. KENNEDY, Cheltenham.

Jan. 15th.
"I have much pleasure in sending you my order after fourteen years' dealing; I have always found your Seeds up to the mark."

ANTIRRHINUM—AMBER QUEEN.

AQUILEGIA.

An exceedingly beautiful class of hardy perennials that will thrive in almost any position where they are not disturbed. Sow in Spring in pots or pans of light sandy soil, and place in a cool pit or frame, and plant out in Autumn, or early in the following Spring, where the plants are intended to remain. The New Long-spurred Hybrids are very elegant, and are highly recommended for cut flowers.

AQUILEGIAS—LONG-SPURRED VARIETIES.

		per pkt.—s. d.
343	**MRS. SCOTT-ELLIOT'S LONG-SPURRED HYBRIDS.** The result of many years' careful selection and hybridising, this is undoubtedly the finest strain in existence of these charming hardy plants. The large beautifully-formed flowers vary in colour through all the delicate shades and tints of white lavender, salmon, mauve, pink, yellow, &c., with the most exquisite blendings .. .. 6d. and	1 0
344	**ALPINA SUPERBA.** Blue and white, 18 inches	0 3
345	**CHRYSANTHA.** Golden yellow, 2½ feet	0 6
346	**GLANDULOSA VERA.** Dark blue and white, 1½ feet ..	1 0
347	**CHOICE MIXED,** in many charming colours, garden varieties	0 3

ARCTOTIS GRANDIS.

348	A pretty, free-flowering, half-hardy annual, about 2 feet in height. White, Marguerite-like flowers with mauve centre	0 6

ASPARAGUS.

349	**PLUMOSUS.** A beautiful greenhouse climber, with finely divided, fern-like foliage. Useful for cutting	1 0
350	**SPRENGERI.** Very handsome foliage. Splendid as a pot plant or for hanging baskets in the greenhouse	1 0

ARALIA SIEBOLDI.

351	This beautiful plant, a native of the far East, forms a handsome pot plant for the greenhouse or for table decoration. Grown outside in a sheltered place it makes a handsome shrub and is quite hardy. New seed supplied end of April.. ..	0 6

AUBRIETIAS.

These charming dwarf-growing hardy perennials are amongst the most beautiful and useful of all plants for Spring gardening, they are of a dwarf-spreading habit of growth, only about 6 inches high and for a long period in Spring are quite covered with bloom, forming perfect cushions of flowers; grown in association with Spring flowering bulbs as edgings to beds, &c., they are very effective and are also admirably suited for growing on rockeries.

		per pkt.—s. d.
352	**LEICHTLINI ROSEA.** Carmine rose, a beautiful Spring bedder. Height 6 inches	1 0
353	**GRÆCA.** Bright blue. Height 6 inches	0 4
354	**VIOLACEA.** Violet blue. Height 6 inches	0 4

AURICULAS.

(PRIMULA AURICULA.)

These deliciously-scented, fine old hardy perennials are worthy of extensive cultivation. Sow the seeds in March or April, in pots or pans of firmly pressed, light rich soil, giving them but a slight covering; and place in a cool pit or frame. Prick the young seedlings off into pots to strengthen soon as large enough to handle, and pot off when large enough, for blooming under glass, or plant out of doors early in Autumn where intended to bloom. The best soil for Auriculas in pots is composed of about four parts loam with about one part leaf soil, and one part well-rotted cow dung. They should be kept comparatively dry during Winter, but have plenty of moisture when growth commences in Spring, and bloom best in a cool pit or frame close to the glass and facing the north. The Alpine varieties are the hardiest and best for out-door growing, and will do well planted on a well-drained, fairly sheltered border, and give a charming display of beautiful flowers in Spring. A position facing west or north-west is preferable.

355	**DANIELS' PRIZE MIXED.** From a fine collection of choice named flowers, including the green-edged and grey-edged sorts; highly recommended	2 6
356	smaller pkt.	1 0
357	**ALPINE.** From a superb collection, including all the most beautiful shades of colour; very hardy and desirable ..	1 0
358	smaller pkt.	0 6
359	**DANIELS' GIANT YELLOW.** A fine strain of Giant Yellow Auriculas, remarkable alike for their all-round vigour as hardy border plants, and their large trusses of handsome and deliciously fragrant flowers	1 0

ABUTILON.

Choice Mixed Hybrids.

360	Very useful for training on the wall in conservatory or greenhouse	1 0

ANAGALLIS.

Beautiful showy half-hardy annuals growing only about 6 inches high.

361	**GRANDIFLORA COCCINEA.** Scarlet	0 3
362	" **CÆRULEA.** Blue	0 3

ANCHUSA ITALICA.

363	**DROPMORE VARIETY.** A splendid hardy perennial growing about 4 feet high with large gentian blue flowers 6d. and	1 0

ANEMONE.

364	**FULGENS.** Brilliant scarlet, very fine. 1 foot ..	0 6
365	**ST. BRIGID.** Very fine strain of beautiful colours. 1 foot ..	0 6

ALONSOA WARSCEWICZI COMPACTA.

366	A brilliant little annual growing about a foot high, and bearing quite a profusion of beautiful scarlet flowers. Very showy	0 4

ARABIS ALPINA.

367	A very useful hardy perennial for early Spring flowering. The plant grows only about 6 inches high, and the pure white flowers afford an excellent contrast to most Spring flowering plants	0 3

AMARANTHUS.

A brilliant class of ornamental foliaged plants, excellent for greenhouse decoration or in a warm spot out of doors.

368	**TRICOLOR SPLENDENS.** Beautiful variety, very superior to the old *tricolor.* 18 inches .. .. 6d. and	1 0

BALSAMS.

These beautiful flowers are well worthy of cultivation, and when well-grown in good-sized pots form handsome objects for the decoration of the greenhouse or conservatory, where they will make a fine display for a long period. Balsams also succeed admirably when planted out of doors in good soil, and in a sheltered position. Sow the seeds in March or April in pots or pans of light rich soil, and place in a gentle heat.

CAMELLIA FLOWERED BAL'AM

DANIELS' CAMELLIA-FLOWERED.

per pkt., s. d.
- 369 AN ASSORTMENT OF 6 SPLENDID VARIETIES, 20 seeds each 2 6
- 370 SALMON QUEEN (new). Brilliant salmon-rose, with large, perfectly formed imbricated double flowers .. 6d. and 1 0
- 371 SNOW QUEEN. Pure white. Splendid double 0 6
- 372 VIOLET SPOTTED 0 6
- 373 WHITE, SHADING TO BLUSH 0 6
- 374 CHOICEST MIXED .. .. 6d. and 1 0
- 375 CAMELLIA-FLOWERED GERMAN. Double; fine mixed .. 0 3

BARTONIA AUREA.

- 376 A free-flowering showy hardy annual, growing about 18 inches high, with rich golden yellow flowers 0 3

BEET.

- 377 DARK-LEAVED BEDDING. Fine dark crimson leaves .. 0 3
- 378 CHILIAN. Variegated. First rate for large beds, &c. The colours are very fine in Autumn 0 4

BRACHYCOME IBERIDIFOLIA.

- 379 The Swan River Daisy, very pretty, small, cineraria-like flowers of a light blue colour. Height 1 foot. May be sown in Spring as a hardy annual 0 3

BROOM.

- 380 CRIMSON AND YELLOW (G. Andreanus). A beautiful hardy shrub, which commences blooming the second year from seed 0 6
- 381 WHITE PORTUGAL. Well-known beautiful hardy shrub, producing long sprays of white flowers in early Summer .. 0 6

BEGONIAS.

Sow the seeds any time from March to May on the surface of well-drained pots or pans of light rich soil, press the surface firm before sowing and sprinkle with tepid water, cover the pot or pan with a sheet of glass to retain the moisture, and place in a heat of about 65°. Transplant as soon as large enough to handle. These will mostly bloom in the Autumn, and will make fine tubers for blooming the following year.

SINGLE FRINGED BEGONIA.

per pkt.—s. d.
- 382 DANIELS' PRIZE SINGLE. Carefully saved from a grand collection of the choicest English varieties, will produce some splendid flowers.. .. .. .. 2 6
- 383 ,, ,, ,, smaller pkt. 1 0
- 384 DANIELS' PRIZE DOUBLE. A superb strain, carefully hybridised, saved from finest varieties. Will produce some grand flowers 2 6
- 385 ,, ,, smaller pkt. 1 6
- 386 FRINGED, SINGLE. Beautifully fringed flowers. Splendid for pot culture .. .. 1s. 6d. and 2 6
- 387 FRINGED, DOUBLE. Handsome, double flowers with elegantly fringed petals, splendid for pot culture.. .. 1 6

FIBROUS-ROOTED BEGONIAS.

A fine class for bedding.
- 388 GRACILIS RUBY (new). Bright metallic brown foliage, with rosy carmine flowers. Height about 10 inches. A splendid variety for bedding 0 6
- 389 SEMPERFLORENS ALBA. Useful for bedding out or edging. Highly recommended 0 6
- 390 ,, ROSEA. Useful for bedding out or edging. Highly recommended.. .. .. .. 0 6
- 391 ,, VERNON COMPACTA (new). Brilliant red flowers and deep red foliage; splendid bedder .. 0 6
- 392 SCHMIDTI. White, shaded with rose. Very free bloomer. Sown in heat in February may be had in bloom throughout the Summer and Autumn 0 6
- 393 REX VARIETIES. Beautiful plants for the stove or greenhouse. Saved from choicest sorts 1 0

For Begonia Tubers see page 112.

CALCEOLARIAS.

We have much pleasure in offering our splendid strain of Calceolaria hybrida, which has been carefully saved from a magnificent collection during the past season, and been awarded many First Prizes. The flowers will be found of large size, beautiful form, and tigred and spotted with the most exquisite and brilliant markings.

CALCEOLARIA—DANIELS' CHOICEST STRAIN.

Sow the seeds of these in May, June, or July, in well-drained pots or seed-pans ; cover the drainage with rough fibrous loam, and fill up the surface with fine light sifted mould and silver sand ; water with a fine rose water-pot, after which sow the seed, placing a piece of glass over the pot to retain the moisture, no covering of soil being required. Place the pots in a cool frame or under a handlight, taking care to shade from the sun. Remove the piece of glass as soon as the plants are up, and when large enough to handle, prick off one inch apart into pots or pans made up as before, placing in a somewhat close situation, and when of sufficient size pot off singly, and treat in a similar manner to that recommended for tender annuals. Calceolarias should, however, be always kept in a cool, moist position, a dry heated atmosphere being very prejudicial to their growth, and they should be kept well supplied with fresh air.

		per pkt.—s. d.
CALCEOLARIA HYBRIDA		
394	**DANIELS' CHOICEST MIXED.** Beautifully spotted and marked flowers	2 6
395	„ „ „ smaller pkt.	1 0
396	**NEW DWARF."** A beautiful strain of handsome varieties growing only about ten inches high, and bearing a profusion of large, brilliantly marked and spotted flowers	2 6
397	„ „ „ „ smaller pkt.	1 0

CALCEOLARIA—Golden Glory.

398   This is a beautiful new hardy hybrid, with bright golden yellow flowers that are produced for a long period. It is an excellent plant for the greenhouse, a capital bedder, and sufficiently hardy for the herbaceous border, where it forms a very attractive object 1 0

From **Mr. J. GLISTER,** Stanley.

July 29th,
"I might say the previous Seeds I had from you have been the best that money could buy."

CALLIOPSIS OR COREOPSIS.

These beautiful free-flowering hardy Annuals are exceedingly valuable for garden decoration. They succeed almost anywhere, but are of especial value for growing in town gardens, where they thrive better than most annuals. They remain in bloom for a long period during the Summer and Autumn, and the blooms of all the taller growing varieties will be found very useful for cutting. The beautiful golden-yellow C. stillmanni blooms within five weeks of the seeds being sown. The Tom Thumb varieties are exceedingly pretty.

			per pkt.—s. d.
399	**DRUMMONDI.** Golden yellow, with brown centre. Fine. 18 inches		0 3
400	**TINCTORIA.** Yellow and chestnut brown, very showy. 2 feet		0 3
401	**CARDIMANIFOLIA NANA.** Dark crimson brown. 18 inches		0 3
402	**STILLMANNI.** Clear golden yellow, very early bloomer. 18 inches		0 3
403	**TOM THUMB, BEAUTY.** Very pretty, free-flowering variety. 1 foot high, bright golden yellow with rich brown centres		0 4
404	„ **CRIMSON KING.** Dark brownish crimson flowers. 1 foot		0 4
405	**TOM THUMB.** Beautiful dwarf-growing varieties, about 1 foot high, and producing quite a profusion of pretty flowers as large as those of tinctoria ; very useful for cutting and excellent for town gardens		0 4
405	**TALL VARIETIES.** Choice mixed, including all the prettiest varieties. A useful selection for cutting		0 3

CALLIOPSIS TINCTORIA.

CALLIOPSIS GRANDIFLORA.

407   A very handsome perennial variety, quite hardy and growing about 3 feet high. The beautiful golden yellow flowers, 3 inches across, are borne on long wiry stems making them of great value for cutting. Seeds sown in March or April will bloom freely in the summer and autumn following. This is a fine showy plant for the garden 0 6

CAMPANULAS.

Campanulas pyramidalis and p. alba form very useful pot plants for the cool greenhouse, whilst C. fragilis is an excellent trailer and very suitable for suspended pots or baskets. Amongst others mentioned, the beautiful persicifolia varieties are very fine and greatly prized for garden decoration, whilst Turbinata is excellent for borders and rockeries. The Campanulas form a splendid group of plants for the garden, and are well worthy of cultivation. They are easily grown, and when in bloom are very charming. They will succeed almost anywhere, but generally speaking thrive best in a light rich sandy soil. Seeds sown from April to end of June.

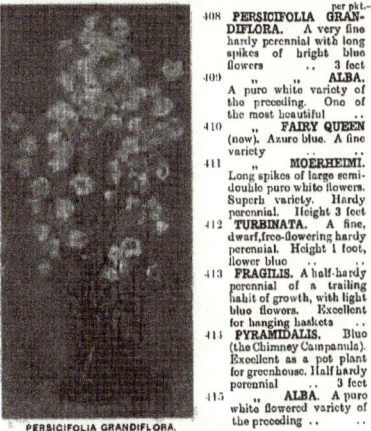

PERSICIFOLIA GRANDIFLORA.

		per pkt.—s. d.
408	**PERSICIFOLIA GRANDIFLORA.** A very fine hardy perennial with long spikes of bright blue flowers .. 3 feet	0 6
409	,, **ALBA.** A pure white variety of the preceding. One of the most beautiful ..	0 6
410	,, **FAIRY QUEEN** (new). Azure blue. A fine variety ..	0 6
411	,, **MOERHEIMI.** Long spikes of large semi-double pure white flowers. Superb variety. Hardy perennial. Height 3 feet	0 6
412	**TURBINATA.** A fine, dwarf, free-flowering hardy perennial. Height 1 foot, flower blue ..	0 1
413	**FRAGILIS.** A half-hardy perennial of a trailing habit of growth, with light blue flowers. Excellent for hanging baskets ..	0 6
414	**PYRAMIDALIS.** Blue (the Chimney Campanula). Excellent as a pot plant for greenhouse. Half hardy perennial .. 3 feet	0 3
415	,, **ALBA.** A pure white flowered variety of the preceding ..	0 3

CELOSIA PLUMOSA
(FEATHERED COCKSCOMB).

These beautiful greenhouse annuals produce long brilliantly coloured plumes of flowers, and are exceedingly useful for decorating the greenhouse or conservatory during the Summer. They may also be planted out of doors towards the end of May on a sheltered border, and will have a very pretty effect.

			per pkt.—s. d.
416	**CELOSIA PLUMOSA COCCINEA.** Brilliant crimson		0 6
417	,, ,, **AUREA.** Golden yellow, height two feet		0 6
418	,, ,, **CHOICEST MIXED.** All shades of yellow and rose to brilliant crimson, &c. .. 6d. and		1 0
419	,, ,, **DWARF MIXED.** Beautiful 6d. and		1 0
420	,, **THOMPSONI MAGNIFICA.** A splendid class of improved feathered cockscombs. Very fine mixed ..		0 6

CENTAUREA CYANUS MINOR.
(CORNFLOWER.)

Highly popular showy hardy annuals; very useful to cut for bouquets and table decoration. The plants grow about 3 feet high. per pkt.—s. d.

421	**EMPEROR WILLIAM.** Bright blue	..	0 3
422	**PURE WHITE.** Large flowers, white	..	0 3
423	**BRIGHT ROSE.** Beautiful colour	..	0 3
424	**CHOICE MIXED.** All colours	..	0 3
425	**SEMI-DOUBLE VARIETIES.** Choice mixed. A very pretty class	..	0 3

From Mr. W. HULL, Cheltenham.

July 17th.
"The Canterbury Bells have been a great picture, and have been much admired."

CANTERBURY BELLS.
(Campanula Medium.)

A beautiful class of free-flowering hardy biennials for garden decoration. The large bells of pure white varieties are very handsome and should be freely grown for the fine contrast they afford with most other flowers. The double-flowered and Calycanthema varieties are exceedingly fine. Young plants potted up in early Autumn and stored in a cool pit for the Winter, may be brought into the greenhouse or conservatory in Spring, and will bloom beautifully without forcing. It should be borne in mind that all the varieties have a tendency to sport and cannot be depended on to come absolutely true from seed, the best selected strains of doubles always producing some single flowers. All the sorts grow about 2 feet high.

			per pkt.—s. d.
426	**NEW PYRAMIDAL.** Beautiful upright growing varieties. Very choice mixed seed		0 6
427	**SINGLE. ROSY CARMINE.** Beautiful bright rose		0 6
428	,, **Pure white, very fine** ..	} Beautiful showy varieties, splendid for garden decoration.	0 3
429	,, **Blue, large-flowered** ..		0 3
430	,, **Rose, large-flowered** ..		0 3
431	,, **Choicest Mixed** ..		0 3
432	**DOUBLE. Pure white, fine** ..	} Large massive blooms, very fine.	0 6
433	,, **Blue** ..		0 6
434	,, **Rose** ..		0 6
435	,, **Choice Mixed** ..		0 6

CALYCANTHEMA VARIETIES.
Cup and Saucer.

436	**BLUE.** Very large flowers	..	0 6
437	**PURE WHITE.** Very beautiful ..	..	0 6
438	**ROSE.** Handsome rose-coloured flowers of great size	..	0 6
439	**CHOICE MIXED**	..	0 6

DOUBLE CANTERBURY BELLS.

CANTERBURY BELLS New Hybrids.

440 A very fine class of beautiful varieties. Shades of pink, lavender, mauve, blush violet, white &c. Very fine 1 0

CANDYTUFT.

An exceedingly useful and showy class of hardy annuals that should be grown freely wherever a good display is desired. The beautiful variety " Rose Cardinal " is particularly fine, as are also those of the new dwarf large-flowered section. " Little Prince " is distinct and charming with its numerous trusses of pure white flowers.

per pkt.—s. d.

				s.	d.
441	DANIELS' MAMMOTH SPIRAL, WHITE.	Immense spikes of large pure white flowers, very fine .. .. 6d. and		1	0
442	ROSE CARDINAL.	Brilliant carmine rose, very showy, and most beautiful colour, 6 inches		0	4
443	CREAMY WHITE.	Large creamy flowers, beautiful. Height 1 foot		0	3
444	DARK CRIMSON.	Selected, very fine colour. Height 1 foot		0	3
445	LILAC.	Pale lilac-purple. 1 foot		0	3
446	CHOICEST MIXED	.. ..		0	3
447	LITTLE PRINCE.	Only 6 inches high, and producing large spikes of pure white flowers. Very pretty and quite distinct		0	3

LARGE-FLOWERED DWARF. A splendid new class of large-flowered beautiful varieties of a dwarf, compact habit of growth. Highly recommended for edgings of large beds or borders. Very showy. Height 9 inches

					s.	d.
448	"	"	"	PURE WHITE. Very fine ..	0	4
449	"	"	"	BRIGHT ROSE. Soft bright rose ..	0	4
450	"	"	"	DARK CRIMSON. Very rich colour ..	0	4
451	"	"	"	LILAC. Pale purplish lilac ..	0	4
452	"	"	"	CHOICE MIXED	0	4

CANDYTUFT DANIELS' MAMMOTH SPIRAL.

CANNA.

A splendid race of handsome foliaged plants suitable for the sub-tropical garden or for greenhouse decoration. The seeds of these, being extremely hard, should be soaked in tepid water a day or two before sowing.

				s.	d.
453	NEW DWARF LARGE-FLOWERED.	A superb strain of large, brilliantly-coloured flowers. Highly recommended for pot culture. Height 3 feet .. .. 6d. and		1	0
454	VARIEGATA.	Beautiful variegated foliage and brilliantly coloured flowers. Very handsome. Height 2 feet 6d. and		1	0
455	CHOICE MIXED VARIETIES	.. .. ..		0	6

COSMEA.

(Cosmos.)

COSMOS, ROSE QUEEN.

A beautiful class of free-flowering, showy, half-hardy Annuals, growing about three feet high, with finely-divided, elegant, fern-like foliage. The flowers, which in form somewhat resemble those of single Dahlias, are borne on long, wiry stems, and are very useful for cutting. If the seed is sown in March under glass and the young plants planted out in May, they will commence blooming in July and continue in full flower quite into late Autumn.

per pkt.—s. d.

				s.	d.
456	ROSE QUEEN (New).	Soft rose, beautiful early-flowering variety, continues in bloom from July till killed by the frost		0	6
457	EARLY-FLOWERING VARIETIES.	Splendid mixed ..		0	4
458	BIPINNATA ALBA.	Large pure white		0	4
459	CHOICEST MIXED.	All colours		0	3

CONVOLVULUS MAJOR.

A fine class of well-known beautiful annual climbers for covering walls, trellis work, &c. Although only half-hardy, may be sown out of doors in April and May with perfect safety.

460	CHOICEST MIXED, in beautiful variety	0	3

CONVOLVULUS MINOR.

Beautiful hardy annuals, growing about 1 foot high and continuing in bloom for a long time.

461	CRIMSON VIOLET.	Splendid colour, quite distinct ..	0	3
462	DARK BLUE OR PURPLE.	Fine	0	3

From Mr. J. HANCOCK, Sulke.

July 24th.
" I enclose you a photo of one of our beds of **Candytuft** grown from your seeds, with which I am highly satisfied."

From Mrs. E. KIDE, Bromley.

July 18th.
" I am delighted with the produce of your Seeds. I took five Firsts and four Seconds at our Show."

DANIELS' SUPERB CINERARIAS.

☞ Carefully saved from a fine collection of named and choicest seedling flowers, which we have every confidence in recommending as unsurpassable. The colours will be found varied and brilliant, combined with a faultless form of flower.

CINERARIA HYBRIDA.

Cultivation.—When required for a general display in early Spring, the seed should be sown in July or early in August, and when for Winter blooming, a few should be sown in March or April. Where the quantity of glass available is somewhat limited, the July sown will, however, be found the most useful. Sow in well-drained pots or pans of light rich soil, giving the seeds but a very slight covering, and place in a cool frame or under a handlight in a shady spot, pot off singly into small pots as soon as the young plants are large enough, and shift as required.

per pkt.—s. d.

463 **DANIELS' CHOICEST MIXED.** A splendid strain of large handsome flowers, including a beautiful variety of colours
 1s. 6d. and 2 6
464 **BLUE.** Fine dark colour 1 0
465 **WHITE.** Very useful variety 1 0

466 **NEW DWARF.** A fine compact-growing class, with large handsome flowers, height about 6 inches, exceedingly floriferous. Choicest mixed .. .. 1s. 6d. and 2 6
467 **DOUBLE-FLOWERED.** Produces a large percentage of handsome double flowers. Choicest mixed .. 1s. 6d. and 2 6

CINERARIA STELLATA (Star Cinerarias).

A magnificent plant for the conservatory or for corridor decoration during the Winter and Spring months. The immense heads of flowers are borne on long stalks, and well above the foliage. The blooms are star-shaped and the colours white, violet, lilac, and red shades. The plants, which grow from 2 to 4 feet in height, are remarkably free-flowering.

468 Per packet, 2s 6d. Smaller packet, 1s. 6d.

CINERARIA STELLATA (New Cactus Varieties).

A splendid new strain of Cineraria Stellata, the petals of the flowers being elegantly twisted and fluted, and comprising a wonderful range of beautiful colours from white, through shades of rose, pink and blue to crimson and purple. The plants are tall and graceful, and form dense masses of flower.
469 Per packet - 1s. 6d.

CINERARIAS FOR BEDDING.

per pkt.—s. d.

470 **CINERARIA MARITIMA "DIAMOND."** A very handsome variety with almost pure white foliage. Height 1 foot .. 1 0

471 **CINERARIA CANDIDISSIMA.** Beautiful silvery cut foliage. Useful bedding plant. Height 1 foot 0 6

CENTAUREA RAGUSINA.
s. d.

472 Handsome, broad silvery foliage, much prized as a bedding plant. Half-hardy perennial. Height 1 foot .. 1 0

CERASTIUM TOMENTOSUM.
s. d.

473 Hardy perennial for dry rockeries, banks, &c. Produces an abundance of white flowers and silvery white foliage. 0 6

CLARKIA—QUEEN MARY.

CACALIA COCCINEA.

per pkt.— s. d.

471 A very useful and pretty hardy annual, growing about 1 foot high, with brilliant scarlet flowers. Excellent for bouquets or decoration 0 3

CALANDRINIA.

475 UMBELLATA. A splendid dwarf growing hardy perennial, only 6 inches high, and producing a profusion of brilliant magenta-crimson coloured flowers. It blooms the first year from seed, and is excellent for dry rockeries, &c. .. 0 4

CALENDULA OFFICINALIS FL. PL.
(Pot Marigolds.)

Free flowering showy hardy annuals, growing about 1 foot high, and continuing in bloom for quite a long period in Summer. The blooms are pleasantly scented, and very useful for cutting.

476 CHOICE MIXED DOUBLE, in beautiful variety of orange, yellow, primrose striped, and other shades 0 3

CHRYSANTHEMUM FRUTESCENS.
(Parisian Daisy.)

477 Exceedingly pretty starry white flowers, very useful for pots or window boxes, or for bedding out. The seeds should be sown in March on a gentle heat, and the young plants potted singly into small pots for planting out towards the end of May 0 6

CELSIA ARCTURUS.

477A A very useful plant for greenhouse or conservatory. The flowers are bright yellow, and borne on tall graceful spikes. Seed sown early in Spring will furnish a supply of flowers throughout the Summer .. .. .. 6d. and 1 0

From Mr. P. OLDS, Newport.

Feb. 20th.
" I won First Prize with flowers grown from your Seeds last year, and they gave every satisfaction."

CLARKIA ELEGANS.
NEW DOUBLE-FLOWERED.

A brilliant and splendid race of free-flowering hardy annuals that should be freely grown in every garden. The beautiful new double-flowered varieties mentioned below, and growing about 2 feet high, are especially worthy of notice for garden decoration, as they continue in bloom for quite a long time, and sown early under glass are excellent as pot plants for the greenhouse.

per pkt. s. d.

478 CLARKIA ELEGANS, QUEEN MARY
A splendid addition to this lovely class of Annuals. The plants grow about 2½ feet high, and the stems and branches are studded with very double brilliant rosy carmine flowers. This is the brightest coloured Clarkia yet introduced, and was much admired at the International Horticultural Exhibition at Chelsea in May last .. .. 6d. and 1 0

479	"	" CHAMOIS QUEEN. Soft chamois rose ..	0 4
480	"	" CARMINE QUEEN (new). Fine sprays of brilliant carmine-red double flowers ; splendid	0 4
481	"	" ORANGE KING. Brilliant orange red	0 4
482	"	" PURPLE PRINCE. Rich purple ..	0 4
483	"	" DOUBLE WHITE	0 4
484	"	" SALMON QUEEN Long sprays of double flowers	0 4
484A	"	" FINEST MIXED	0 4

CLARKIA PULCHELLA AND INTEGRIPETALA.

These beautiful hardy annuals are very showy when grown in clumps, they are more compact than the Elegans type, growing only about 1 foot in height. The Tom Thumb varieties make a good lasting edging to beds.

485	INTEGRIPETALA, DOUBLE ROSE. Bright rose ..		0 3
486	" ALBA. Double white..		0 3
487	" MARGINATA. Rose edged with white, very pretty		0 4
488	PULCHELLA, DOUBLE CRIMSON. Bright crimson purple..		0 4
489	" SINGLE WHITE. Pure white ..		0 3
490	" Choice mixed.. ..		0 3
491	" TOM THUMB, double white ..		0 4
492	" " " mixed ..		0 3

CINERARIA STELLATA. (See page 51)

CARNATIONS.

SEEDLING CARNATIONS, FROM OUR COLLECTION OF CHOICE VARIETIES

Carnation seed may be sown from March to May in well-drained pans of good rich soil, and these should be kept shaded until the seeds have germinated, when the plants should be gradually hardened off by admitting air and light. Prick off the seedlings about nine inches apart in boxes or prepared borders, and let them stay there until the Autumn, when they may be permanently planted in the positions they are to occupy.

The Perpetual or Tree varieties are a very valuable class, giving as they do a charming display in Winter, when flowers are so much valued.

The "Marguerite" Section is a special favourite with amateurs, as the plants when raised from Seed early in the Spring, produce an abundance of flowers during the Summer, if sown in June, carefully lifted in Autumn and potted up, they will continue to bloom right into the Winter.

	per pkt.—s. d.
493	**DANIELS' CHOICEST MIXED.** A very fine strain of beautiful varieties, saved from stage flowers, and will produce a high percentage of double blooms 2 6
494	smaller pkt. 1 6
495	**DANIELS' PERPETUAL or TREE.** A fine strain of beautiful flowers. Fine for pot culture 2 6
496	smaller pkt. 1 6
497	**AMERICAN PERPETUAL** A fine class for pot culture, very choice mixed 1 6
498	**PICOTEES.** Yellow, ground varieties, very fine 1 6
499	„ White, ground varieties, very beautiful .. 1 6
500	**DANIELS' CHOICEST MIXED.** From stage flowers, in splendid variety 2 6
501	smaller pkt. 1 6
502	**MARGUERITE, NEW LARGE-FLOWERED.** Handsome, double, fringed flowers, deliciously scented. Sown early will bloom freely the first year from seed; splendid for pots; a highly improved strain. Very choice mixed .. 6d. and 1 0
503	**MARGUERITE, PURE WHITE.** Very useful for cut flowers 1 0
504	**GARDEN PINK, " ARGUS."** A splendid strain of beautiful double, sweet-scented flowers; bloom first year from seed 1 0

ANNUAL CHRYSANTHEMUMS.

An exceedingly useful and showy class of hardy annuals for garden decoration. The single-flowered varieties are especially valuable to cut for vases and large bouquets, and will last for a long time in water. Sow the seeds in March or April in the open ground and thin out to 6 or 8 inches.

	per pkt.—s. d.
505	**MORNING STAR.** Beautiful large pale yellow flowers, a gem for cutting. Height 18 inches.. .. .. 0 6
506	**NORTHERN STAR** (new). Very large flowers, with soft yellow centres, clear white edges and black disc. Fine for cutting 0 6
507	**EVENING STAR.** Large, rich golden yellow flowers. 18 in... 0 6
508	**CORONARIUM PRINCESS MAY.** Large, beautiful single white flowers, with primrose centre, very handsome .. 0 4
509	**CARINATUM ATROCOCCINEA.** Crimson. 2 feet.. .. 0 3
510	**BURRIDGEANUM.** Beautiful flowers with bands of crimson yellow, &c. 2 feet 0 3
511	**CHAMELEON.** Very handsome flowers, with variously coloured bands. 2 feet 0 3
512	**SEGETUM GLORIA** (new). Pale yellow centre with pure white edge. Large flowers, splendid variety. Height 18 inches.. 0 6
513	**DANIELS' CHOICEST MIXED.** Single. A beautiful strain of handsomely coloured flowers, splendid for garden decoration or cut flowers .. .. .. 3d. and 0 6
514	**INODORUM, "BRIDAL ROBE"** (new). Large double snow-white flowers, very fine. Height 9 inches 1 0

ANNUAL CHRYSANTHEMUMS, CHOICEST MIXED.

CHRYSANTHEMUM MAXIMUM
(The Speaker). Hardy Perennial.

515 Very large, splendid pure white flowers. Sown in March under glass will bloom beautifully out doors in the Autumn.

Per packet 0 6

COBÆA SCANDENS.

per pkt.—s. d.

516 Well-known useful climber for the conservatory or sheltered walls. It is a half-hardy perennial, but blooms the first year from seed and is easily raised in a gentle heat 0 6

COCKSCOMB (Celosia cristata).

Sow the seeds in February or March in pots or pans of light rich soil and plunge in a good heat. The object being to keep the plants in free growth without a check, the young plants should be carefully pricked out into small pots as soon as they can be handled, and as these fill with roots they should be shifted into larger pots.

517 **DANIELS' GIANT PRIZE.** A splendid strain, saved from combs of the richest crimson colour .. .. 6d. and 1 0

COLEUS.

These beautiful and highly interesting ornamental-foliaged plants are easily raised, and grown from a really good strain of seed will produce plants of great beauty. Sow the seeds in February or March in light rich soil and place in a good heat. When the young plants are large enough, pot off singly into small pots, keeping near the light, and shift into larger pots as required. Those of about six or seven inches diameter being ample for a final potting.

518 **NEW LARGE-LEAVED HYBRIDS, Choicest Mixed.** This is a grand strain of large-leaved and brilliantly coloured varieties, invaluable for the decoration of the greenhouse or conservatory. The seed offered will produce a splendid variety of beautiful foliage .. 1s. 6d. and 2 6

519 **SALICIFOLIUS.** A beautiful and quite distinct class, with long narrow willow-like foliage and a great variety of handsome colours 1 6

SEEDLING COLEUS.

CYCLAMEN.

CYCLAMEN—SALMON KING.

A beautiful class of plant for the greenhouse, blooming freely in Winter and early Spring. The seed should be sown in January or February in a gentle heat, for blooming the following year. For earlier flowering sow in November.

per pkt.—s. d.

520 **DANIELS' GIANT MIXED.** A magnificent strain of a highly improved type, having large, beautifully mottled coriaceous leaves and stout flower-stalks. The blooms, which are carried well above the foliage, are of splendid size, each flower frequently measuring from two and a half to three inches in length 2 6

521 smaller pkt. 1 0

522 **SALMON KING.** Large beautiful flowers of a clear salmon-pink colour. A very fine variety 1 6

523 **DANIELS' GIANT WHITE.** Pure white, large flowers. Splendid 1 0

524 **PURE WHITE CRESTED.** Beautifully crested, pure white flowers, very handsome, and quite novel .. 1 0

525 **FRINGED.** A beautiful class of handsomely fringed or crested flowers, choicest mixed 1 0

526 **PERSICUM.** Choice mixed 0 0

DAISY, Double-flowered.

Well-known useful hardy perennial plants for Spring bedding, edgings, &c. The plants grow only about 3 inches high and are exceedingly pretty when in bloom. Sow in March or April for blooming the same year, and sow in June for blooming the following Spring.

527 **NEW GIANT WHITE.** Large double pure white flowers, very fine 0 6

528 **DARK ROSE.** Double 0 6

529 **CHOICEST MIXED.** Double 0 6

DIANTHUS.

DIANTHUS HEDDEWIGI—SNOWDRIFT.

These constitute one of the most brilliant and splendid groups of hardy biennials in cultivation. The large, beautifully coloured flowers vary from pure white to the darkest crimson, some of the double flowers being almost equal to carnations in size. All the varieties are easily raised from seed, and sown in March under glass and transplanted they will bloom freely the first season and make charming beds during the Summer and Autumn. The Heddewigi section produces the largest flowers and are perhaps the most beautiful, but all are deserving of extensive cultivation. The plants vary in height from 8 inches to 1 foot.

DIANTHUS HEDDEWIGI, Double-flowered.

VERY USEFUL FOR CUT FLOWERS.

		per pkt.—s. d.
538	FIREBALL. Dark crimson, splendid	0 6
539	SNOWDRIFT. Pure white, beautifully fringed flowers, charming	0 6
540	FRINGED, DOUBLE. Splendid mixed. The petals of these are elegantly laciniated. Excellent for cutting	0 6
541	DANIELS' CHOICEST MIXED, DOUBLE. A charming variety of beautiful colours .. 6d. and	1 0

DIANTHUS HEDDEWIGI, Single-flowered.

		per pkt.—s. d.
542	PURE WHITE. Large flowers, very freely produced	0 6
543	SALMON QUEEN. Brilliant salmon pink, one of the most beautiful, makes a splendid bed	0 6
544	DARK CRIMSON. Very rich colour	0 6
545	CHOICEST MIXED SINGLE. Very showy and beautiful varieties	0 6
546	CHINENSIS (Indian Pink). Finest double mixed. Very choice .. 3d. and	0 6
547	,, ALBA FL. PL. White, double	0 6

DAHLIA.

Sow the seeds of these in February or March in a gentle heat, pot the young plants singly into small pots and plant out towards the end of May. In a favourable season an abundance of fine bloom will be produced from July till the plants are killed by the frost.

		per pkt.—s. d.
530	LARGE-FLOWERED SHOW AND FANCY. Saved from our fine collection of choice named flowers ..	1 0
531	CACTUS-FLOWERED. From named flowers, very choice ..	1 0
532	POMPONE. Fine dwarf varieties from choicest named flowers	1 0
533	SINGLE FLOWERED. From a very fine collection of named sorts .. .. 6d. and	1 0

DIASCIA BARBERÆ.

534	A beautiful little half-hardy annual growing about 9 inches high and bearing a profusion of pretty terra-cotta red flowers. Excellent for pots in the greenhouse or for borders ..	1 0

DIMORPHOTHECA AURANTIACA.

535	A beautiful and showy half-hardy annual growing about a foot high with brilliant orange yellow Marguerite-like flowers. Sow in Spring under glass and transplant .. 3d. and	0 6
536	NEW HYBRIDS, beautiful varieties, ranging in colour from yellow and orange to maize and pure white .. 6d. and	1 0

DODECATHEON MEADIA.

(American Cowslip.)

537	Beautiful hardy perennial, about 9 inches high, with elegant cyclamen-like flowers of a bright purplish rose colour	1 0

From Mr. G. RAYNER, Durham.
June 11th.
"I received Dahlias quite safe and sound. I am very pleased with them; they are in perfect condition."

From Mr. H. CHAMBERS, Legbourne, Louth.
Oct. 22nd.
"The Asters raised from your Seed have charmed us with a most beautiful blending of colours and delicate tints we have never seen before."

DELPHINIUM.

These beautiful hardy border Perennials, when grown in clumps on the herbaceous border, are strikingly effective when in bloom. Their handsome spikes of flowers ranging in colour from white through all the richest shades of blue and purple, furnish some rare colours not found in any other class of plant. The new Dwarf Hybrids and the Formosum varieties are very fine, whilst the scarlet Nudicaule and the pale yellow Sulphureum, provide some novel colours amongst these charming flowers.

		per pkt.—s. d.
548	CARDINALE. Bright scarlet. 18 inches ..	0 6
549	FORMOSUM. Rich dark blue. Very fine. Height 4 to 5 feet ..	0 4
550	COELESTINUM. Beautiful sky blue	0 6
551	NUDICAULE. Bright scarlet flower. Height 1 foot. Very pretty	0 6
552	SULPHUREUM. Long spikes of beautiful clear yellow flowers. Height 3 feet	1 0
553	NEW DWARF HYBRIDS A splendid new class, growing only about 3 ft. and producing a beautiful variety of handsome spikes of bloom ..	1 0
554	CHOICEST MIXED SINGLE. In beautiful variety. From our fine collection of named flowers .. 3d. and	0 6
555	DOUBLE-FLOWERED CHOICEST MIXED. Fine new varieties 6d. &	1 0

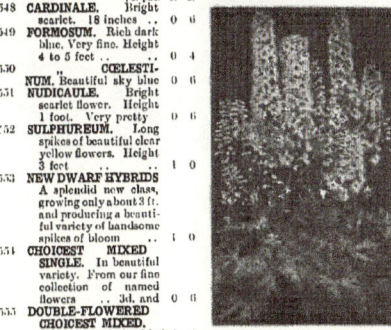

DELPHINIUM SINGLE FLOWERED.

From Mr. J. FOX, Holloway, N.
Aug. 14th.
"Your Wallflower Seed turned out splendid, in four days they were up in hundreds, and looked a great picture of colour."

From Mr. T. MOORE, Histon.
Feb. 12th.
"Your Seeds have given great satisfaction in the past. Shall be pleased to recommend them to all."

ESCHSCHOLTZIA.

A brilliant class of showy hardy biennials growing about 1 foot high and blooming freely the first year from seed. They may be sown and treated as hardy annuals and will give a beautiful display within a few weeks of the seeds being sown. These are certainly amongst the most delightful of our summer flowers and should certainly find a place in every garden. The beautiful frilled varieties of *E. caniculata* are very charming, whilst such fine sorts as "Mandarin," "Carmine King," and "Rose Cardinal" are exceedingly brilliant.

ESCHSCHOLTZIA -ROSE CARDINAL

		per pkt.	s.	d.
556	**CANICULATA MIKADO** (new). Intense crimson scarlet suffused with orange; most brilliant variety	..	1	0
557	**,, ROSEA.** Bright rose ..	..	0	4
558	**CARMINE KING.** Brilliant carmine, splendid colour	..	0	6
559	**CROCEA ALBA.** Large white, single	..	0	3
560	**,, ,, FL. PL.** Double white flowers, very showy	0	4
561	**,, ,, FL. PL.** Orange, double	..	0	4
562	**MANDARIN.** Orange, scarlet ..	..	0	3
563	**,, COMPACTA** (new). Brilliant orange scarlet	..	0	6
564	**ROSE CARDINAL.** Beautiful rose	..	0	4
565	**CALIFORNICA.** Pale yellow	..	0	2
566	**CHOICE MIXED.** In beautiful variety ..	..	0	3

ERYSIMUM.

E. perofiskianum, with its bright rich orange coloured flowers, is very effective when sown in good clumps or patches on the mixed border. Whilst the dwarf Golden Gem, sown in June and planted out in Autumn, makes one of the best of Spring flowering plants.

557	**PEROFFSKIANUM.** Showy hardy annual. Height 18 inches. Flowers bright orange	..	0	2
558	**GOLDEN GEM.** A beautiful dwarf compact biennial, resembling a miniature yellow wallflower, makes a splendid edging for wallflower beds	..	0	6

ECCREMOCARPUS SCABER.

		per pkt.—s.	d.
569	Very useful half-hardy perennial climber of quick growth. The flowers are of a bright orange scarlet colour. Height about 10 feet	0	6

EUCALYPTUS.

570	**GLOBULUS** (Australian Blue Gum). Glaucous green foliage, fine for sub-tropical garden ..	0	6
571	**CITRIODORA.** Lemon-scented foliage, makes a capital pot plant for the greenhouse. Deliciously fragrant ..	1	0

GERBERA.
(The Transvaal Daisy.)

572	**JAMESONI.** A beautiful plant for pots in the greenhouse or a warm dry position out of doors. The plants grow about 15 inches high, and the Marguerite-like flowers are orange or yellow	1	6
573	**,, New Hybrids.** A magnificent strain of new varieties of this charming and interesting plant from the Transvaal. The colours of the flowers are of incomparable delicacy and richness, with almost an infinity of tints ranging from pure white through all the shades of yellow, orange, salmon, rose, cerise, scarlet, ruby, and violet. The beautiful light starry flowers are borne on long rigid stems, and are delightful as cut flowers, lasting a long time in perfection. They are easily raised from seeds grown in pots of sandy peat, and placed in a gentle heat. The young plants must be kept only moderately moist, and if potted on into sandy peat and loam, and re-potted as growth advances, may be had in bloom in from seven to nine months. The plants will thrive in the greenhouse, or may be planted in a sunny sheltered spot in the garden	1	6

GERBERA JAMESONI—NEW HYBRIDS.

All Flower Seeds quoted in 3d. packets may be had at 2/6 per dozen.

FOX-GLOVE—DIGITALIS.

A very beautiful and showy class of hardy perennials, of fine effect for shrubbery borders, and first class for planting in any odd corner of the garden. The large-spotted varieties are exceedingly handsome. They grow about 5 to 6 feet in height, with long spikes of beautiful Gloxinia-like flowers that continue for a long period when the plants are partially shaded by trees, &c. The seeds should be sown somewhat thinly out of doors in May or June, and the young plants should be planted out where intended to bloom, in Autumn or early Spring.

		per pkt. s. d.
574	DANIELS' SUPERB SPOTTED. Magnificent varieties with large, Gloxinia-like spotted flowers	0 6
575	MONSTROSA. Splendid mixed. Beautiful shades of rose and white	0 4
576	LARGE WHITE. Very fine	0 3

GODETIA DOUBLE ROSE.
(See page 88.)

FUCHSIAS.

Sow in February or March on a gentle heat, and treat as recommended for tender annuals. These beautiful free-flowering plants will bloom well the first year from seed, and plants raised from a first-class strain will produce the most satisfactory results.

577	CHOICEST MIXED. Single	1 6
578	Double	1 6
579	BOLIVÏANA. A fine species, with long racemes of splendid scarlet flowers	1 0

GAILLARDIA.

A splendid class of showy hardy perennials. If sown under glass in March, will bloom freely the first year from seed, and continue quite into late Autumn. First-class for cut flowers.

GAILLARDIA LARGE-FLOWERED SINGLE.

		per pkt. s. d.
580	LARGE-FLOWERED SINGLE. Saved from our splendid strain of choice named flowers. 2 to 3 feet 6d. and	1 0
581	LARGE-FLOWERED DWARF SINGLE. Beautiful new compact growing varieties	0 6
582	LORENZIANA. Double mixed. Very fine for cutting	0 3
583	SULPHUREA. Pale yellow, very showy	0 4
584	AMBLYODON. Half-hardy annual, flowers dark red. Height 2 feet	0 3

GENTIANA ACAULIS.

585	A splendid hardy dwarf-growing perennial, first-rate for rockeries or edgings, beautiful deep blue flowers in Spring. Height 6 inches	0 6

GILIA.

Very pretty free-flowering hardy annuals, useful for patches on mixed beds or borders. Excellent for bees.

586	ALBA. White. 18 inches	0 3
587	TRICOLOR. Lavender white and black. 1 foot	0 3

GLADIOLUS PRÆCOX.

588 A fine new class of large beautifully blotched flowers of the richest colours. Sown in February or March under glass, and the young plants planted out in May, will bloom in early Autumn with excellent results, and if the bulbs are allowed to remain in the ground, they will bloom finer still the second year, being quite hardy ... 1 0

GLOXINIA.

GLOXINIA—SPOTTED HYBRID.

These, the most exquisitely beautiful of all greenhouse plants, bloom freely the first year from seed, and should be grown largely by every one having accommodation for them. Sow in February or March on a good moist heat, in the way recommended for Calceolarias. Pot off singly into small pots as soon as the young plants can be handled, and shift into larger as required, keeping the plants going with a good liberal warmth, and finally shift into pots of about six inches diameter, using a light and rich soil, and continuing with a moderate heat and giving air on warm days. Treated in this way, a charming display of bloom may be had during July and August, and some really grand flowers will be the result.

		per pkt.—s.	d.
589	DANIELS' PRIZE MIXED. A splendid strain of large, beautifully coloured flowers, including the newest colours..	2	6
590	„ „ smaller pkt.	1	0
591	GIANT-FLOWERED, MIXED. Very large flowers, more than four inches across and of the most splendid colours	1	6
592	SPOTTED HYBRIDS. Flowers beautifully spotted	1	0

GEUM.

A very useful hardy perennial, growing about 2 feet high, with brilliant scarlet ranunculus-like flowers. Excellent for cutting. Sown early under glass will bloom freely the same year.

593	ATROSANGUINEA FL. PL. Deep rich scarlet double flowers	0	3
594	MRS. BRADSHAW. Beautiful double scarlet flowers, very fine variety ..	0	6

GREVILLEA ROBUSTA.

595	Beautiful greenhouse shrub with handsome fern-like foliage..	0	6

GYPSOPHILA.

596	PANICULATA. A hardy perennial with elegantly branched panicles of small white flowers. Fine for bouquets. Height 2 ft.	0	4
597	ELEGANS GRANDIFLORA ALBA. An exceedingly pretty hardy annual, with finely branched elegant stems of white flowers. Splendid for bouquets. 18 inches .. 3d. and	0	6
598	„ „ ROSEA. Rosy pink and very pretty „ „ .. 3d. and	0	6

GODETIA.

A magnificent class of brilliant, large-flowered, showy hardy annuals that should be grown freely in every garden where a bold display is desired. They are very effective for mixed beds or borders, and when grown in masses are very charming. For a general display sow thinly in the open ground from early in March to the end of April. If sown in Autumn and transplanted in Spring they will bloom much earlier and finer. Excepting where mentioned the plants grow about 1 foot high.

		per pkt.—s.	d.
599	CRIMSON GLOW (new). Intense dark crimson, splendid ..	0	6
600	CARMINEA AUREA. Crimson and yellow ..	0	4
601	DUKE OF FIFE. Brilliant crimson ..	0	4
602	DUCHESS OF FIFE. White and carmine ..	0	4
603	DUCHESS OF ALBANY. Pure white ..	0	3
604	DUKE OF YORK. Vivid carmine ..	0	3
605	BRIDESMAID. Rose and white ..	0	3
606	GLORIOSA. Dark crimson ..	0	3
607	DWARF CARMINE. Brilliant carmine, splendid. Height 6″	0	4
608	DWARF WHITE. Beautiful pure white satiny flowers. Height 6 inches ..	0	4
609	DANIELS' LARGE-FLOWERED. Mixed, in beautiful variety	0	4
610	ROSEA GRANDIFLORA FL. PL. Beautiful double rose-coloured flowers. 2 feet ..	0	4
611	THE BRIDE. White petals with crimson base 2 feet ..	0	6
612	COLLECTION OF 6 SUPERB VARIETIES ..	1	6

LARGE-FLOWERED GODETIAS.

HELICHRYSUM.
(Everlasting.)

HELICHRYSUM.

A brilliant and splendid class of showy hardy annual everlasting flowers, that remain in bloom for a long period. The handsome globular flowers vary in colour from dark crimson or purple, orange scarlet and yellow, to delicate rose and pure white. In association with ornamental grasses these are excellent for the decoration of vases in Winter. The plants grow about 3 feet in height.

		per pkt.—s.	d.
613	FIREBALL. Deep crimson red, fine	0	3
614	PURE YELLOW. Clear golden yellow	0	3
615	PURPLE. Purplish crimson	0	3
616	ROSE. Beautiful clear rose	0	3
617	WHITE. Silvery white, beautiful	0	3
618	LARGE-FLOWERED. 6 separate varieties	1	3
619	Choicest mixed, all colours.. 3d. and	0	6
620	DWARF VARIETIES. Choice mixed	0	3

OTHER EVERLASTING FLOWERS.

For preserving, the blooms should be cut before they are fully expanded and be hung up to dry in a cool place with the flowers downwards.

			per pkt.—s.	d.
621	ACROCLINIUM. Double, rose	Beautiful hardy annuals	0	4
622	„ Single, rose	growing about 15 inches	0	3
623	„ white	in height	0	3
624	CATANANCHE BICOLOR. Hardy perennial, height about 2½ feet. Flowers blue and white		0	3
625	HELIPTERUM SANDFORDI. Half-hardy annual. 18 inches. Bright yellow		0	3
626	RHODANTHE ATROSANGUINEUM.	Half-hardy annuals.		
	Crimson	Height 1 foot.	0	4
627	„ MACULATA. Rose	Very useful and	0	3
628	„ „ ALBA. White	pretty.	0	3
629	STATICE SINUATA HYBRIDA. Half-hardy annual. Height 18 inches. Flowers mauve, white, and yellow; very fine..		0	6
630	„ SUWOROWI. Bright rose. 15 inches		0	3
631	WAITZIA AUREA GRANDIFLORA. Half-hardy annual. 1 foot. Orange		0	3
632	XERANTHEMUM SUPERBISSIMUM.	Hardy annuals. 1 ft.	0	4
	Bright purple	Very handsome and		
633	„ Choice mixed	free flowering.	0	3

HOLLYHOCK, DOUBLE.

These magnificent hardy perennials form grandly conspicuous objects in the flower garden during Summer and Autumn, and should always be grown where convenient. They are easily raised from seed sown in May or June out of doors, and will provide some strong plants for planting out in Autumn for blooming the following year.

		per pkt.—s.	d.
634	BRIGHT SCARLET. Fine colour	1	0
635	DEEP PINK. Lovely deep rosy pink	1	0
636	SALMON ROSE. Rosy apricot	1	0
637	YELLOW. Bright clear yellow	1	0
638	ROSY CARMINE. Splendid colour	1	0
639	PURE WHITE. Beautiful variety, comes quite true from seed	1	0
640	DANIELS' PRIZE MIXED. A superb strain of beautifully coloured, large double flowers ..	2	6
641	smaller pkt. 6d. and	1	0
642	SINGLE-FLOWERED. An attractive and beautiful class, producing some rare and charming colours .. 6d. and	1	0

SEEDLING HOLLYHOCK.

HELIOTROPE.

Although classed as half-hardy perennials, these deliciously scented and highly popular flowers bloom freely the first year from seed, and sown in February or early March in a gentle heat and planted out in May will furnish some nice plants for pot or garden culture. These will commence blooming in July and continue to flower till late in Autumn. The plants grow about 18 inches high.

		per pkt.—s.	d.
643	QUEEN MARGUERITE. Rich dark blue, deliciously scented, very large heads of bloom 6d. and	1	0
643A	VERY CHOICE VARIETIES. Mixed 6d. and	1	0

HEUCHERA SANGUINEA.

644 A charming hardy perennial, growing about 18 inches high, with long slender panicles of brilliant coral red flowers. A first-rate plant for rockeries and borders, and exceedingly useful for cut flowers   0   6

HONESTY.

Very useful early flowering hardy biennial. Fine for shrubbery borders, and valued for its dried silvery seed pods.
645	CRIMSON. Bright red, very fine	..	..	0	6
645A	PURPLE. Bright purplish lilac ..	..	..	0	3
646	WHITE. Pure white, pretty	..	..	0	3

HUMULUS.

The Japanese Hop. Half-hardy annuals of rapid growth and first class for covering trellises.
| 647 | JAPONICUS VARIEGATUS. Handsomely variegated leaves with silvery white markings. Height 8 to 10 feet | .. | 0 | 4 |
| 648 | JAPONICUS. Large green foliage, a rapid grower. Height 10 feet | .. | .. | 0 | 3 |

HUNNEMANNIA FUMARIÆFOLIA.

649 A beautiful hardy perennial, growing about 2 feet high, and bearing bright yellow poppy-like flowers. Sown out of doors in March or April, and treated as a hardy annual, will bloom freely in August and September   0   3

ICE PLANT.

(Mesembryanthemum crystallinum.)

650 A trailing half-hardy annual of singular appearance. The stem and foliage being covered with icy-looking points. Useful for garnishing   0   3

INCARVILLEA DELAVAYI.

651 Splendid hardy perennial, with large gloxinia-like rosy carmine flowers. The plants grow about 18 inches high, and bloom in June and July. Is easily raised from seeds. Sown out of doors in May or June   0   6

JACOBEA.

Free-flowering hardy annuals, growing about 9 inches high, with numerous handsome double flowers. Very useful for bouquets.
652	DWARF, PURPLE. Fine colour	..	..	0	3
653	DWARF, WHITE. Very fine ..	..	..	0	3
654	DWARF, CRIMSON. Very showy	..	..	0	3
655	DWARF, CHOICE MIXED. All colours ..	..	..	0	3

From Mr. F. S. Moore, Ilford.

Sept. 8th,
"I thought I might interest you to know what good results I have had from your Kochia Trichophylla."

KOCHIA TRICHOPHYLLA.

(Summer Cypress, The True Variety.)

This is undoubtedly one of the most interesting and beautiful plants of recent introduction. The plant which is of an elegant upright habit of growth, with pale green fern-like foliage, attains a height of about eighteen inches, and forms a charming plant for the centres of small beds, or as a "dot" plant on borders amongst dwarfer growing subjects. In the Autumn, the foliage changes to a deep bright crimson colour, when it has a very novel and striking effect. It is easily raised and grown as a half-hardy annual, and may be sown in the open ground in April, and thinned out or transplanted, whilst potted up into six or eight inch pots, it forms a charming plant for the greenhouse.
656 Per packet   ..   ..   3d. and 6d.

LARKSPUR.

A very fine class of beautiful showy hardy annuals that are of great value for garden decoration. The tall-growing varieties are especially handsome, and the flowers being produced on long, graceful spikes, are very useful for cut flowers.

STOCK-FLOWERED LARKSPUR, CARMINE.

			per pkt.—s.	d.
657	STOCK-FLOWERED, CARMINE. Splendid colour. Height 3 feet	..	0	6
658	" PALE BLUE (new). Beautiful colour. Height 3 feet	..	0	6
659	" CHOICEST MIXED. Fine, tall varieties. Height 3 feet	..	0	4
660	TALL VARIETIES. Choice mixed	..	..	0	3
661	EMPEROR, CHOICE MIXED. Free-flowering branching varieties. Height 2 feet	..	0	4
662	BLUE BUTTERFLY. Very pretty. Height 1 foot ..	..	0	6
663	DWARF ROCKET, CHOICE MIXED. Beautiful early-flowering varieties. Height 1 foot ..	..	0	3

LANTANA.

A half-hardy shrubby perennial, with heads of brilliantly coloured flowers. Excellent for bedding out, or as a pot plant for the greenhouse.

per pkt.—s. d.

664 **NEW DWARF HYBRIDS, MIXED.** Beautiful varieties, of compact habit. Height 9 inches 0 6

LAYIA ELEGANS.

665 A pretty hardy annual from California, about 1 foot high, with large round yellow flowers edged with white 0 3

LEPTOSIPHON.

Free-flowering and exceedingly pretty hardy annuals. L. densiflorus and albus are very useful for beds or borders. The dwarf-growing sorts are well suited for edgings or rockwork.

666 **DENSIFLORUS.** Lilac. 1 foot 0 3
667 ,, **ALBUS.** Pure white, sweet-scented. 1 foot 0 3

LEPTOSYNE STILLMANNI.

668 A beautiful hardy annual, growing about 15 inches high, with bright golden-yellow flowers. This is one of the quickest annuals to bloom from seed and may be had in perfection within five weeks of sowing 0 4

LINARIA MAROCCANA.

A charming class of beautiful hardy annuals, growing about 18 inches high, and throwing up elegant spikes of small Antirrhinum-like flowers. The colours vary from crimson, rose, yellow and pink to the purest white. These are splendid as cut flowers for table decoration.

669 **CHOICE HYBRIDS, MIXED** 0 3
670 **EXCELSA HYBRIDS.** Splendid new strain of beautiful varieties 0 6

LINUM.

671 **GRANDIFLORUM RUBRUM.** Very showy hardy annual, producing a profusion of brilliant crimson-scarlet flowers. Height 1 foot 0 3

LOVE-LIES-BLEEDING.

672 **AMARANTHUS CAUDATUS.** A fine showy hardy annual with long drooping stems of crimson-scarlet flowers. 2 to 3 feet 0 3

LUPINUS.

Handsome and easily-grown showy hardy annuals that well deserve their high popularity. All the varieties are free-flowering and have a very pretty effect on mixed beds or borders.

673 **HYBRIDUS ATROCOCCINEUS.** Scarlet and white, very showy. 2½ feet 0 3
674 **CRUIKSHANKI.** Fine dark blue. Height 3 feet 0 3
675 **SULPHUREUS SUPERBUS.** Bright yellow, fine. 2 feet .. 0 3
676 **SUBCARNOSUS.** Dark blue and white, very pretty. 1 foot 0 3
677 **LUTEUS ROMULUS.** Rich bright yellow, very distinct. 2 ft. 0 4
678 **NANUS.** Blue. 1 foot 0 3
679 ,, **ALBO-COCCINEUS.** Bright carmine tipped with white, charming variety. 1 foot 0 4

HARDY PERENNIAL LUPINS.

680 **ARBOREUS** (The Tree Lupin). Handsome shrubby variety, flowers yellow. Height 4 feet 0 4
681 ,, **SNOW QUEEN.** Long spikes of beautiful pure white flowers, splendid variety. Height 4 feet .. 0 4
682 **POLYPHYLLUS.** Blue. Height 4 feet 0 3
683 ,, White. Height 4 feet 0 4
684 ,, Choice Hybrids. Fine varieties. Mixed 0 6

LYCHNIS HAAGEANA.
(New Hybrids.)

A splendid class of dwarf-growing hardy herbaceous perennials, growing about 1 foot high. The flowers vary in colour from the most intense and brilliant scarlet to the brightest orange and salmon shades, and are very effective when grown in good clumps on the border.

685 **CHOICE MIXED HYBRIDS,** in beautiful variety 0 4

LOBELIA.

LOBELIA.—DANIELS' WHITE BEDDING.

To secure fine plants for bedding out the following May, some prefer to sow the seed in Autumn, but February or March is good time for sowing if the plants have careful attention and are grown on freely. Sow the seeds thinly in pans or pots of sandy loam, cover very lightly, and place in a heat of about sixty degrees, keep moist, and soon as the young plants can be handled, pot off singly into small pots of light rich soil, keep near the glass in a gentle heat, and give plenty of air on fine days. Carefully picking off all the flower-buds will greatly assist their growth, and they should on no account be allowed to suffer from want of moisture. Other excellent methods are to prick the young plants five or six in a five-inch pot, or, better still, to plant them thinly in shallow trays of rich soil, keeping in gentle heat, giving air, etc., as recommended. These will generally form compactly grown, sturdy plants, that will quickly produce a beautiful effect when planted out. Lobelias intended for pots or window-boxes succeed best when planted out thinly in good soil in an open situation, and carefully lifted when they have formed nice tufty plants; these will at once commence blooming, and produce an effect that could not be otherwise obtained. For bedding out, we strongly recommend Daniels' Dark Blue and Daniels' White Bedding as most compact in growth and reliable in colour. Royal Purple and Barnard's Perpetual are also very fine, whilst for pot culture, hanging baskets, and greenhouse decoration, the beautiful Tenuior and the varieties of Ramosa are by far the best.

per pkt.—s. d.

686 **DANIELS' DARK BLUE.** A very fine dark blue, compact-growing variety; splendid for edgings and carpet bedding. For a really good dark blue bedder, we recommend this as the best variety for garden decoration 1 0
687 **DANIELS' WHITE BEDDING.** Pure white dwarf; a beautiful variety for bedding 1 0
688 **ROYAL PURPLE.** Deep rich blue with distinct white eye, splendid 0 6
689 **BARNARD'S PERPETUAL.** Bright ultramarine blue, white at base of lower petals; splendid dwarf variety 0 6
690 **COMPACTA, WHITE LADY.** Pure white, very compact .. 0 6
691 **SPECIOSA** (true). Fine dark blue, excellent bedder .. 0 6
692 **COBALT BLUE.** Fine and distinct colour 0 3
693 **ERINUS ALBA.** White, very useful 0 3
694 **PAXTONI.** Blue and white, dwarf 0 3
695 **TENUIOR.** A charming variety, growing about one foot high, with very large flowers, cobalt blue, with white centre; very graceful in habit and makes a beautiful pot plant, and is excellent for vases and hanging baskets 0 6
696 **RAMOSA BLUE** ⎫ A beautiful upright growing class 9 in. to 0 4
697 ,, **WHITE** ⎬ 1 ft. high, very useful for pot culture 0 4
698 ,, **ROSE** ⎭ in the greenhouse. 0 4

LOBELIA CARDINALIS VICTORIA.

This beautiful perennial, growing about two feet high, with its rich dark metallic foliage and brilliant scarlet flowers, comes quite true from seed, and sown in February or March on a gentle heat will make nice plants for bedding out in May or June for blooming the following Autumn.

699 Per packet .. .. 1s.

LAVATERA.

LAVATERA ROSSA "SUNSET."

Exceedingly beautiful and showy hardy annuals, growing about 3 feet high and bearing for a long period quite a profusion of large, beautifully coloured flowers. Sow in April in the open garden and thin out the young plants to 6 or 8 inches apart. L. rosea splendens is especially fine, and this and the pure white Alba splendens are first-class to cut for the decoration of large vases, etc., in which they are very effective. The new L. rosea "Sunset," in consideration of its fine colour, is highly recommended for garden decoration.

per pkt—s. d.

700   **SPLENDENS "SUNSET"** (new). A very fine improvement in this beautiful class of mallows. The flowers are exceedingly bright and of the most beautiful deep rose colour, having the most charming effect. The plants grow only about 2 to 2½ feet high, and the flowers are very lasting when cut   1 0

701   **ROSEA SPLENDENS.** A very beautiful tall growing hardy annual, with large bright rosy-pink flowers that continue in bloom for a long time. Very showy and effective in large beds or borders. 3 feet   0 4

702   **ALBA SPLENDENS.** Large glossy pure white flowers. This and the preceding are excellent as cut flowers. Height 3 feet   0 4

LAYIA ELEGANS.

703   A charming hardy annual from California. It grows only about nine inches high and bears quite a profusion of pretty round yellow flowers edged with white ..   0 3

LOPHOSPERMUM SCANDENS.

704   Very useful half-hardy perennial climber, with large blush-pink flowers. Height 8 to 10 feet ..   0 6

LIMNANTHES DOUGLASI.

705   A free-flowering and useful hardy annual, about six inches high, of a spreading habit, with white and yellow flowers ..   0 3

MARIGOLD.

Seeds of these fine half-hardy annuals should be sown under glass, not earlier than the beginning of April, or the plants are apt to get too forward before planting out, which can only be done with safety when all danger from Spring frosts is over. The African varieties grow about two feet high, and their large showy flowers are very effective in late Summer and Autumn. The French striped are very handsome for garden decoration, whilst the new dwarf varieties are splendid little plants for edgings of beds or borders.

per pkt.—s. d.

706   **ORANGE AFRICAN.** A magnificent selection from a prize strain, bearing immense, brilliant orange-coloured, perfectly double flowers 0 6

707   ,,   ,,   smaller pkt.   0 3

708   **LEMON AFRICAN.** The same as preceding in size and form of flower and habit of plant, but varying slightly in colour   0 6

709   ,,   ,,   smaller pkt.   0 3

710   **DANIELS' STRIPED FRENCH (Scotch Prize).** A fine strain of beautifully striped flowers of the most perfect form and doubleness. Grown expressly for our retail trade. Height 1 foot

     6d. and   1 0

711   **NEW DWARF, Golden Yellow**   ⎫ Very dwarf and double.   0 6
712   ,,   ,,   **Sulphur Yellow**   ⎬ Splendid for edgings.   0 6
713   ,,   ,,   **Brown and Yellow**   ⎭   0 6
     The above three varieties grow only four inches in height

714   **TALL FRENCH.** A very showy strain ..   .. 3d. and   0 6

715   ,,   ,,   **METEOR** (new). A beautiful variety of tall French marigold, with double yellow flowers striped with orange 0 6

716   **DWARF FRENCH.** Striped and blotched   .. 3d. and   0 6

717   **DWARF BROWN FRENCH.** Dwarf and double 0 3

718   **SIGNATA PUMILA.** Single, golden yellow flowers   ..   0 3

719   **SILVER KING.** Single, pale yellow flowers, prettily marked with maroon. Height 9 inches 0 4

720   **LEGION OF HONOUR.** Single, golden yellow with crimson blotch, very pretty, splendid bedder. Height 9 inches   ..   0 3

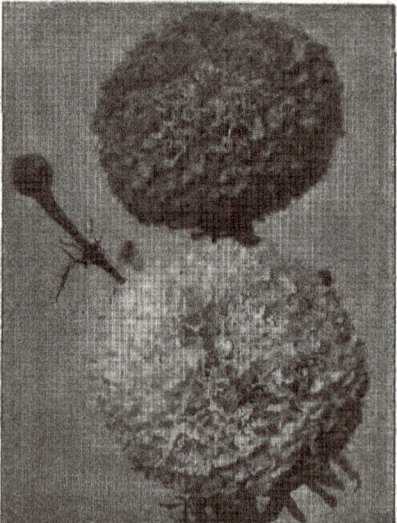

AFRICAN MARIGOLDS.

We beg to intimate that we cannot "break" packets quoted in this list.

MALOPE.

Showy hardy annuals growing about 2 feet high. Very useful for large borders or beds.

		per pkt.—s. d.
721	**GRANDIFLORA ROSEA.** Bright rose	.. 0 3
722	„ **ALBA.** Pure white ..	.. 0 3
723	„ **PURPUREA.** Red ..	.. 0 3
724	„ **MIXED.** Various ..	.. 0 3

MALVA.

725 **MOSCHATA ROSEA.** A fine hardy perennial. 18 inches high, and blooming the first year from seed. With bright rose sweet-scented flowers 0 3
726 **MOSCHATA ALBA.** A pure white-flowered variety of the preceding. Very free flowering 0 3

MATRICARIA.

727 **GOLDEN BALL.** Hardy perennial. Height 1 foot. Beautiful double yellow flowers. Excellent for beds or borders .. 0 6

MATHIOLA BICORNIS.
(Night-Scented Stock.)

728 One of the most deliciously-scented of all annuals, especially in the evening. Should be grown freely in every garden. Although classed as half-hardy it is best sown in April and treated as a hardy annual.. .. .. .. 0 3

MECONOPSIS.

Seeds of these fine perennial poppies should be sown in April or May, and the plants potted into small pots and sheltered, in a cold pit, during the following Winter. These may be planted out in March, and will produce some fine flowers in June and July.

729 **INTEGRIFOLIA.** The Giant Yellow Poppy from Thibet. Very large, beautiful, pale yellow flowers in June. Height about 3 feet 1 6
730 **WALLICHII.** The large Blue Himalayan Poppy. A magnificent flower. 3 to 4 feet 1 6

MESEMBRYANTHEMUM.

731 **CORDIFOLIUM VARIEGATUM.** Dwarf-growing variety of spreading habit, foliage yellowish with small purplish-crimson flowers. Excellent for carpet bedding. Half-hardy perennial 0 6
732 **TRICOLOR.** A capital dwarf-growing, half-hardy annual. Flowers crimson, white and purple. Height 3 inches. Excellent for dry sunny rockeries 0 3

MIMULUS.

A splendid and profuse-flowering class of brilliant half-hardy perennials, blooming the first year from seed, and thriving in damp or shady positions.

733 **DANIELS' LARGE-FLOWERED.** A grand strain of large beautiful flowers of the richest colours. Height 1 foot (d. and 1 0
734 **NANUS ROSEUS.** A charming variety growing only 4 inches high, with bright salmony-rose coloured flowers 0 6
735 **HOSE-IN-HOSE VARIETIES.** Choice mixed 0 6
736 **CHOICE MIXED.** In good variety 0 3

MUSK PLANT.
(Mimulus moschatus.)

737 **NEW DWARF.** A fine compact growing variety. A great improvement on the old variety for pot culture. Very free-flowering and powerfully fragrant. Half-hardy perennial, 4 inches high 0 6

MARVEL OF PERU.

737A A half-hardy tuberous-rooted perennial, growing about 2½ ft. high. Sown early will bloom the first year from seed. Choice mixed 0 3

From **S. A. SIMON,** Birkdale.
Sept. 12th.
" The Mignonette have done splendid this year and has been much admired."

MIGNONETTE.

MIGNONETTE—DANIELS' GIANT RED.

These well-known, deliciously scented, hardy annuals are extremely easy of cultivation. Sow the seeds in the open border where intended to flower any time from the middle of March to the end of June, and thin out the plants to four or six inches apart as soon as they are large enough to handle. For Winter blooming sow any time in August, in pots of five or six inches diameter, and thin out the plants to three or five in a pot, keeping them as hardy as convenient before placing under glass for the Winter. The following list includes the finest varieties of recent introduction for garden or pot culture.

		per pkt. s. d.
738	**AUREA MAGNIFICA.** A splendid variety far in advance of any other yellow-flowered Mignonette yet sent out. The plants, which attain a height of about one foot, throw up numerous fine spikes of beautiful bright yellow deliciously scented flowers .. .. .. 6d. and	1 0
739	**DANIELS' CRIMSON KING.** About one foot high, with rich green foliage, and gigantic spikes of the darkest bright red blooms. It is of the most delicious fragrance, and will prove a decided acquisition .. .. 6d. and	1 0
740	**DANIELS' GIANT RED.** Grand variety, growing two feet high, and throwing up very large spikes of red, highly-scented flowers .. .. .. 6d. and	1 0
741	**DANIELS' GIANT WHITE.** A superb variety of robust habit, growing about 18 inches high, and bearing very large spikes of almost pure white deliciously fragrant flowers. Undoubtedly by far the finest of all white Mignonettes 6d. &	1 0
742	**DANIELS' GOLDEN QUEEN.** A beautiful compact-growing variety, with numerous sweet-scented spikes of yellow flowers .. .. .. 6d. and	1 0
743	**MACHET.** A fine, sturdy, compact-growing variety ; one of the best for pots .. .. .. 3d. and	0 6
744	**GIANT MACHET, SALMON-RED.** Splendid variety, a great improvement .. .. .. 6d. and	1 0
745	**A COLLECTION OF SIX CHOICE VARIETIES** ..	2 0
746	**LARGE-FLOWERED** .. — per lb. 6s. per oz. 6d.	0 2

From Mr. **G. HICKS,** St. Ives.
July 15th.
" The Sweet Pea seed I bought off you this Spring has given the most satisfactory results."

MYOSOTIS.
(Forget-me-not.)

MYOSOTIS—RUTH FISCHER.

A free-flowering and beautiful class of easily grown hardy perennials, which are in great request for Spring gardening. They will thrive in almost any soil, but prefer a partially-shaded and rather damp position. By sowing in June or July and potting-up, some charming flowers may be had in the greenhouse during the Winter and early Spring.

per pkt.—s. d.

747 **DANIELS' SKY BLUE.** A charming dwarf-growing variety, 6 inches high, with a profusion of lovely sky-blue flowers. A gem for pots ..   1 0

748 **DANIELS' INDIGO BLUE.** A very fine upright-growing variety, with long sprays of deep indigo blue flowers. First-rate for cutting. Height 1 foot ..   1 0

749 **STAR OF LOVE.** A beautiful compact-growing variety, only 5 inches high, covered with large bright blue flowers. A gem for pots..   1 0

750 **RUTH FISCHER.** A very beautiful variety of compact habit, with very large beautiful flowers of the most intense sky blue   1 6

751 **DISSITIFLORA, Large-flowered.** Sky blue. Height 9 inches. The best variety for Spring gardening ..   0 6

752 **DISSITIFLORA ALBA.** White, very fine ..   0 6

753 **PALUSTRIS SEMPERFLORENS.** The true marsh Forget-me-not. Height 9 inches. A continuous bloomer from Spring to Autumn ..   0 3

754 **RUPICOLA.** Deep sky blue, very dwarf. Exceedingly pretty and charming for pots ..   1 0

MYOSOTIDEUM NOBILE.

755 **THE NEW ZEALAND GIANT FORGET-ME-NOT.** A magnificent variety growing 18 inches to 2 feet high, with fine sprays of large deep blue flowers edged with white. The seed should be sown in a gentle heat, the plants pricked out and finally planted in open ground. Succeeds best in a somewhat shady position. Is easily grown ..   1 0

From Mr. F. LAYTHAM, Garsfield.
August 25th.
"Your Sweet Peas have done very well and look very beautiful, and people are admiring them every day."

MAURANDYA.
per pkt.—s. d.
Beautiful climbers for the greenhouse or conservatory.
756 **PURPUREA GRANDIFLORA.** Purplish blue ..   0 6

MAIZE.

757 **VARIEGATED JAPANESE.** A beautiful variety for pots in the greenhouse or for garden decoration. The plants grow about 4 feet high, and the broad green leaves are elegantly striped with white. Half-hardy annual..   0 3

758 **NEW GIANT VARIEGATED.** A fine variety growing about 6 feet high, with foliage handsomely striped with white, pink and yellow. Fine for sub-tropical garden ..   0 6

NEMOPHILA.

Extremely pretty early-flowering hardy annuals. Very useful for Spring gardening, beds or borders, or for pots in the greenhouse. The beautiful sky blue "Insignis" is very fine.

759 **INSIGNIS.** Lovely sky blue with conspicuous white eye. Charming. Height 6 inches ..   0 3

760   **ALBA.** Pure white ..   0 3

761 **MACULATA GRANDIFLORA.** White, spotted with violet blue. Height 6 inches ..   0 3

NIGELLA.
(Love in a Mist.)

A very pretty class of hardy annuals, blooming freely from seeds sown in March or April.

762 **MISS JEKYLL.** An attractive and beautiful annual, growing about 18 inches high, with lovely clear blue flowers and delicately divided elegant foliage. Excellent as a cut flower ..   0 6

763 **DAMASCENA FL. PL.** Light blue double flowers surrounded with finely divided foliage. Hardy annual. Height 9 inches   0 3

764 **HISPANICA ALBA.** White flowers. Hardy annual. Height 18 inches ..   0 3

NIGELLA—MISS JEKYLL.

NASTURTIUMS.

An exceedingly brilliant and indispensable class of easily grown half-hardy annuals. To obtain the best results the seeds should be sown in Spring on rather poor soil in the open ground, and in an exposed sunny position where they will continue in bloom for a long time. Grown in long lines as edgings or in beds or patches they are very showy. The following varieties grow about 1 foot high, and are best treated as hardy annuals.

TOM THUMB VARIETIES.

per pkt.—s. d.

		s	d
765	EMPRESS OF INDIA. Intense crimson scarlet, with dark leaves. Splendid variety of dwarf habit	0	3
766	SNOW QUEEN (new). Very compact and free-flowering variety. The blooms opening creamy and changing to pure white	0	4
767	QUEEN OF TOM THUMBS. Dark crimson flowers, with silver variegated foliage. Very pretty	0	6
768	CARMINE KING. Bright carmine	0	3
769	CÆRULEA ROSEA. Bluish rose	0	3
770	CRYSTAL PALACE GEM. Primrose, spotted maroon	0	3
771	FELTHAM BEAUTY. Rich brilliant scarlet	0	6
772	FIREBALL. Brilliant orange scarlet	0	6
773	GOLDEN KING. Rich yellow with dark foliage	0	3
774	KING OF TOM THUMBS. Brilliant scarlet	0	3
775	KING THEODORE. Dark crimson	0	3
776	LADY-BIRD. Golden yellow with scarlet spots	0	3
777	RUBY KING. Rosy carmine with dark foliage, fine	0	3
778	TERRA COTTA. Terra cotta tinted salmon	0	3
779	VESUVIUS. Rich apricot with dark foliage	0	3
780	YELLOW. Bright golden yellow	0	3
781	CHOICE MIXED. In splendid variety of colours	0	3

CLIMBING VARIETIES.

Brilliant and rapid growing annual climbers of splendid effect. First-class for walls or trellises or for covering rough fences or banks.

782	BUTTERFLY. Golden yellow with scarlet spots, fine	0	4
783	DEFIANCE. Brilliant scarlet	0	4
784	MIDNIGHT. Crimson maroon with dark foliage, splendid	0	4
785	MOONLIGHT. Pale yellow, beautiful	0	4
786	SUNLIGHT. Bright golden yellow	0	4
787	VESUVIUS. Deep apricot with dark foliage, very pretty	0	4
788	IVY-LEAVED. Scarlet flowers	0	4
789	SCARLET. Bright scarlet	0	3
790	GOLDEN YELLOW. Very fine	0	3
791	CHOICEST MIXED. In beautiful variety of colours	0	3

CANARY-BIRD NASTURTIUM.

(Tropæolum canariense.)

792	Well-known useful annual climber of elegant growth with singularly formed yellow flowers	0	3

NEMESIAS.

A magnificent class of beautiful half-hardy annuals, producing flowers of the most rare and brilliant colours. They are easily raised by sowing the seeds in boxes or pans of light soil, in March, and placing in a gentle heat or in a cool frame. Plant out in May 5 or 6 inches apart in an open sunny position.

per pkt.—s. d.

793	STRUMOSA GRANDIFLORA, ORANGE KING. Deep orange yellow, fine	1	0
794	" SCARLET BEAUTY. Rich brilliant scarlet	1	0
795	" Mixed. Beautiful shades of crimson, yellow, orange and rose to pure white. Height 12 to 15 inches	1	0
796	COMPACTA, BLUE GEM. Beautiful myosotis blue flowers, charming variety	0	6
797	" WHITE GEM. Pure white	0	6
798	" FIRE KING. Brilliant scarlet	0	6
799	" Mixed. A fine class of brilliant varieties. Height 9 inches	1	0

NIGHT-SCENTED STOCK.

See *Mathiola Bicornis*, page 93.

From Mr. N. WATSON, Wilton.
April 3rd.
"I'm pleased to say everything turned out remarkably well last year. The Tobacco Plants being greatly admired."

From Mr. J. Clemen's, Muryhill.
July 24th.
"The Seeds and Plants I had from you in the Spring have done well especially the Nasturtium."

NASTURTIUM, VESUVIUS.

NICOTIANA.

Beautiful half-hardy annuals for pots in the greenhouse, large beds or borders or for sub-tropical gardening. The Sanderæ and Affinis hybrids are very fine.

per pkt.—s. d.

800	AFFINIS. Large, white tubular flowers, deliciously fragrant in the evening. Height 3 feet	0	4
801	AFFINIS. New hybrids, mixed. Beautiful shades of pink, violet, mauve, &c. Very sweet scented. Height 3 feet	0	6
802	MACROPHYLLA GIGANTEA. The Giant Tobacco. Flowers pink. Height 6 feet	0	3
803	SANDERÆ HYBRIDS, Mixed. A splendid race of fine varieties. The flowers vary in colour from white, rose and lilac to dark crimson. Height 3 feet	0	6
804	SYLVESTRIS. A very fine variety growing 6 feet high, and bearing a profusion of pure white tubular flowers throughout the Summer	0	6

ŒNOTHERA.

(Evening Primrose.)

805	MACROCARPA. A fine hardy perennial with large pale yellow flowers. Height 6 inches	0	4
806	LAMARCKIANA. Splendid hardy perennial, with large primrose-yellow flowers. Height 4 feet	0	3

OXALIS.

807	ROSEA. Very pretty half-hardy perennial. Excellent for rockwork or pot culture. Flowers bright rose. Height 6 inches	0	3

DANIELS' EXHIBITION GIANT PANSIES.

DANIELS' SHOW & BEDDING PANSIES.

These beautiful, free-flowering, hardy plants are easily raised from seed, and will richly repay the small cost and trouble required to grow them to perfection. For blooming in Summer and Autumn, sow in February, March, and April, in pans or boxes of light rich soil placed in a gentle heat, and as soon as the young plants are large enough, prick out about two inches apart on rich soil to strengthen, and finally plant out six or eight inches apart, in ground into which a good quantity of well-decayed manure has been worked. Pansies delight in a somewhat shady position, and plenty of moisture in dry weather. The finest blooms are produced the second year, and grand flowers may be had by sowing in July or August in the open ground, and planting out in the following Spring into good rich soil.

		per pkt.—s.	d.
808	**DANIELS' EXHIBITION GIANT.** A superb strain of extra large and beautifully coloured flowers of the highest type, and including the most charming and richly coloured stained and blotched flowers. Many of the blooms from this strain will be found equal to the finest named varieties. Very choice mixed seed	5	0
809	„ „ „ „ „	2	6
810	„ „ „ „ smaller pkt.	1	6
811	**DANIELS' PRIZE BLOTCHED.** A splendid strain of brilliantly coloured flowers of the most exquisite shades of colour, the petals being handsomely stained or blotched, very choice	1	0
812	„ „ smaller pkt.	0	6
813	**DANIELS' GIANT WHITE.** Very large flowers, pure white, with dark purple eye; splendid	0	6
814	**DANIELS' GIANT YELLOW.** Very large, pure yellow, a very fine variety	0	6
815	**DANIELS' GIANT PURPLE.** Dark purple, very fine	0	6
816	**DANIELS' GIANT STRIPED.** Beautifully formed flowers, handsomely striped. The perfection of all striped varieties	0	6
817	**BUGNOT'S CHOICE MIXED.** Fine blotched varieties	1	0
818	**CARDINAL.** Bright red with darker blotch, the brightest red of all the Pansies, very fine	0	6
819	**GOLDEN YELLOW.** Fine spotted; a beautiful and distinct variety	0	6

		per pkt.—s.	d.
820	**LORD BEACONSFIELD.** Purple violet, the top petals shading off to white; splendid	0	6
821	**ORCHID-FLOWERED.** Large beautiful flowers, including some rare and attractive shades	6d. and 1	0
822	**ODIER'S FINE SPOTTED.** A superb strain of beautifully blotched flowers	6d. and 1	0
823	**PEACOCK.** A strikingly handsome and very distinct variety. The upper petals are a beautiful peacock blue, the flower shading off to velvety maroon and crimson	0	6
824	**PSYCHE.** Beautiful variety with handsome undulating petals, colour a rich velvety violet, the petals broadly margined with white	0	6
825	**TRIMARDEAU or GIANT.** A fine strain of beautiful large-flowered varieties	6d. and 1	0
826	„ **GOLDEN QUEEN** (new). Deep golden yellow with black eye	1	0
827	„ **CANDIDISSIMA.** A giant, pure white	0	6
828	„ **LIGHT BLUE.** Very fine	0	6
829	**MADAME PERRET, "The Wine Pansy."** A very fine and quite distinct class of large beautiful flowers that continue in bloom throughout the Summer. The colours may be described as a series of wine shades varying from deep port to claret and delightfully fragrant	6d. and 1	0
830	**MIXED GERMAN.** Ordinary varieties	0	3

BEDDING PANSIES.

The following varieties will be found exceedingly useful for making showy beds in Spring, where distinct colours are desirable, all the sorts being of compact habit and very free-flowering

		per pkt.—s.	d.
831	**CLIVEDEN YELLOW.** Bright yellow	0	6
832	„ **PURPLE.** Purplish maroon	0	6
833	„ **WHITE.** Fine	0	6
834	**EMPEROR WILLIAM.** Ultramarine blue	0	6
835	**SNOW QUEEN.** Pure satiny white; beautiful	0	6
836	**LIGHT BLUE.** Beautiful	0	6

		per pkt.—s.	d.
837	**YELLOW GEM.** Golden yellow	0	6
838	**RICH PURPLE.** Fine dark	0	6
839	**GOLD-MARGINED.** Splendid	0	6
840	**KING OF THE BLACKS.** Jet black	0	6
841	**PURPLE AND GOLD.** Golden yellow, the upper petals purple; very showy	0	6

842 Six choice varieties, 1s. 6d.

BEDDING VIOLAS OR TUFTED PANSIES.

A PROFUSE-FLOWERING and invaluable class of hardy perennial bedding plants, continuing in bloom from early Spring till late in the Autumn months. Highly desirable for Spring gardening, and afford some charming effects in association with Spring-flowering Bulbs, &c. The following list includes the finest varieties in cultivation, and which we highly recommend. For blooming the same year, sow the seeds in early Spring in a gentle heat, prick out to strengthen, harden off, and plant out in April or May where intended to flower. For Spring flowering the following year, sow the seeds in May or June, prick out on Nursery beds and plant out in Autumn or early Spring where intended to flower.

		per pkt.—s.	d.
843	**AN ASSORTMENT OF 6 SPLENDID VARIETIES**	2	6
844	**ADMIRATION.** Splendid dark violet, yellow eye	0	6
845	**ARDWELL GEM.** Large rayless primrose-coloured flowers. A fine bedder	0	6
846	**BLUE PERFECTION.** Bluish purple	0	6
847	**GOLDEN GEM.** Rich golden yellow	0	6
848	**MAGNIFICENT.** Deep rich purple	0	6
849	**MARCHIONESS.** Pure white, very fine	0	6
850	**SNOWFLAKE.** Splendid pure white	0	6
851	**CHOICEST MIXED**	1	0
852	„ „ smaller pkt.	0	6

DANIELS' SUPERB PETUNIAS.

Petunias in their many beautiful varieties form a highly interesting and desirable class of free-flowering plants for pot or garden culture; those of the Grandiflora section, both single and double-flowered, being especially valuable. The blooms of these are of immense size, beautifully formed, and of the most charming and delicate colours; some of the flowers are exquisitely veined or pencilled, others blotched or striped. The new "Fringed" varieties, both double and single, produce some charming flowers, the edges of the petals being elegantly cut or fringed, whilst the colours are most varied and beautiful. The seed we offer has been carefully saved from fecundated flowers of the finest varieties; but as Petunias raised from seed have a tendency to "sport," we cannot guarantee more than sixty or seventy per cent. of flowers true to description. All will, however, be found well worth growing, and occasionally some fine novelties may be secured. Petunias for indoor cultivation may be sown in January or early in February, but those intended for bedding out do not require to be sown before March. A soil composed of two parts leaf-mould and one part loam, with the addition of a little sharp sand, forms an excellent compost for these, but the seeds being very small require special care in sowing. Fill your pots or seed-pans to near the rim and press the soil down firmly and evenly, sow thinly, and cover the seeds very slightly with fine soil, sprinkle gently with a fine rose water-pot, and place in a gentle heat of sixty or sixty-five degrees, not higher, and keep nicely moist. As soon as the young plants can be handled, prick them out about one inch apart in pots to strengthen, and when sufficiently advanced in growth pot off singly into small pots, gradually harden off when established, and plant out about the middle of May, or shift into large pots as required. In planting Petunias, out of doors, ground should be selected that has not been freshly manured, otherwise a superabundant foliage will retard the flowering.

PETUNIA, HYBRIDA GRANDIFLORA.

PETUNIAS—Daniels' Superb Fringed.

A beautiful class, producing large and strikingly handsome flowers, the edges of the petals being elegantly laciniated or fringed.

			per pkt.—s.	d.
853	SINGLE, PURE WHITE. Beautiful		1	0
854	" BRILLIANT ROSE AND WHITE. Splendid variety		1	0
855	" VERY CHOICE MIXED		2	6
854	" " smaller pkt.		1	0
857	DOUBLE, AN ASSORTMENT OF 6 SUPERB VARIETIES		2	6
858	" BRILLIANT ROSE. Beautiful bright rose; most charming variety		1	0
859	" LADY OF THE LAKE. Beautiful large fringed, pure white, double flowers, superb		1	0
860	" CHOICEST MIXED		2	6
861	" " smaller pkt.		1	0

DOUBLE-FLOWERED PETUNIAS.

Saved from carefully hybridised flowers, will produce a good percentage of large, handsome, double flowers.

			per pkt.—s.	d.
862	VERY CHOICE MIXED		2	6
863	" smaller pkt.		1	0
864	AN ASSORTMENT OF 6 CHOICE SORTS		2	6
865	PURE WHITE. Beautiful		1	0
866	BRILLIANT ROSE. Splendid		1	0
867	MINIATURE. Small, double flowers, charming variety		1	0

PETUNIA HYBRIDA GRANDIFLORA.

A fine and distinct class of beautiful, large-flowering varieties producing blooms of immense size, and of the most charming colours; much superior to the old varieties of Petunia hybrida. The plants are robust in habit of growth, and admirably suited as pot-plants for the greenhouse or conservatory or for garden decoration.

			per pkt.—s.	d.
868	AN ASSORTMENT OF 6 BEAUTIFUL VARIETIES		2	6
869	ALBA GRANDIFLORA. Immense pure white flowers; beautiful		0	6
870	BRILLIANT ROSE. With white eye; superb variety		0	6
871	PURPUREA. Immense flowers of the deepest blood crimson colour; magnificent		0	6
872	MACULATA. Very large flowers handsomely blotched or striped		0	6
873	VIOLACEA. Rich velvety violet blue; fine		0	6
874	VERY CHOICE MIXED, IN BEAUTIFUL VARIETY		2	6
875	" " " " smaller pkt.		1	0
876	" " " " "		0	6

DWARF BEDDING PETUNIAS.

A very pretty free-flowering class of dwarf compact-growing varieties, exceedingly useful for massing in beds, or as an edging to shrubbery borders, &c. The plants grow only about 6 or 8 inches high.

			per pkt.—s.	d.
877	DWARF, PURE WHITE. Beautiful variety, with pure satiny-white flowers		1	0
878	DWARF, ROSY CARMINE. Brilliant rosy-carmine, with white throat		1	0
879	DWARF, STRIPED. Beautiful bright rosy-purple, striped with white		1	0
880	DWARF, MIXED		6d. and	1	0

PETUNIAS—Ordinary Class.

			per pkt.—s.	d.
881	CHOICEST MIXED. Beautiful showy varieties for beds or borders		0	6
883	" " smaller pkt.		0	3

From D. HUTCH, Esq., Butterant.

July 2nd.

"I am very pleased with the Petunia Plants you sent me, they are grand."

PINKS—Garden.

883   **MRS. SINKINS.** A fine double-flowered pure white, deliciously scented; quite hardy .. .. .. per pkt. 1s. 0d.

884   **HOMER.** A fine double dark rose with a crimson centre. A fine variety .. .. per pkt. 1s. 0d.

All Flower Seeds quoted in 3d. packets may be had at 2/6 per dozen.

DANIELS' SELECTED POPPIES.

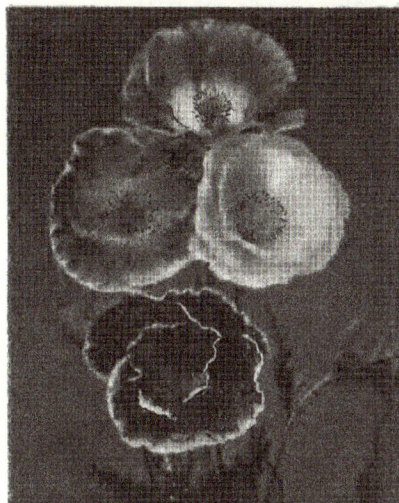

SHIRLEY POPPIES DANIELS' SELECTED.

ANNUAL POPPIES.

A brilliant and charmingly effective group of hardy annuals of great value for garden or shrubbery decoration. The single-flowered varieties are especially valuable as cut flowers, and if cut when the blooms are just beginning to expand, will retain their beauty for a long period. The beautiful Shirley Poppy, sown at intervals from early Spring to the end of June, will give a charming display quite into the Autumn

		per pkt.—s. d.
885	**DANIELS' SELECTED SHIRLEY.** The fine strain we offer has been carefully selected and includes all the most brilliant and exquisite shades of colour. Highly recommended for cut flowers. Height 2 feet. Choicest mixed .. 3d. and	0 6
886	**THE TULIP POPPY** (Papaver glaucum). Vivid scarlet, very effective. Height 15 inches	0 3
887	**CARDINAL.** Large double flowers, beautifully fringed, of an intense scarlet colour. Height 18 inches ..	0 3
888	**CHAMOIS-ROSE, Double.** Large, beautiful double flowers of a lovely salmony-pink shade and handsomely fringed ; charming variety. Height 2 feet	0 6
889	**WHITE SWAN.** Large, double, pure white flowers, beautifully fringed. Height 2 feet	0 3
890	**CARNATION-FLOWERED, Double.** Fine double flowers in many brilliant colours. 2 feet.. ..	0 3
891	**FRENCH RANUNCULUS.** A very fine class of handsome brilliantly-coloured double flowers. Height 18 inches ..	0 3
892	**PÆONY-FLOWERED, Double.** A fine race of large handsome double flowers in beautiful variety of colour. Height 3 feet. Choice mixed	0 3

PERENNIAL POPPIES.

The seeds of the beautiful Nudicaule varieties, for blooming the same year from seed, should be sown in February or March in a gentle heat, and planted out in May. The large-flowered Orientale varieties are best sown thinly in the open ground in May or June, and transplanted in Autumn or early Spring where intended to bloom. The same treatment will apply to the dwarf Alpinum and other perennial sorts.

NUDICAULE (The Iceland Poppy)—
Charming dwarf-growing hardy perennial, with beautifully coloured single flowers on long slender stems. Will bloom the first year from seed. Height 1 foot.

			per pkt.—s. d.
893	"	**MINIATUM.** Brilliant orange scarlet	0 6
894	"	**ALBUM.** Pure white	0 6
895	"	**CROCEUM.** Bright yellow	0 6
896	"	**VERY CHOICE MIXED**	0 6
897	"	**NEW EXCELSIOR STRAIN.** Many exquisite shades of colour	1 0
898	**ALPINUM.** Beautiful little hardy perennial, growing only 6 inches high. Flowers of various pretty colours. Excellent for rockwork		0 6
899	**ORIENTALE HYBRIDS, Choice Mixed.** Magnificent hardy perennials, with large single flowers, including beautiful shades of red, rose, lilac, mauve, &c. Height 3 feet ..		0 6
900	**ORIENTALE.** Immense, brilliant scarlet flowers, very hardy. Height 3 feet		0 6

PORTULACA.

A brilliant class of half-hardy annuals. The plants are of a dwarf spreading habit and are first rate for dry rockeries or an edging on warm borders. The seeds may be sown out of doors in April where intended to bloom. Height 6 inches.

			per pkt.—s. d.
901	**GRANDIFLORA ALBA FL. PL.** White, double flowers ..		0 6
902	"	**AUREA FL. PL.** Golden yellow ..	0 6
903	"	**SPLENDENS FL. PL.** Brilliant crimson ..	0 6
904	"	**DOUBLE, Choice Mixed** .. 6d. and	1 0
905	"	**SINGLE, Choice Mixed** ..	0 6

PERILLA.

Valuable plants for bedding with richly coloured dark foliage.

906	**ATROPURPUREA LACINIATA.** Handsome laciniated foliage, deeper in colour than P. nankinensis. 2 feet ..	0 3
907	**NANKINENSIS.** Fine dark leaves. 2 feet ..	0 3

PHACELIA CAMPANULARIA.

908	A showy hardy annual from California, growing about 1 foot high, with bell-shaped flowers of a bright blue colour, which continue for a long time	0 3

PYRETHRUM—GOLDEN FEATHER.
(Pyrethrum parthenifolium aureum.)

Exceedingly useful for bedding. Sow the seeds under glass in February or March and plant out in May for the best results. The plant is a hardy perennial, but plants that have withstood the Winter are not satisfactory.

909	**GOLDEN FEATHER, Selected.** Bright yellow foliage. Fine for bedding. Height 6 inches ..	0 3
910	**LACINIATUM PERFECTION.** Bright yellow, finely cut bright yellow leaves ; very pretty. Height 6 inches ..	0 6
911	**SELAGINOIDES.** A beautiful fern-leaved variety with bright golden foliage. A splendid bolder. Height 6 inches ..	0 6

PYRETHRUM HYBRIDUM.

Very fine hardy herbaceous perennials. Excellent for mixed borders, and useful for cut flowers.

912	**DOUBLE-FLOWERED, Choicest Mixed.** Double and semi-double flowers. Height 2 feet.. ..	1 6
913	**SINGLE-FLOWERED.** Splendid mixed, saved from a fine collection. Height 2 feet	0 6

PHLOX DRUMMONDI.

All the varieties of this beautiful class of annuals are worthy of extensive cultivation, especially those of the grandiflora class, which produce such a profusion and diversity of their large beautifully formed and brilliantly coloured flowers. Those of the compacta section growing only about four to six inches in height are also highly desirable for massing or beds, or for edgings, producing an effect that can probably be attained by no other plant.

Cultivation.—Sow the seeds in February, March, or early in April, in pans or boxes of light rich soil; sow thinly, press down firmly, cover lightly, water, and place in a gentle heat. The young plants will be up in a few days, and soon as they can be fairly handled they should be pricked out about two inches apart in pans or boxes to strengthen, or potted singly into small pots; keep close for a few days, and when they are established give abundance of air, placing close to the glass to induce a sturdy growth. May is soon enough for planting out, and a rather dry and sunny position is to be preferred. The dwarf kinds should be planted about eight inches apart; the others, which grow from nine inches to one foot in height, with a spreading habit, may be planted one foot or more apart. Towards the end of April and during May, the seeds may be sown where intended to bloom in the open ground, and in an ordinary season a fine display may be had quite into the Autumn

PHLOX DRUMMONDI GRANDIFLORA

PHLOX DRUMMONDI GRANDIFLORA.

☞ The grandiflora varieties form a magnificent class; the plants are robust in habit, and the flowers, which are of various rich and beautiful colours, have in many of the varieties large, conspicuous white eyes; the individual blooms are of fine substance and scarcely inferior in size to the perennial sorts. A decided improvement on the old varieties of P. Drummondi. The plants grow about one foot high.

				per pkt.—s.	d.
910	AN ASSORTMENT OF 12 SPLENDID VARIETIES			3	6
920	" 8 " "			2	6
921	ALBA. Pure white	..	..	0	4
922	ATROPURPUREA. Dark purple	..	..	0	4
923	CARMINEA. Beautiful carmine, white eye	..	..	0	4
924	COCCINEA. Brilliant scarlet	..	..	0	4
925	ROSEA. Delicate rose, white eye	..	..	0	4
926	VIOLACEA. Violet blue, white eye	..	..	0	4
927	SPLENDENS. Fine vivid crimson	..	..	0	4
928	CHOICEST MIXED. In beautiful variety			1	0
929	" "	..	smaller pkt.	0	6

PHLOX DRUMMONDI.
Dwarf Compact Varieties.

A charming class of beautiful dwarf-growing varieties. The plants grow 4 to 6 inches in height and 6 or 8 inches across, and are almost covered with bloom. Splendid for edgings or beds.

				per pkt.—s.	d.
930	FIREBALL. An exceedingly fine dwarf-growing and profuse-flowering variety, height six inches, brilliant scarlet; fine for pots or edging			0	6
931	SNOWBALL. Same height and habit as the preceding, but bearing quite a profusion of large, pure white flowers	..	..	0	6
932	ROSY GEM. Bright rose with white eye. Charming variety		..	0	4
933	CARMINEA. Beautiful carmine..	..	..	0	4
934	ATROPURPUREA. Dark purple	..	..	0	4
935	DELICATA. Blush, very charming	..	..	0	4
936	SPLENDENS. Vivid crimson, with white eye	..	..	0	4
937	EXTRA CHOICE MIXED. In beautiful variety			1	0
938	" "	..	smaller pkt.	0	6
939	SIX BRILLIANT VARIETIES			2	0

PHLOX DRUMMONDI CUSPIDATA.
The New Star Phloxes.

A very pretty class, with neat, stellate flowers of the most beautiful colours; very useful as cut flowers.

				per pkt.—s.	d.
940	CHOICEST MIXED. In beautiful variety			1	0
941	" "	..	smaller pkt.	0	6

PHLOX DRUMMONDI—Original Class.
VERY SHOWY AND FREE-FLOWERING.

				per pkt.—s.	d.
942	CHOICEST MIXED. In beautiful variety			0	6
943	" "	..	smaller pkt.	0	3

PHLOX DRUMMONDI, Intermediate.

An exceedingly free-flowering and beautiful class of great value for showy beds or borders. The plants, which are of a compact habit of growth, attain a height of about 8 inches.

			per pkt.—s.	d.
914	BRILLIANT SCARLET. Splendid	..	0	6
915	ROSE. Beautiful colour	..	0	6
916	PURE WHITE. Very fine	..	0	6
917	DARK PURPLE. Rich violet purple	..	0	6
918	VERY CHOICE MIXED. All colours	..	0	6

PERENNIAL PHLOX.

Splendid hardy perennials for large beds or borders. The seed we offer has been saved from a fine collection of beautifully coloured named flowers.

			per pkt.—s.	d.				per pkt.—s.	d.
944	TALL VARIETIES. Very choice mixed. Height 3 feet		1	0	945	DWARF VARIETIES. Choice varieties. Height 2 feet		1	0

PENTSTEMONS.

These beautiful free-flowering plants succeed admirably when treated as half-hardy annuals, and sown in February or March on a gentle heat and planted out in May they will commence blooming in July and continue to throw up their lovely spikes of flowers till late Autumn. The new large-flowered hybrids produce some charming flowers, many of them being equal to the finest named sorts. The plants grow about 18 inches high.

		per pkt.—s. d.
946	NEW LARGE-FLOWERED HYBRIDS. Choicest mixed, from a magnificent strain	1 0
947	smaller packet	0 6

PASSIFLORA CÆRULEA.
(The Passion Flower.)

948	GRANDIFLORA. Splendid hardy climber, with large pale blue flowers. Much superior to the old variety	0 6

PEA, EVERLASTING.
(Lathyrus latifolius.)

Splendid hardy perennial climbers for walls, trellises, &c.

949	RED or SCARLET	0 4
950	WHITE. Pure white	0 4
951	ROSE. Pale rose, charming	0 4

PELARGONIUMS—GERANIUMS.

Sow in February or March in pots or pans of light rich soil, covering the seeds to the depth of about a quarter of an inch, and place in a heat of about sixty-five or seventy degrees. Pot off the young plants singly into small pots, and shift into larger as these fill with roots. With liberal treatment these will bloom the first year, and, although many will not be up to the standard of first-class florists' flowers, some really beautiful varieties may be expected from a good strain of seed.

952	FRENCH BLOTCHED or REGAL. Beautiful large-flowered varieties, with handsomely blotched petals	2 6
953	smaller pkt.	1 6
954	FANCY VARIETIES. Very choice mixed	1 6
955	ZONAL. Single-flowered, from finest named sorts	1 0
956	IVY-LEAVED. Single and double-flowered varieties. Choice mixed	1 6

POLYANTHUS.

A beautiful free-flowering class of hardy perennials which has been highly improved of late years. The plants are about six inches high, and bloom about the same time as primroses. The large-flowered varieties in their many beautiful colours are very charming and should be used extensively for Spring gardening. The blue varieties are very fine.

		per pkt.—s. d.
957	LARGE-FLOWERED, CHOICEST MIXED. A very fine strain of beautiful varieties, very free-flowering	1 0
958	smaller pkt.	0 6
959	POLYANTHUS-PRIMROSE (bunch-flowered). Choicest mixed hybrids, special selection	1 6
960	" New blue flowered. Beautiful varieties, producing large heads of lovely dark blue and purple flowers. Very handsome and distinct	1s. 6d. and 2 6
961	NEW GIANT, Crimson	Fine showy varieties for	1 0
962	" White	bedding out, &c.	1 0
963	" Yellow		1 0
964	GOLD-LACED. Fine varieties, from a choice collection of beautifully laced flowers	6d. and 1 0
965	HOSE-IN-HOSE VARIETIES. Choice mixed	1 0

LARGE-FLOWERED POLYANTHUS.

HARDY PRIMROSES.

Profuse flowering and very charming hardy perennials, growing six inches high, invaluable for Spring gardening. The hybrid varieties vary in colour from the palest and most delicate sulphur yellow, through all the soft shades of rose and purple to the most intense and brilliant crimson. From the beginning of April to the middle of May they are generally in full bloom, and present a most lovely appearance. A partially shaded border, with a westerly aspect, will grow them to perfection in almost any moderately rich soil.

966	LARGE-FLOWERED HYBRIDS. Grand strain of beautiful high-coloured flowers, all of the true Primrose type, with the flowers large and brilliant; very fine	1 6
967	VERY CHOICE MIXED. From a good collection	1 0
968	WHITE QUEEN. Pure white, beautiful	1 0
969	BLUE-FLOWERED (G. F. Wilson's). Rich purple blue, very fine and quite distinct	1 6
970	COMMON YELLOW	0 6

DANIELS' SUPERB FRINGED PRIMULAS

☞ It is with very much pleasure that we offer the grand strains of Primulas named below, all of which have been specially grown for our retail trade, and will give the highest satisfaction. The flowers will be found of great size and perfect form, combined with the most brilliant and charming colours, and a habit of plant which leaves nothing to be desired.

The beautiful varieties of Primula sinensis may be sown in March, April, May, and June. The earlier sown are, however, to be preferred for making fine strong plants with an abundance of bloom. Great care must be taken to have a well-drained pot or seed-pan filled to within half an inch of the top, with sifted leaf-mould : leave the surface rather rough, and sprinkle the seeds thinly upon it. The most successful raisers do not cover with soil, but after sowing the seed press down the surface tolerably firm, and place a square of glass over the pot. Place in a good strong heat, shaded from strong light, and water very gently when the soil becomes dry. The seeds will germinate in two or three weeks, after which remove the glass and keep in a shady position. Pot off into small pots when the young plants are about half an inch above ground, and place near the glass in the frame or greenhouse. In their after culture Primulas should be kept as near as convenient to the glass, have plenty of fresh air, and never be kept for a long period in a high temperature or in a dry heated atmosphere.

DANIELS' WHITE PERFECTION.

		per pkt.—s. d.	
974	"KING GEORGE V." (new). Very large, beautifully fringed flowers, of the most intense crimson, the darkest variety yet offered .. .. 1s. 6d. and	2	6
975	ALBA MAGNIFICA. Beautifully fringed, pure white flowers	1	6
976	ORANGE KING (new). A superb variety of quite a new colour in Primulas. The beautiful orange colour in the bud and the orange salmon shade around the edge of the terra-cotta coloured petals give the flower a most pleasing and distinct appearance .. .. 1s. 6d. and	2	6
977	"QUEEN MARY" (new). A magnificent new variety of the true giant type. The colour is a most lovely rose-pink, the flowers are of great size with large and very stout petals, whilst the plant is of a fine erect habit of growth, and very free flowering .. .. .. 1s. 6d. and	2	6
978	NEW GIANT PINK. The finest of the Giant Primulas, blooms nearly 3 inches across, of a lovely bright rosy pink colour with petals of great substance. Magnificent .. 1s. 6d. and	2	6
979	NEW GIANT SALMON. Beautiful salmon pink; immense flowers .. .. 1s. 6d. and	2	6
980	THE DUCHESS (new). Beautiful white, with rosy-carmine zone surrounding a yellow eye ; splendid .. 1s. 6d. and	2	6
981	CRIMSON KING (new). The darkest coloured and richest of all Crimson Primulas, splendid flowers, with a black ring round the centres ; most superb variety .. 1s. 6d. and	2	6
982	DANIELS' QUEEN OF ROSES. Beautiful soft rosy pink, a flower of great size and substance .. 1s. 6d. and	2	6
983	DANIELS' WHITE PERFECTION. A beautiful pure white of the fern-leaved type, of splendid habit .. 1s. 6d. and	2	6
984	DANIELS' SUPERB BLUE. Carefully saved from beautifully fringed flowers of perfect form and of the deepest shade of blue ; splendid colour .. .. 1s. 6d. and	2	6
985	DANIELS' EMPRESS, GIANT WHITE. Immense white flowers, borne on strong stems, with very robust foliage ; a grand variety .. .. .. 1s. 6d. and	2	6
933	DANIELS' CHOICEST MIXED. In beautiful variety. Including some of the finest .. .. 1s. 0d. and	2	0

DOUBLE-FLOWERED FRINGED VARIETIES.

Exceedingly useful for flowering in the greenhouse during Winter.

987	DOUBLE, PURE WHITE FRINGED. Useful for cutting ..	1	6
988	" CHOICEST MIXED. In splendid variety 1s. 6d. and	2	6
989	PRIMULA FORBESI RUBER. A beautiful little plant, with bright rosy purple flowers. Blooms 3 months from sowing	1	0
990	" MALACOIDES. Whorls of pale lilac flowers, very early blooming	1	0
991	" ALBA. A pure white-flowered variety of the beautiful little lilac primrose	1	0

PRIMULA STELLATA (Star Primula).

An improved form of the Star Primula, differing only in the formation of its flowers, which are nearly equal in substance and size to some of the best of the Chinese varieties. The snow-white flowers are beautifully fringed, and stand well above the dark foliage and purple stems, which make it even more attractive than those of the older type.

		per pkt.—s. d.	
971	KING OF THE STARS. Magnificent variety, immense heads of deep crimson-carmine flowers	1	6
972	CHOICEST MIXED STAR. A charming mixture	1	6
973	GIANT WHITE STAR. The grandest White Star Primula yet raised. The pure white massive flowers are produced in great abundance, and contrast admirably with the rich dark foliage ; splendid for cutting	1	6

HARDY AND HALF-HARDY PRIMULAS.

PRIMULA OBCONICA.

A beautiful class of free-flowering half-hardy perennials growing about eight inches high, admirably suited for pot culture in the cool greenhouse. The blooms are very useful for cutting.

		per pkt.—s. d.	
992	ALBA GRANDIFLORA. Pure white, with small yellow eye	1	0
993	ROSEA Large, finely-formed, bright rosy lilac flowers	1	0
994	VERY CHOICE MIXED. In beautiful variety	1	0

PRIMULA JAPONICA.

		per pkt.— s. d.	
995	A very fine hardy plant, growing about 18 inches high, with whorls of various coloured flowers. Choice mixed seed ..	0	6
996	PRIMULA KEWENSIS. Beautiful half-hardy Autumn and Winter bloomer for the greenhouse Flowers bright yellow, 1 ft.	1	0

PRIMULA ROSEA GRANDIFLORA.

997	A charming dwarf hardy species, with very pretty bright rose-coloured flowers. The plant grows only about six inches high, and is an excellent subject for dry rockeries ..	1	6

REHMANNIA ANGULATA.

per pkt.—s. d.

998 **PINK PERFECTION.** A charming half-hardy herbaceous
perennial of fine effect for conservatory decoration .. 1 0

ROCKET, SWEET.
(Hesperis matronalis.)

Deliciously fragrant Spring-flowering hardy herbaceous perennial

999 **EARLY DWARF WHITE.** Very free-flowering and sweet-
scented. Height 1 foot 0 6
1000 **PURPLE.** Bright purple. Height 2 feet .. 0 3
1001 **WHITE.** Very sweet-scented. Height 2 feet .. 0 3

RUDBECKIA NEUMANNI.

1002 A splendid hardy perennial growing about 2 feet high, with
bright golden yellow flowers and black disc. An almost
continuous bloomer, and excellent for cut flowers .. 0 6

SAPONARIA.

1003 **SCARLET QUEEN.** A compact-growing hardy annual, with
numerous bright rosy scarlet flowers. Excellent for beds or
edgings. Height 6 inches 0 3

SCABIOSA.

1004 **CAUCASICA.** Splendid hardy perennial producing large bluish
mauve flowers. Sown early under glass and planted out will
bloom the first year from seed. Height 2 feet .. 1 0
1005 ,, **ALBA.** Splendid large pure white flowers,
excellent for cutting 1 0

SENSITIVE PLANT.
(Mimosa pudica.)

1006 A beautiful greenhouse shrub with handsome acacia-like
foliage 0 6

SILENE.

Brilliant, profuse-flowering hardy annuals of dwarf compact growth.
1007 **COMPACTA, DWARF ROSE.** Beautiful bright rose, very
compact. The best for Spring bedding 0 4

STREPTOCARPUS.

SALPIGLOSSIS.

A charming class of half-hardy annuals of great value for large beds
or borders, and exceedingly useful for cut flowers. The large blooms are
beautifully veined, and vary in colour from dark purple and crimson to
orange, golden yellow and scarlet. Sow in the open ground in March to
April, and thin out. Height 3 feet.

SALPIGLOSSIS—LARGE-FLOWERED VARIETIES.

LARGE-FLOWERED VARIETIES— per pkt.—s. d.
1008 **CRIMSON.** Veined with gold 0 6
1009 **GOLDEN YELLOW.** Very fine 0 6
1010 **RICH PURPLE.** Fine colour 0 6
1011 **BLUE.** Veined with gold, beautiful 0 6
1012 **SIX BEAUTIFUL VARIETIES.** Separate 1 6
1013 **VERY CHOICE MIXED** .. .. 6d. and 1 0

SOLANUM HYBRIDUM.

1014 Half-hardy compact-growing shrub, bearing pretty orange-
scarlet fruit. Very useful for table decoration .. 0 6

STREPTOCARPUS.

1015 **DANIELS' LARGE-FLOWERING HYBRIDS.** A very fine
strain of large beautiful flowers, varying in colour through
all the shades of pink, lavender-blue, purple, &c., to pure
white. Greenhouse perennials. Height 9 inches .. 1 6

From **H. SKEGGS,** Stevenage.
Aug. 8th.
" I took eleven Prizes at our Show with your **Seeds,** and second Prize being second
with your **Flowers.**"

From **W. J. SHABBOTT,** Oxon.
Aug. 13th.
" I may say that I took First and Second at our Flower Show, so I can recommend
your Seeds to my friends."

SALVIA.

Beautiful free-flowering half-hardy perennials, splendidly effective for beds or borders in Summer and Autumn.

per pkt.—s. d
1016 **MINIATURE, New Dwarf.** A splendid variety, with large pure scarlet flowers. First class for pot culture or for bedding. Height 1 foot
1017 **SPLENDENS.** Brilliant scarlet. Height 2 feet   ..   0 6
1018 **ARGENTEA.** Silvery white foliage, very fine. Height 6 inches 0 4
1019 **PATENS.** Intense pure blue. A fine variety for beds. Height 2 feet 1 0

SALVIA—BLUE BEARD.

1020 A showy hardy annual growing about 18 inches high, with spikes of bright bluish purple bracts, very showy   .. 0 3

SCABIOUS—SWEET.

Beautiful hardy biennials with large fragrant flowers of many rich and beautiful shades of colour, blooming the first year from seed. Sow in March under glass and transplant or sow in April in the open ground and treat as hardy annuals.

1021 **THE BRIDE.** Large double pure white flowers, very sweet. Height 3 feet   ..   0 3
1022 **FIRE KING.** Deep crimson, large double flowers. A splendid variety   ..   0 6
1023 **ROSE PINK.** Beautiful variety. Height 3 feet   ..   0 6
1024 **BLACK PRINCE.** Large double flowers of the richest dark purple colour. Height 3 feet   ..   0 6
1025 **MAUVE QUEEN.** Fine double flowers of a beautiful lilac-mauve colour. Height 3 feet   ..   0 6
1026 **6 LARGE-FLOWERED VARIETIES, Separate.** Our selection 1 0
1027 **LARGE-FLOWERED,** Splendid double mixed. Height 3 feet 3d. and 0 6

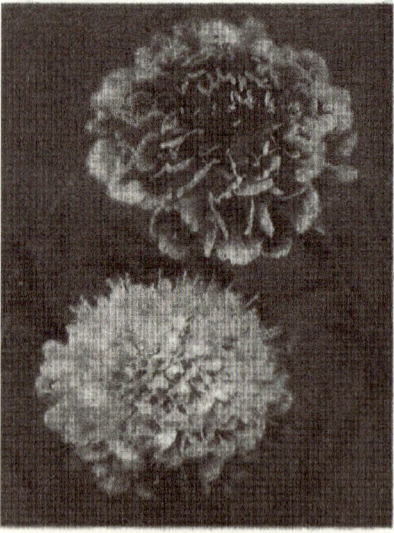

LARGE-FLOWERED SWEET SCABIOUS.

SCHIZANTHUS.

A beautiful class of half-hardy annuals of elegant growth which succeed well grown out of doors. They are also of great value for pots in the greenhouse where they are charmingly effective. The flowers vary in colour from delicate pink and rose to carmine-yellow, apricot, mauve, crimson and other lovely shades. The long sprays of bloom being very useful when cut, and last a long time.

The outdoor cultivation is very easy; the seed should be sown thinly in clumps during April or May, and the plants thinned out to about 6 or 8 inches apart, these will give a profusion of flowers all summer, for earlier blooming the seed may be sown in February or March in a slight heat for planting out in May. For pot culture seed may be sown at almost any time, and splendid specimens may be had by sowing in August or September for Winter blooming, about five plants in a six inch pot being most suitable.

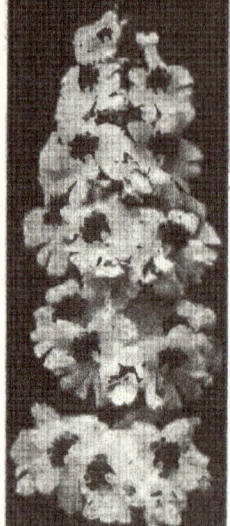

SCHIZANTHUS WISETONENSIS EXCELSIOR.

per pkt.—s. d.
1028 **WISETONENSIS, Daniels' Excelsior Strain.** This magnificent strain has been grown and specially selected for us at Wiseton during the past Summer by Mr. Musk, who rightly claims this as the finest strain of these beautiful flowers in existence. The plants, which grow from 1½ to 2 feet high, are more robust in their habit of growth, and the flowers are much larger than those of those hitherto offered. The individual blooms, which are of good substance, frequently measure 1½ to 1¾ inches across, and have a wonderful range of the most beautiful colours known in this class, and which contrast admirably with the elegant fern-like foliage. The lighter coloured varieties, which largely predominate, have a ground colour of buff, white, pink, rose, yellow, etc., marked and surrounded by a deeper shade, and are exquisitely beautiful. This strain is a grand acquisition, and will be found splendid for pot culture or for exhibition   .. 1s. 6d. and 2 6
1029 **WISETONENSIS.** Daniels' Selected strain, charming shades of beautiful colours, very fine. Height 18 inches 6d. and 1 0
1030 **HYBRIDUS GRANDIFLORUS.** Very fine large-flowered varieties. Height 18 inches 0 6
1031 **PINNATUS.** Lilac spotted. Height 18 inches   ..   0 3
1032 Dwarf rose, very pretty. Height 1 foot   .. 0 6
1033 **RETUSUS ALBUS.** Flowers large pure white, blotched with yellow. Height 18 inches 0 4
1034 **CHOICE MIXED.** Showy varieties 0 3

SWEET PEAS.

See pages 71 to 74.

SWEET WILLIAM.

We have given great attention for several years past to our splendid strain of these, which we have much pleasure in offering. The sorts embrace a great variety of the choicest Auricula-eyed, margined, selfs, &c., of the most brilliant types. The flowers are beautifully formed, of good substance, and are almost invariably awarded First Prize wherever exhibited. Sow the seeds thinly, in any sheltered place out of doors, in May or early in June, and plant out one foot apart in August or September where intended to bloom.

per pkt.—s. d.
1035 **DANIELS' GIANT PRIZE AURICULA-EYED.** A magnificent strain of the choicest large-flowered Auricula-eyed varieties. The flowers perfectly formed and of the most brilliant and beautiful colours. Highly recommended; mixed seed .. 1 0
1036   smaller pkt. 0 6
1037 **DARK CRIMSON.** Splendid colour 0 3
1038 **PINK BEAUTY.** Large heads of lovely salmony-rose coloured flowers 0 6
1039 **SCARLET BEAUTY** (new). Intense scarlet, very showy .. 0 6
1040 **PURE WHITE, DOUBLE.** Fine 0 3
1041 **MIXED.** Beautiful varieties, including Auricula-eyed and self coloured flowers .. .. .. 3d. and 0 6

The "HORTICULTURAL ADVERTISER" for July 6th, referring to our Strain of Sweet Williams says :—

"The Auricula-Eyed forms are delightful, and represent one of the best strains we have seen for years past. The trusses are good, and most of the pips 1½ inches in diameter ; the rich crimson and purple markings leave no opening for criticism by the most exacting florist, being perfectly even, and showing no tendency to run into the pure white of the ground colour. It is pleasing to find these old-fashioned favourites still receive in some quarters the attention they richly merit."

SWEET WILLIAM—DANIELS' PRIZE AURICULA-EYED.

TITHONIA SPECIOSA.
(THE RED SUNFLOWER.)

per pkt. d.
1042 This fine new variety forms, when well-grown, a striking object on large borders; the plant grows about 5 feet high with large orange-red flowers; seed is best sown in March, in pots, and the young plants planted out when a fair size 1 0

SWEET SULTAN.
(Centaurea.)

SWEET SULTAN—GIANT VARIETIES.

Very fine hardy annuals, deliciously scented, and very useful for cut flowers, remaining fresh for a long time in water.

The giant flowered varieties are exceedingly fine.

per pkt.—s. d.
1043 **GIANT WHITE.** A superb variety, with large pure white, sweet-scented flowers, quite double the size of the old sort. Height 2 feet 0 6
1044 **GIANT BLUE.** Large bluish mauve flowers. Very fine. Height 2 feet 0 6
1045 **NEW GIANT HYBRIDS** (Centaurea Imperialis). A superb strain of giant flowered Sweet Sultans, growing about 2½ feet high, producing very large, sweet-scented flowers of the most beautiful and novel shades of colour .. .. 6d. and 1 0
1046 **YELLOW.** Bright yellow. 18 inches 0 3
1047 **PURPLE.** Height 2 feet 0 3
1048 **WHITE.** Useful for cutting 0 3
1049 **MIXED.** Sweet-scented varieties 0 3

TORENIA FOURNIERI.

1050 Free-flowering greenhouse annual. Flowers purple and white. Makes an excellent pot plant 1 0

From **T. HAWKINS**, Chard.

July 8th.
" I find a grand show of **Sweet William** grown from your Seeds, which was very much admired."

SUNFLOWER.

SUNFLOWER—STARLIGHT.

A very fine class of hardy annuals of great value for garden decoration. Those of the "Giant" type are of stately growth and very fine when planted amongst shrubs, on large beds, or at the back of the herbaceous border: whilst the dwarfer growing sorts are excellent decorative plants for the garden, the smaller flowering kinds furnishing some very useful cut flowers.

		per pkt.—s.	d.
1051 GIANT YELLOW, Double. Enormous flowers, very double		0	3
1052 GIANT YELLOW, Single. Immense flowers, yellow with black disc. Height 6 to 8 feet		0	3
1053 PALLIDUS PLENUS (new). Enormous double pale yellow flowers, very fine. Height 5 to 6 feet		0	6
1054 PRIMROSE DAME. Large flowers. Primrose-yellow with black disc. Height 5 to 6 feet		0	3
1055 DWARF, Double. Deep yellow double flowers. Height 4 feet		0	4
1056 MINIATURE, Single. Small bright yellow flowers, very useful		0	4
1057 STARLIGHT, Single. Pale primrose with pointed petals. Height 3 feet. Charming for cut flowers	6d. and	1	0
1058 STELLA, Single. Long bright yellow petals, with small black centre. First rate for cutting. Height 4 feet		0	4

TACSONIA VAN VOLXEMI.
(The Scarlet Passion Flower.)

1059 A superb evergreen climber for the greenhouse, with brilliant crimson-scarlet flowers 1 0

THUNBERGIA.

Beautiful annual climbers for pots in the greenhouse. The plants grow about 4 feet high, with pretty flowers of yellow shades and white with black centres.
1060 VERY CHOICE MIXED SEED 0 4

VERBENA.

VERBENA—LARGE FLOWERED VARIETIES.

Beautiful free-flowering half-hardy perennials, producing an abundance of bloom during the Summer and Autumn. Exceedingly useful for beds or borders. The plants grow about one foot high. Sow in February or March, in pans or trays of light rich mould, and place in a gentle heat. As soon as the young plants have made three or four leaves pot them off singly into small pots, keep close till established, when they should be placed near the glass and have plenty of air, gradually harden off and plant out in May where intended to flower. Seedling Verbenas are almost invariably very vigorous in growth, and if raised from a good strain of seed will produce some charming flowers.

			per pkt.—s.	d.
1061 LARGE-FLOWERED, Pure White. Beautiful trusses of pure white flowers			0	6
1062 " " Rose and Carmine. Lovely shades			0	6
1063 " " Scarlet and Crimson. Very rich colours			0	6
1064 " " Purple shades. Very fine			0	6
1064A HELEN WILLMOTT. A lovely bright salmon rose with white eye. This variety now comes fairly true from seed			1	0
1065 EXTRA CHOICE MIXED, includes the most brilliant varieties			6d. and	1	0
1066 DWARF COMPACT. Brilliant scarlet, splendid bedder			0	6
1067 AURICULA-FLOWERED. Beautiful large-flowered varieties, with conspicuous white eyes, very showy. Choice mixed			0	6
1068 A lovely bright salmon rose with white eye. This variety now comes fairly true from seed			1	0

VERBENA VENOSA.

1069 A handsome hardy perennial about one foot high. Blooms first year from seed if sown under glass in March and bears numerous trusses of bright purple flowers till late in Autumn 0 6

VENUS' NAVEL-WORT.

1070 A pretty hardy annual with silvery leaves and white flowers. Height 1 foot 0 3

DANIELS' SELECTED WALLFLOWERS.

The single-flowered varieties of this beautiful class of hardy flowers should be freely-grown wherever there is room for them. No plant is easier of cultivation, and their charming colours and delicious perfume, added to their profusion of bloom render them highly desirable for Spring gardening. The splendid varieties—Eastern Queen, Vulcan, Cloth of Gold, Selected blood-red, and the New White Queen are particularly worthy of notice, as are also the New Tom Thumb varieties which make a fine edging for large beds or borders. May and June are the best months for sowing the seeds. Excepting where mentioned, the plants grow about 18 inches high.

DANIELS' SELECTED BLOOD-RED WALLFLOWER.

SINGLE-FLOWERED VARIETIES.

		per pkt.—s.	d.
1071	ELLEN WILLMOTT (new). Ruby-red, a distinct and beautiful variety	0	6
1072	VESUVIUS (new). Orange scarlet buds, expanding a rich bronzy orange. A fine and quite distinct colour..	0	6
1073	WHITE QUEEN. The plants grow only about one foot high, and are very free-flowering. The sweet-scented blooms, when first open, are of a delicate palo primrose colour, changing in a day or two to almost pure white ..	0	6
1074	GOLDEN MONARCH. Magnificent variety. Large, rich, golden yellow flowers .. 6d. and	1	0
1075	DANIELS' EARLY QUEEN. Beautiful golden yellow flowers tinged with brown; remarkably early, sown in March will bloom the first year from seed..	0	6
1076	EASTERN QUEEN. A peculiar shade of chamois, changing to salmon rose, giving a most pleasing and striking effect ..	0	6
1077	VULCAN. Splendid variety, with large velvety-crimson flowers	0	6
1078	PRIMROSE DAME. Clear primrose, very pretty ..	0	6
1079	RUBY GEM. Rich satiny ruby violet	0	6
1080	HARBINGER. Rich dark brown, early ..	0	3
1081	BLOOD RED. Daniels' Selected. Splendid colour 3d. and	0	6
1082	CLOTH OF GOLD. Dwarf, large-flowered .. 3d. and	0	6
1083	BLUE or VIOLET. Beautiful colour ..	0	6
1084	DANIELS' CHOICEST MIXED. Including the most beautiful varieties ..	1	0
1085	,, ,, smaller pkts. 3d. and	0	6
1086	TOM THUMB Golden yellow .. } Large flowered,	0	6
1087	,, ,, Dark brown } compact class,	0	6
1088	,, ,, Purple or Violet } about 9 inches high.	0	6
1089	,, ,, Choicest mixed .. 6d. and	1	0

DOUBLE GERMAN WALLFLOWERS.

The Double German Wallflowers produce grand spikes of handsome double blooms in April and May, but being less hardy than the single varieties, require to be planted in a more sheltered position.

1000	AN ASSORTMENT OF 6 CHOICE VARIETIES. Separate ..	2	0
1091	TALL VARIETIES, Splendid mixed. Large double sweet-scented flowers. Height 2 feet .. 6d. and	1	0
1092	DWARF VARIETIES, Choicest mixed. Stout spikes of large double sweet-scented flowers. Height 1 foot .. 6d. and	1	0

VENUS' LOOKING-GLASS.

Useful free-flowering hardy annuals, growing about 9 inches high, with pretty bell-shaped flowers

		per pkt.—s.	d.
1003	BLUE. Bluish purple with white throat ..	0	3
1004	WHITE. Pure white, very pretty ..	0	3

VIRGINIAN STOCK.

Early flowering hardy annuals, much grown for their pretty effect in beds, &c. Excellent for Autumn Sowing.

1005	CRIMSON KING. Bright rosy-crimson. Height 6 inches ..	0	3
1006	WHITE Large-flowered. Height 6 inches ..	0	3
1007	RED. Bright, rosy-red. Height 9 inches ..	0	3
1008	MIXED. Various colours ..	0	3

VIOLET.

1099	PRINCESS OF WALES. Large deep-blue flowers with long stems, deliciously fragrant. Height 9 inches ..	1	0
1100	THE CZAR. Deep purple flowers, fine scented ..	0	6
1101	WHITE. Large flowered, very sweet scented ..	0	6

VISCARIA.

Brilliant, free-flowering hardy annuals of easy cultivation. Very showy when grown in masses. Height 1 foot.

1102	CARDINALIS. Brilliant crimson-scarlet, very showy ..	0	3
1103	ELEGANS PICTA. Pale rose with crimson eye ..	0	3
1104	OCULATA CÆRULEA. Bright, deep lavender-blue, fine ..	0	3
1105	Dwarf Carmine. Bright carmine red flowers, very pretty. Height 6 inches ..	0	4

WINTER CHERRY.

1106 GIANT SCARLET (Physalis Franchetti). A splendid hardy perennial, growing about 2 ft. high, producing very large globular pods of a bright orange-scarlet colour .. 0 6

Aug. 14th. From J. FOX, Holloway, N.
"Your Wallflower Seed turned out splendid, in four days they were up in hundreds and looked a great picture of colour."

May 17th. From J. T. W. COOLING, Newport, Mon.
"Your Vulcan Wallflower Seed turned out a splendid colour, and they were admired by all."

ZINNIA.

These splendid half-hardy annuals are of great value as bedding and border plants, and should always be grown for their brilliant and beautiful colours. The middle of March is quite soon enough to sow the first batch of Zinnias under glass. Successive sowings may be made till the latter part of April. Sow the seeds in pans or pots of light, rich, finely made soil, and place in a moderate heat. Soon as the young plants are large enough to handle, they should be potted off singly into small pots or pricked out into larger pots or pans to strengthen. To prevent the plants drawing up too much, keep as close as convenient to the glass, give plenty of air on fine warm days, and if the leading flower buds are pinched out as they make their appearance, a more bushy and vigorous growth will follow. Planting out should not take place till all danger from May frosts is over. An open sunny position with fairly rich soil should be chosen and the plants should not be less than a foot apart. Weak liquid manure given once or twice a week before the plants come into flower, will assist in the development of some fine blooms. The flowers of Zinnias have a tendency to sport, and although the seeds of these have been carefully saved we cannot guarantee that the flowers will be absolutely true to the colours mentioned.

DANIELS' LARGE-FLOWERED ZINNIAS.

per pkt.—s. d.

DANIELS' LARGE-FLOWERED. A splendid strain of beautiful varieties, growing about two foot high, with large, handsome, double flowers of the most splendid colours.

			s.	d.
1107	**AN ASSORTMENT OF 6 SPLENDID VARIETIES** ..		1	0
1108	**BRILLIANT SCARLET.** Splendid colour ..		0	4
1109	**WHITE.** Creamy white		0	4
1110	**ROSE.** Delicate rose		0	4
1111	**YELLOW.** Clear yellow ..		0	4
1112	**PURPLE.** Rich colour ..		0	4
1113	**STRIPED VARIETIES.** Large double blooms, handsomely striped		0	6
1114	**DANIELS' CHOICEST MIXED.** A splendid strain, including the most beautiful varieties		1	0
1115	,, ,, ,, smaller pkts. 3d. and		0	6

DANIELS' GIANT-FLOWERED. A superb class of a robust habit of growth, producing beautiful double flowers of an immense size and of the most charming colour. Height 2 to 2½ feet.

			s.	d.
1116	**VERY CHOICE MIXED,** including the most beautiful colours		1	0
1117	,, ,, smaller pkt.		0	9
1118	**FIRE KING** (new). A magnificent variety, growing about 18 inches high; very free-blooming, with splendid double flowers of a deep rich scarlet colour		1	0
1119	**DWARF, DOUBLE.** Compact-growing varieties, about 15 inches high, with handsome double flowers in many beautiful colours. Choicest mixed		0	6
1120	**MINIATURE or POMPONE.** A pretty class of very dwarf compact growing varieties, only nine inches high, with brilliantly-coloured double flowers. Very choice mixed		0	6
1121	**GIPSY GIRL.** A beautiful dwarf growing variety producing for a long period a profusion of double and semi-double flowers, bright crimson-brown with golden yellow edged petals. Very pretty ..		0	6

From Mr. C. H. DYKE, Thornton Heath.
March 9th.
"The Zinnias we had from you last year were admired by everyone."

ORNAMENTAL GRASSES.

The following hardy annual ornamental grasses are amongst the best of their class for the flower garden. They are one and all of a graceful and elegant habit of growth, and highly interesting. If the heads are cut before they arrive at full maturity, they are charming for bouquets or table decorations.

		per pkt.—s. d.			per pkt.—s. d.
1122	**AGROSTIS NEBULOSA.** One of the most elegant	0 3	1128	**ERAGROSTIS ELEGANS.** Fine for decoration	0 3
1123	,, **PULCHELLA.** Beautiful small variety	0 3	1129	**HORDEUM JUBATUM.** Very handsome	0 3
1124	**AVENA STERILIS.** Animated oats, very quaint ..	0 3	1130	**LAGURUS OVATUS.** The "hare's tail" grass	0 3
1125	**BRIZA MAXIMA.** The great quaking grass ..	0 3	1131	**LAMARCKIA AUREA.** Pretty dwarf variety	0 3
1126	,, **GRACILIS.** The "Maiden-hair" grass	0 3	1132	**PENNISETUM LONGISTYLUM.** Very fine	0 3
1127	**BROMUS BRIZÆ FORMIS.** Fine for decoration ..	0 3	1133	**SETARIA ALOPECUROIDES NIGRA.** Graceful black spikes	0 3

1134 One Packet of each 12 fine varieties, 2s. 6d.

From Mr. T. HAWKINS, Chard.
July 8th.
"I had a grand show of Sweet Williams grown from your seed, which were very much admired."

From J. DRAKE, Abingdon.
August 10th.
"I took 1-4 with your Zinnias grown from your seed."

FLOWER SEEDS IN PENNY PACKETS.

For the convenience of those having but small gardens, or requiring only small quantities, we have much pleasure in offering the following popular varieties of Flower Seeds in Penny Packets, all being of the same good quality as those quoted at higher rates for larger packets.

In ordering from the following list the numbers only will be sufficient.

1200	Acroclinium (*Everlasting*), mixed
1201	Alyssum, sweet
1202	Anemone, fine mixed
1203	Antirrhinum (*Snapdragon*), mixed
1204	,, tall mixed
1205	,, dwarf mixed
1206	Aquilegia (*Columbine*), mixed
1207	Aster, Comet, choice mixed
1208	,, ,, white
1209	,, Victoria, choice mixed
1210	Balsam, double mixed
1211	Bartonia aurea
1212	Briza maxima (*Quaking Grass*)
1213	Carnation, Margaret
1214	Candytuft, dark crimson
1215	,, white rocket
1216	,, mixed
1217	Canterbury Bells, mixed
1218	Calandrinia speciosa
1219	Calliopsis Burridgi
1220	,, Drummondi
1221	,, tinctoria
1222	Clarkia elegans, double mixed
1223	,, pulchella, mixed
1224	Collinsia bicolor
1225	,, ,, candidissima
1226	Convolvulus major
1227	,, minor, dark purple
1228	Chrysanthemum tricolor, mixed
1229	Cyanus minor (*Cornflower*), mixed
1230	,, ,, dark blue
1231	Dahlia, single mixed
1232	Delphinium, choice mixed
1233	Dianthus Heddewigi, mixed
1234	Eschscholtzia crocea
1235	,, choice mixed
1236	Erysimum Perofiskianum
1237	Forget-me-not, blue
1238	Foxglove, mixed
1239	Gaillardia Lorenziana
1240	Gilia tricolor
1241	Godetia, The Bride
1242	,, Lady Albemarle, carmine
1243	,, large-flowered, mixed
1244	Helichrysum (*Everlasting*), fine mixed
1245	Honesty, purple
1246	Ice plant
1247	Jacobæa, double crimson
1248	Larkspur, double dwarf rocket
1249	,, tall branching, mixed
1250	Lavatera rosea
1251	Layia elegans
1252	Leptosiphon densiflorus
1253	Linum grandiflorum rubrum

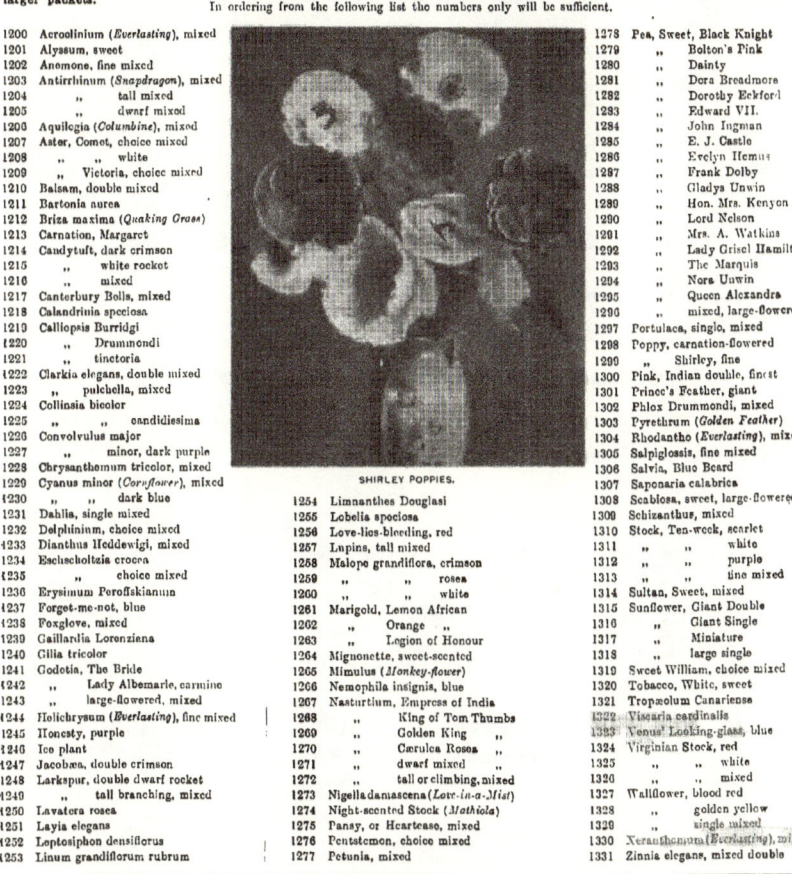

SHIRLEY POPPIES.

1254	Limnanthes Douglasi
1255	Lobelia speciosa
1256	Love-lies-bleeding, red
1257	Lupins, tall mixed
1258	Malope grandiflora, crimson
1259	,, ,, rosea
1260	,, ,, white
1261	Marigold, Lemon African
1262	,, Orange ,,
1263	,, Legion of Honour
1264	Mignonette, sweet-scented
1265	Mimulus (*Monkey-flower*)
1266	Nemophila insignis, blue
1267	Nasturtium, Empress of India
1268	,, King of Tom Thumbs
1269	,, Golden King ,,
1270	,, Cærulea Rosea ,,
1271	,, dwarf mixed
1272	,, tall or climbing, mixed
1273	Nigella damascena (*Love-in-a-Mist*)
1274	Night-scented Stock (*Mathiola*)
1275	Pansy, or Heartsease, mixed
1276	Pentstemon, choice mixed
1277	Petunia, mixed

1278	Pea, Sweet, Black Knight
1279	,, Bolton's Pink
1280	,, Dainty
1281	,, Dora Breadmore
1282	,, Dorothy Eckford
1283	,, Edward VII.
1284	,, John Ingman
1285	,, E. J. Castle
1286	,, Evelyn Hemus
1287	,, Frank Dolby
1288	,, Gladys Unwin
1289	,, Hon. Mrs. Kenyon
1290	,, Lord Nelson
1291	,, Mrs. A. Watkins
1292	,, Lady Grisel Hamilton
1293	,, The Marquis
1294	,, Nora Unwin
1295	,, Queen Alexandra
1296	,, mixed, large-flowered
1297	Portulaca, single, mixed
1298	Poppy, carnation-flowered
1299	,, Shirley, fine
1300	Pink, Indian double, finest
1301	Prince's Feather, giant
1302	Phlox Drummondi, mixed
1303	Pyrethrum (*Golden Feather*)
1304	Rhodantho (*Everlasting*), mixed
1305	Salpiglossis, fine mixed
1306	Salvia, Blue Beard
1307	Saponaria calabrica
1308	Scabiosa, sweet, large-flowered
1309	Schizanthus, mixed
1310	Stock, Ten-week, scarlet
1311	,, ,, white
1312	,, ,, purple
1313	,, ,, fine mixed
1314	Sultan, Sweet, mixed
1315	Sunflower, Giant Double
1316	,, Giant Single
1317	,, Miniature
1318	,, large single
1319	Sweet William, choice mixed
1320	Tobacco, White, sweet
1321	Tropæolum Canariense
1322	Viscaria cardinalis
1323	Venus' Looking-glass, blue
1324	Virginian Stock, red
1325	,, ,, white
1326	,, ,, mixed
1327	Wallflower, blood red
1328	,, golden yellow
1329	,, single mixed
1330	Xeranthemum (*Everlasting*), mixed
1331	Zinnia elegans, mixed double

THE COTTAGER'S PACKET OF CHOICE FLOWER SEEDS.

Containing Twelve selected varieties, including Aster, Stock, Sweet Peas, Mignonette, Scarlet Linum, &c. *(REGISTERED.)*

Post Free, One Shilling; Twelve Packets, 10s. 6d.

DANIELS' COMPLETE COLLECTIONS OF

Choice Flower Seeds for Amateurs

Carefully arranged to ensure a fine display of flowers throughout the Summer and Autumn, and specially adapted to the requirements of the Cottage, Villa, or large Garden.

Collection A.—Price 5s. 6d. Post Free.

Contains the following choice selection.

8 Distinct vars. Aster, Ostrich Plume	6 Choice vars. Sweet Peas, new large-flowered Spencers	12 Packets Choice Hardy and Half-hardy Annuals, including Godetias, Shirley Poppy, Candytuft, Dwarf Nasturtiums, Mignonette, Salpiglossis, Clarkia elegans, new double
6 „ „ Stock, large-flowered Ten-week	1 Packet Petunia, large-flowered	
1 Packet Phlox Drummondi Grandiflora	1 „ Zinnia, finest double	

Collection B.—Price 7s. 6d. Post Free.

6 Choice vars. Comet Aster	1 Packet Dianthus, choice mixed	1 Packet Petunia, finest mixed
1 Packet Aster, Dwarf Scarlet	6 Half-hardy Annuals, including Phlox, Marigold, Portulaca	1 „ Zinnia, finest double
6 Choice vars. Large-flowered Ten-week Stock	9 Distinct varieties Sweet Peas, new large-flowered	1 „ Helichrysum, mixed
8 Choice Hardy Annuals		1 „ Mignonette, new Giant Red
		1 „ Salpiglossis, mixed

Collection C.—Price 10s. 6d. Post Free.

8 Choice vars. Victoria Aster	12 Choice Hardy Annuals, the most useful and showy kinds	1 Packet Verbena, choice mixed
6 „ „ Large-flowered Ten-week Stock, distinct colours	3 Choice varieties Everlasting Flowers	1 Ounce Mignonette, large-flowered
6 Varieties Zinnia elegans, double	1 Packet Petunia, choice mixed	12 Choice varieties Sweet Peas, new large-flowered Spencers
6 Choice Half-hardy Annuals for bedding out, &c.	1 „ Nemesia, choice mixed	

Collection D.—Price 21s. Carriage Free.

6 Choice vars. Aster, Ostrich Plume	6 Choice varieties Half-hardy Annuals, for bedding out, pots, &c.	1 Packet Petunia, choice mixed
6 „ „ „ Victoria	6 Hardy Perennials and Biennials	1 „ Verbena, fine mixed
1 Packet Aster, Dwarf Scarlet	3 Choice varieties Everlasting Flowers	1 „ Calceolaria, choicest mixed
6 Choice vars. Ten-week Stock Large-fld	18 Choice varieties Sweet Peas, new large-flowered Spencers	1 „ Cineraria, choice mixed
6 „ „ Double Zinnia	1 Packet Dianthus Heddewigi, mixed	1 „ Primula, choice fringed
6 „ „ Phlox Drummondi	1 „ Salpiglossis Grandiflora	1 Ounce Nemophila insignis
12 „ „ Showy Hardy Annuals, for borders, &c.		1 „ Mignonette, Giant

Other Collections of Choice Flower Seeds, 31s. 6d., 42s., 63s., 84s., and 100s.

THE AMATEUR'S PACKET OF CHOICE FLOWER SEEDS. *(REGISTERED.)*

Price 2s. 6d. Post Free.

Contains the following Choice Assortment in full-sized packets, with cultural directions. This is a very cheap and splendid collection, which we can highly recommend.

Sweet Peas, New Large-flowered Six distinct and beautiful varieties, one packet each.	Stock, Large-flowered Ten-week, mixed	Sweet Sultan, Giant mixed
	Phlox Drummondi, mixed	Godetia, Large-flowered, mixed
Aster, "Ostrich Plume," choicest mixed	Shirley Poppy, selected strain	Mignonette, Giant Crimson
	Nasturtium, Empress of India	Clarkia, double, Queen Mary

Biennials and Perennials.			Everlasting Flowers.			Ornamental Grasses.		
	s.	d.		s.	d.		s.	d.
12 Selected Hardy Varieties	3	6	12 Very Fine Varieties	2	6	12 Fine Annual Varieties	2	6
6 „ „ „	2	0	6 „ „ „	1	6	6 „ „ „	1	6

FLOWER SEEDS BY WEIGHT.

The following popular annuals, &c., which are often required in larger quantities, we shall be pleased to supply by weight at the following moderate rates, all of the same high class excellence as sold in packet.

	per oz.—s. d.		per oz.—s. d.
ALYSSUM, SWEET . .	0 9	LUPINUS NANUS. Blue . .	0 6
" LITTLE GEM. Splendid for edgings	1 0	LUPINS. Tall, mixed . .	0 4
ANTIRRHINUM. Tall, choice mixed . .	1 0	MAIZE. Variegated, Japanese	0 6
" SEMI-DWARF, OR INTERMEDIATE. Choice mixed	1 6	MALOPE GRANDIFLORA. Rose	0 6
" TOM THUMB. Dwarf mixed	2 0	" Scarlet	0 6
ASTER. Daniels' Improved Victoria, mixed . .	10 6	" White	0 6
" Giant Comet, pure white . .	10 6	" Mixed	0 6
" mixed	10 0	MATHIOLA BICORNIS. Night-scented Stock . . per lb. 6s.	0 6
" Ostrich Plume, pure white . .	10 6	MIGNONETTE. Machet, selected Giant Crimson	1 6
" mixed	10 0	" Crimson Pyramidal . .	1 0
" Dwarf Chrysanthemum, mixed	8 6	" Golden Queen	1 0
BARTONIA AUREA. Orange yellow	0 9	" Large-flowered . . per lb. 6s.	0 6
CALLIOPSIS TINCTORIA . .	0 6	NASTURTIUM. Tom Thumb, Carmine King . .	0 9
" TOM THUMB. Mixed . .	0 9	" " Crystal Palace Gem	0 9
" DRUMMONDI	0 6	" " Empress of India	0 6
" Tall varieties. Choice mixed	0 6	" " Golden King	0 9
CANDYTUFT. Empress, pure white . .	1 6	" " King . .	0 9
" Creamy white	0 9	" " Vesuvius	0 9
" Large-flowered, dwarf mixed . .	1 6	" " Mixed, all sorts . . per lb 6s.	0 6
" Rose Cardinal, carmine	1 6	" CLIMBING. Finest mixed . . 6s.	0 6
" Extra dark crimson . .	0 6	" Dark crimson . .	0 9
" Mixed, all colours . . per lb 6s.	0 6	" Bright yellow . .	0 9
CANTERBURY BELLS. Single, choice mixed . .	1 0	NEMOPHILA INSIGNIS. Blue . .	0 6
" Double, choice mixed . .	4 0	" MACULATA	0 6
" Calycanthema varieties, mixed . .	6 0	NICOTIANA AFFINIS. Sweet-scented ·	1 0
CENTAUREA IMPERIALIS. Giant white	2 0	NIGELLA DAMASCENA (Love-in-a-Mist)	0 6
" Giant blue	2 0	PERILLA NANKINENSIS . .	0 6
CHRYSANTHEMUM BURRIDGEANUM	0 6	PHLOX DRUMMONDI GRANDIFLORA. Mixed	2 0
" CARINATUM CHAMELEON	0 6	PANSY. Daniels' Prize Blotched	12 6
" ANNUAL. Daniels' splendid mixed	0 9	" German mixed . .	2 6
CLARKIA INTEGRIPETALA. Rose . .	0 9	POPPY. Shirley, selected, very fine strain . . per lb 10s. 6s.	1 0
" White	0 9	RICINUS GIBSONI (Castor Oil Plant) . .	0 4
COLLINSIA BICOLOR. Lilac and white	0 9	RHODANTHE MACULATA. Mixed, charming everlasting	2 0
" CANDIDISSIMA Pure white	0 9	SALPIGLOSSIS. Large-flowered, mixed . .	2 6
CONVOLVULUS MAJOR. Mixed . .	0 6	SAPONARIA CALABRICA. Pink . .	0 6
" MINOR. Dark blue . .	0 6	SCABIOUS. Large-flowered, very useful for cutting . .	0 9
CYANUS MINOR (Cornflower). Dark blue	0 6	SCHIZANTHUS HYBRIDUS GRANDIFLORUS. Choice mixed.	2 0
" Choice mixed	0 6	SILENE PENDULA COMPACTA. Double Rose . .	0 6
DELPHINIUM. Hybrid Perennial, choice mixed	2 6	STOCK. Daniels' Large flowered Ten-week, choice mixed . .	10 0
DIANTHUS HEDDEWIGI. Choice mixed, single	2 0	" Perpetual Perfection, choice mixed . .	10 6
" CHINENSIS (Indian Pink). Finest double, mixed	1 0	" Dwarf German, finest mixed . .	7 6
DIGITALIS (Foxglove). Finest spotted, mixed	1 6	" Brompton. Choicest mixed . .	12 6
ESCHSCHOLTZIA CROCEA. Yellow . . }	0 6	SUNFLOWER. Miniature . .	0 9
" Extra choice, mixed	0 6 Splendid	" Giant double	0 9
" MANDARIN. Orange scarlet } Showy Annuals	0 9	" Single, Primrose Dame	0 6
" Rose cardinal, bright rose . . }	1 0	" Giant Yellow . .	0 6
GAILLARDIA HYBRIDA GRANDIFLORA. Mixed	0 9	SWEET PEAS. Daniels' Special Mixed Spencers per pint 7s. 6d.	0 9
GILIA TRICOLOR. Very pretty Annual	0 4	" Good mixture . . . . " 2s. 6d.	0 4
GODETIA. Bridesmaid	1 0	SWEET SULTAN. Purple, white, and yellow . . each	0 4
" Duchess of Fife . . } Splendid large-flowered varieties	1 0	" Fine mixed . .	0 6
" Duke of York " } for beds or borders	1 0	SWEET WILLIAM. Daniel's Prize Auricula eyed, very fine strain	1 6
" Duchess of Albany	1 0	TROPÆOLUM CANARIENSE . .	1 0
" Choicest mixed, large-flowered	1 0	VENUS' LOOKING GLASS. Blue . .	0 6
" Lady Satin Rose. Dwarf	1 6	VERBENA HYBRIDA Choice mixed	4 0
GYPSOPHILA GRANDIFLORA ALBA. . .	1 6	VIRGINIAN STOCK. Red or white . . each	0 6
HELICHRYSUM. Choice mixed, beautiful varieties	1 3	" Mixed . . per lb. 5s.	0 6
LARKSPUR. Dwarf Rocket . .	0 6	VISCARIA CARDINALIS. Scarlet . .	0 9
" Tall, branching . .	0 6	WALLFLOWER, SINGLE. Blood Red . .	1 6
LAVATERA ROSEA SPLENDENS . . } Very showy	1 0	" Golden Yellow . .	1 6
" ALBA " }	1 0	" Primrose Dame . .	1 6
LEPTOSIPHON DENSIFLORUS. Lilac and white	0 9	" Extra choice mixed . . per lb. 12s.	1 6
" ALBUS. White	0 9	" Eastern Queen . .	1 6
LIMNANTHES DOUGLASI. Yellow and white . .	0 6	" Ruby Gem . .	1 6
LINUM GRANDIFLORUM RUBRUM. Brilliant scarlet . .	0 6	" DOUBLE GERMAN. Splendid mixed	10 6
LOVE-LIES-BLEEDING. Red . .	0 4	ZINNIA ELEGANS. Choicest double mixed . .	1 6

Choice Flower Seeds in Mixture.

FOR SOWING ON BANKS, ROCKERIES, WASTE PLACES, &c.

We offer a splendid mixture of the choicest dwarf-growing Hardy Annuals, suitable for the above purposes, and which will make a very pretty display for a long period. The mixture includes :—Godetias, Clarkias, Candytufts, Mignonette, Poppies, Gilias, Viscarias, and other free-flowering subjects, and will give the highest satisfaction.

MIXED FLOWER SEEDS, Choicest Dwarf Varieties, per lb. 5s. ; per oz. 6d.

TUBEROUS-ROOTED BEGONIAS.

We have much pleasure in offering tubers of our grand strains of Tuberous-rooted Begonias. These have been grown and selected at our Nurseries during the past season, and for form, size, substance of flower, and beauty and variety of colouring are second to none.

DANIELS' DOUBLE-FLOWERED BEGONIAS (Dry Tubers).

The Double-flowered Begonias are especially recommended for pot culture. The colours of the flowers vary from the darkest crimson and scarlet, through all the most beautiful shades of salmon, rose, and yellow, to the purest white. They are easily grown, and with their large massive blooms form strikingly handsome objects for the greenhouse or conservatory.

per doz.—s. d.

FOR POT CULTURE. A superb collection of choice sorts, equal to named varieties, the flowers being of the most perfect form, and of the most varied and beautiful colours. Highly desirable for conservatory or greenhouse decoration .. .. 6s., 9s. and 12 0

MIXED DOUBLES FOR BEDDING. A capital variety of large, full, double flowers, in beautiful variety of colour .. .. per 100, 25s. 3 6

DOUBLE BEGONIAS IN DISTINCT COLOURS FOR POTS OR BEDDING OUT.

Fine double flowers, carefully selected when in bloom, and first class for pot culture or the garden.

| DARK REDS AND SCARLETS | PURE WHITE | YELLOW SHADES | per doz.—s. d. |
| ROSE SHADES | ORANGE AND SALMON SHADES | RED SHADES | per 100, 30s. 5 0 |

DANIELS' SINGLE BEGONIAS FOR BEDDING.

IN DISTINCT COLOURS (Dry Tubers).

Distinct and beautiful colours, specially selected for effective bedding, all of the large-flowered erect growing class, and good strong tubers. Highly recommended.

DANIELS' BRILLIANT SCARLET	DANIELS' PURE WHITE	DANIELS' DARK RED AND CRIMSON	per doz.—s. d.
DANIELS' SALMON ROSE SHADES	DANIELS' ORANGE SHADES	DANIELS' YELLOW SHADES	per 100, 21s. 3 0
CHOICE MIXED SEEDLINGS. In beautiful variety, all approved flowers from our fine collection ..		per 100, 15s.; per doz. 2s. 6d

SINGLE-FLOWERED BEGONIAS FOR POT CULTURE (Dry Tubers).

per doz.—s. d.

FOR GREENHOUSE AND CONSERVATORY. A very fine mixture of choice selected flowers, mostly equal to the named sorts, the flowers being perfect in form and of the most beautiful colours .. .. 6s. and 9 0

FOR POT CULTURE. A capital mixture of beautiful colours, the varieties all being carefully selected and really good. Considering the high-class quality, we consider these remarkably cheap .. .. per 100, 30s. 4 6

BEGONIAS—NEW FRINGED SINGLE.	BEGONIA ERECTA CRISTATA.
A remarkably fine new strain of handsomely fringed flowers. The large finely-formed blooms, which are elegantly frilled and crested, are borne on stiff, erect stems, carried well above the foliage, and are possessed of the most beautiful variety of colouring known amongst Begonias. This splendid class will be found first-class for pot culture.	A remarkable strain of great beauty. The plants are of a dwarf, sturdy, upright growth, and first-class for pot culture. The petals are of great substance, and the flowers of the most charming colours, each petal carrying on its upper surface a handsome crest resembling a Cockscomb. Singularly beautiful, and quite unique.
PURE WHITE, beautiful .. Dry Tubers, each 1s.; per doz. 10s. 6d.	VERY CHOICE MIXED, in beautiful variety
VERY CHOICE MIXED, in fine variety .. each 6d.; per doz. 5s.	Dry Tubers, per doz. 5s.; each 6d.

☞ The prices quoted above are for dormant tubers, and these can only be supplied to the end of April.

In May and June we supply strong plants from single pots at the following rates :—

SINGLE-FLOWERED, choice mixed, per 100, 30s.; doz. 4s. 6d.   DOUBLE-FLOWERED, choice mixed, per 100, 42s.; doz. 6s.

GLADIOLI.

These beautiful flowers succeed well in almost any soil or situation, and planted in association with Dwarf or Standard Roses, with hardy herbaceous plants, or on the shrubbery border, they have a very fine appearance. They also do well as pot plants, and are capitally suited for growing in outside window boxes.

We would strongly recommend all who have not yet grown them to procure the new Giant-flowered hybrids, the varieties of Nanceianus and Lemoinei, all of which can be highly recommended for making a display of rare beauty in the garden. The hybrids of G. Gandavensis are also well known and very popular. Plant the corms or roots firmly, three or four inches deep and eight or nine inches apart, in clumps of three, five, or more as required, and put a neat stake to each when the flower buds make their appearance. March is the best month to plant for blooming in July and August, and by a few successive plantings in April and the early part of May, a succession of handsome flowers may be had to the end of September.

Gladioli are of especial value as cut flowers for decorative purposes. If the flower spikes are cut and placed in water just as the blooms are beginning to expand, they will all open in succession to the topmost bud, and will retain their beauty for a longer time than if remaining on the plant.

NEW GIANT-FLOWERED HYBRIDS.

We strongly recommend the following varieties, which have proved highly satisfactory with us in our trials during the past season. The flowers are of great substance and gigantic size.

AMERICA. Great substance, colour soft flesh pink, slightly tinged with lavender. Each 3d.; per doz. 2s. 6d.

CARDINAL. Intense scarlet. Each 6d.; per doz. 5s.

*DAWN Shell pink, most pleasing. Each 8d.; per doz. 7s. 6d.

*EMPRESS OF INDIA. Very dark rich maroon. A.M. Each 7d.; per doz. 6s.

*GLORY OF HOLLAND. Splendid white. A.M. Each 7d.; per doz. 6s

GOLDEN WEST. Orange red, overlaid with gold, blotched. Each 8d.; per doz. 7s. 6d.

HALLEY. Lovely salmon pink, blotched yellow. Each 3d.; per doz. 2s. 6d.

*HENRY GILMAN. Deep salmon scarlet, white band. Each 6d.; per doz. 5s.

LILY LEHMAN. White, slightly edged with rose, very fine. Each 7d.; per doz. 6s.

*NIAGARA. Canary yellow, very tall. A.M. Each 10d.; per doz. 9s.

PEACE. White, blotched with pale lilac. Each 10d.; per doz. 9s.

*PRINCEPS. Enormous flowers of dazzling scarlet, with a small white vein; a most remarkable variety. Each 4d.; per doz. 3s.

WHITE GIANT SEEDLINGS A splendid strain, varying slightly in shade, very large blooms. Each 4d.; per doz. 3s.

*WILLY WIGMAN. Enormous flowers, 6 to 8 inches across, creamy white with large crimson blotches. F.C.C. Each 6d.; per doz. 5s.

One of each of the above 14 Superb Varieties for 6s. 6d.

* One each of Seven Varieties for 3s. 6d.

Splendid mixture of Giant-flowered Hybrids - per doz. 1s. 6d.; per 100 10s. 6d.

GLADIOLUS GANDAVENSIS HYBRIDS.

A very fine free-flowering class, growing about three feet high and producing long, handsome spikes of lovely flowers, ranging in colour through all the shades of scarlet and crimson, mauve, rose, pink and yellow to pure white.

CHOICE NAMED VARIETIES IN COLLECTIONS.
Our own selection.

	s.	d.
24 in 12 fine varieties	8s.	6d.
18 in 18 choice sorts	6s.	6d.
12 in 12 choice sorts	4s.	6d.
12 in 12 good varieties	3s.	6d.

Gladiolus Gandavensis.
Finest Named and Seedling Sorts. Mixed.

We highly recommend our mixture of these, which includes a splendid variety of the most beautiful colours, varying from the most intense scarlet and crimson through all the shades of rose, salmon, pink, yellow, and carmine to the purest white.

Choicest Mixed, per 100, 10s., per doz. 1s. 6d.

EARLY FLOWERING GLADIOLI.

Beautiful showy varieties, blooming in June and July. Splendid for cut flowers.

	per 100.		per doz.	
	s.	d.	s.	d.
ACKERMANNI. Salmon, flaked carmine, with violet eye	4	6	0	9
BLUSHING BRIDE. Lovely white, with pink and carmine flakes on lower petals, beautiful	3	6	0	6
CARDINALIS ELEGANS. Bright scarlet, flaked white	7	6	1	0
COLVILLEI ALBA. "THE BRIDE." Pure white	3	6	0	6
NON PLUS ULTRA. Large rosy-red, flaked with white	5	0	0	9
PEACH BLOSSOM. Delicate peach-pink, extra fine	5	0	0	9
QUEEN VICTORIA. Vermilion scarlet, flaked with white	10	6	1	6
WILHELMINA. Pure white, blotched with rosy red; very pretty	8	6	1	3
ROSY GEM. Delicate rosy pink; splendid for cutting	4	0	0	8
SALMON QUEEN. Beautiful salmon-red	8	6	1	3
VERY CHOICE MIXED	4	0	0	8

GLADIOLUS LEMOINEI.
Hardy Hybrid Gladioli.

This fine new race of Hybrid Gladioli blooms somewhat earlier than those of the Gandavensis section, and are much more hardy, so hardy in fact, that their bulbs do not need to be lifted in Winter. The flowers are very striking and handsome in appearance, all having conspicuous blotches on the lower petals, whilst the colours are very diversified and beautiful. These will be found splendid alike for garden decoration or for cut flowers.

BARON HULOT. A quite novel and very beautiful variety of the hardy Lemoinei class of Gladioli. The large flowers, which are produced on handsome spikes, are of a lovely rich dark violet blue. A colour quite unique amongst Gladioli and of striking effect. Each 3d.; per doz. 2s. 6d.

GELRIA STRAIN. A beautiful strain, containing mostly pale blue, yellow, and heliotrope shades. Per doz. 1s. 6d.; per 100, 10s. 6d.

LEMOINEI VARIETIES. Choice mixed, in beautiful variety. Per doz. 1s. 6d.; per 100, 10s. 6d.

GLADIOLUS BRENCHLEYENSIS.

A well-known and splendid variety of fine effect for massing; the flowers are of a rich bright scarlet colour, and being produced in handsome spikes are first-class to cut for church and other decorations.

Good flowering roots, per doz. 1s.; per 100, 7s. 6d.

Extra fine roots, per doz. 1s. 6d.; per 100, 10s. 6d.

GLADIOLUS HOLLANDIA.

Equally as useful as Brenchleyensis for cut work. Flowers of a lovely rosy salmon.

Per doz. 1s. 6d.; per 100 10s. 6d.

GLADIOLUS NANCEIANUS.

A magnificent class of beautiful flowers, producing large, brilliantly coloured blooms. Very Choice Mixed, in beautiful variety.

Per doz. 1s. 6d.; per 100, 10s. 6d.

LILIES (Lilium) for Spring Planting.

For growing Lilies in pots a compost of about equal parts of sandy loam, leaf mould, and peat, is, perhaps, the best. Fine Lilies may however, be grown in almost any good light and rich soil, especially those of the Auratum type. For single specimens use pots of about six inches diameter. These will be found very useful for house decoration ; but pots of eight or ten inches diameter, with five or six bulbs in each, form grand objects for the conservatory when in bloom. Pot firmly, any time during Spring, with the bulbs about two inches below the surface, and plunge the pots with their rims about six inches deep in some light material, such as ashes or cocoa-nut fibre, in some sheltered position out of doors. When the stems have pushed their way well through the plunging material, they may be lifted and removed to a cool pit or frame till the flower-buds are developed, when they may be removed to the greenhouse or conservatory.

All the sorts mentioned in the following list are suitable for Spring planting out of doors. For pot culture, however, we strongly recommend the beautiful varieties of Auratum and Speciosum, with the addition of the fine Longiflorum Giganteum as the most suitable.

LILIUM AURATUM.

			each—s.	d.
AURATUM (The Golden-rayed Lily of Japan). Large white flowers with yellow stripes and brownish-red spots ; deliciously fragrant, extremely hardy ; a very free bloomer, and first rate for pot culture.				
No. 1.	Extra selected large roots	per doz. 15s.	1	6
No. 2.	Very fine roots	,, 10s. 6d.	1	0
No. 3.	Large roots	,, 7s. 6d.	0	9
No. 4.	Good flowering roots	5s.	0	6
,,	rubro-vittatum. Immense flowers, petals white, with a distinct broad band of deep crimson	per doz. 15s.	1	6
,,	virginale. Very large flowers, white, with pale yellow bands ; most beautiful variety	per doz. 15s.	1	6
,,	platyphyllum (macranthum). Gigantic flowers, broad petals, white, with yellow bands, spotted : very fine	per doz. 12s.	1	3
,,	WITTEI. A pure white Auratum with yellow hands ; very scarce	per doz. 2s.	2	0
SPECIOSUM. A fine hardy class ; excellent for pot culture ; deliciously scented.				
,,	Album, pure white	per doz. 6s.	0	8
,,	Krœtzeri. Pure white ; finest variety for pot culture	,, 10s. 6d.	1	0
,,	melpomene. Most beautiful variety ; flowers large ; splendid form, and of a lovely purplish crimson colour ; heavily spotted, makes a splendid pot plant	per doz. 7s. 6d.	0	9
,,	punctatum. White, rose-spotted	,, 5s.	0	6
,,	rubrum. White, spotted and shaded crimson	5s.	0	6
,,	roseum. White, crimson-spotted	6s.	0	6
HENRYI (Orange-yellow Speciosum). Stems six feet high, bearing 15 to 20 flowers, of a rich deep orange-yellow colour, well set off by the deep green foliage		per doz. 27s. 6d.	2	6
HUMBOLDTI. A fine species, growing about five feet high, with large golden-yellow flowers, spotted purple			2	0
KRAMERI. Similar to Auratum, but of a beautiful pink colour ; deliciously scented		per doz. 7s. 6d.	0	9
LONGIFLORUM FORMOSUM. Very strong growing, dwarf and free flowering		per doz. 5s.	0	6
,,	**GIGANTEUM.** Early-flowering species, trumpet-shaped flowers, pure white	per doz. 4s. 6d.	0	6
LEICHTLINII. Citron-yellow spotted purple ; very handsome	per doz. 10s. 6d.	1	0
MARTAGON (Turk's Cap). Purple	per doz. 4s. 6d.	0	6
,,	**ALBUM.** Pure white-flowered form of the preceding ; extremely scarce		2	0
,,	**DALMATICUM.** A magnificent variety, with deep velvety crimson purple flowers		3	6
PARDALINUM. Bright scarlet shading to orange, spotted maroon ; large flowers		per doz. 5s.	0	6
POMPONIUM VERUM. An elegant species, with bright scarlet flowers		per doz. 7s. 6d	0	9
PYRENAICUM (the Yellow Martagon). Deliciously scented flowers, yellow, spotted black		per doz. 7s. 6d.	0	9
SUPERBUM. A fine yellow Lily with purple spots. Flowers often fifteen to twenty on a stem		per doz. 6s.	0	8
TESTACEUM (Excelsum). Nankeen-coloured flowers, delightfully fragrant ; four feet high		per doz. 15s.	1	6
THUNBERGIANUM ATROSANGUINEUM. Scarlet, spotted black		per doz. 5s.	0	6
,,	**ORANGE QUEEN.** Bright orange, dark spots	,, 12s.	1	3
TIGRINUM SPLENDENS FORTUNEI. The finest of the Tiger Lilies. Orange scarlet, black spots		per doz. 4s. 6d.	0	6
,,	**FL. PL.** Scarlet, spotted brown, very double	,, 4s. 6d	0	6

	each—s.	d.
BATEMANNIÆ. Apricot-yellow	per doz. 10s. 6d.	1 0
BROWNI. Large, creamy white trumpet-shaped flowers, the outside of the petals being of a rich purplish brown colour		2 6
CHALCEDONICUM (Scarlet Turk's Cap). Splendid old variety, flowers medium sized, reflexed, and of a deep rich scarlet colour ; finely effective	per doz. 21s.	2 0
COLCHICUM (Szovitzianum). Pale yellow, spotted with black ; finely scented	per doz. 10s. 6d.	1 0
CROCEUM. Light orange, spotted black	per doz. 5s.	0 6
DAVURICUM FULGIDUM. Deep orange red flushed with yellow, very showy	per doz. 5s.	0 6
GIGANTEUM (the noble Himalayan Lily). White, with broad bands of crimson violet	3s. 6d., 5s. and	7 6
HANSONII. Golden yellow, spotted black	per doz. 10s. 6d.	1 0

We can supply many other species and varieties of choice Lilies, which from want of space we are unable to enumerate here.

Lilies in Collections—our own selection.

Carefully arranged Collections of Lilies, 6s., 9s., 12s., and 18s. per dozen. Carriage Free.

Oct. 27th.

From Mr. G. JACKSON, Millom.

"I was very pleased with the Lilium Auratum and Begonias which I had in the Spring. The former were wonderfully fine."

Jan. 24th.

From Mr. C. BEAN, Camden Town.

"I had Lily Blooms measuring 10 inches across from the Bulbs I bought of you. I think, considering the plants were grown due north, also partly overhung by Lime trees, that the Bulbs have done exceedingly well."

TWO FINE LILIES for Pot Culture.

Lilium Speciosum Melpomene and Lilium Speciosum Krætzeri. *(See opposite page.)*

APPLES.

Our fine stock of Apples are principally worked on the Crab Stock, but we have a large collection of the most suitable kinds worked on the broad leaved Paradise Stock, the varieties we can supply of these being marked with an asterisk (*). The best time for planting is as early as convenient in October or November, after the young trees have shed their leaves, but planting may be done with safety any time to the end of March if the weather is fairly open.

Dwarf Apples on the Paradise Stock are of especial value both for large or small gardens, and have come very much into favour of late years. They are much dwarfer in growth, come into bearing and profit much sooner, are easier to thin and spray, and they produce almost continuously abundant crops of much finer fruit. For small holdings, or where the tenure is uncertain, they are specially recommended.

PRICES OF APPLES.

In all cases where customers leave the selection of varieties to us, they may rely on only good trees of the best kinds being supplied. It is most important, however, that the style or shape of trees required should be clearly stated when ordering. Orders entrusted to us in this way are invariably filled to the entire satisfaction of our clients.

ON ORDINARY CRAB STOCK.

	each. s. d.	per doz. s. d.
MAIDENS ..	1 0	10 0
DWARFS OR BUSHES	1 6	15 0
PYRAMIDS. Good ..	2 0	20 0
„ Selected ..	2 6	25 0
„ Extra Strong Fruiting	3 0	30 0
DWARF TRAINED ESPALIERS .. 3s. 6d. to	5 0	36 0
STANDARDS. Good	1 6	15 0
„ Selected ..	2 0	20 0
„ Extra Strong Fruiting	2 6	25 0
CORDONS, SINGLE ..	1 6	17 0

Special Quotations for Larger Quantities.

ON PARADISE STOCK.

Highly Recommended.

	each. s. d.	per doz. s. d.
MAIDENS	1 0	10 0
DWARF FRUITING BUSHES	2 0	20 0
PYRAMIDS. Strong	2 6	25 0
„ Extra Strong ..	3 6	35 0
CORDONS, SINGLE ..	1 6	17 0

Special Quotations for Larger Quantities.

When it is proposed to form new Orchards or to plant a quantity of Fruit Trees, for market purposes, we shall be most happy to quote special prices on our customers naming the varieties and styles they desire to have.

NEW AND VERY CHOICE APPLES.

Those marked (*) can be supplied on Paradise Stock. Those marked (†) can be supplied as Single Cordons.

ARD CAIRN RUSSET. This is an Irish Apple, one of the best of the Russet family ; a good bearer and long keeper, of delicious flavour.
Maidens, 1s. 6d. each ; Bush, 3s. 6d. each.

BENS RED. A most valuable dessert Apple of a brilliant bronzy-red colour and of first-class flavour.*
Maidens, 1s. 6d. each ; Bush, 2s. 6d. each.

ELLISON'S ORANGE (D). This is a delicious dessert Apple approaching closely in appearance and flavour to Cox's Orange Pippin, and possessing equally good keeping qualities. We have every confidence in recommending this variety.
Maidens, 1s. 6d. each ; Two Year Trees, 2s. 6d. each.

***FELTHAM BEAUTY** (new). A splendid new highly coloured early dessert variety, raised from Cox's Orange Pippin and Mr. Gladstone. The fruit is of fair size, flesh crisp, sweet, and of rich aromatic flavour.
One Year old Trees, 1s. 6d. each ; Two Year old Trees, 2s. 6d. each.

RED VICTORIA. This is not a red form of the popular "Early Victoria," but a very highly coloured early culinary variety ; flesh white and juicy, a good cropper and free grower. We can very highly recommend this variety to our customers.
Maidens, 1s. 6d. ; Bush, 2s. 6d.

RENOWN. A very fine variety of excellent habit, a regular and heavy cropper ; the flesh is solid, crisp, juicy, and of pleasing flavour, and possesses every good point either for cooking or dessert purposes.
Maidens, 2s. each ; Bush, 3s. each.

REV. W. WILKS (K). A very large, culinary apple of fine form ; the colour is a creamy yellow dotted with brown and scarlet specks, flesh white and juicy and of pleasant flavour ; a good grower and free bearer.
Maidens, 2s. each ; Bush, 3s. each.

WM. CRUMP. A beautiful new dessert Apple, the fruit is of medium size, conical bright red on the exposed side, and heavily streaked with russet marking round the stalk, flesh crisp and of rich flavour.
Maidens, 2s. each ; Bush, 3s. each.

From Mr. E. A. LANGFORD, Valentia Island.

Aug. 1st.
"The Fruit Trees you supplied me with a few years since are doing splendidly and giving fine crops ; I am well satisfied with them."

From Mr. J. LINES, Warwick.

Dec. 6th.
"Fruit Trees to hand safely. I thank you for your grand selection, and am more than pleased with them. Great praise is due for the excellent way in which they were packed."

From H. LANE, Esq., Lichfield.

March 1st.
"The Apple Trees arrived safely and in excellent condition, and I must say I am much pleased with the stud you have sent."

From Mr. A. HUBBELL, Meopham.

March 11th.
"I would like to say I am very pleased with the Apple Trees you have sent me."

APPLES—General List of Select Varieties.

D denotes dessert. K Kitchen. Those marked (*) can be supplied on Paradise Stock. Those marked (†) can be supplied as Single Cordons.

*ALFRISTON (K). A large and useful variety. Nov. to April.

†ALLINGTON PIPPIN. A splendid medium-sized Apple introduced a few years ago, and which has taken a position in the front rank as a first-rate dessert variety and a reliable bearer. Maidens, each 1s. ; Dwarfs on Paradise Stock, 3s. ; Pyramids, 3s. 6d. ; Standards, 2s.

*ANNIE ELIZABETH (K). A very fine late Apple of excellent keeping qualities. Dec. to May.

*BARON WOLSELEY (K). An enormous fruit of the Warner King type, but larger and with more colour, being flushed with bronzy red. A good grower and free bearer. A splendid Exhibition Apple. One Year Trees on Paradise, 1s. 6d. each ; Two Year Trees on Paradise, 2s. each ; Cordons, 2s. 6d. each ; Standards, 3s. 6d. each.

†BEAUTY OF BATH (D). A very handsome early variety, has a brisk sub-acid flavour. July and Aug.

*BEAUTY OF KENT (K). A handsome, large, and first-rate culinary Apple ; excellent bearer. Oct. to Feb.

†BISMARCK (K). One of the best varieties in cultivation for market or the private garden. Oct. to Dec.

†*BLENHEIM ORANGE (D.K). Well-known and splendid variety ; large handsome fruit. Dec. to Feb.

†BRAMLEY'S SEEDLING (K). A large handsome fruit, resembling Blenheim Pippin. Sept. to Jan.

CELLINI (D.K). A fine, showy, and handsome Apple of the first quality. Oct. and Nov.

†CHARLES ROSS (new). A cross between Cox's Orange Pippin and Peasgood's Nonsuch. One of the finest dessert Apples yet raised. Nov. to Jan.

*CHELMSFORD WONDER (K). Fruit large, skin smooth, deep yellow shaded with brilliant crimson. Nov. to Jan.

*CHRISTMAS PEARMAIN (D). Medium, of excellent flavour, rich scarlet cheek and russet markings, an enormous cropper. The tree is a good grower, free from canker. We consider it will take the place of the King of Pippins for dessert or market, as the latter is subject to canker and can only be grown well in few localities. Nov. to Dec.

*CLAYGATE PEARMAIN (D). A valuable variety. Nov. to March.

†*COX'S ORANGE PIPPIN (D). A highly popular and first-rate dessert Apple ; fruit medium-sized, finely coloured, rich, crisp and juicy, and of delicious flavour. Oct. to Mar.

†CRIMSON BRAMLEY (K). Similar in every respect except colour to the well-known Bramley Seedling, equally hardy, robust grower, and heavy bearer. Standards 2s. 6d. each.

DEVONSHIRE QUARRENDEN (D). A fine hardy, free-bearing variety of excellent quality ; fruit small. Aug. and Sept.

*DUMELOW'S SEEDLING (K). A large and excellent variety ; one of the most useful of culinary Apples ; a strong grower, and an excellent bearer. Nov. to May.

*EARLY VICTORIA (K). A pale lemon-coloured, very early variety of the Codlin type ; very free bearer. July and Aug.

†ECKLINVILLE SEEDLING (K). A large and useful sort ; flesh white and tender ; a great bearer Oct. to Dec.

†*EMPEROR ALEXANDER (K.D). Very large, handsome ; free cropper, Oct.

*ENCORE (K). A very large and handsome cooking variety. In colour it is yellow streaked and flushed with red, flesh crisp and juicy, strong grower and free bearer. Bush Trees, 2s. each.

†*GASCOIGNE'S SCARLET (K). A remarkably handsome Apple of very fine quality ; very large. Nov. to Jan.

*GOLDEN NOBLE (K). Large, handsome, yellow, tender, juicy ; a valuable culinary Apple. Nov. to Jan.

†*HAMBLING'S SEEDLING (K.D). A very large and most remarkable late-keeping variety. First-rate in every way. Dec. to March.

†IRISH PEACH (D). One of the best early dessert Apples. July and Oct.

†*JAMES GRIEVE (D). Medium-sized fruit ; flavour of "Orange Pippin." Oct. to Dec.

†*KERRY PIPPIN (D). Small fruit, sweet, crisp, juicy, and richly flavoured ; one of the best dessert Apples. Sept. and Oct.

†KESWICK CODLIN (K). One of the earliest and most useful of kitchen Apples ; very prolific. Aug. and Sept.

†*KING OF PIPPINS (D). Fruit medium-sized ; a richly flavoured and excellent dessert variety ; in season during Aug. and Sept.

*LADY HENNIKER (K). Large, handsome fruit ; a free bearer, and good keeper. Oct. to Feb.

*LADY SUDELEY (D). Large, yellow with crimson streaks ; very fine Summer Apple. Sept.

†*LANE'S PRINCE ALBERT (K). Large, handsome fruit ; a great bearer, and one of the very best kitchen Apples. Oct. to March.

†*LORD DERBY (K). Large, handsome, heavy cropper ; one of the best. Nov. and Dec.

LORD GROSVENOR (K). A large and handsome culinary Apple. Sept. to Nov.

†LORD SUFFIELD (K). A fine variety of the Keswick Codlin type. It is an early and prolific bearer, and one of the very best of early cooking Apples. Aug. and Sept.

MOTHER (D). Medium, a most delicious conical fruit, rich and aromatic ; does admirably as a pyramid, and is good even in the North. One of the best flavoured kinds with soft flesh.

†*MR. GLADSTONE (D). Medium, mottled red, yellow streaks ; the earliest dessert, free-bearer ; fine flavour. July and Aug.

†NEWTON WONDER (K). Large ; a valuable new kind, between "Wellington" and "Blenheim" ; a handsome fruit, keeping soundly, free grower and bearer ; one of the best among recent sorts.

†*NORFOLK BEAUTY (new) (K). A cross between "Warner's King" and "Dr. Harvey." Fruit large, pale green changing to yellow. In appearance, intermediate between the two parents. Maidens, each 1s. ; Pyramids, 2s. 6d. and 3s. 6d. ; Standards, each 2s.

†*NORWICH PIPPIN (D). A splendid variety resembling Cox's Orange but brighter in colour. It is a splendid keeper and may be had in good condition up to April or May, whilst the flavour is excellent. Maidens, each 1s. ; Pyramids, 2s. 6d. and 3s. 6d. ; Standards, 2s.

*OLD NONPAREIL (D). A richly flavoured and first-rate dessert Apple of excellent keeping qualities. Jan. to May.

†*PEASGOOD'S NONSUCH (D.K). A large, handsome Apple of the Blenheim Orange type ; excellent for dessert or kitchen. Sept. to Jan.

POTT'S SEEDLING (K). Large, angular, yellow ; very heavy cropper. Aug. and Sept.

RED ASTRACHAN (K.D). Large, brilliantly coloured ; handsome. Aug. and Sept.

REINETTE DU CANADA (D.K). A large and excellent Apple, suitable for dessert or culinary purposes. Nov. to April.

†*RIBSTON PIPPIN (D). Well-known splendid old sort, but tree rather subject to canker. Nov. to March.

*SCARLET NONPAREIL (D). A capital dessert Apple of first-rate quality ; in season from Jan. to March.

STONE'S APPLE (K) (syn. Loddington). A large and handsome kitchen Apple ; an immense bearer. Sept. to Dec.

*STIRLING CASTLE (K). An early and free-bearing Apple ; a great bearer, and well suited for dwarf culture. Aug. and Sept.

THE HOUBLON (D). Similar to Cox's Orange Pippin, but higher colour, and will keep much longer. Dec. to Feb.

*THE SANDRINGHAM (D). A fine, large, and very handsome Apple of excellent quality. Feb. to May.

†*VICAR OF BEIGHTON (K). One of the handsomest, most prolific, and best keeping Apples in cultivation. The fruit is large and roundish, and of a deep bright crimson colour, mottled and striped with yellow and green. Nov. to May.

*WARNER'S KING (K). A very large and splendid Apple of first-rate quality ; the tree is a free and vigorous grower, a great bearer, and not subject to disease. Nov. to March.

†*WORCESTER PEARMAIN (K.D). Handsome early variety, suitable for kitchen or dessert ; a great favourite in the market. Aug. and Sept.

YORKSHIRE BEAUTY (K). Large ; fine kitchen Apple. Aug. to Oct.

CRABS (Pyrus baccata).

The following varieties, which we consider by far the best and most useful, are excellent for making preserves. They are also very pretty as ornamental trees, the bright-coloured fruits hanging in abundance, as they generally do, for a long time in Autumn, being very handsome and effective amongst other ornamental trees, shrubs, &c.

			Standards, each 2s.		Maidens, each 1s.
DARTMOUTH. Very handsome dark crimson fruit ; an abundant bearer					
JOHN DOWNIE. Bright crimson, conical fruit of good size and quality ; very handsome	..	..	,, 2s.	,,	,, 1s.
YELLOW SIBERIAN	..	..	,, 2s.	,,	,, 1s.
RED SIBERIAN. Bright scarlet fruit, round and resembling those of the Cherry	..	..	,, 2s.	,,	,, 1s.

If desired we can supply "Acme" Labels for all Fruit Trees.   For Prices see page 60.

SELECT PEARS.

Pears should be much more freely grown than they are. The young trees come into bearing much earlier than is generally supposed, especially when worked on the Quince stock. Many of the varieties are exceedingly prolific, whilst the fruit are more valuable than Apples, choice sorts always finding a ready sale at good prices.

PRICES OF PEARS ON QUINCE OR PEAR STOCK.

			each s. d.	per doz. s. d.				each s. d.	per doz. s. d.
MAIDENS	..	On Quince and Pear Stock	1 0	10 0	STANDARDS. Good	..	On Pear Stock only	1 6	15 0
DWARFS OR BUSHES	,,	,,	1 5	15 0	,, Selected	..	,, ,,	2 0	20 0
PYRAMIDS Good	,,	,,	2 0	20 0	,, Extra Strong Fruiting	,,	,,	2 6	25 0
,, Selected	..	,,	2 6	25 0	STANDARDS, TRAINED	..		5 0	—
,, Extra Strong Fruiting	,,	,,	3 6	35 0	CORDONS, SINGLE.	On Quince and Pear Stock		1 6	17 0
DWARF TRAINED ESPALIERS	..	3s. 6d. and	5 0	—		Special Quotations for Larger Quantities.			

Those marked (†) can be supplied in single cordons.   *Those marked (*) highly recommended for early bearing.*

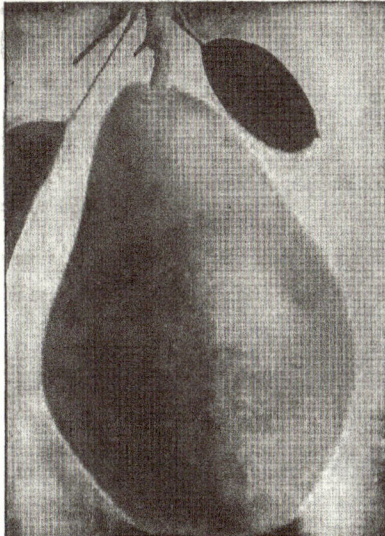

PITMASTON DUCHESS

Our Pears are mostly worked on the ordinary pear stock. Those marked with an asterisk (*) we can, however, supply in dwarfs and pyramids on the quince. These come into bearing and profit much earlier than those worked on the ordinary stock, and are specially recommended to the notice of allotment holders or where the tenure is uncertain.

SELECT PEARS—General List.

BERGAMOTTE ESPEREN. A most delicious late pear; melting, juicy, and sugary; medium-sized fruit. Feb. to April.

†**BEURRE D'AMANLIS.** Fruit large, one of the best early pears. Sept.

BEURRE CAPIAUMONT. A good hardy variety, succeeds well as a standard, and is a great bearer. Oct.

BEURRE D'AREMBERG. A highly-flavoured rich juicy pear, of medium size. Dec. and Jan.

BEURRE BOSC. A large, delicious half-melting dessert pear. It does best in a warm soil and situation, when it is a very free bearer. Nov.

†**BEURRE DIEL.** Fruit very large, does well on a wall. A hardy and vigorous variety of first-rate quality. Oct. and Nov.

BEURRE HARDY. A fine, large dessert pear of most excellent quality. As a pyramid it is a very great bearer. Oct.

BEURRE RANCE. A valuable late dessert pear; an excellent bearer. Feb. to May.

BEURRE SUPERFIN. One of the best pears in cultivation; fruit large, very handsome, and of splendid quality. Sept. and Oct.

†***CATILLAC.** Fruit large; one of the best stewing pears. Does not succeed well as a Pyramid or Standard unless well sheltered. Dec. to April.

†**CLAPP'S FAVOURITE.** A medium-sized good early pear. Aug.

CONFERENCE. Fruit large; very prolific, a valuable market sort. Nov.

CONSEILLER DE LA COUR. Fruit large, one of the finest pears in cultivation. Oct. and Nov.

†**DOYENNE DU COMICE.** Fruit large and of first-rate quality; a healthy grower and a good bearer. Oct. and Nov.

DOYENNE BOUSSOCH. A very large lemon-coloured pear of good quality, juicy, and melting; good bearer. Oct.

†***DUCHESSE D'ANGOULEME.** A delicious dessert pear of great excellence. An abundant bearer. Oct. and Nov.

†***EMILE D'HEYST.** A very useful and good pear. Fruit large, juicy, and finely flavoured. Tree hardy and a prolific bearer. Nov. and Dec.

GENERAL WAUCHOPE (new). Fruit of medium size, pale green changing to yellow, with small brown dots and russet blotches, flesh soft and of delicious flavour. Award of Merit, R.H.S. Dec. Two-year Bush Trees on Pear Stock, 2s. 6d. Large Fruiting, 2s. each.

†***GLOU MORCEAU.** A very fine dessert pear. Dec. and Jan.

HESSLE. Well-known good market sort; abundant bearer. Oct.

†***JARGONELLE.** A large handsome pear of excellent quality; first-class for wall culture in the Northern Counties. Aug.

†***JOSEPHINE DE MALINES.** A fine pear of most delicious flavour; the tree is hardy and an excellent bearer. Jan. to May.

†***LOUISE BONNE OF JERSEY.** Fruit medium-sized and of most delicious quality; very free bearing. Oct.

LE LECTIER. Very large, flesh fine, melting and very juicy. A new variety. Dec. to Feb.

†**MARIE LOUISE.** A large-fruited and exceedingly fine sort, of the highest merit as a dessert pear. Oct. and Nov.

MARIE LOUISE D'UCCLE. A large useful pear of first-rate quality; a great cropper. Oct.

†***MARGUERITE MARILLAT.** Very large and showy, with aromatic flavour; handsome in colour and shape; the finest in its season. Sept.

†***PITMASTON DUCHESS.** A very fine pear indeed, the fruit is very large and handsome, and of first-rate quality. Oct. to Dec.

†***PRINCESS.** A handsome pear; large, melting, flavour very good; the fruit will keep good until Christmas. Nov.

†***ROOSEVELT.** A new pear of immense size, sometimes measuring 16 inches in circumference, skin smooth, yellow-tinted with salmon pink, and of delicious flavour; highly recommended. One-year Trees on Quince, 1s. 6d. each; Two-year Trees on Quince, 2s. each; Fruiting Cordons, 2s. 6d. each; Stout Standards, 2s. 6d. each.

SANTA CLAUS (new). Ripe at Christmas, and certainly the finest pear fit for use at that season. Two-year Trees on Quince, 2s. 6d. each; Maidens, 1s. 6d. each; Stout Standards, 2s. 6d each.

SOUVENIR DU CONGRES. A splendid pear of first size and handsome appearance, capital bearer. Aug. and Sept.

UVEDALE'S ST. GERMAIN. A very large pear, first-class for stewing. Jan. to April.

VICAR OF WINKFIELD. A very handsome and excellent pear, of large size, but requires a wall to ripen it well. Nov. to Jan.

†***WILLIAMS' BON CHRETIEN.** Well-known splendid old dessert pear; very hardy and a good bearer. Aug. and Sept.

†**WINTER ORANGE.** A large stewing pear of first-class quality, yellow covered with russet brown; a good grower and bearer. Feb. to Mar.

WINTER NELIS. Fruit small but of most delicious flavour; quite hardy and an excellent bearer Nov. to Feb.

If desired we can supply permanent "Acme" Labels for all Fruit Trees. For prices see page 60

SELECT PLUMS.

Although as a rule, Plums attain the greatest perfection when grown as wall fruit, most of the varieties will succeed admirably when grown as Pyramids or Standards. Dwarf trees should be lifted and root-pruned from time to time, if making too strong a growth, and the branches should be thinned out to admit air and induce the formation of fruit buds. For growing on walls the following are highly recommended :—Green Gage, Golden Gage, Coe's Golden Drop. For general purposes the following are amongst the very best :—Cox's Emperor, Early Prolific, Diamond, Jefferson's, Magnum Bonum, Victoria, Sultan, Pond's Seedling, The Czar, Grand Duke.

DWARFS OR MAIDENS	each 1s. 0d. ;	per doz. 10s. 0d.
DWARF TRAINED	,, 3s. 6d. ;	,, 35s. 0d.
STANDARDS	,, 1s. 0d. ;	,, 17s. 6d.
TRAINED (list of sorts on application)		each 5s. 0d.
PYRAMIDS	each 2s., 2s. 6d. and 3s. 6d. ;	per doz. 20s., 25s. and 35s.

PLUM—THE CZAR.

General List.

D denotes dessert, K kitchen.

BELLE DE LOUVAIN (K). Very large handsome fruit, red, of rich flavour. A good strong-growing orchard or garden variety.

COE'S GOLDEN DROP (D). Large oval fruit, pale yellow spotted with red ; one of the very best for dessert or preserving. End of Sept.

COX'S EMPEROR (K). Large dark reddish-purple fruit, firm flesh, sweet, rich, and juicy. A very fine bearer. Sept.

DAMSON PRUNE (K). Small oval fruit, a great bearer. Sept.

DENNISTON'S SUPERB (D). Large oval fruit, greenish-yellow blotched purple ; a delicious dessert plum, and an abundant bearer. Aug.

DIAMOND (K). Large oval, dark purple fruit ; an excellent variety for cooking or preserving. Sept.

EARLY PROLIFIC (D). A certain bearer ; very valuable market sort ; ripens middle of July on a wall, and when fully ripe is good for dessert, and one of the best flavoured when cooked. July.

GIANT PRUNE (new) (Burbanks). A very large, long oval fruit of dark red colour, with yellow flesh of excellent flavour. The tree is a splendid grower, hardy and a good bearer. Fruit firm and does not split. A valuable plum for market purposes.

One-year trees, 1s. 6d. each ; two-year trees, 2s. 6d. each.

GOLDEN GAGE (D). Large fruit, of very rich and delicious flavour ; a most excellent and prolific sort. Sept.

GREENGAGE (D). Well known to be the very best and richest of all. In common with all the Gages, this race requires vigorous root pruning, and then bears freely ; as Pot trees they succeed in an Orchard House, but as Standards they are not satisfactory, the birds taking the best buds in Winter. Aug.

JEFFERSON'S (D). A large and delicious plum, hardy, and a good bearer. Sept.

KIRKE'S (D). One of the very best of the blue plums, the fruit is medium-sized and richly flavoured ; a first-class dessert variety. Sept.

MAGNUM BONUM, WHITE (K). Large yellow fruit ; an excellent kitchen variety. Sept.

MONARCH (K). One of the best late plums, of large size and splendid flavour, dark purplish blue ; it is a heavy bearer and fruit does not crack with rain. A valuable late market plum. Sept.

ORLEANS (K). A good cooking or preserving plum ; a great bearer. Aug.

POND'S SEEDLING (K). Very large, good bearer and a sturdy grower. Forms a spreading tree ; fruit is enormous from a wall ; valuable for late market or garden culture. Early in Sept.

PRIMATE (Rivers). A splendid new late plum, purplish red in colour, dotted with good bloom ; very large and late variety. A valuable addition.

REINE CLAUDE DE BAVAY (D). Large, round, greenish-yellow fruit of the " gage " type, rich and delicious flavour ; the tree is hardy and a great bearer. Beginning of October.

SULTAN (K). Fruit above medium size, skin dark purple ; covered with a thick blue bloom. A culinary plum of great excellence. Middle of August.

THE CZAR (D.K.). Very large, purple fruit of rich flavour ; it is an abundant bearer, and will prove most valuable to market growers on account of its earliness, fine appearance, and excellent quality. End of July.

VICTORIA (K). A well-known and very fine variety ; the tree is hardy and an almost constant bearer. The most useful kind of the season. Early in Sept.

CHERRIES.

DWARFS OR MAIDENS	each 1s. ;	per doz. 10s.
DWARF TRAINED	each 3s. 6d. and 5s. ;	per doz. 35s.
STANDARDS	each 2s. and 2s. 6d. ;	per doz. 20s. and 25s.
STANDARDS, TRAINED (list of names on application)		each 5s.
PYRAMIDS	each 2s., 2s. 6d., and 3s. 6d. ;	per doz. 20s., 25s., and 35s.

BIGARREAU. Large and of first-rate quality ; a capital bearer. July.

BIGARREAU NAPOLEON. Good bearer, hardy and excellent, follows the Bigarreau ; valuable as extending the season ; first rate for market, handsome, and indispensable for garden culture.

BLACK BIGARREAU. Fruit large and good ; an excellent variety.

BLACK EAGLE. Fruit of good size and flavour ; excellent. July.

BLACK HEART. A capital early black cherry of good quality, free bearer.

EARLY RIVERS. Large, shining black, very handsome, rich flavour ; one of the best for forcing or cherry house, and valuable for wall. As an orchard tree it requires close pruning for three or four years, and then forms a grand tree. The fruit makes a very high price in the market.

DOWNTON. Fruit above medium size, flesh pale amber, mottled with deep red, very rich and high flavour. July.

ELTON. Large, rich and excellent. July.

FROGMORE EARLY PROLIFIC. A capital early sort, very prolific.

GOVERNOR WOOD. Large, yellow, mottled with red, sweet and rich ; a good bearer ; excellent. July.

KNIGHT'S EARLY BLACK. Flesh deep purple, tender, rich, and juicy ; a delicious early cherry. End of June.

MAY DUKE. Large, juicy, rich, and excellent ; an abundant bearer as a standard or a bush. July.

MORELLO. Valuable for preserving and bottling. Pyramid trees produce fruit equal to that from a wall. Succeeds on north walls, and is occasionally planted as a Standard.

THE NOBLE. Very large, flesh firm, of rich flavour. This new variety is a great addition both for Garden or Market culture. It is a profuse bearer, and the fruit keeps well after gathering. It proves quite distinct from others in our collection.

WHITE HEART. Flesh firm, sweet and pleasant.

SELECT PEACHES.

MAIDENS, 2s. each. DWARF TRAINED, 5s. and 7s. 6d. each. STANDARD TRAINED, marked (*), 8s. 6d., 10s. 6d., and 15s. each.

PEACH—ROYAL GEORGE.

*ALEXANDRA NOBLESSE. Very large fruit, flesh tender, juicy, and richly flavoured. Middle of Aug.
*ALEXANDER. A very early Peach. Brilliant colour. July.

*BARRINGTON. Large fruit of rich vinous flavour, and first-rate quality The tree is hardy and a good bearer. Sept.
BELLEGARDE. Fruit round, deep red all over; flesh pale yellow. Middle of Sept.
CONDOR. Large bright crimson fruit, handsome and of rich flavour; a capital variety for forcing. Early in Aug.
CRAWFORD'S EARLY. Very large fruit, of splendid colour; very tender and melting, remarkably succulent and delicious. Aug. and Sept.
CRIMSON GALANDE. Large; deep crimson; flesh tender, melting, rich, and deliciously flavoured. Aug.
*DR. HOGG. Large, fruit remarkable for its high colour; it is firm yet melting, and of rich sugary flavour. Middle of Aug.
DUKE OF YORK. Large free stone, fruit well coloured and of excellent flavour; ripe about the same time as Alexandra. Maidens 2s. 0d. Dwarf trained 7s. 6d.
DYMOND. Fruit large, skin greenish yellow; flesh white, rich, melting, juicy. Middle of Sept.
*EARLY RIVERS. Large, pale straw-coloured fruit, very rich and fine flavour; first-rate for forcing. End of July.
EARLY LOUISE. Medium size, bright red; melting, very juicy. July.
EARLY GROSSE MIGNONNE. Medium size, melting; one of the finest early Peaches. Aug.
GOSHAWK. Large fruit of exquisite flavour, good bearer; colour pale with red flesh, very hardy. Sept.
*GROSSE MIGNONNE. Large, melting, excellent fruit; one of the finest in cultivation. Early in Sept.
*HALE'S EARLY. Large size; melting and very good. July.
LADY PALMERSTON. Large, melting, and very good skin, greenish yellow marbled with crimson; very handsome, flesh pale yellow. End of Sept.
LATE ADMIRABLE. Fruit very large; skin yellowish green, flesh greenish white. End of Sept.
LORD PALMERSTON. The largest of Peaches, skin creamy white with pink cheek, flesh firm, melting, and juicy. Sept.
*NOBLESSE. Large, melting, and excellent; one of the best either for forcing or the open wall. Sept.
PEREGRINE. Distinct Mid-season variety of fine constitution, fruit large and handsome with brilliant crimson skin, flesh rich and highly flavoured, and parting readily from the stone. Maidens 2s. 0d. Dwarf trained 7s. 6d.
PRINCE OF WALES. Large, rich melting fruit; an excellent late variety.
PRINCESS OF WALES. One of the largest Peaches and best; skin cream with a rosy cheek, melting and rich End of Sept.
*ROYAL GEORGE. Large, melting, and excellent; a good variety for the open wall. Sept.
*SEA EAGLE. A very large Peach of good flavour; remarkable for its brilliant colour and size. End of Sept.
*STIRLING CASTLE. A fine hardy Peach of the *Royal George* type, large, skin deep red on sunny side, rich and highly flavoured. Aug.
*WATERLOO. A superior first early variety; bears freely in pots and is hardy when grown outside. Six weeks earlier than *Royal George*.

SELECT APRICOTS.

MAIDENS, 2s. each. DWARF TRAINED, 5s. and 7s. 6d. each. STANDARD TRAINED, 10s. 6d. and 15s. each.

BREDA. Small, rich, vinous, and agreeably flavoured. Aug.
HEMSKERK. Flesh tender, juicy, and richly flavoured. July and Aug.
KAISHA. Middle size, flesh deep orange, juicy and rich. Aug.
LARGE EARLY. Very rich and juicy. July and Aug.

MOORPARK. One of the best. Aug. and Sept.
PEACH. Very large, rich, and juicy; one of the finest of all. Aug. and Sept.
ROYAL. Large, rich and juicy. July and Aug.

SELECT NECTARINES.

MAIDENS, 2s. 0d. each. DWARF TRAINED, 5s. and 7s. 6d. each. STANDARD TRAINED, marked (*) 10s. 6d., 15s., and 21s. each.

*EARLY RIVERS. A seedling Nectarine, raised by Mr. T. F. Rivers, ripening twenty-one days before *Lord Napier*. It is a certain and heavy cropper, and promises to be one of the most valuable Nectarines yet introduced.
*DOWNTON. Fruit large, oval, skin greenish in the shade, dark red on sunny side; melting, juicy, rich, and highly flavoured; an excellent variety. End of Aug.
*ELRUGE. Medium-sized fruit, melting, rich and juicy; one of the best. Aug. and Sept.
HUMBOLDT. A very large Nectarine of splendid flavour. Sept.
*LORD NAPIER. Medium size; pale cream with red cheek, flesh melting, very early, one of the best.

NEWINGTON. Fruit large, rich, sweet, and finely flavoured. Early in Sept.
*PINEAPPLE. Large, bright red on the sunny side, very rich and sweet. Sept.
*PITMASTON ORANGE. Large bright orange, dark brownish-red on the sunny side; melting, juicy, and rich; an excellent Nectarine, a good bearer. Aug. and Sept.
RIVERS' ORANGE. Similar to *Pitmaston Orange*, but earlier.
ROMAN. Large, deep red; juicy, rich, highly flavoured. Sept.
VICTORIA. Very rich, large, and sugary; a fine fruit when grown under glass.
VIOLETTE HATIVE. Medium-sized, melting, rich, and excellent. Aug.

CURRANTS.

CURRANT. BOSKOOP GIANT BLACK.

Generally speaking, the Black Currant thrives best on a damp soil and the Reds and Whites on a light soil, but with good cultivation they will succeed in almost any soil. Trained on a north wall or fence the Reds and Whites are exceedingly prolific and splendid fruit may be had well into September. Liquid manure is very beneficial where extra fine fruit are desired.

BLACKSMITH (new). One of the largest Black Currants in cultivation, fruit enormous size and fine flavour.

1 year plants, 1s. 6d. each ; 15s. doz.
2 year plants, 2s. 0d. each ; 21s. doz.

BOSKOOP GIANT BLACK. The finest black currant yet introduced. It is of extraordinary vigorous growth with long bunches of enormous fruit. Flavour, sweet and rich. A first-rate variety for exposed situations, and although it flowers late it ripens early. F.C.C.

per 100, 30s. ; per doz. 4s. ; each 6d.

FAY'S PROLIFIC. One of the best Red Currants. The bush is a strong grower, wonderfully prolific, and comes into bearing early. The fruit is large, bright red, and of excellent flavour.

per doz. 4s. ; each 6d

VICTORIA BLACK. This is one of the finest and largest black currants in cultivation. The fruit is of great size, splendid quality and flavour ; and the plant is a most abundant bearer. A first-rate market sort.

Strong young bushes, per doz. 4s. ; each 6d.

OTHER VARIETIES—
Strong Bushes   per 100, 21s. and 30s. ; per doz. 3s. and 4s.

BLACK—	RED—	WHITE—
Black Grape	Cherry	White
Lee's Prolific	Raby Castle. Fine	Dutch
Naples	Red Dutch	Transparent
Baldwin's Black	Victoria	White

We have a fine lot of Fan-trained Currant Bushes. Our selection from the above named varieties 1s. 9d. each, 18s. per doz.

From Mr. W. Ling, Gardener, Rockland.
August 20th.
"I have done well with your Currant Trees, taking first Prize for Black and first for White at our Show."
From Mr. D. A. TALLACH Oban.
April 25th.
"I won first Prize for Gooseberries from the trees supplied by you at our Show."

GOOSEBERRIES.

LANCASHIRE PRIZE VARIETIES.

A very fine class, much esteemed for the splendid size of their fruit and their value for exhibition or dessert. When well ripened they are of delicious flavour and equal to many forced fruits.

LANCASHIRE PRIZE GOOSEBERRIES.

RED—	WHITE—	YELLOW—
Bobby	Careless	Broom Girl
Lancashire Lad	Hero of the Nile	Criterion
Roaring Lion	Mitre	High Sheriff
Rifleman	Snowdrift	Leader
Speedwell	White Eagle	Pilot
Victoria	White Swan	Ringer

GREEN—General—Langley Gage, Langley Green, Queen Victoria, Turnout.

And many other first-class varieties.

Our own selection in choice variety in strong 2 and 3 year old bushes.

per doz. 6s. ; per 100, 40s.

We have a few Standards on about 3 feet stems, 2s. 6d. each.

Other Varieties.

NORWICH LATE RED (New). Fruit very large, the bushes are of free growth and good habit, very heavy bearer.

2 and 3 year old bushes, 9d. each ; per doz. 6s.

MAY DUKE. One of the earliest gooseberries in cultivation. It is a heavy cropper, and the fruit is large and handsome ; colour deep red, thin skin.

per doz. 4s. ; each 6d.

WHINHAM'S "INDUSTRY." A superb variety, bearing a wonderful profusion of large handsome fruit, which are of a dull red colour when ripe. Strong bushes, per 100, 27s. 6d. ; per doz. 4s.

KEEPSAKE. A very large straw-coloured variety of excellent flavour, and one of the best and earliest for gathering green.

Strong bushes, per 100, 27s. 6d. ; per doz. 4s. ; each 6d.

OTHER VARIETIES. Strong Bushes—

Our selection, per 100, 24s. to 30s. ; per doz. 3s. 6d., 4s. 6d.

We can supply Fan-trained Gooseberries from the above varieties

1s. 9d. each ; 18s. per doz.

Standards, 2s. 6d. each. Single Cordons, 1s. 6d. each.

GOOSEBERRY, WHINHAM'S "INDUSTRY."

RASPBERRIES.

Ground intended for these should be deeply trenched and heavily manured. The canes should be planted (not too deeply) about 2 feet apart and the rows should be 5 or 6 feet apart, and after planting, a mulching of well-decayed manure should be placed on the surface. Newly planted canes should be cut back to 2 feet to encourage the formation of suckers for the following season.

RED ANTWERP. WHITE ANTWERP. Per 100, 12s. ; per doz. 2s.
BAUMFORTH'S SEEDLING. A fine variety ; fruit very large, of the most beautiful crimson colour; an abundant bearer of good habit.
per 100, 12s. ; per doz. 2s.
HORNET (Rivers.) A very fine Raspberry, fruit deliciously flavoured, and the most juicy of any variety. A splendid cropper, and will be largely grown when better known. First Class Certificate, Royal Horticultural Society   ..   .. per 100, 15s. ; per doz. 2s. 3d.
LOWE'S PERPETUAL. This is a grand new Red variety of great size and perpetual bearer, good flavour, will fruit from middle of June to September   .. Strong Canes, per 100, 30s. ; per doz. 5s.
NOVEMBER ABUNDANCE. A splendid Autumn bearing variety. The fruit, which is borne in large clusters, is large, of a deep red colour and of excellent flavour, while the canes are strong and vigorous
per 100, 15s. ; per doz. 2s. 3d.
PERFECTION. This is an absolutely new and distinct variety. It is an exceptionally strong grower and makes a better plant the first year than any other variety. It is a good cropper, producing fruit from base to top of cane of a bold size, firm, fine, acidulous flavour, and brilliant scarlet colour, the high colour being retained even when the fruit is fully ripe
per 100, 15s. ; per doz. 2s. 3d.
SUPERLATIVE. Fruit very large, mostly freely produced ; au excellent variety   ..   ..   .. per 100, 12s. ; per doz. 2s.
YELLOW SUPERLATIVE (new). The largest and strongest growing yellow variety, very large fruit.
Strong fruiting Canes, per 100, 21s. ; per doz. 3s.

BLACKBERRIES.

PARSLEY-LEAVED. Very ornamental cut-leaved variety, which bears large fruit, good and productive   ..   .. per doz. 5s. ; each 6d
WILSON JUNIOR. One of the finest and most prolific in cultivation, producing very large, glossy black fruit of delicious flavour
per doz. 5s. ; each 6d.

RASPBERRY, SUPERLATIVE.

STRAWBERRY PLANTS—Prepared Runners.

KING GEORGE V. This is a fine new early forcing and outdoor Strawberry. It is a really magnificent fruit, quite as large as Royal Sovereign, but ripens a week earlier.
Strong Plants from open ground, per 100, 30s. ; per doz 5s

LAXTON'S MAINCROP—Fine New Maincrop Strawberry. The following is the raiser's description :—" Undoubtedly the largest and firmest Strawberry we have yet raised, a cross between Bedford Champion and The Laxton ; a vigorous grower, throwing out very bold, large trusses in the greatest profusion. Undoubtedly the ' Maincrop' Strawberry of the future ; good in all respects, both in colour, size, flavour, and vigour of plant."
Strong Plants from open ground, per 100, 30s. ; per doz. 5s.

" PROFIT," This is a main crop fruit which we have confidence in recommending for size, firmness, flavour, and cropping.
Strong open ground Plants, per 100, 16s. ; per doz. 2s. 6d.

EATON GROVE FAVOURITE. This splendid variety ripens ten to fourteen days earlier than Royal Sovereign. The fruit is not quite so large, but is much sweeter in flavour. We can highly recommend this.
Open ground Plants, per 100, 6s. 6d. ; per doz. 1s.

GEORGE MUNRO. A cross between Royal Sovereign and Sir Chas. Napier. Award of Merit, R.H.S.   Per 100, 6s. 6d. ; per doz. 1s.

" THE EARL " (Laxton). Waterloo × Royal Sovereign. The Raisers say :—" This may be best described as a much-improved ' Viscountess H. de Thury.' In colour, shape and flavour it is almost identical ; but it is larger in size of fruit, and more vigorous and free cropping in habit ; the flavour is very similar to that well-known sort, being rich yet juicy, and it should make a useful preserving variety owing to its specific density."
Strong Plants from open ground, per 100, 30s. ; per doz. 5s.

The following Varieties all at 5s. per 100 ; 9d. per doz. Not less than 50 supplied at the rate per 100.

BEDFORD CHAMPION. One of the largest fruits in commerce, often 2½ to 3 ozs. in weight and 6 ins. circumference. Bright scarlet skin, flesh white.
BRITISH QUEEN. Well-known superb variety ; the finest flavoured Strawberry in existence ; requires good cultivation.
FILLBASKET. The colour is a good bright scarlet similar to Royal Sovereign, the flesh is white and firm.
GIVON'S LATE PROLIFIC. A fine new variety raised from Waterloo and Latest of All. Large, wedge-shaped fruit of rich colour, and splendid flavour. Award of Merit, R.H.S.
LAXTON'S LATEST. A very late variety. The fruit is large, conical wedge-shaped, deep crimson in colour and of fine flavour.
PRESIDENT. A great cropper, colour crimson, of superior flavour.
PROGRESS. A splendid variety of full rich flavour. Large flattish wedge-shaped fruit.
REWARD. Very large, wedge-shaped fruit of most excellent quality, being of the richest " Queen " flavour.

ROYAL SOVEREIGN. This fine early variety possesses all the qualities required in a really good Strawberry. The best variety for pot culture.
SENSATION. An enormous second early or mid-season variety of good flavour, and one of the largest Strawberries ever introduced.
SIR JOSEPH PAXTON. Hardy early variety.
" ST. ANTOINE DE PADOUE." Said to be by far the finest perpetual bearer yet raised. Superior to " St. Joseph."
THE CROPPER. A very prolific main crop variety of a rich crimson colour, the flesh is white and of tho most luscious flavour.
THE LAXTON. A cross between Royal Sovereign and Sir Joseph Paxton. One of the finest and best early.
WATERLOO. Fruit large and of a fine dark crimson colour, almost black when ripe, a good grower.

100 in 10 choice varieties, our own selection   ..   ..   .. 5s. 6d.

GRAPE VINES.

The best time for the Spring planting of these, either on inside or outside borders, is in March or April, when the sap is beginning to flow and the buds show signs of bursting into leaf. Ground intended for growing Grapes should be carefully drained, if the soil is wet, and should be well broken up to a depth of two feet, and well mixed with some old well-rotted manure and rough loam, with the addition of some old lime rubbish, if procurable.

Our stock of Grape Vines for the present season is very fine. The canes have all been grown from eyes and are well-ripened, strong and healthy. The buds are thoroughly matured and plump.

The fruiting canes we offer are extra strong and stout, from eight to ten feet in length; and if cultivated in pots should bear from eight to twelve bunches each next season.

H. denotes those varieties that require a heated vinery.   C denotes those suitable for growing in a cool vinery.

BLACK ALICANTE (H). One of the largest and handsomest grapes in cultivation. The fruit is of oval form and carries a fine bloom. It is of excellent flavour and very prolific. Its flavour is at the best when allowed to hang till Christmas.
BLACK HAMBURGH (C). Berries large, round, sweet and juicy. Large broadly shouldered bunches. A well-known most excellent variety and probably the most popular in cultivation. The best for general use.
BUCKLAND'S SWEET WATER (C). Large bunches and berries of amber colour. An excellent variety for a cool vinery.
FOSTER'S SEEDLING (C). Pale amber, an excellent variety.
GROS COLMAR (H). Bunches and berries very large. Dark purple with beautiful bloom. A very handsome and deservedly popular variety.
GROS MAROC (H). An exceedingly handsome large-fruited grape of delicious flavour and one that ripens early.
LADY DOWNE'S SEEDLING (H). Large black berries of good flavour. This is a splendid keeper and will hang till March.
MADRESFIELD COURT MUSCAT (H). Long bunches and large black berries of delicious Muscat flavour, will hang for a long time without shrivelling.
MUSCAT OF ALEXANDRIA (H). Long and large bunches of large red amber-coloured berries of the most delicious Muscat flavour. The most popular of all the "Muscats."
ROYAL MUSCADINE. A fine hardy white grape that will succeed well on a south wall   each 3s. 6d., 5s., and 7s. 6d.

Prices for the above varieties, with the exception of Royal Muscadine
   STRONG PLANTING CANES, in pots   ..   ..   each 3s. 6d. and 5s.
   FRUITING CANES, in pots, very fine   ..   ..   each 5s., 7s. 6d. and a few at 10s. 6d.

FIGS.

BROWN TURKEY. Most abundant bearer; the finest for out-door culture, and very free setter in pots for forcing.
    Strong Plants, Fan Trained, not in pots.   each 5s.
NEGRO LARGO. Very luscious, free bearer, strong grower; large rich chocolate purple fruit; splendid for second crop under glass, but not fertile outside.   F.C.
WHITE ISCHIA. Small, sweet and delicious; produces three crops a year in heat; forces well; great bearer; for indoor culture only.
   STRONG PLANTS, in pots, Trained, flat   ..   each 3s. 6d.
   FRUITING   "   "   ..   each 5s., and 7s. 6d.

ALMONDS.
STANDARDS   ..   ..   each 1s. 6d. and 2s. 6d.

MEDLARS.
STANDARDS   ..   ..   each 2s. 6d.

NUTS AND FILBERTS.
We have a very fine stock of these in good strong plants.
DREADNOUGHT (new). A very large and excellent cob nut of excellent flavour. Very prolific.
   STRONG FRUITING BUSHES   ..   3 for 2s. 6d. ; each 1s.
NORWICH PROLIFIC. An excellent variety and a great bearer.
    per doz. 10s. 6d. ; each 1s.
Also the following sorts :—Cosford, Kentish Cob, White Filbert, Red Filbert, Purple Leaved Filbert, &c.
STRONG FRUITING DWARFS or BUSHES in first-class condition for removal   per doz. 9s. ; each 1s.

WALNUTS.
FINE STANDARDS   ..   each 2s. 6d., 3s. 6d., and 5s.

QUINCE.
STANDARDS   ..   ..   each 2s. 6d.

PHENOMENAL BERRY.
(Novelty.)

A further cross between the Logan Berry and the Raspberry, the shape and colour of the Logan Berry, with the flavour of a Raspberry. Without the hard core of the Logan Berry, and will be a most suitable fruit of the future for dessert or preserving, which will ripen before the "Lowberry." This is a very strong grower and should be planted in the same way as the Logan Berry.   In pots, 1s. 6d. each.   From open ground, 1s. each.

LOGAN BERRY.

This fine American fruit has proved a decided acquisition and is now being extensively grown for market purposes. Grown in the same way as Raspberries. It is a strong grower and will often succeed where those fail. It is of very strong growth and makes a capital plant for poles or pillars; is also makes an excellent fence, and is very useful for pergolas. Plant 6 or 8 feet apart.
STRONG PLANTS from layers, the true variety each 9d. ; per doz. 7s. 6d.

THE LOWBERRY.

A very fine new variety of the Logan Berry, producing an abundance of handsome black fruit without core, and of delicious flavour.
    In pots, 1s. 6d. each.

THE HIMALAYA BERRY.

A new berry from California, said to have been found growing on the mountains. It is a very strong grower, plants at our Nurseries have made a growth of 15 feet; the plants have fruited well, producing large clusters of beautiful black berries, said to be free fruiting.
    Strong plants, 1s. 6d. each.

MULBERRIES.
STANDARDS   ..   ..   each 5s. to 7s. 6d.

For plants of Asparagus, Herbs, Rhubarb, & Sea Kale. *See page 61.*

OUR GUINEA COLLECTION OF CHOICE FRUITS.

We have much pleasure in offering the following liberal Collection of Fruits, which will be found admirably suited to the requirements of a small garden, or where the space for fruit growing is limited. The fruit Trees will in all instances be Dwarfs, and only good varieties will be sent, but the selection of sorts must be left to us. We make no charge for packages, but in consequence of the extreme cheapness of this Collection, we cannot pay carriage, and must ask that all orders be accompanied by a remittance.

OUR GUINEA COLLECTION OF FRUITS CONTAINS.

6 APPLES. Best sorts for succession.	2 CHERRIES. Two varieties.	2 LOGAN BERRIES.
4 PEARS. In good variety.	12 GOOSEBERRIES. In variety.	12 RASPBERRIES. Best sorts.
4 PLUMS. Most useful sorts.	18 CURRANTS. Red, Black, and White.	50 STRAWBERRIES. In four sorts.

We supply half the above Collection for 11s. 6d.

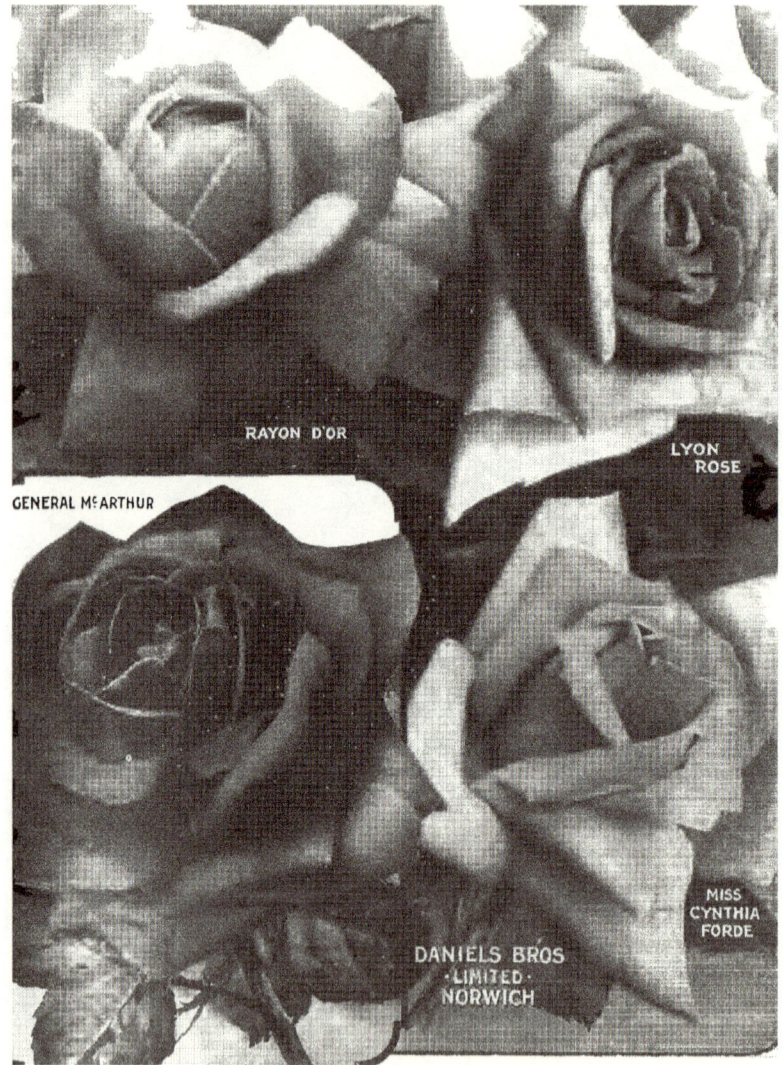

RAYON D'OR

LYON ROSE

GENERAL McARTHUR

MISS CYNTHIA FORDE

DANIELS BROS
·LIMITED·
NORWICH

HYBRID PERPETUAL & H. T. ROSES.

These magnificent and beautiful Roses are better adapted than any others for exhibition and pot culture. They continue in flower from the early part of June to the end of October, and are by far the most desirable for general cultivation.

The "NORWICH" Collection
of 12 Champion Bush Roses, 10/6 Carr. Paid.

CAROLINE TESTOUT	HUGH DICKSON	LYON ROSE	MRS. J. LAING
CAPTAIN HAYWARD	JULIET	MADAME ABEL CHATENAY	RAYON D'OR
FRAU KARL DRUSCHKI	LADY HILLINGDON	MISS C. FORDE	RICHMOND.

The "TOWN CLOSE" Collection
of 18 Very Choice Bush Roses for Exhibition, 15/- Carr. Paid.

ALFRED COLOMB	FRAU KARL DRUSCHKI	LYON ROSE	MRS. A. R. WADDELL
BESSIE BROWN	GENL. JACQUIMINOT	MADAME RAVARY	PRINCE CAM DE ROHAN
CAPT. HAYWARD	GUSTAVE REGIS	MARQUIS DE LITTA	SIR ROWLAND HILL
CAROLINE TESTOUT	KILLARNEY	MRS. JOHN LAING	
DEAN HOLE	LA FRANCE	MRS. S. CRAWFORD	

The "NORFOLK" Collection
of 24 Choice and Well-known Bush and Climbing Roses for 20/- Carr. Paid.

ABEL CARRIERE	FRAU KARL DRUSCHKI	LYON ROSE	PEACE
ALFRED COLOMB	GENERAL McARTHUR	MADAME CHARLES	PRINCE CAM DE ROHAN
BARONESS ROTHSCHILD	G. C. WAUD	MADAME RAVARY	PRINCE DE BULGARIA
*CRIMSON RAMBLER	*HIAWATHA	MARIE BAUMANN	RICHMOND
*DOROTHY PERKINS	J. B. CLARKE	MRS. SHARMAN CRAWFORD	ULRICH BRUNNER
DUKE OF EDINBURGH	*LADY GAY	MRS. J. LAING	*WHITE DOROTHY PERKINS

*Those marked * are Climbers.*

The "POPULAR" Collection
of 12 Dwarf Roses, in 12 Varieties (our selection) 7/6 Carr. Paid.

The "CLIMBING" Collection
for Pergolas or Arches, 12 of the best for 10/6 Carr. Paid.

BLUSH RAMBLER	DOROTHY PERKINS	LADY GAY	TAUSENDSCHON
CARMINE PILLAR	EXCELSA	MADAME ALFRED CARRIERE	THALIA
CRIMSON RAMBLER	HIAWATHA	MRS. F. W. FLIGHT	WHITE DOROTHY PERKINS

The "WALL" Collection
for Walls and Pillars, 12 of the best for 10/6 Carr. Paid.

AIMEE VIBERT	CHESHUNT HYBRID	GLOIRE DE DIJON	REINE M. HENRIETTE
BOUQUET D'OR	CLIMBING LA FRANCE	GRUSS AN TEPLITZ	TRIER
CELINE FORESTIER	„ CAROLINE TESTOUT	J. B. CLARKE	WM. ALLEN RICHARDSON

HYBRID PERPETUAL AND OTHER ROSES.
Choice New Roses.

BRITISH QUEEN (H.T.). The finest pure white Hybrid Tea Rose in existence, surpassing in purity and elegance of form " Frau K. Druschki "; very free, opening well in all weathers. Bush, each 3s.

CARINE (H.T.). Colour orange-carmine, suffused buff; a good addition to this class ... ... Standards, each 2s. 6d.; Bush, each 2s.

CLAUDIUS (H.T.). Colour bright glowing rose, of uniform shade throughout, strong and sturdy growth, flowers carried erect on stout stems; sweetly scented ... Standards, each 2s. 6d.; Bush, each 2s.

CORONATION (Wichuriana). Bright crimson, shaded scarlet, splashed with small white streaks. Climbing Polyantha Bush, each 3s. 6d.

EARL OF GOSFORD (H.T.). Strong, vigorous growth, very hardy, colour dark crimson, heavily shaded, after the style of " Victor Hugo," very free and perpetual ... ... Bush, each 3s. 6d.

GEORGE DICKSON (H.T.). Strong, vigorous, upright growth; flowers large, perfect in shape and unique in colour, which is a velvety black crimson, the back of the petals being heavily veined with pure crimson maroon. Bush, each 3s.

DUCHESS OF WESTMINSTER (H.T.). First-class exhibition variety; colour mad.-pink, fine Standards, each 2s. 6d.; Bush, each 2s.

KING GEORGE V. (H.T.). A rich blackish crimson Hybrid Tea Rose; the flower is very large and full, beautifully shaped; it keeps its colour in the hottest sun and does not turn blue as so many of our dark roses do. The perfume is very strong and pleasing. Bush, each 3s. 6d.

LOUISE CATHERINE BRESLAU (Rose Pernetiana). A very vigorous grower. Large oval-shaped bud of coral red tint shaded with chrome yellow; flower very large, full and globular; superb colouring, shrimp pink shaded with reddish coppery orange and chrome yellow on the reverse of petals Standards, each 3s. 6d., Bush, each 2s. 6d.

MADAME CHARLES LUTAUD (H.T.). Reddish green bronzed foliage, fine long bud of a nice ochre carmined tint and carried on long flower stalks. Very large flower, full and globular, colour middle chrome yellow slightly blended with bright rosy scarlet on the outer petals. Bush, each 2s.

Choice New Roses H. P. & H. T. Roses *(continued.)*

MADAME EDMOND ROSTAND (H.T.). Vigorous grower; deep green bronzed foliage, fine long and elegant bud opening to very large flower, quite full and globular, with large outcircling petals; colour pale flesh shaded with salmon and reddish orange yellow in the centre. Bush, each 2s.

MADAME EDOUARD HERRIOT (Daily Mail Rose). A very vigorous grower, quite hardy, of spreading branching habit with many long thorns, green bronzed foliage; coral red bud shaded with yellow on the base; flower of medium size semi-double, superb colouring coral red shaded with yellow and bright rosy scarlet passing to prawn red. Bushes only. Strong plants, each 15s.; smaller plants, each 6s. 6d.

MRS. AMY HAMMOND (H.T.). This is perhaps best described as a highly improved Madame A. Chatenay. It is a better grower, a freer bloomer, its flowers are longer and more pointed, the colour a blend of amber and apricot .. .. Bush, each 2s.

MRS. SAM ROSS (H.T.). A pale, straw-coloured Hybrid Tea of immense size and great refinement. The flowers are carried on stiff erect footstalks and last a very long time in good condition. Bush, each 3s.

MRS. E. ALFORD (H.T.). After the style of "Mad. A. Chatenay," but of a more soft pink colour; the flowers are large, full, and of excellent form, each petal being gracefully reflexed. Bush, each 3s. 6d.

MRS. CHAS. E. RUSSELL (H.T.). This rose is the nearest approaching yet to a continuous blooming Hybrid Perpetual; it has vigour, large foliage, productive, and all the flowers are good. Colour rose-carmine, with centre of rose-scarlet, fragrant, a large flower of good form, an exhibition as well as a forcing rose. Bush, each 3s. 6d.

MRS. RICHARD DRAPER (H.T.). Colour bright rosy satin-pink on the outside of the petals, inside very pale silvery flesh, which shows a delightful contrast as the flowers expand; sweetly perfumed. A magnificent exhibition rose, and one of the most perpetual blooming of garden roses. Gold Medal of N.R.S., 1911 .. Bush, each 3s.

OPHELIA (H.T.). Salmon-flesh shaded with rose, large and of perfect shape, standing up well on long stiff stems; growth vigorous, very free flowering. A fine decorative variety. Bush, each 2s. 6d.

RICORDO DI GIOSUE CARDUCCI. Rosy white, tinted and edged bright rose, reverse of petals deeper, very large, very double, long bud, opening well; very vigorous .. Standards, each 3s.; Bush, each 2s.

SUNBURST (H.T.). Fine long pointed bud, generally borne singly on long stout stems; flowers large, fairly full and of nice elongated cupped form; the colouring is a superb cadmium yellow with orange yellow centre .. .. Standards, each 3s.; Bush, ground plants, 2s.

SYLVIA (H. Wich.). Buds pale and lemon-yellow, changing when opening to pure white, double, produced in elegant sprays Summer and Autumn. In pots, 3s. 6d. each; Bush, each 1s. 6d.

WILLOWMERE (Rosa Pernetiana). A very vigorous grower of erect branching habit with few thorns, light green foliage, long carmined coral red bud carried on long stout flower stalks, very large flower, full and of elongated shape, colouring of a rich shrimp pink-shaded yellow in the centre and toning to carmine pink towards the edges of petals. This superb novelty was greatly admired at the Royal International Horticultural Exhibition, London, last year; Bush, each 4s.

H. P. & H. T. ROSES—General Select List.

In ordering from the following list, please give a few supplementary names of varieties to be sent in case of our being sold out of those first named. The prices quoted in this list are for dwarf or bush plants from open ground.

STANDARD ROSES. We can supply those varieties of H. P. and H. T. marked (*) at 18s. per dozen, our selection 15s. per doz. **HALF-STANDARDS**, 15s. per dozen, our own selection. Carriage Paid if 1 dozen is taken.

In all cases where one dozen or more Roses of any one variety are ordered, we will supply them as follows:—Those priced at 9d. each, at 8s. per doz.; at 1s. each, at 10s. 6d. per doz.; at 1s. 6d. each, at 16s. per doz., &c., pro rata.

	Dwarfs—s. d.
*ABEL CARRIÈRE. Deep velvety crimson	0 9
*ALFRED COLOMB. Brilliant fiery red	0 9
*ALFRED K. WILLIAMS. Fine carmine red	1 0
ALICE GRAHAME (H.T.). Flower of large size, enormous substance, and perfect form; colour ivory white tinted salmon ..	1 0
BARONESS ROTHSCHILD. Delicate rose, beautiful form; splendid	0 9
BEAUTY OF WALTHAM. Bright red, large; splendid form ..	0 9
BEN CANT (H.P.). Deep clear crimson with dark shading ..	0 9
BESSIE BROWN (H.T.). Creamy white; the blooms are perfectly formed and of large size; highly perfumed ..	1 0
BETTY. Coppery rose, overspread with golden yellow ..	1 0
*CAROLINE TESTOUT (H.T.). Bright satiny-rose, with brighter centre; large, full, and globular, very free and sweet ..	1 0
*CAPTAIN HAYWARD (H.P.). A scarlet crimson, long pointed flowers, perfectly formed	0 9
CHARLES LEFÈVRE. Velvety crimson	0 9
COUNTESS OF DERBY (H.T.). Colour salmon centre, outer petals rose; flowers large, full, and of perfect shape ..	1 0
COUNTESS OF GOSFORD (H.T.). Clear salmon pink, the base of petals suffused with yellow; large, full and free ..	1 0
COUNTESS OF SHAFTESBURY (H.T.). Bright silvery carmine, one of the most perfect type of Hybrid Teas in habit and growth; an ideal exhibition Rose. Gold Medal, N.R.S.	3 0
*DEAN HOLE (H.T.). This is a most distinct and magnificent Rose; colour silvery carmine, shaded salmon ..	1 0
DOROTHY (H.T.). Clear bright flesh colour, shading to delicate blush at the edges of petals; large and splendidly formed ..	1 0
DOROTHY PAGE ROBERTS (H.T.). Coppery yellow with apricot yellow at base of petals ..	1 0
DOROTHY RATCLIFF (H.T.). A perfect rose for bedding and massing; the colour of the blooms in bud state is a coral red, shaded yellow and fawn, becoming paler when expanding ..	2 6
DUCHESS OF WELLINGTON (H.T.). In the young stage it is an intense saffron yellow, stained with rich crimson, which as the flower develops becomes a deep coppery saffron yellow—a shade hitherto unknown among roses .. per doz., 15s.	1 6
*DUKE OF EDINBURGH. Rich vermilion	1 0
*DUKE OF TECK. Vivid bright crimson scarlet	0 9
DUKE OF WELLINGTON. Bright red, shaded crimson, very lovely	0 9
EARL OF DUFFERIN. Flowers of large size; colour rich brilliant velvety crimson, shaded with dark maroon ..	1 0
*EARL OF WARWICK (H.T.). Colour soft salmon-pink, with deeper centre; large, perfectly formed flowers	1 0

	s. d.
ELIZABETH BARNES (H.T.) (new). Large full flowers with pointed centre, most perfectly formed and delightfully fragrant. The colour is a satiny salmon rose with a fawn centre ..	1 0
ETOILE DE FRANCE (H.T.). The flowers are very large; colour brilliant velvety crimson. Very sweet scented	1 0

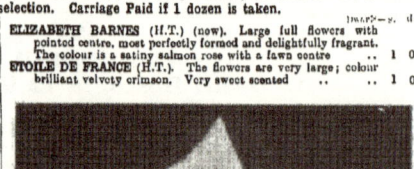

MRS. GEORGE SHAWYER.

Hybrid Perpetual and H. T. Roses—General List (continued).

SUNBURST.

	Dwarfs—s.	d.
EDWARD MAWLEY (H.T.). A superb Rose of a rich velvety crimson colour (with huge petals of the type of Melaine Soupert), in fact, in form it resembles that grand rose only much larger. A splendid grower, and a gorgeous variety for the garden and the exhibitor	2	6
FLORENCE PEMBERTON (H.T.). The colour is creamy white, with "suspicion" of pink, the edges of the petals occasionally flushed peach	1	0
*✉ **FRAU KARL DRUSCHKI.** Flowers large, perfectly formed with shell-shaped petals, and of the purest white, opening well	1	0
FRAU LILA RAUTENSTRAUGH (H.T.). Apricot orange, suffused yellow, tinted rose; flowers large and very full	1	0
***GENERAL JACQUIMINOT.** Brilliant crimson scarlet	0	9
***GENERAL McARTHUR** (H.T.). Dark velvety scarlet, very sweet scented	1	0
GEORGE C. WAUD (H.T.) (new). A remarkably distinct and beautiful variety. The flowers are large, full, perfectly-formed, with high-pointed centre, and of a brilliant orange-vermilion colour that does not fade, and is highly perfumed	1	0
GRACE MOLYNEAUX (H.T.). Creamy apricot flesh in the centre; the outer petals, when fully developed, are creamy white inside A splendid rose for garden decoration and button-holes	1	0
GUSTAVE REGIS (H.T.). Nankeen yellow, very long pointed buds of perfect shape; first-rate for button-holes	1	0
HARRY KIRK (H.T.). Deep sulphur yellow; splendid	1	0
HEINRICH SCHULTHEIS. Delicate purplish-rose with a white shading, bold form; a distinct rose	0	9
HERZOGIN MARIE ANTOINETTE (H.T.). Pure orange and golden yellow, large, very full, fine form, sweetly scented, long bud opening well; fine for cutting, forcing, and decoration	2	6
*✉ **HUGH DICKSON** (H.P.). In colour it is an intense brilliant crimson shaded scarlet. It is deliciously fragrant	0	9
✉ **HUGH WATSON** (H.P.). The blooms are very large, full, and most perfect shape, quite exhibition form. Very sweetly perfumed. Colour crimson, shaded carmine	0	9
JEANNIE DICKSON. Colour rosy pink, edged with silvery pink, perfectly formed large flowers	0	9
***J. B. CLARKE** (H.T.). Bright deep scarlet; flowers extra large, with perfect pointed centre. Gold Medal, N.R.S.	1	0
***JULIET.** Outside old gold, interior rich rosy red, base of petals deep yellow; large flowers distinct Standards 2s.	1	0

	Dwarfs—s.	d.
✉ **KAISERIN AUGUSTA VICTORIA** (H.T.). Lemon delicately shaded with cream; very large, of most perfect form	1	0
***KILLARNEY.** Flesh colour, shaded white, and suffused pale pink; blooms large, buds long and pointed	1	0
✉ **LADY BATTERSEA** (H.T.). Bright rosy crimson tinged with orange, and changing to soft pure rose; long oval buds	1	0
***LA FRANCE.** Bright lilac rose; beautiful	1	0
LADY GREENALL (H.T.). Intense saffron orange, heavily zoned and overspread on deep creamy-white each	1	6
***LADY ASHTOWN** (H.T.). Colour very pale rose, shading to yellow at base of petals, reflex of petals silvery pink	1	0
LESLIE HOLLAND (H.T.). Deep scarlet crimson, heavily shaded deep velvety crimson; it is a flower of immense size and great substance, sweetly scented. Gold Medal, N.R.S.	2	0
LIBERTY (H.T.). Brilliant crimson, large, elongated, beautifully formed buds; a splendid Rose for forcing	1	0
LYON ROSE (H.T.). Edges of petals shrimp pink, centre coral red or salmon pink shaded with chrome yellow; growth vigorous, distinct and quite first rate	1	0
MABEL DREW (H.T.). Deep ochre passing to canary yellow; a distinct and lovely novelty	1	6
***MADAME ABEL CHATENAY** (H.T.). Bright carmine rose shaded to deep salmon; long pointed full-sized flowers	1	0
MADAME A. ULLIET (H.T.). Clear yellow with golden yellow centre, edges of petals creamy white, very large, very full and cupped, vigorous erect growth; seedling of "Antoine Rivoire"	1	6
MADAME LEONE PAIN (H.P.). Similar in every way to Madame Abel Chatenay, but do not fade in the hot sun	1	0
MADAME MELAINE SOUPERT (H.T.). Colour pale saffron yellow, suffused with pink and carmine; flowers large, full and of perfect form	1	0
MADAME RAVARY (H.T.). Golden yellow, shaded orange; a continuous bloomer and splendid bedder	1	0
***MARGARET DICKSON** (H.P.). Apricot flesh centre, very large, stout shell-shaped petals	0	9
MARQUISE LITTA (H.T.). Carmine rose with vermilion red centre, very large, of perfect shape	1	0
✉ **MILDRED GRANT** (H.T.) The blooms are of immense size and substance, with high-pointed centres, the petals unusually long. Ivory white, flushed with pale peach	1	0
MME. SEGOND WEBER (H.T.). Clear bright salmon rose, extra large fine petals, lasting well	1	0
MONS. JOSEPH HILL (H.T.). Salmon pink, shaded yellow. The buds are long, and the flowers large and of perfect shape	1	0
MONS. PAUL LEDE (H.T.). Deep rose shaded yellow, large, full, perfect shape	1	0
MRS. E. G. HILL (H.T.). Colour alabaster white inside the petals, the reverse coral red, long pointed buds, borne on long stalks	1	0
MRS. PETER BLAIR (H.T.). Lemon yellow with golden yellow centre; full perfectly-shaped flowers	1	0
***MRS. J. LAING** (H.P.). A seedling from Francois Michelon; flowers large and finely shaped; colour a beautiful soft pink	0	9
***MRS. R. G. SHARMAN CRAWFORD.** Deep rosy pink, the outer petals shaded with pale flesh; the flowers are large, perfectly formed, and abundant	0	9
***MRS. W. J. GRANT** (H.T.). Imperial pink, of very good form, large flowers borne on good stout stems, retaining perfect form	1	0
MRS. GEORGE SHAWYER. Colour deep carmine rose pink; bud long of elegant form. A good forcing variety	1	6
MRS. AARON WARD (H.T.). Colour Indian yellow, similar to Catherine Mermet in form, one of the best yellow Roses	1	0
PHARISAER (H.T.). Rosy white shaded salmon, bud long, opening into a large, full, and well-formed flower, growth vigorous	1	0
***PRINCE CAMILLE DE ROHAN.** Dark crimson maroon, fine form	0	9
RAYON D'OR (Rose Pernetiana). A pure yellow Rose resembling in colour Persian Yellow, the buds are orange yellow with crimson flush, the open flower is clear yellow. Faintly Tea Scented. Splendid bedder. Gold Medal, N.R.S., 1910	1	6
REYNOLDS HOLE. Dark maroon	0	9
SIR ROWLAND HILL. Rich deep port wine colour, with violet shading, changes to claret	0	9
SOUVENIR DE PIERRE NOTTING (H.T.). Blooms very large; surpassing in form and beauty those of Maman Cochet. Colour, deep apricot yellow shaded with orange. Splendid	1	0
***ULRICH BRUNNER.** Cherry crimson; fine	0	9
WHITE KILLARNEY (H.T.) (new). A pure white sport from the well-known old pink favourite, with the same splendid size and beautiful form of flower. A valuable acquisition	1	6

STANDARD ROSES. We can supply those varieties of H. P. and H. T. marked (*) at 18s. per dozen, our selection 15s. per doz. **HALF-STANDARDS,** 15s. per dozen, our own selection. **Carriage Paid if 1 dozen is taken.**

ROSES—TEA-SCENTED AND NOISETTE.

ROSE, LADY HILLINGDON.

Dwarfs—s. d.
LADY HILLINGDON. Fine golden yellow novelty, a cross between "Papa Goutier" and "Lady Roberts," with long pointed buds, producing a glorious effect Standards 2s. 6d.; Dwarfs, doz. 15s. 1 6
LADY ROBERTS. Rich apricot, shaded pale orange, buds long pointed, blooms large and of perfect form Stds. 2s. 6d. 1 6
MADAME CONSTANCE SOUPERT (T). Colour yellow with pretty peach shading, large full pointed flowers, freely produced 1 6
MADAME CUSIN. Rosy purple, with pale yellow at base of petals, exquisitely formed 1 6
MADAME FALCOT. Apricot yellow, very distinct Stds. 2s. 6d. 1 0
MADAME JULES GRAVEREAUX. Lemon yellow with rosy peach centre; buds large, long, and beautifully formed .. 1 6
MADAME LAMBARD. Salmon shaded rose, variable Stds. 2s. 1 6
MADAME DE WATTEVILLE. Salmony white edged with bright rose and pink; beautiful and distinct variety .. 1 6
MAMAN COCHET. Clear flesh mingled with salmon rose, outer petals splashed with bright rose; flowers very large and well formed .. .. Standards 2s. 6d. 1 6
MARECHAL NIEL (Noisette). Beautiful golden yellow. Stds. 2s. 6d. 1 0
MARIE VAN HOUTTE. Lemon yellow edged with lively rose, medium size, good form, beautiful 1 6
MOLLY SHARMAN CRAWFORD (T). A splendid rose of sturdy growth and branching habit, flowering most profusely and continuously. The colour is a delicate eau-de-Nil white, which, as the flower expands, becomes a dazzling pure white. It is delicately perfumed, and will be a great acquisition .. 1 0
MRS. E. MAWLEY. Bright carmine, shaded salmon. Large blooms of great substance and beautiful form. A variety of marvellous beauty .. .. Standards 2s. 6d. 1 6
MRS. FOLEY HOBBS (T). Tea scented variety of sterling quality. Grand flower of delicate ivory white tinged pink on edges of petals 1 6
MRS. HERBERT STEVENS (T). A hardy variety said to withstand our winters in this climate. The bloom is as long and even more pointed than that of the Maman Cochet family, faultless in shape and form, a flower of exquisite grace and refinement, unsurpassed by any in its class; colour white, with a distinct fawn and peach shading towards centre. The petals are of great depth and substance 1 6
NIPHETOS. Pale lemon, changing to white .. 1s. 6d. and 2 0
PAPA GONTIER. Rosy crimson buds, excellent to force for cutting .. .. .. Standards 2s. 6d. 1 6
PERLE DES JARDINS. Straw colour 1 6
REVE D'OR (Noisette). Deep yellow .. Standards 2s. 1 6
SAFRANO. Bright apricot; beautiful 1 6
SOUVENIR DE S. A. PRINCE. The finest white .. Stds. 2s. 1 6
SOUVENIR DE STELLA GRAY (T). Very novel shade, orange splashed yellow and salmon; medium flowers .. 1 6
SUNRISE. The outer petals are of a lovely salmony-carmine shading to a delicate fawn and apricot 1 6
THE BRIDE. A pure white sport from "Catherine Mermet" .. 1 6
VICOMTESSE FOLKESTONE. Creamy pink 1 6
WHITE MAMAN COCHET. A white sport from the well-known "Maman Cochet." This is a fine addition Stds. 2s. 6d. 1 6
WILLIAM ALLEN RICHARDSON (Noisette). Fine, deep orange yellow, very showy 1 6

Dwarfs—s. d.
ANNA OLIVIER. Flesh-coloured rose .. Standards 2s. 6d 1 6
BOUQUET D'OR (Noisette). Deep yellow, coppery centre Stds. 2s. 1 6
CATHERINE MERMET. Flesh-coloured rose .. „ 2s. 1 6
CELINE FORESTIER (Noisette). Pale yellow 1 6
CORALLINA. Deep rosy crimson, large petals, very beautiful .. 1 6
DEVONIENSIS. White, tinted yellow beautiful 1 6
ENCHANTRESS. Flowers large creamy white, tinted with buff in the centre; a splendid Tea Rose 1 6
FRANCISCA KRUGER. Copper yellow, shaded peach .. 1 6
HOMER. Rose, centre salmon 1 6

Our own selection, in choice variety, plants mostly established in 5 in. pots, per doz. 15s., 18s. and 21s.

DWARF POLYANTHUS ROSES.

s. d.
BABY DOROTHY. Dorothy Perkins colour, dwarf growing .. 1 0
CECIL BRUNNER. Blush, shaded pale pink, small pointed buds.. 0 9
JESSIE. Bright orange red, in clusters 2 0
MADAME TURBAT (new). Flowers of a soft china rose colour .. 1 6
MRS. W. CUTBUSH. Bright pink, distinct, most valuable bedding rose 1 0
LEONIE LAMESCH. Bright copper red with golden centre .. 0 9

s. d.
ORLEANS. Clear rose colour, large trusses freely produced, and the very best for forcing .. .. .. Ground plants 1 0
PERLE D'OR. Nankeen yellow, pointed bud, best of this class .. 0 9
WHITE PET. Creamy white, a profuse bloomer 0 9
YVONNE RABIER (new). The best of all white dwarf polyanthus; an excellent grower 1 6

We have some Short Standard Polyanthus Roses, our selection, 2 to 2½ ft. stems, 1s. 6d. each, 15s. per doz.

ROSES IN POTS.

In April, May, and June, we supply the following Roses in pots for flowering under glass, or late planting in the garden, at prices as below. The pots vary in size from six to seven inches.

CAROLINE TESTOUT	LADY ROBERTS	MRS. GEO. SHAWYER	RICHMOND
CAPTAIN HAYWARD	LADY HILLINGDON	MRS. J. LAING	SOUVENIR DE GUSTAVE PRATT
FRAU KARL DRUSCHKI	LA FRANCE	MRS. SHARMAN CRAWFORD	SUNBURST
EDWARD MAWLEY	MADAME GABRIEL LUIZET	MOLLY SHARMAN CRAWFORD	and other varieties in 6 and
HUGH DICKSON	MRS. CORNWALLIS WEST	PRINCE CAMILLE DE ROHAN	7 inch pots.

HYBRID PERPETUAL AND HYBRID TEA.	TEA-SCENTED AND NOISETTE.	STRONG CLIMBING VARIETIES, RAMBLERS,
Our selection .. .. per doz. 18s. to 21s.	Our selection .. .. per doz. 18s. to 21s.	AND OTHER SORTS.
		Our selection, ea. 2s 6d., 3s. 6d., 21s. & 30s. doz.

CLIMBING, PILLAR AND WEEPING ROSES.

The following list of Climbing Roses includes the most beautiful and useful sorts in cultivation.

NOTE:—Climbing Roses priced at 2/6, 3/6 and 5/- are large plants in pots with shoots 6 to 12 feet in length; those quoted at 1/- being plants from the open ground.

AGLAIA (Yellow Rambler). Large trusses of canary-yellow flowers ... 1s., 2s. 6d., and 3 6

AIMEE VIBERT (Noisette). Pure white flowers in clusters ... 1 0

ALLISTER STELLA GRAY. Pale yellow with orange centre ... 1 0

AMERICAN PILLAR. Very strong climbing Rose; a lovely rosy pink colour ... 1s., 2s. 6d., and 3 6

BANKSIA ALBA. Pure white, in pots ... 1 6

LUTEA. Fine yellow, in pots ... 1 6

BLUE RAMBLER. Steel blue, very distinct and pleasing. Strong 1 0

BLUSH RAMBLER (Polyantha). Beautiful soft blush 1s., 2s. 6d., & 3 6

BUTTERCUP. Small single flowers, deep yellow in the bud, lemon and white when open ... 2 0

CAROLINE TESTOUT. A very strong growing, climbing sport from Caroline Testout, making strong shoots 1s., 2s. 6d., and 3 6

CHESHUNT HYBRID. Bright cherry carmine, large open flowers; a very hardy and strong grower ... 1s., 2s. 6d., 3s. 6d., and 3 6

CLIMBING DEVONIENSIS (T). Flowers creamy white with blush centre; deliciously scented ... 5 0

CLIMBING KAISERIN AUGUSTA VICTORIA. Cream shaded lemon, good climber ... 5 0

CLIMBING NIPHETOS. Pure white 1s. 6d., 2s. 6d., 3s. 6d., and 5 0

CRIMSON RAMBLER. A splendid free-growing variety, with bright glossy-green foliage, and large pyramidal trusses of bright crimson flowers ... 1s., and 3 0

DOROTHY PERKINS (Hybrid Wichuriana). Clear soft pink flowers in large clusters, very fragrant and lasting 1s., 2s. 6d., and 3 6

DR. VAN FLEET (new). Flesh pink variety, foliage very glossy. In pots ... 2 6

EXCELSA. The Red Dorothy Perkins. This is without doubt the prince of Ramblers, it is equally as brilliant as Hiawatha 1s., 2s. 6d., and 3 6

STANDARD WEEPING ROSE, DOROTHY PERKINS.

FLOWER OF FAIRFIELD. The perpetual flowering crimson Rambler ... 1 0

FRAU KARL DRUSCHKI. Flowers similar to the dwarf-growing variety, but a stronger grower ... 1s., 2s. 6d., and 3 6

GARDENIA (W). Colour bright yellow, paler as flowers expand 1 0

GLOIRE DE DIJON (T). Buff, with orange centre, well-known superb variety ... 1s., 2s. 6d., 3s. 6d., and 5 0

GOLDFINCH. Strong growing Rambler, producing large clusters of yellow flowers ... 1s., 2s. 6d., and 3 6

HIAWATHA (POLYANTHA). A seedling from Crimson Rambler. The flowers are single, deep crimson, shading to white at the base of the petals ... 1s., 2s. 6d., and 3 6

LA FRANCE. A climbing form of the well-known La France 1s., 2s. 6d., and 3 6

LADY GAY (Wichuriana). A brilliant and lovely shade of rose-pink ... 1s., 2s. 6d., 3s. 6d., and 3 6

L'IDEAL (Noisette). Yellow and metallic red, streaked and tinted golden yellow ... 1s., 2s. 6d., 3s. 6d., and 5 0

LONGWORTH RAMBLER. A fast growing continuous bloomer, producing wreaths of brilliant crimson flowers 1s., 2s. 6d., and 3 6

JERSEY BEAUTY (Wichuriana). Single flowers, pale yellow, with bright yellow stamens, produced in great profusion ... 1 0

LADY GODIVA (Wichuriana). Soft pale flesh pink like a carnation; a sport from "Dorothy Perkins," of same habit of growth ... 1 0

MINNEHAHA (Wichuriana). Deep rose, very double flowers produced in small panicles ... 1 0

MARECHAL NIEL (Noisette). Beautiful golden yellow of the most lovely form and delicious fragrance; well-known superb variety 1s., 2s. 6d., 3s. 6d., and 5 0

MONSIEUR DESIR. Velvety crimson, shaded with violet, large and double; a good dark climber ... 1 0

MRS. F. W. FLIGHT. Pink with white centre, semi-double, and of fair size, produced in enormous trusses ... 1s., 2s. 6d. and 3 6

MRS. W. J. GRANT. A vigorous growing free-flowering sport from Mrs. W. J. Grant. A great acquisition to the Climbers ... 1s., 2s. 6d., and 3 6

PAUL'S CARMINE PILLAR. Bright rosy carmine single flowers, produced very freely, charming ... 1 0

PERLE DES JARDINS. Colour same as the dwarf growing variety, but a good climber ... 1s. 6d., 2s. 6d., and 3 6

PHILADELPHIA RAMBLER. A fuller, larger, and brighter form of Crimson Rambler, earlier, and retains its colour better ... 1 0

REINE MARIE HENRIETTE. Bright cherry carmine, long pointed flowers; fine for cutting ... 1s., 2s. 6d., and 3 6

STARLIGHT. White, suffused rose-violet, a single variety recommended for pillars or pergolas ... 1 0

SWEETHEART. Vigorous. Pure white, double, very good. In pots 1s. and 2 6

SYLVIA (Wichuriana) (new). Buds pale lemon yellow, opens to pure white, produced in very large sprays ... 1s. 6d., 2s. 6d., and 3 6

TAUSENDSCHON. Bright satin-pink flowers, two inches in diameter, produced singly and in trusses of three to five on long stems, standing well out from the plant ... 1s., 2s. 6d., and 3 6

THALIA (White Rambler). A multiflora Rose, double-white flowers ... 1 0

TRIER (Multiflora). Large pyramidal trusses of white flowers 1s., 2s. 6d., and 3 6 F.C.C.

WALTHAM BRIDE (new). Snow-white sprays or clusters, very fragrant. F.C.C. of Merit ... 1s. 6d., 2s. 6d., and 3 6

WHITE DOROTHY PERKINS. A splendid white sport from the well-known Dorothy Perkins, the same style of flower but pure white; a great acquisition ... 1s. 6d., and 3 6

WILLIAM ALLEN RICHARDSON (Noisette). Fine deep orange yellow, very showy ... 1s. 6d., 2s. 6d., 3s. 6d., and 5 0

STANDARD WEEPING ROSES.

The varieties named below can be supplied on tall Standards. These are the very best and most suitable varieties for this purpose. All who have seen these charming subjects will at once acclaim their worth.

AMERICAN PILLAR	HIAWATHA	MRS. F. W. FLIGHT
BLUSH RAMBLER	LADY GAY	PARADISE
CRIMSON RAMBLER	LADY GODIVA	TAUSENDSCHON
EXCELSA	LONGWORTH RAMBLER	TRIER
GOLDFINCH	MINNEHAHA	WH. DOROTHY PERKINS

4 to 5 feet stems, 3s. 6d. each.   5 to 6 feet stems, 5s. each.
A few sorts can be supplied on 8 to 10 feet stems. Prices and varieties on application.
Wire Frames for Weeping Roses, 2 feet in diameter, 3s. 6d. each.
Acme Labels can be supplied for all rose trees See page 60.

CLEMATISES.

These magnificent hardy climbers are highly popular amongst amateur growers, and, considering their great beauty, freedom of blooming, and the facility with which they may be trained on any kind of wall, trellis, verandah, or pillar, and in almost any aspect, it is surprising that Clematises are not found in abundance in every garden. The plants we offer are established in pots, and can be removed at any time of the year. The sorts blooming after June are the best for bedding purposes ; they flower on the young wood, and therefore require, before growth commences in Spring, to be cut down to within six or twelve inches of the ground, as likewise do all the late-flowering kinds ; and early sorts, flowering from May to July on the old wood, should be pruned similarly to Roses. When the selection of sorts is left to ourselves customers may rely on our sending a really good variety.

A richly manured soil is indispensable if the best result is aimed at. Manure ought to be well mixed with the soil when planting, and used annually as a mulch for Winter protection, forking it in very lightly in the Spring. The addition of chalk or lime to the soil when planting is also beneficial.

CLEMATISES. *From a Photograph. One-third in size.*

	Months of each. Flowering s. d.
COUNTESS OF LOVELACE. Bluish lilac, double	Ju Jy 1 6
DUKE OF EDINBURGH. Rich violet purple	My Jy 1 6
DUCHESS OF EDINBURGH. The best of all the double whites, deliciously scented	Ju Jy 1 6
EARL OF BEACONSFIELD. Rich royal purple	Jy Oc 1 6
FAIRY QUEEN. Pale flesh, pink bar	Jy Oc 1 6
FLAMMULA. Sweet scented, white	— 1 6
GIPSY QUEEN. Dark velvety purple	Jy Oc 1 6
HENRYI. Beautiful large creamy white	Jy Oc 1 6
JACKMANII. Intense violet purple	Jy Oc 1 6
JACKMANII, RED. A fine new red variety of true Jackmanii type	Jy Oc 1 6
JACKMANII SUPERBA. Similar to "Jackmanii," but the colour more intense	Jy Oc 1 6
KING EDWARD VII (new). Beautiful pucy violet with crimson bar down the centre of each petal, large flowers	Jy Oc 2 0
LA FRANCE. Deep violet purple, dark anthers	Jy Oc 1 6
LADY NORTHCLIFF (new). Beautiful deep lavender, tinted bright blue, with purple bars and white stamens	Jy Oc 2 0
LORD NEVILLE. Very bright heliotrope blue, with white filaments and chocolate anthers	— 1 6
LANUGINOSA. Pale lavender	Jy Oc 1 6
LUCIE LEMOINE. Double, white	Ju Jy 1 6
MADAME EDOUARD ANDRE. Beautiful bright velvety red ; very distinct and free-flowering	Jy Oc 1 6
MISS BATEMAN. White, red anthers	My Jy 1 6
MRS. CHOLMONDELEY. Lavender	My Ju 1 6
MRS. HOPE. Satiny mauve ,	Ju Au 1 6
MRS. GEO. JACKMAN. Satiny white, beautiful	Ju Oc 1 6
MRS. QUILTER. Pure white, very fine	Jy Oc 1 6
NELLY MOSER. Light mauve, with bright red bars	Jy Oc 1 6
PAPA CHRISTEN. Large flowers, colour, a delicate mauve with broad band of deep carmine down the centre of each petal	Jy Oc 1 6
PRESIDENT. Purple, suffused with claret, good	Jy Oc 1 6
PRINCESS OF WALES. Deep bluish mauve	Jy Oc 1 6
PURPUREA ELEGANS. Deep violet purple	Jy Oc 1 0
QUEEN ALEXANDRA. Beautiful pale lavender lilac, purple base, silvery white down centre of each sepal. Very pretty	Jy Oc 1 6
SNOW WHITE JACKMANII. The flowers are pure white, about the same size as those of the old purple Jackmanii but produced in greater profusion. Superb variety	— 1 0
VENUS VICTRIX. A fine double-flowered variety, delicate lavender blue, beautiful form	Jy Oc 1 6
VILLE DE LYON. Bright carmine, red	Jy Oc 1 6
VILLE DE PARIS. Pale flesh, pink bar, of great merit	Jy Oc 1 6
WILLIAM KENNETT. Deep lavender, fine	Jy 1 6

	Months of each. Flowering s. d.
ALBA MAGNA. Large white broad sepalled flowers, sometimes very faintly tinted lavender	— 1 6
BEAUTY OF WORCESTER. Large and handsome, producing double and single flowers on same plant, lovely bluish violet	Ju Oc 2 0
BELLE OF WOKING. Silvery grey, double	Ju 1 6
BLUE GEM. Pale cerulean blue	Jy Oc 1 6
COCCINEA. Very elegant bell-shaped flowers, cream inside and crimson outside	— 1 6

Choice named varieties from the above list, our own selection, 15s. per doz.

Clematis montana –Rubens.

A very charming new variety, very hardy. The flowers, which are produced in great abundance, are of a soft bright rosy lilac with white.

Each 2s.

Clematis montana grandiflora.

A beautiful early free-flowering variety, blooming in May and June, and producing a profusion of large, pure white starry flowers. Splendid for covering trellises, porches, &c.

Each 1s. 6d.

CLEMATIS MONTANA   Each 1s.

HARDY CLIMBING & OTHER PLANTS.

SUITABLE FOR TRAINING ON WALLS, &c.

These are mostly grown in pots, and can be supplied and planted at any time of the year with perfect safety.

each—s. d.

AKEBIA QUINNATA. Purplish brown flowers 1 6

AMPELOPSIS (Virginian Creepers). Well-known beautiful climbers, the leaves changing to a deep crimson in Autumn.

" **HENRYANA,** A strikingly handsome variety, each leaflet is marked by a silvery band 1 6

" **LOWII** (new). A beautiful new Ampelopsis with small Palmata leaves and a delightful graceful habit. The foliage going red as Autumn advances 1 6

" **VEITCHII.** Small-leaved, very beautiful variety. Clings to walls with great tenacity .. 1s. and 1 6

" **PURPUREA.** A beautiful dark-leaved variety 1 6

" Hedcracea, Common Virginian Creeper 1 0

" Sempervirens. Evergreen .. 1 6

ARISTOLOCHIA SIPHO. Deciduous .. 1 6

AZARA MICROPHYLLA. Beautiful plant for walls 1 6

BIGNONIA RADICANS (Trumpet Flower) .. 1 6

BRIDGESIA SPICATA .. .. 1s. 6d. and 2 6

BUDDLEA GLOBOSA. Orange globose flowers 1 6

CEANOTHUS, GLOIRE DE VERSAILLES. Large panicles of sky blue flowers, fine 2 0

" Azureus. Pale blue 2 0

" Divaricatus. Very pale blue .. 1 6

" VEITCHII. Blue, very fine. In pots 1 6

CHIMONANTHUS FRAGRANS. Very sweet-scented 1 6

COTONEASTER MICROPHYLLA Very handsome with scarlet berries in Autumn.. 1 6

CRATÆGUS LÆLANDII. Red-berried and splendidly effective in the Autumn and Winter .. .. 1s. 6d. and 2 6

ESCALLONIA MACRANTHA. Evergreen, with bright rosy crimson flowers, very pretty .. .. .. 1s. 6d. and 2 6

GARRYA ELLIPTICA. A beautiful plant for the wall .. .. 1s. 6d. and 2 6

IVY (Hedera)—Cavendishii. Silver-margined 1 6

" Clouded Gold. Fine 1 6

" Crippsi. One of the most beautiful silvery-leaved Ivies 1 6

" CHRYSOPHYLLA. Medium sized leaf, bright sulphur yellow, not affected by smoke 1 6

" Palmata. Handsome variety .. 1 0

" PURPUREA. Hardy and smoke resisting. Leaves purplish bronze .. 1 6

" DENTATA. Very large dark-green foliage, strong growing variety .. 1 0

" VARIEGATA. The finest and most striking golden variegated Ivy in commerce 1 6

" Emerald Green. Beautiful glossy bright leaves ; very distinct .. 1 0

" MADERIENSIS VARIEGATA. Fine robust-growing variety, beautiful silver edged foliage .. 1s. 6d. and 2 6

" IRISH. A fine quick-growing variety, very useful for covering large trellises, walls, &c. Strong plants from open ground per 100, 21s. ; per doz. 3s. 0 — Fine plants in pots, 4 to 6 ft., per doz. 10s. 6d.

" RÆGNERIANA (The Giant Ivy). Very large, beautiful foliage, quite distinct 1 0

" Tricolor. Very pretty 1 6

12 Ivies, distinct sorts, in pots, for 12s.

JASMINUM (Jasmine)—

" Nudiflorum. Yellow, blooms in December and January 1 0

each—s. d.

JASMINUM Officinale. White, very sweet-scented 1 0

" **BUSCARIA.** Scarlet flowering variety 1 6

" **REVOLUTUM.** An evergreen variety with bright golden flowers ; hardy. In pots 1 6

KERRIA JAPONICA FL. PL. Double yellow.. 1 0

LONICERA (Honeysuckle)—

" **Aurea reticulata.** Golden-veined foliage, fast growing variety .. 1 6

" **EARLY DUTCH.** Not quite so fast a grower as late Dutch ; hardy .. 1 0

" **Flexuosa.** Evergreen 1 6

" **HALLII.** Pure white, evergreen, fine 1 6

" **Late Red Dutch.** Well-known .. 1 0

" **SCARLET TRUMPET.** Beautiful and free, should be extensively grown .. 1 6

" **SPLENDIDISSIMA.** Very free flowering, sweet-scented variety, with large trusses of orange-coloured flowers tinged with yellow, and fine glaucous foliage 2 0

MAGNOLIA GRANDIFLORA. Exmouth variety, very fine .. 3s. 6d. to 7 6

" **SOULANGEANA.** Very fine, sweetly scented variety, bearing purplish tinted flowers with white centre 3s. 6d. and 5 0

" **LENNE.** Beautiful flowers of a purplish colour, with blush-white centre 5 0

MUHLENBECKIA COMPLEXA. A distinct plant of good growth, with handsome Maiden Hair like round leaves ; fine for border or wall 1 6

PASSIFLORA CÆRULEA. Common blue Passion flower 1 0

" **"CONSTANCE ELLIOTT."** Flowers pure white ; sweet-scented .. 1 6

PERIPLOCA GRÆCA. Rapid climber .. 1 6

PIPTANTHUS NEPALENSE. Called the Evergreen Laburnum. A very handsome early flowering Climber 1 6

POLYGONUM BALDSCHUANICUM. A splendid free-flowering climber for covering old buildings or arbors ; panicles of pale pink flowers 1 6

PYRUS JAPONICA. Valuable early Spring-flowering plant, rich scarlet, exceedingly handsome 1 6

" **ALBA.** White form of the above. In pots 1 6

" **ATRO-COCCINEA.** Double flowered variety. In pots 1 6

" **RUBRA GRANDIFLORA.** In pots 1 6

" **MAULEI.** Very beautiful plant, bearing bright light red flowers in Spring and golden yellow fruit in Autumn .. 1 6

ROSES, CLIMBING. See page 131.

VITIS. Ornamental Vines, with large handsome foliage.

" **Coignetiæ,** The Crimson Glory Vine, Brilliant scarlet in Autumn .. 2 6

" **HETEROPHYLLA.** A vigorous and hardy climber ; violet berries .. 1 6

" **VARIEGATA.** Speckled ivory and cream 1 6

" **Purpurea.** Large claret-coloured foliage, handsome 2 6

" **THUNBERGII.** Leaves nine to twelve inches across, upper surface rich dark green passing to richest crimson in Autumn ; most handsome .. 2 6

WISTARIA SINENSIS. Large clusters of lilac mauve coloured flowers .. 1s. 6d. to 3 6

" **SINENSIS ALBA** .. 1s. 6d. and 3 6

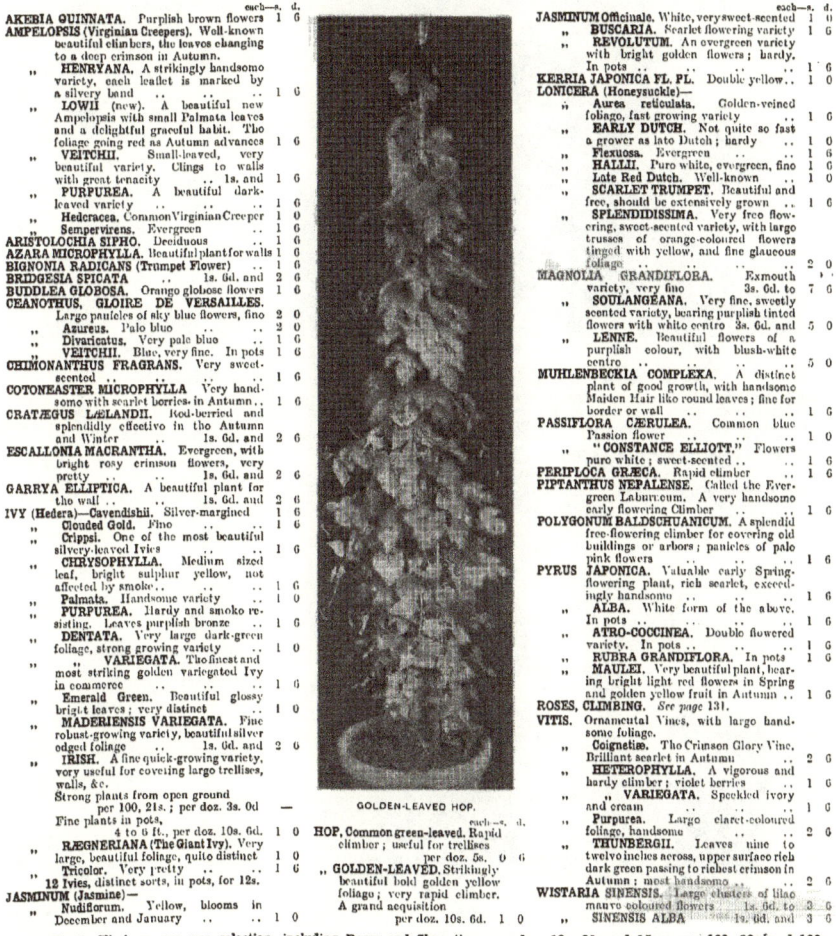

GOLDEN-LEAVED HOP.

each—s. d.

HOP, Common green-leaved. Rapid climber ; useful for trellises per doz. 5s. 0 6

" GOLDEN-LEAVED, Strikingly beautiful bold golden yellow foliage ; very rapid climber. A grand requisition per doz. 10s. 6d. 1 0

Choice Hardy Climbers, our own selection, including Roses and Clematises, per doz. 12s. 6d. and 15s. ; per 100, 80s. and 100s.

HARDY ORNAMENTAL TREES AND SHRUBS.

ROW OF SPECIMEN MOP-HEADED ACACIA GROWING IN OUR NURSERIES.

This class includes the loveliest and most charming trees for the garden, pleasure grounds, shrubberies and park. Many of them are remarkable for their graceful form and flowers, and for the highly ornamental effect produced by their delightful tints. We take great pains to ensure the trees being of the best possible quality. Careful attention is also given to pruning and staking, and our stock is regularly transplanted to ensure their safe removal. There is scarcely any spot, even under the greatest natural disadvantages, which cannot be made to look bright by the judicious planting of Ornamental Trees.

This list is not by any means exhaustive of our stock, and we shall welcome inquiries for anything not included herewith.

A separate list of Rhododendrons and Azaleas will be found on page 137, and of Conifers on page 138. These classes can be usefully employed in ornamental borders, either alone or mixed with other shrubs and trees.

We are continually engaged in carrying out alterations to gardens and pleasure grounds, and shall be most happy to advise as to the best manner to treat any proposed alterations, or to prepare plans and designs for new gardens.

NEW AND RARE ORNAMENTAL TREES AND SHRUBS.

APPLE (Weeping). A fine fruit bearing variety, and good flavour. Standards only, 5/- each.

BAY (Sweet Golden). Fine golden variety. Height 1½ ft. 1/6 each.

BUDDLEA VARIABILIS MAGNIFICA. A deep shade of rosy purple, the best of its class, 1/6 each.

CATALPA SYRINGAEFOLIA AUREA. Large Ornamental tree, golden leaves, 3/6 and 5/-.

DIMORPHANTHUS MANDSCHURICUS FOLIUS AUREUS VAR. Handsome, 5/- each.

CYTISUS ANDREANUS PROSTRATA. A very fine weeping variety. Half Standards 7/6 each.

  „ **PENDULA PURPUREA.** A charming variety with rosy purple pea-shaped flowers. Dwarfs 1/6 each. Standards 3/6 each.

LABURNUM VOSSII. Distinct yellow flowers, the best of this class. Bush plants 2/- each. Standards 2/6 each.

PAMPAS GRASS (Rose Queen). Enormous plumes of a magnificent shade of rose. 3/6 each.

PRIVET (Ligustrum) CORIACEUM. A very interesting species of slow growth, leaves leathery and densely crowded on short shoots. Height 1½–2 ft. 1/6 each.

RIBES SPECIOSUM. Fuchsia flowering Gooseberry, flowers deep red, spreading growth. Height 3–4 ft. 2/6 each.

SPIRÆA CRISPIFOLIA. Very dwarf habit, carmine red flowers. Height 12–15 inches 1/6 each.

WILLOW, WEEPING (New Golden Barked). Very fine orange-coloured wood. 3/6 each.

General List.

ACACIA (Robinia).

  „ **HISPIDIA (Rose Acacia).** Dwarfs, height 3–4 ft. 1/6 each. Standards, 3/6 each.

  „ **INERMIS (Mop-headed Acacia).** Stds. 3/6 ea.

ACER (Maple). NEGUNDO CALIFORNICUM AUREUM. This is a specially good variety, with large, broad golden foliage. Standards, with 3–4 ft. stem, 2/- each, 21/- per doz.

ÆSCULUS. *See Horse Chestnuts.*

ALMOND Purple-Leaved. Dwarfs, 1/- each, Standards 2/- each.

  „ **Common.** Dwarfs, 9d. each, Standards, 1/6 ea.

ALTHÆAS. In choice variety, 1/6 each.

ANDROMEDA FLORIBUNDA. Dwarf compact growing shrubs, pure white bell-shaped flowers, Height 9–12 in. 1/6 ea, 12–18 in. 2/- ea.

  „ **JAPONICA.** Pure white flowers, often called the Lily of the Valley Tree, 3/6 each.

ASH (Fraxinus). EXCELSIOR PENDULA. (Weeping). This is a splendid weeping tree. Standards, 5/- and 7/6 each.

  „ **MARGINATA PENDULA.** Gold leaved, Weeping, 3/6 each.

AUCUBA JAPONICA VARIEGATA. 1½–2 ft. 10/6 per doz, 70/- per 100. Larger specimens 1/6 and 2/6 each.

BAY (Sweet) (*Laurus Nobilis*), 1½–2 ft., 1/6 each; 2–3 ft., 2/- each. We also have a supply of strong plants in Tubs, grown as Pyramids and Standards from 10/6 each.

BEECH (Fagus) ATROPURPUREA. Height 7–8 ft. 2/6 each, 10–12 ft. 3/6, 5/- each.

  „ **FERN LEAVED.** 2/- and 3/6 each.

  „ **PENDULA PURPUREA.** Purple leaved Weeping, 5/- and 7/6 each.

  „ **WEEPING.** 5s. and 7s. 6d.

BERBERIS STENOPHYLLA. One of the best, very graceful, small evergreen leaf, and covered with bright yellow flowers. Height 1–1½ ft. 5/- per doz., 2–3 ft 7/6 per doz.

  „ **THUNBERGII.** Pretty early blooming species. White flowers; leaves in Autumn are tinted crimson. Height 1–1½ ft. 6/- per doz., 2–2½ ft. 8/- per doz.

  „ **VULGARIS (Common Barberry).** All are very hardy shrubs with pretty foliage. Height 2–3 ft. 8/- per doz.

BIRCH (Betula). *See also page 138.*

  „ **PENDULA (Weeping Birch).** Standards, 2/- each.

  „ **YOUNGII.** Beautiful fern-leaved form, very distinct. Ht. 7–8 ft. Standards. 3/6 each

BOX (Buxus). HANDSWORTHII. This is the best of the green varieties of Box, close growing and of erect habit. Height 12–18 in. 6/- per doz., 40/- per 100, 18–24 in. 7/- per doz., 45/- per 100, 2–3 ft. 15/- per doz., 80/- per 100. Larger Specimens, 1/6 and 2/- each.

BIRCH, SILVER BARKED.

Hardy Ornamental Trees and Shrubs (*continued.*)

WEEPING ELM. True Camperdown variety.

BOX EDGING. One Nursery yard plants 3 yards. 8d. per Nursery yard.

BROOM (Cytisus).
,, **ANDREANUS.** Most distinct and beautiful, maroon-crimson and yellow flowers. In pots, 1/- and 1/6 each. Std. 3—4 ft. 3/6 ea.
,, **PRÆCOX.** Free flowering early. Dwarfs in pots 1/6 each. Standard Variety, 2/6 and 3/6 each.
,, **WHITE PORTUGAL.** Free flowering, most effective. 6d. each, 5/- per doz.
,, **COMMON YELLOW.** 6d. each, 4/- per doz.
,, **SPANISH YELLOW.** In pots, 1/- each.

BUDDLEIA GLOBOSA. Orange globose flowers. 1/6 each.
,, **VARIABILIS VEITCHI.** In pots, 1/6 each.

CALYCANTHUS (Allspice). Maroon colour flowers, very fragrant. Height 2 ft. 1/- each.

CARYOPTERIS MASTACANTHUS (Blue Spiræa). Height 12—18 in. 9d. each.

CHERRY (Cerasus).
,, **RHEXII FLORE PLENA.** Double white cherry. Dwarf Bush 1/-, Standards 2/-.
,, **ROSEA PLENA,** Double Rose. Beautiful rose. 2/6 and 3/6 each.
,, **JAMES H. VEITCH.** The finest variety yet introduced. Height 4—5 ft. 1/3 each, Standards 2/6 each.
,, **SINENSIS ROSEA (Weeping).** Beautiful weeping tree of graceful habit. Stds. 2/6 ea.

CERCIS SILIQUASTRUM (Judas Tree). Flowers early in Spring. Height 2—3 ft. 9d. each.

CHOISYA TERNATA. Lovely white, sweet-scented. In pots, 1/6 each.

CISTUS LADANIFERUS (The Gum Cistus). A handsome shrub. In pots, 1/- each.

CORNUS AUREA TRICOLOR. Most beautiful variegated trees. Dwarfs 1/6 each.
,, **SPATHII AUREA.** Dwarfs 1/- each.

CO?ONEASTER, HORIZONTALIS. Fan shaped for rockeries. In pots, 1/6 each. Open ground, 9d. each.
,, **MICROPHYLLA.** Fine for rockeries or walls, one of the best. Height 12—18 in. 1/- each.
,, **SIMONSII.** Tall growing scarlet berries. Height 2—3 ft. 9d. each. 7/6 per doz.

CRABS. *See Pyrus, page 136.*
CRATÆGUS. *See Thorns.*

CYDONIA JAPONICA. Japanese Quince, bright scarlet, splendid for walls, 1/- and 1/6 each.
,, **ALBA.** White form of the above. In pots, 1/6 each.

DAPHNE CNEORUM (The Garland Flower). Very sweet evergreen, trailing. 1/6 each.
,, **MEZEREUM.** Of fragrant purple flowers, early. 1/- and 1/6 each.
,, **ALBUM.** White, fragrant. 1/3 & 1/6 ea.

DEUTZIA, CRENATA. Single white, June and July. 6d. each, 5/- per doz.
,, **FL. PL.** Double rose-coloured flowers. 6d. each, 5/- per doz.
,, **GRACILIS.** White, 6d. ea. 4/- per doz.
,, **LEMOINEI.** Beautiful white variety. 6d. each, 5/- per doz.

ELÆAGNUS PUNGENS AUREA PICTA. In pots, 2/- each.

ELDER (Sambucus).
,, **SERRATIFOLIA FOLIUS AUREUS.** Magnificent fern-like leaf, bright golden in colour. Height 2 ft. 1/- each. Other varieties. *See page 139.*

ELM, ENGLISH. (Ulmus Campestris.) Height 6—7 ft. 9d. each 7/6 per doz., 7—8 ft. 1/- each 10/6 per doz.
,, **WEEPING.** The true Umbrella Elm. 5/- and 7/6 each.
,, **DAMPIERI AUREA.** This is a splendid Golden Elm in habit and growth and colour. Height 5—6 ft. 2/6 each.
,, **LOUIS VAN HOUTTE.** Golden. Height 5—6 ft. 1/6 each.
,, **WHEATLEYII.** Height 6—8 ft. 1/6 each, 16/- per doz.
,, **HUNTINGDON.** Height 6—8 ft. 1/6 each, 15/- per doz.

ESCALLONIA INGRAMI. Erect growth, pink flowers, 1/6 each.
,, **LANGLEYENSIS.** Long slender branches producing flowers of a bright rose carmine, in pots, each 1/6.

EUONYMUS EUROPÆUS (Spindle Tree). Very pretty in Autumn. Height 4—5 ft. 10/6 doz.
,, **JAPONICUS.** Green-leaved variety, 7/6 doz. Various gold and silver variegated varieties. 9/- per doz.
,, **RADICANS,** 4/- per doz.
,, **VARIEGATUS.** Hardy dwarf variety, for edging. 4/6 each, 5/- per doz.

FAGUS. *See Beech.*

FORSYTHIA SUSPENSA. Suitable for wall or rockwork. 9d. each.
,, **FORTUNEI.** 9d. each.
,, **VIRIDISSIMA.** 9d. each.

FRAXINUS. *See Ash.*

GORSE (Ulex) EUROPÆUS. Double, in pots, 1/- each 10/6 per doz.

HAZEL, Purple Leaved. Fine broad leaved variety. 1/- each 10/6 per doz. *See also p. 139*

HEATH (See Eric?). *See page 137.*

HOLLY (Ilex) ARGENTEA MARGINATA. Broad-leaved, silver, free grower and hardy. Height 2—2½ ft. 2/6 each, 2½—3 ft. 3/6 each.
,, **REGINA (Silver Queen),** Height 2—2½ ft. 2/6 each.
,, **AUREA PENDULA.** Waterer's Gold Weeping. 7/6 and 10/6 each.
,, **GOLDEN QUEEN.** Height 2—2½ ft. 2/6 each, 3—4 ft. 5/- each.
,, **FEROX FRUCTO LUTEA.** Golden-fruited Holly. Height 2 ft. 3/6 each.

HORSE CHESTNUT (Æsculus).
,, **SCARLET.** Splendid subject for avenues, or for planting as park specimens. Height 4—5 ft. 1/6 each. Specimen Standards 2/6 each.
,, **BRIOTI.** Bright red. Early-blooming variety of the well-known scarlet chestnut. Height 7—8 ft. 2/6 each.
,, **DOUBLE WHITE.** Height 7—8 ft. 2/6 each. For Common Chestnuts. *See page 139.*

HYDRANGEA PANICULATA GRANDIFLORA. Quite hardy, panicles of white flowers. Height 2—3 ft. 9d. each 7/6 per doz.

HYPERICUM (St. John's Wort).
,, **MOSERIANUM.** Handsome evergreen shrub. 5/- per doz.
,, **TRICOLOR,** in pots. Height 12—15 in. 1/3 each 12/- per doz.

ILEX. *See Holly.*

KALMIA GLAUCA. Very free flowering lilac flowers. Height 1½-2 ft. 2/- each.
,, **LATIFOLIA.** Rose coloured flowers. Height 1½—2 ft. 2/- each.

KERRIA JAPONICA. Yellow shrub, free-flowering. 9d. each.
,, **FLORA PLENA.** Double. 1s. each.

LABURNUM ADAMI (Purple). Ht. 6—8 ft. 2/-.
,, **ALPINUM (Scotch).** Standards, 2/- each.
,, **VOSSI.** Distinct yellow flowers, the best of this class. Standards, 2 6 each.

LAUREL, CAUCASICA. Rich green foliage, very compact habit. Height 1½—2 ft. 4/- per doz. 2½/- per 100, 2—3 ft. 6/- per doz. 40/- per 100.
,, **COLCHICA.** This is one of the best varieties for seaside. 1—1½ ft. 4/- per doz. 25/- per 100, 1½—2 ft. 5/- per doz. 30/- per 100.
,, **LATIFOLIA.** Fine broad-leaved variety. Height 1½—2 ft. 4/- per doz. 25/- per 100, 2—3 ft. 6/- per doz. 40/- per 100.
,, **ROTUNDIFOLIA.** Height 1½—2 ft. 4/- per doz. 30/- per 100, 2—2½ ft. 6/- per doz. 40/- per 100, 4—5 ft. 1/6 each.
,, **PORTUGAL (Lusitanica).** Height 2—2½ ft. 1/6 each 15/- per doz., 3—4 ft. 2/6 each. Standard Laurels, with nice clear stems and good heads. 3/6 and 5/- each.

LAURUSTINUS. Height 2—3 ft. 1/6 each.
LAURUS NOBILIS. *See Bay (Sweet)*

LAVENDER, COMMON (Lavendula). 6d. each. 4/- per doz. 30/- per 100.
,, **NANA (Dwarf Lavender).** 6d. each, 4/- per 100.

LEYCESTERIA FORMOSA. Beautiful Spring flowering Shrub, very handsome. Height 2—3 ft. 9d. each 7/6 per doz.

LILAC ALBA. The common single white lilac. Height 3—4 ft. 1/- each 10/6 per doz.
,, **CHARLES X.** Single deep purplish lilac. 1/3 each 12/- per doz.
,, **LEMOINEI.** Double, rose, changing to bluish lilac, with white centre. Ht. 2—3 ft. 1/6 ea.

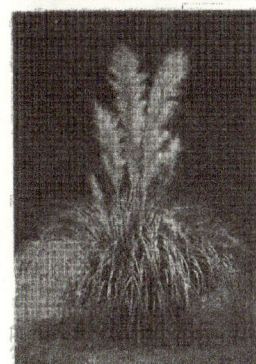

PAMPAS GRASS. *See page 133.*

Hardy Ornamental Trees and Shrubs *(continued).*

GOLDEN LEAVED PRIVET

LILAC, MADAME CASIMIR PERIER. Double creamy white, extra good flower. Ht. 2—3 ft. 1/6 each.
" **MADAME LEMOINE.** Double, compact, spike of the purest white. Height 2—3 ft. 1/6 each.
" **MARIE LEGRAYE.** Height 2—3 ft. 1/6 each, 3—4 ft. 2/- each.
" **PRESIDENT GREVY.** Double blue, shaded rose, large. Height 2—3 ft. 1/6 each.
" **VULGARIS.** The common single purple lilac. Height 2—3 ft. 1/- each, 3—4 ft. 1/6
" **SOUVENIR DE LOUIS SPATH.** Height 2—4 ft. 2/6 each.
LIMES. Red Twigged from Layers. Standards, 1/-, 1/6, 2/6 each. Smaller sizes. *See page 139.*
LIQUIDAMBAR STYRACIFLUA (Sweet Gum). Leaves very fragrant and thrives well on damp situations. Height 3—4 ft. 1/6 each.
MAGNOLIA GRANDIFLORA. Large white flowers and very fragrant, requires a south aspect. In pots, height 2—3ft. 3/6 and 5/- each.
" **LENNE.** Beautiful flowers of a purplish colour with white blush centre. In pots, height 2—3 ft. 3/6 and 5/- each.
" **SOULANGEANA.** Very fine sweetly scented variety, purplish tinted flowers. In pots, height 2—3 ft. 3/6 each.
MAPLES, JAPANESE (Acer) In pots.
" **JAPONICA AUREA.**
" **PURPUREA.**
" **PALMATA.**
" " **ATRO-PURPUREA.**
" " **DISSECTUM.**
" " **RUBRUM.**
" " **ROSEA MARGINATA.**
" " **SANGUINEUM.**
" " **SEPTEMLOBEN.**
Extremely handsome, may be grown in pots for conservatory, or planted out of doors; colours ranging from yellow to rich dark crimson and purple, broadly palmate and delicately cut leaves. Purchaser's selection, 2/6 and 3/6 each. Our selection, 2/- each.
MAPLES, NORWAY.
" **FOLIUS ARGENTEUS.** Silver. Leaf beautifully variegated, a most effective tree. Pyramids, 3—4 ft. 1/6 each, 15/- per doz. Standards, 2/6 each.
" **PLATINOIDES.** This is also a beautiful form, very effective. Standards, 1/6 ea.

MOCK ORANGE (Syringa).
" **CORONARIUS.** Useful for shrubberies; flowers freely. Ht. 2—4 ft. 7/6 & 10/6 doz.
" **GRANDIFLORUS.** Very large-flowered variety. Height 2—4 ft. 7/6 and 10/6 per doz.
" **LEMOINEI.** Ht. 2—4 ft. 7/6 and 10/6 doz.
" " **BOULE D'ARGENT.** Dwarf habit, flowers very large. Ht. 2—4 ft. 7/6 & 10/6 doz.
" **GERBE DE NEIGE.** Large white flowers, sweet. Ht. 2—4 ft. 7/6 & 10/6 doz.
OAK (Quercus). COCCINEA (Scarlet Oak). The Scarlet Oak is one of the finest of our ornamental trees. 6—8 ft. 1/6 each 15/- doz.
" **CONCORDIA (Golden Oak).** Fine trees. Height 5—6 ft. 2/6 each.
" **ILEX (Holm, or Evergreen Oak).** Grown specially in pots. Height 1—1½ ft. 1/- each 10/6 per doz., 3—4 ft. 2/6 each.
OLEARIA HAASTII. Height 12—18 in. 1/- each 10/6 per doz.
" **GUNNIANA.** Heads of white flowers in great profusion. In pots, 1/6 and 2/- each.
OSMANTHUS ILICIFOLIUS. Height 1½-2 ft. 1/6 each 15/- doz.
PERNETTYA. A hardy evergreen shrub, covered with red berries. 1/6 each.
PLANE, LONDON (Platanus Acerifolia). 7—8 ft. 2/- each, 8—10 ft. 2/6 each. Larger specimens, extra good heads, 3/6 & 5/- each.
PRIVET (Ligustrum).
" **JAPONICUM.** Large, broad, shining green foliage. 1/6 each.
" **OVALIFOLIUM FOLIUS AUREUS (Golden-Leaved Privet).** A most showy hardy plant, foliage broadly margined with bright gold; useful alike for hedges, or for planting singly in borders. Height 1½—2 ft. 9d. each, 7/6 per doz., 2—3 ft. 1/- each, 10/6 per doz. Selected Standards, 1/6 and 2/6 each. Selected Half-stds., 1/6 each. *See also page 139.*
PRUNUS PISSARDII (Purple Leaf Plum). Stds, 3—4 ft. stems and good heads, 1/6 and 2/- each. Pyds. 3—5 ft. 1/3 ea. 12/- per doz.
" **TRILOBA.** Double pink, useful for forcing. Bush, 2—3 ft. 1/6 each. Stds., 2/6 each.
PYRUS (Apple).
" **FLORIBUNDA.** Dwarfs. 1/6 each 15/- per doz. Stds., 6—7 ft. 2/- each 21/- doz.
" **MALUS, Dartmouth Crab.** Very fine, Std. 1/6
" " **JOHN DOWNIE.** A beautiful variety. Standards, 1/6 each.
QUERCUS. *See Oak.*
RIBES SANGUINEUM (Flowering Currant). 2—3 ft. 6d. each 5/- per doz.
" **FLORA PLENA.** Flowers double red. Height 2—3 ft. 9d. each 7/6 per doz. Standards, height 3—4 ft. stems 2/- each.
SKIMMIA JAPONICA. Female variety. Height 12—15 in. 1/6 each.
SNOWDROP TREE (Halesia Tetraptera). Height 1½—2 ft. 1/- each.
SNOWY MESPILUS (Amelanchier Canadensis). Standards 1/6 and 2/- each.
SPIRÆA AUREA. The golden-leaved variety. 6d. each 5/- per doz.
" **ARGUTA.** 9d. each 7/6 per doz.
" **CALLOSA.** Free flowering, red flowers. 6d. each 5/- per doz.
" " **ALBA.** 6d. each 5/- per doz.
" **CONFUSA.** 9d. each 7/6 per doz.
" **DOUGLASII.** Rose-coloured flowers, free-flowering. 6d. each 5/- per doz.
" **ANTHONY WATERER.** Dwarf-growing. Crimson flowers 9d. each 7/6 per doz.
STAPHYLEA COLCHICA. Pretty creamy white flowers. 9d. each 7/6 per doz.
SUMACH, VENETIAN (Rhus Cotinus). Lovely foliage which deepens in Autumn. Height 2 ft. 9d. each 7/6 per doz.
" **ATROPURPUREA.** Very ornamental with purple flowers. 2 ft. 9d. each 7/6 per doz.
" **GLABRA LACINIATA.** Pretty fern-like foliage. 1½—2 ft. each 10/6 per doz.

SYCAMORE (Acer).
" **ALBA VARIEGATA.** Very beautiful. Ht. 4—5 ft. 1/- each, 5—6 ft. 1/6 each, 6—8 ft. 2/- each ; Larger specimens 3/6 and 5/- each.
" **LEOPOLDII.** Beautiful purple, flesh coloured. Standards, 7—8 ft. 2/6 each.
THORNS (Crataegus).
Handsome free-flowering trees. Double Crimson, Paul's Pyramids, 1/3 each. Stds. 1/6 and 2/- each.
" Single Scarlet, Pyrds. 1/6 ea., Stds. 1/6 & 2/-.
" Double White (Paul's), Standards. 2 - each.
TULIP-TREE (Liriodendron Tulipifera). A deciduous tree allied to the Magnolia. Standards. Height 6—8 ft. 2/6 each.
VERONICA TRAVERSII. 6d. each 5/- per doz.
VIBURNUM OPULUS STERILE (Snowball Tree). Beautiful flowering Shrub with large globular white flowers. Height 2—3 ft. 9d. each 7/6 per doz.
" **PLICATUM.** One of the best. Height 2—3 ft. 1/6 each 15/- per doz.
VINCA (Periwinkle). MAJOR, Blue, 5/- per doz.
" **MINOR,** Small leaves and blue flowers. 5/- each.
" **ELEGANTISSIMA.** With beautiful variegated foliage. 7/6 per doz.
WEIGELIA. A very handsome and desirable class of beautiful flowering Shrubs, blooming in June; highly recommended.
" **AMABILIS.** Bright pink, 9d. each 7/6 per doz.
" **ABEL CARRIERE.** Rosy carmine, very free. 9d. each 7/6 per doz.
" **ALBA.** Pure white, 9d. each 7/6 per doz.
" **EVA RATHKE.** A very beautiful variety, flowers dark red. 1/- each 10/6 per doz.
" **ROSEA.** Rose coloured, 9d. each 7/6 per doz.
WILLOW (Salix). *See also page 139.*
" **ALBA (White Willow).** 5 ft. 6d. each.
" **CŒRULEA (Bat Willow)** *See page 139.*
" **BABYLONICA (Weeping Willow).** Standards. Height 6—8 ft. 1/- each
" **NIGRA.** Black barked. Ht. 4 ft. 6d ea.
" **HUNTINGDON WILLOW.** Ht. 4—5 ft. 6d. ea.
" **KILMARNOCK.** This is a splendid Weeping variety. Height 6—8 ft. 2/- each.
WISTARIA SINENSIS. Standards 5/- each.
" **ALBA.** Standards 5/- each.
WYCH HAZEL (Hamamelis). Flowers in mid-Winter. 3/6 each.
YUCCA FILAMENTOSA. Most useful plant, flowers freely. 9d. each 6 - per doz.

VIBURNUM PLICATUM.

RHODODENDRONS.

RHODODENDRON, PINK PEARL.

The cultivation of these beautiful hardy evergreen flowering shrubs has been greatly on the increase since the discovery that peat soil is not absolutely necessary for their successful growth. Sandy peat suits them best, but they do well in sandy loam or even clayey loam, if free from calcareous matter, whilst we have seen beautiful specimens growing in ordinary light garden soil. The colours of flowers range from most intense crimson to the most delicate shades of rose and pure white.

CHOICE HYBRIDS.

	each—s.	d.
BARCLAYANUM. Deep rosy crimson, fine truss	2	6
BEAUTY OF SURREY. Scarlet spotted	2	6
BOULE-DE-NEIGE. Pure white	2	6
BRAYANUM. Deep rosy scarlet	2	6
CHARLES BAGLEY. Cherry red	2	6
COUNTESS OF NORMANTON. Pale pink, almost white	2	6
CYNTHIA. Rosy crimson	2	6
DONCASTER. Intense scarlet, fine trusses, superb variety	3	6
DR. HOGG. Bright crimson. This variety was the leading feature in the Royal bed at the Royal Agricultural Show, Norwich, June 26th, 1911	2	6
FATUOSA FLORA PLENA. Mauve, large and double flowers	2	6
GENERAL GRANT. Scarlet	2	6
JAMES MASON. Bright scarlet	2	6
JOHN WATERER. A fine dark crimson variety	2	6
KATE WATERER. Rosy crimson, large yellow centre	2	6
LADY ARMSTRONG. Pale rose	2	6
LADY ELEANOR CATHCART. Red, crimson spot	2	6
MRS. JOHN CLUTTON. The best hardy white Rhododendron	2	6
MRS. JOHN WATERER. Bright rose, spotted	2	6
MRS. TOM AGNEW. Blush white with lemon blotch	2	6
PINK PEARL. F.C.C., R.H.S. The most remarkable and finest variety of Rhododendron that has ever been introduced. The colour is a beautiful flesh tinted pink, a shade that makes it absolutely unique.		
Fine Plants, set with buds .. 5s., 7s. 6d., and 10		6
SNOWFLAKE. Pure white, large truss	2	6
SIR JAMES CLARKE. Dark crimson, shaded purple	2	6
SURPRISE. Light rose, very free	2	6
VANDYKE. Bright crimson, fine truss	2	6

In Choice Varieties, our selection, 25s. per doz.

RHODODENDRONS.

These have amongst them all the colours of the named varieties, the seed being gathered from a collection of named sorts only, but the colour of each plant cannot be guaranteed as in named varieties.

For general effect in the borders they are most excellent, and being of very hardy and robust constitution are in very great demand. We strongly recommend them to our customers.

CHOICE HYBRID SEEDLINGS.
Height 12—18 in. 12/- per 100, 85/- per 100, 18—24 in. 15/- per doz. 105/- per 100.

CUNNINGHAMII. The best white for forcing. Height 12—15 in. 12/- per doz. 75/- per 100, 18—24 in. 18/- per doz. 125/- per 100.

JACKSONII. Good strong stuff, extra bushy. Height 1½—2 ft. 2/- each.

PRÆCOX. Rosy lilac, dwarf and very early, often seen in bloom in February in sheltered borders. Height 12—15 in. 1/6 each 18/- per doz., 15—18 in. 2/- each 21/- per doz.

PONTICUM. All good bushy stuff, well rooted. Height 12—15 in. 6/- per doz. 40/- per 100, 15—18 in. 8/- per doz. 60/- per 100, 24—30 in. 12/- per doz. 70/- per 100.

STANDARDS.

These are very beautiful for lawns. We can supply a few of the best sorts with good heads, 10/6 and 15/- each.

These are excellent for forcing, or for out-door planting.

AZALEAS.

These are excellent for forcing, or for out-door planting.

MOLLIS. In fine shades of orange, flesh pink, rose, and salmon. Nice bushy plants, well set with buds. Height 12—15 in. 15/- per doz. 1/6 each, 15—18 in. 18/- per doz. 2/- each. We can also supply as Standards, 5/- and 7/6 each.

GHENT VARIETIES.
Bouquet de Flore. Salmon Pink.
Daviesii. White (good for forcing).
Gloria Mundi. Vermilion Red.
Melanie. Soft Pink.
Pallas. Red.
Unique. Yellow.
Nice plants, well set with buds, 24/- doz. ea. 2/6 Standards, with nice heads, 5/- and 7/6 each.

RUSTICA (Flora Plena).
A most lovely section, flowers double, of fine shape, colours from pure white to dark red, and sweetly scented; very easy to force.
Nice plants, set with buds, 2/6 each, 24/- doz. Larger plants, 5/- each.

PONTICA. Orange yellow, sweetly scented, very free. Height 12—15 in. 60/- per 100 9/- per doz., 15—18 in. 75/- per 100 12/- per doz.

From **C. W. PAINE, ESQ.**, Pickering.

"The Azaleas you sent me were very beautiful, and have been much admired."

HARDY HEATHS.
(ERICAS.)

These beautiful plants are most useful for edging beds of Azaleas and Rhododendrons.

ALPORTI. The best crimson. 7/6 per doz. 60/- per 100.

AUREA. Golden foliage. 7/6 per doz. 60/- per 100.

CARNEA. Abundance of reddish flesh-coloured flowers in March and April. 9/- per doz.

„ **ALBA.** White variety of above. 9/- per doz.

HAMMONDII. The lucky White Heath. 7/6 per doz. 60/- per 100.

SEARLEII. White, very distinct. 7/6 per doz. 60/- per 100.

HARDY BAMBOOS.

ARUNDINARIA FORTUNEII, variegata. Beautiful bright green leaves, striated white, 1/6 and 2/- each.

„ **JAPONICA (Bambusa Metake).** Stems 15 ft. long with dark green sharply pointed leaves. 1/6 and 2/- each.

„ **SIMONII.** Tall, straight, slender stems, runs very freely at the root. 2/6 and 3/6 each.

BAMBUSA TESSELLATA. The largest leaved of all the hardy Bamboos. 2/- each.

PHYLLOSTACHYS AUREA. Stems yellow, very straight, erect growing close round the base. 2/6 and 3/6 each.

„ **NIGRA.** Stems glossy black after the first year. 3/6 and 5/- each.

CONIFERÆ.

In the following list we have aimed at offering only the most popular and useful kinds. They are most striking objects either planted singly, or in groups, and if rightly placed amongst deciduous and ornamental trees the effect is very pleasing.

All have been recently transplanted so as to ensure as far as possible safety in removal, abundance of room and attention have been given so that each tree may be a perfect specimen. Our trees are all hand pruned with a knife, which is a most important point. We offer well shaped plants, suitable for potting or window boxes, in good variety, our selection.

12 to 18 inches, 6s. per doz., 45s. per 100.   18 to 24 inches, 9s. per doz., 60s. per 100.

ABIES CANADENSIS (Hemlock Spruce). Very graceful tree, grows well, and well worthy of a prominent sheltered place in the pleasure grounds. Height 2–3 ft. 1/3 each.

" NORDMANNIANA. Very handsome tree, and should be more extensively planted. Height 1—1½ ft. 1/6 each, 2—3 ft. 3/6 each.

" PINSAPO. Very thick-growing, and most distinct. Height 2—3 ft. 2/6 each.

ARAUCARIA IMBRICATA. This is a most distinct tree, and specimens should be planted more extensively. Height 2–3 ft. 5/- each.

CEDRUS ATLANTICA. This is a very fast-growing and ornamental tree with silvery foliage, and of more upright habit than Libani. Ht. 2—3 ft. 2/6 each, 3—4 ft. 3/6 ea.

" DEODARA. Height 2—3 ft. 2/- each, 3—4 ft. 3/6 each.

" LIBANI (Cedar of Lebanon). A handsome bold tree. 2—3 ft. 3/6 each.

CRYPTOMERIA JAPONICA (Japanese Cedar). Bright green foliage, and very rapid growth. 2—3 ft. 3/6 each.

" ELEGANS. Plumose habit, very ornamental, with bronzy crimson foliage in Winter. Height 2—3 ft. 2/6 each.

CUPRESSUS LAWSONIANA. See page 139.

"   "   ALBA-SPICA. The young, beautiful foliage tipped with white. Height 1½—2 ft. 1/6 each.

" ALLUMII. Very hardy, compact, upright habit, foliage rich silver blue. 1½—2 ft. 1/3 each 12/- per doz., 2½—3 ft. 2/- each.

" ERECTA VIRIDIS. Good Cupressus of erect habit. Height 1½—2 ft. 1/- each 10/6 per doz., 2—3 ft. 1/6

" LUTEA. A beautiful golden form of the Lawson's Cypress. Height 2—2½ ft. 3/6 ea.

" MACROCARPA (In pots). A very handsome variety, of rapid growth. Height 2—3 ft. 2/6 each.

PICEA PUNGENS GLAUCA KOSTERIANA.

CUPRESSUS MACROCARPA LUTEA (In pots). A very good golden Cupressus. Height 1½—2 ft. 1/6 to 2/6 each.

GINKGO (Maiden Hair Tree) (Salisburia adiantifolia). Height 1½—2 ft. 6d. each, 3—4 ft. 1/- each, 3—4 ft. 1/6 each.

JUNIPERUS (Juniper).

" COMMUNIS FASTIGIATA (Irish Juniper). A beautiful and effective Conifer for landscape planting, of close, upright growth. Height 1—1½ ft. 1/3 each, 1½—2 ft. 1/9 each.

" VIRGINIANA (Red Cedar). Good hardy variety of upright growth. Ht. 2½—3 ft 1/6 ea.

PICEA PUNGENS. Height 2—2½ ft. 1/6 each.

" GLAUCA (Blue Spruce). A lovely Spruce, with glaucous leaves. Height 1½—2 ft. 2/6 each.

PINUS CEMBRA. Very distinct species of conical growth. Height 2—3 ft. 1/6 each.

" AUSTRIACA. See Austrian Pine, page 139.

" PINASTER. Valuable tree for seaside planting, stands breeze well and good shelter tree. Height 2—2½ ft. 1/- each.

RETINOSPORA PISIFERA. Height 1½—2 ft. 1/6 each.

"   " AUREA. Very beautiful. Height 1—1½ ft. 1/9 each.

" PLUMOSA AUREA. Soft, dense habit, should be regularly clipped. Height 2—3 ft. 2/- each.

TAXODIUM DISTICHUM (Deciduous Cypress). Very ornamental, light feathery foliage, should be closely pruned when transplanting, changing to rich brown in Autumn. Height 2—3 ft. 1/- each.

TAXUS AUREA (Golden Yew). Height 1½—2 ft. 2/6 each, 2—3 ft. 3/- each.

" FASTIGIATA (The Irish Yew). Very dark foliage, with upright habit. Height 1½—2 ft. 1/6 each, 2—3 ft. 2/- each.

" AUREA (Golden Irish Yew). Resembling the above in shape and habit, but golden colour. Height 1—1½ ft. 1/6 each, 2—3 ft. 3/6 each.

" BACCATA (Common Yew). See page 139.

THUJOPSIS DOLABRATA. This is a beautiful Conifer, compact habit, most pleasing appearance, massive bright glossy green foliage. Height 1—1½ ft. 9d. each.

THUJA LOBBII. A very hardy, ornamental shrub, suitable for any position. Height 2½—3 ft. 1/- each 10/6 per doz., 3—4 ft. 1/6 each 15/- per doz.

" VERVAENEANA. Beautiful golden tinted variety. Height 2—3 ft. 1/6 each.

TRANSPLANTED FOREST TREES, HEDGING AND UNDERWOOD PLANTS FOR GAME COVERTS.

To meet the demand for Forest Trees we have considerably increased our Stock in this direction, and it will be found to comprise all the best varieties for Forest and Estate planting; further, we make it a practice to grow our trees thinly in wide rows, which ensures their being thoroughly hardened when moved to exposed situations. We shall be pleased to give estimates, free of cost, for all kinds of planting, Forest or otherwise, and will carry out the entire work if desired.

Our prices, taking quality into consideration, are exceedingly moderate, and we are prepared to compete with any respectable firms in the trade. Extra Selected Plants, and smaller quantities than quoted, will be charged proportionally higher.

We shall be pleased to submit samples of any Forest Trees, Carriage Free.

ACACIA, Common. See also page 134.

Very ornamental tree, growing freely on poor sandy soil. Height 2—3½ ft. 5/- per 100 45/- per 1000. Specimen Trees, 1/-, 1/6, and 2/- each.

ALDER, Common. Grows well on wet, undrained soils. Height 2—3 ft. 4/6 per 100 40/- per 1000, 3—5 ft, 6/- per 100 50/- per 1000. Specimen Trees, 1/-, 1/6, and 2/6 each.

ARBOR-VITÆ (Thuya Occidentalis). Very compact and hardy. Height 1½—2 ft. 25/- per 100, 2—3 ft. 35/- per 100, 3—4 ft. 9/- per doz.

ASH, Common. See also page 134.

Requires good land; timber very valuable when well grown. Height 2—3 ft. 4/- per 100 35/- per 1000, 3—4 ft, 6/- per 100 50/- per 1000, 4—6 ft. 7/- per 100 65/- per 1000, 10 —12 ft. 1/6 and 2/6 each.

" MOUNTAIN. Very ornamental tree, most valuable for exposed situations; fruit valued by many for making preserves for eating with game. Height 4 —5 ft. 10/- per 100 90/- per 1000, 6—8 ft. 12/- per doz. Specimen Trees, 1/6 and 2/6 each.

BEECH, Common. Makes a splendid hedge. Height 1½—2 ft. 7/- per 100 60/- per 1000, 2—3 ft. 10/- per 100 80/- per 1000.

BERBERIS AQUIFOLIUM. This is one of our finest shrubs for underwood; flowers and seeds freely, excellent for game covers and shrubberies. Height 1½—2 ft. 15/- per 100.

" DARWINII. 12—18 in. 6/- per doz. 30/- per 100. Specimens, 9d. and 1/- each.

BIRCH, Common. See also page 134.

Timber fine-grained and valuable. Makes the best charcoal for gunpowder. Height 2—3 ft. 5/- per 100 45/- per 1000, 3—4 ft. 6/- per 100 55/- per 1000, 6—10 ft. 9/- per doz.

" SILVER. One of the most beautiful of our forest trees. Succeeds in moist situations. Height 3—4 ft. 9/- per 100, 9—12 ft. 1/6, 2/6, 3/6 each.

Forest Trees *(continued)*

BLACKTHORN or SLOE. A splendid plant for Fox covers and for hedges. Height 1½—2 ft. 6/- per 100 45/- per 1000.

BOX TREE. This forms a handsome hedge. Height 1½–2 ft. 25/ per 100, 2–3 ft. 40/ per 100.

BRAMBLES. 6/- per 100 50/- per 1000.

BRIAR, DOG. 6/- per 100 50/- per 1000.

,, **SWEET.** Height 2—3 ft. 6/- per doz. 30/- per 100.

BROOM, Common. Seedlings, 3/6 per 100 30/- per 1000. Transplanted, 7/6 per 100.

CHESTNUT, SPANISH. Highly ornamental and rapid grower. Requires a sheltered situation. Height 2—3 ft. 6/- per 100. Specimen Trees, 1/- and 1/6 each.

,, **HORSE.** *See also page* 135. Very handsome flowering tree. Splendid for avenues or parks, requires good land. Height 3—4 ft. 12/6 per 100, 5—6 ft 15/- per 100. Specimen Trees, 1/-, 1/6, 2/6 each.

COTONEASTER SIMMONDII. Very rapid growing. Ht. 1½—2 ft. 4/- per doz. 30/- per 100.

CUPRESSUS LAWSONIANA. The most popular of all the Cupressus. Height 1½—2 ft. 5/- per doz. 35/ per 100, 3–4 ft. 1/6 ea. 15/ per doz.

DOGWOOD, Scarlet. Very effective for massing. Ht. 2—3 ft. 3/- per doz. 10/6 per 100.

ELDER, Golden Leaved. Height 3—4 ft. 9d. each 10/6 per doz.

,, **Silver variegated.** Ht. 2-3 ft. 6d. each 5/- doz.

ELM, ENGLISH. This is a tall and elegant tree of rapid and erect growth. Height 2—3 ft. 4/6 per 100 40/- per 1000, 3—4 ft. 6/- per 100.

FIR, DOUGLAS (Abies Douglasii). This is a fast-growing, magnificent timber tree, its foliage is a rich green. Height 1½—2 ft. 20/- per 100, 3—4 ft. 6/- per doz.

,, **SCOTCH.** The true Highland Pine is now much planted, grows freely on all exposed late districts. Height 12—15 in. 3/6 per 100 30/- per 1000, 15—18 in. 4/6 per 100 40/- per 1000, 1½—2 ft. 6/- per 100 50/- per 1000.

,, **SPRUCE (Pinus excelsa).** Height 12—18 in. 6/- per 100 50/- per 1000, 18—24 in. 10/- per 100 70/- per 1000. Xmas trees in various sizes, from 3—8 ft. Prices on application.

HAZEL. Ht. 2—3 ft. 4/- per 100 35/- per 1000.

HYPERICUM CALYCINUM. An excellent covert plant for growing under the shade of large trees, beautiful when in flower, and not liked by Rabbits. Transplanted, 3/- per doz. 20/- per 100

HOLLY, Green. Forms a beautiful hedge if planted in double rows, leaving 12 ins. between each row, also well adapted for mixing with thorn. Height 1½—2 ft. 6/- per doz. 50/- per 100, 2—2½ ft. 12/- per doz.

HORNBEAM. Grows very close and rapidly. Height 1½—2 ft. 4/6 per 100 40/- per 1000.

IVY, IRISH. Open ground. Transplanted, 3/- per doz. 21/- per 100.

LABURNUM, Common. *See also page* 135. Very handsome early-flowering tree, covered with yellow blossom. Height 2½—3 ft. 12/- per 100. Specimens, 1/-, 1/6 and 2/6 each.

LARCH, Native. The above are all grown from Seed had from the North of Scotland, and are splendidly rooted. Height 1—1½ ft. 3/- per 100 25/- per 1000, 1½—2 ft. 4/- per 100 35/- per 1000, 2—2½ ft. 5/- per 100.

,, **JAPANESE.** This variety is coming more into demand, owing to its rapid growth and being late in showing leaf is not so apt to be cut down with late Spring frosts. Height 1—1½ ft. 8/- per 100, 2—2½ ft. 10/6 per 100.

LIMES. Red Twigged from Layers. Very ornamental tree when grown singly, most useful for Parks or Avenue planting, very hardy and large specimens, transplants safely. Height 2—3 ft. 3/- per doz. 15/- per 100, 5—6 ft. 6/- per doz. 45/- per 100, 6—7 ft. 9/- per doz. 60/- per 100. Specimen Standards, 1/-, 1/6, 2/6, 3/6 each.

MAPLE, NORWAY. *See also Acers, page* 136. Height 3—4 ft. 7/6 per 100 70/- per 1000, 8—10 ft. 9/- per doz. 70/- per 100 Large specimens, 1/-, 1/6 and 2/6 each

OAK, ENGLISH. Height 2—3 ft. 7/- per 100 65/- per 1000. Specimen Trees, 1/- and 1/6 ea.

,, **SCARLET.** One of the most beautiful trees, scarlet foliage with rich Autumn tint. Specimen Trees, 1/-, 1/6, and 2/- each.

PINE, AUSTRIAN. Succeeds on high, dry, exposed situations, and on sea-shore. All well transplanted trees. Height 1—1½ ft. 12/6 per 100, 3—4 ft. 2/6 each 24/- per doz., 2—3 ft. 12/- doz. 90/- 100.

,, **WEYMOUTH (Pinus Strobus).** The White Canadian Pine of soft and delicate appearance, with silky foliage. Height 1½—2 ft. 6/- per doz. 30/- per 100, 3—4 ft. 1/- each 15/- per doz.

PERIWINKLE (Vinca). 5/- per doz. 30/- per 100.

PRIVET, Common. Height 2—3 ft. 6/- per 100 50/- per 1000.

,, **EVERGREEN.** Ornamental when cut well back. Height 1½—2 ft. 4/6 per 100 40/- per 1000, 2—3 ft. 6/- per 100 50/- per 1000.

,, **OVAL-LEAVED.** Invaluable for planting in towns, no plant stands smoke better and makes a beautiful ornamental hedge. Height 1½—2 ft. 6/6 per 100 50/- per 1000, 2—3 ft. 10/- per 100 90/- per 1000, 3—4 ft. 12/- per 100 100/- per 1000.

POPLAR ABELE, Silver. Very valuable quick-growing tree, useful for exposed situations, with silvery leaf; grows freely on the coast. Height 4—6 ft. 20/- per 100, 8—10 ft. 9/- per doz. Specimen Trees, 1/- and 1/6 each.

,, **BLACK ITALIAN.** The most rapid growing of all our forest trees, grows fully in most soils and is invaluable for shelter. Height 4—6 ft. 10/- per 100, 8—9 ft. 7/6 per doz. 50/- per 100. Specimen Trees, 9d., 1/6, and 2/6 each.

,, **DELTOIDEA (Canadensis).** This is undoubtedly the coming Poplar for Street, Park, or Avenue planting. It does splendidly in smoky towns and is of fine pyramidal habit with bold shining foliage. Height 8—10 ft. 7/6 per doz. 50/- per 100. Very large specimens for parks or planting singly, 1/-, 1/6 and 2/6 each.

ENGLISH YEW.

POPLAR AUREA. This variety is becoming a favourite, grows very freely, with rich golden foliage, Standards. Height 6—8 ft. 1/6 each, 8—10 ft. 2/- each.

,, **LOMBARDY.** Very ornamental upright growing tree, often introduced in Landscape with effect, grows well in almost any soil, and most useful for close planting to act as a block. Height 5—6 ft. 8/- per 100, 8—10 ft. 7/6 per doz. 50/- per 100. Specimens, 1/-, 1/6 and 2/- each.

,, **BALSAM.** Very early to bud in Spring, with large fragrant foliage. Height 8—10 ft. 6/- per doz. 30/- per 100. Large Specimens, 6/- doz., 1/-, 1/6 and 2/- each.

ROSA RUGOSA. One of the finest hardy and ornamental berried shrubs introduced from Japan. 6/- per doz. 35/- per 100.

SEA BUCKTHORN. Height 1½—2 ft. 6/- per doz. 40/- per 100.

SNOWBERRY. Height 2—3 ft. 4/6 per 100 40/- per 1000.

SERVICE TREE. A beautiful tree, handsome dark green foliage; splendid avenue tree and should be more grown. Specimen Trees, 1/- and 1/6 each.

SYCAMORE. Very hardy, and stands the sea winds better than most other trees; grows freely in any soil, very ornamental, and excellent timber. Height 2—3 ft. 4/6 per 100 35/- per 1000, 3—4 ft. 6/- per 100 50/- per 1000, 5—6 ft. 10/- per 100. Specimen Trees, 1/-, 1/6 and 2/6 each.

THORNS or QUICKS. This is the best of all plants for an efficient hedge. Height 1—1½ ft. 3/- per 100 25/- per 1000, 1½—2 ft. 4/- per 100 30/- per 1000, 2—2½ ft. 6/- per 100, extra strong.

WILLOW, BAT (Salix alba cœrulea). Fine selected standards, 8—10 ft. per doz. 12/- per 100 80/-. Strong two-year old plants, 5—6 ft. per doz. 9/- per 100 60/-. Strong one-year old, well rooted, per 100 25/-. Unrooted sets, 3—5 ft. 17/6 per 100.

,, **BITTER OSIER.** Splendid for covers, not liable to be destroyed by Rabbits. Height 3—4 ft. 4/6 per 100 40/- per 1000.

,, **HUNTINGDON.** Makes valuable timber, ornamental, and of rapid growth. Height 3—4 ft. 6/6 per 100.

,, **YELLOW OSIER.** Very ornamental when planted near water. Height 3—4 ft. 4/6 per 100.

WHIN, GORSE, or FURZE. Seedlings, 3/- per 100 20/- per 1000. Transplanted, 4/- per 100 30/- per 1000.

YEW, Common. This is the most Ornamental of all evergreen hedges, it should not be planted in any situation accessible to animals that might eat it. It is hardy and a compact grower. Height 1—1½ ft. 5/- per doz. 30/- per 100, 1½—2 ft. 7/6 per doz. 50/- per 100, 2—2½ ft. 10/6 per doz. 80/- per 100.

MYROBELLA
or CHERRY PLUM.

This is the quickest growing hedge plant and largely used in England. Extra fine, well rooted, 6/6 per 100, 60/- per 1000. Second size, 5/6 per 100, 50/- per 1000. Very scarce.

The best time for planting is in November or early Spring, or it may be done in open weather at any time during the Winter months, but in fairly moist weather successful plantings may be made as late as the middle or end of April. In planting plant firmly, placing the sets from six to nine inches apart, according to size. When growth commences, they should be cut down to eight or ten inches in height. It should be cut at least twice a year—about the end of July and in Spring whilst in a dormant state.

ANEMONES—Single and Double-flowered.

ANEMONE, ST. BRIGID.

ANEMONE, St. Brigid.

A brilliant and very beautiful class of large semi-double flowers of the most striking and charming shades of colour, ranging from crimson and scarlet to rose, lilac, dark blue, &c., to the purest white. Nearly all the blooms have conspicuous white centres, which add greatly to their beauty. They are first-class for cut flowers, and if out when the bloom is beginning to open and the stems placed in water, they will retain their beauty for a long time.

Very Choice Mixed. In beautiful variety

per 1000, 45s. ; per 100, 5s. ; per doz. 9d.

NEW PINK SPIRÆAS.

These grand varieties are suitable alike for forcing or planting in the open ground, when planted outside the colours will be much deeper.

QUEEN ALEXANDRA. Bright pink   per doz. 15s. ; each 1s. 6d.
PEACH BLOSSOM. Pale pink ..   ,, 15s. ; ,, 1s. 6d.
These made quite a sensation when exhibited at Holland House, and were awarded the Gold Medal of the Royal Horticultural Society.

ANEMONES.
SUPERB DOUBLE-FLOWERED.

Producing large, handsome, double flowers of various beautiful colours some of the varieties are strikingly brilliant.

	per 100. s. d.	per doz. s. d.
CHOICE NAMED SORTS, our selection	7 6	1 0
CHOICEST MIXED, from named sorts	6 0	1 0

GIANT FRENCH SINGLE.
(Poppy Anemones.)

A magnificent class, producing immense double and semi-double flowers of the most beautiful colours ; splendid for garden decoration.

	per 100. s. d.	per doz. s. d.
Very Choice Mixed. Single	5 0	0 9

DUTCH ANEMONES.

		per 100. s. d.	per doz. s. d.
DOUBLE, finest mixed, fine roots .. .. per 1000, 35s.	4 0	0 8
SINGLE, ,, ,, ... ,, 30s.	3 0	0 6
SCARLET, FINEST DOUBLE. Fine roots	5 0	0 9
,, SINGLE. Strong roots	2 6	0 6
PURE WHITE, SINGLE, "THE BRIDE." Splendid ..	2 6	0 6

ANEMONE SPECIES.

Beautiful large-flowered varieties with dazzling vermilion scarlet blooms. Particularly valuable for cut flowers. Planted in September may be had in bloom in February. Quite hardy.

	per 100. s. d.	per doz. s. d.
APPENINA. Blue mountain wind flower ..	4 0	0 9
FULGENS. Single scarlet ; very fine ..	7 6	1 0

RANUNCULI.

The Ranunculi are very free-flowering and beautiful. They will succeed in almost any soil or position, and planted any time up to the middle of April will bloom abundantly during the Summer ; very useful for cutting.

	per 100. s. d.	per doz. s. d.
TURBAN, DANIELS' GIANT. A splendid and robust-growing class, very superior to the common Turban varieties ; grows to the height of eighteen inches ; each plant producing from forty to fifty splendid double flowers .. per 1000, 35s.	4 6	0 9
,, SCARLET. Admirably adapted for filling beds, ribbon borders, or massing .. .. per 1000, 21s.	2 6	0 4
,, MIXED. All colours ; a beautiful variety ..	2 0	0 4
FRENCH GIANT. Very fine .. .. per 1000, 35s.	4 6	0 9
PERSIAN, CHOICEST MIXED. In beautiful variety ,, 1000, 20s.	2 6	0 4

TIGRIDIAS—TIGER FLOWERS.

Beautiful showy plants growing about one foot high ; quite hardy.

	per doz. s. d.	each s. d.
CANARIENSIS. Yellow, spotted with scarlet ..	1 3	0 3
CONCHIFLORA. Brilliant yellow, spotted with scarlet ..	2 0	0 3
PAVONIA. Scarlet and orange	1 3	0 3
GRANDIFLORA ALBA. Creamy white, spotted with red, and having a violet centre ; a fine and beautiful form..	1 3	0 3

EREMURUS HIMALAICUS.

A magnificent hardy plant, throwing up stately spikes of white campanulate flowers 6 or 8 feet high. Splendidly effective when planted in groups amongst shrubs, &c. .. .. .. each 3s. 6d., 5s., and 7s. 6d.

HYACINTHUS CANDICANS.

A splendid hardy bulbous-rooted plant, blooming in August, and throwing up fine spikes of white bell-shaped flowers three to four feet high. It makes a capital plant for pots in the greenhouse, and is finely effective when planted out of doors in association with Gladiolus Brenchleyensis, which blooms at the same time. Fine Bulbs, per 100, 5s. 6d. ; per doz. 10d.

MISCELLANEOUS BULBS, ROOTS, &c.

LILY OF THE VALLEY.

For early forcing, single crowns of these should be planted about twelve in a five-inch pot, with the buds well above the surface. Cover the crowns with a little moss or an inverted flower-pot and place them in a good heat of say 85 to 90 degrees; water frequently with tepid water, and if judiciously looked after they will bloom in four or five weeks from time of potting. Good single crowns are much the best for this purpose.

SELECTED SINGLE CROWNS FOR FORCING

per 1000, 50s.; per 100, 6s.; per doz. 1s.

LILY OF THE VALLEY.
Fortin's Giant-flowered.

A very fine variety with remarkably large handsome bells on long sturdy stalks. It is not so early and does not force so well as the ordinary variety, but will bloom splendidly out of doors in a sheltered position. Quite hardy.

STRONG FLOWERING CROWNS .. per 100, 12s. 0d.; per doz. 2s. 0d.
GOOD PLANTING CROWNS .. .. ,, 7s. 6d. ,, 1s. 6d.

MONTBRETIAS.

Beautiful showy plants, producing graceful spikes of brilliantly coloured flowers which are exceedingly useful for cutting. Planted in Spring they will bloom freely during August and September, and form permanent clumps that will increase in beauty from year to year. The plants grow 18 inches to 2 feet high and will thrive anywhere.

	per 100.		per doz.	
	s.	d.	s.	d.
GEORGE DAVISON. Pale orange yellow, a very fine variety ..	7	6	1	3
GERMANIA. Orange-scarlet, large flowers, beautiful	15	0	2	0
KOH-I-NOOR. Rich pure orange, on apricot base, extra fine ..	13	6	2	0
NORVIC (new). Large pure yellow, stained red outside each 1s.	—		10	6
PROMETHEUS (new). Deep orange, with carmine central ring		*		
each 2s. 6d.	—		24	0
STAR OF FIRE. Bright vermilion, centre yellow, outside blood red	5	0	0	10
CHOICE MIXED SEEDLINGS, containing many beautiful colours	4	0	0	8

MONTBRETIAS GERMANIA.

LARGE-FLOWERED CANNAS.

These magnificent plants with their beautiful spikes of brilliantly coloured Gladiolus-like flowers and handsome foliage, have become highly popular for bedding out on lawns, &c., and for greenhouse and conservatory decoration. They are as easily grown as most bedding plants, and are generally effective in groups or centres of beds. Break up the ground and manure as for Dahlias, and plant out in May as soon as danger from frost is over. They will soon start into growth and bloom, and if mulched with short well-rotted manure and well watered should the weather be dry, they will give a splendid show of beautiful flowers till killed by the frost in Autumn. In October or November they may be taken up, and after a short period of rest, divided and potted, when they will again start into growth and bloom in the greenhouse; or the roots may be kept dormant till Spring, when they should be divided and potted up for turning out again in May. If grown for their beautiful foliage alone they are well worth growing, and with additional charm of their gorgeous spikes of beautiful flowers they cannot be too highly recommended.

We have a very fine collection of these, including the most brilliant and beautiful colours.
CHOICE NAMED VARIETIES, our selection .. .. per 100, 75s.; per doz. 10s. 6d.; each 1s.
CROZY'S DWARF VARIETIES, CHOICE MIXED IN BEAUTIFUL VARIETY. Splendid for massing in large beds, &c.
per 100, 35s.; per doz. 5s.; each 6d.

DAHLIAS, POT ROOTS (Dry Tubers).

We offer as below, dry tubers from our splendid collection of choice named Dahlias, which includes the finest varieties in commerce. Considering the low prices at which these are quoted, it must be distinctly understood that the selection of varieties must, in all instances, be left to ourselves.

CACTUS-FLOWERED. Choice named sorts, carefully selected, beautiful varieties .. .. per 100, 30s.; per doz. 4s. 6d.
SHOW AND FANCY. Finest named exhibition varieties .. .. ,, 3s. 6d.
POMPONE. From our choice collection .. .. ,, 3s. 6d.

TUBEROSES.

These deliciously fragrant and exceedingly useful flowers are much more easily grown than is generally supposed, and will well repay the little trouble that is necessary to have them in perfection. For early forcing pot singly into five or six-inch pots, as early in the season as the bulbs can be obtained, and plunge in a good moist heat, withholding water till the foliage makes its appearance, when water may be given abundantly till the flower-buds are formed, when they may be removed to the greenhouse or conservatory and less water given. For Autumn blooming pot singly into five or six-inch pots in March or April, using a light rich compost, and plunge the pots about six inches above their rims in cocoa-nut fibre, coal ashes, or any light material, under the stage of a greenhouse or in a cool pit or frame; when the foliage of these makes its appearance they should be removed and plunged under a south wall, removing them to the greenhouse or indoors as the flower buds are formed. Dry roots may also be planted in sheltered places in the open ground, from the middle of April to the latter part of May, and will produce beautiful flowers in Autumn if taken up and potted when coming into flower, and will furnish a supply of beautiful bloom in the greenhouse almost up to Christmas.

DOUBLE, "AMERICAN PEARL." Fine new dwarf variety from the United States; deliciously fragrant, with large double flowers, pure white.
Selected roots, per 100, 12s. 6d.; per doz. 2s. 0d.; each 3d

DAHLIAS—Cactus-flowered.
NEW AND SELECT VARIETIES.

The following varieties, which are all of the true Cactus type, include what we consider the very choicest flowers for exhibition or decorative purposes, and cannot fail to give the highest satisfaction.

Strong Plants from single pots ready in May.

	each—s. d.
ARGONAUT. Orange-scarlet with lighter centre, very fine and distinct	0 6
CARRIE HAMMOND (1913). White in centre, changing to clear pink, which on older petals becomes deeper. Blooms remain good late into Autumn	2 0
C. E. WILKINS. A magnificent variety. The colour is an exquisite shade of bright clear salmon pink overlaying yellow	0 6
CHARLES H. CURTIS. A noble flower, large, full and strikingly incurved in form. The colour is a rich crimson scarlet	0 6
CORAL. Large beautiful flowers. The base of the florets chrome yellow, the upper part light red	0 6
DOROTHY. Deep and well-formed flowers of good size and with full centres. The colour is a lovely bright silvery pink	0 6
FLAME. A large and splendid flower of a brilliant orange-scarlet colour of a very rich and telling shade	0 6
FREDERICK WENHAM (1912). Very large flowers on long stiff stems, colour a warm fawn pink with soft salmon at centre	1 0
F. W. FELLOWES (new, 1913). A splendid variety producing large flowers with surprising freedom. The plants have a capital style of growth, the flower stems being long and wiry. The colour is a bright orange scarlet throughout. A fine exhibition flower	2 0
GOLDEN WAVE (1912). Rich deep golden yellow, splendid variety	1 0
HAROLD PEARMAN. A deep pure yellow, one of the most constant and free-flowering yet introduced	0 6
H. H. THOMAS. Beautifully formed incurving flowers of good size; colour a deep rich crimson. Splendid exhibition variety	0 6
H. L. BROUSSON. A first-class flower of great depth with long, narrow slightly incurved florets. The colour is a deep, rich rose, lighter at the tips	0 0
INDOMITABLE. Long incurved narrow florets and well-formed large blooms; the colour is a beautiful lilac mauve	0 6
IOLANTHE. Deep coral red, every floret distinctly tipped with gold. A charming variety and first-class for exhibition	0 6
J. B. RIDING. The blooms are large and splendidly formed, the centre a rich yellow, with apricot red outer petals	0 6
J. H. JACKSON. Brilliant crimson maroon, long narrow pointed and incurving petals; splendid dark variety of good form	0 6
JOHANNESBURG. A gigantic flower with splendid centre, borne on long, stout stems. Colour a bright rich golden yellow. A fine exhibition flower	0 9
JOHN RIDING (new 1913). For exhibition this is one of the finest introductions of recent years. Its exceptional size, perfect form, great depth and deep rich crimson colour, placing it easily in the front rank. It is a good bloomer and sturdy grower. F.C.C., N.D.S., and A.M., R.H.S.	2 0
Choice selected sorts, our selection	
Showy and popular varieties, our selection	

	each—s. d.
MRS HOGHTON (new 1913). Lovely rich coral pink, perfectly distinct in colour from any other Cactus Dahlia; blooms well above the foliage	2 0
MISS STREDWICK (1912). One of the finest yet introduced. Soft yellow at base, changing to a lovely tint of deep rosy pink	1 0
MONARCH. Bright bronzy red with yellow centre; very fine	0 6
MRS. DOUGLAS FLEMING. The finest white Cactus Dahlia yet raised. A splendid exhibition flower, of good constitution, and free blooming	0 9
MRS. HENRY RANDLE (new 1913). One of the best all-round varieties in existence. The blooms are of medium size, deep and prettily incurved. The colour is a pale cream changing to a lovely rosy tint and distinctly tipped rosy white	2 0
MRS. H. SHOESMITH. One of the finest pure whites yet sent out	0 6
MRS. J. J. CROWE. Beautiful clear canary yellow; undoubtedly the best yellow Cactus-flowered	0 6
MRS. STEPHENS (1912). Soft primrose yellow, a charming flower	1 0
NEW YORK. A magnificent flower of great size and splendid form, orange yellow in the centre, shading off to deep bronzy salmon. First class	0 9
RED ADMIRAL. One of the most brilliant Dahlias in existence. The blooms are large, well formed, and of the richest fiery scarlet colour	0 6
REV. T. W. JAMIESON. Magnificent variety with large incurved blooms, yellow, edged with rosy lilac, very striking	0 6
SATISFACTION. Most beautiful variety, and one of the very best of the incurved type. The colour is a lovely rose pink, approaching to white in the centre	0 6
SAXONIA. A splendid new deep crimson that will prove of great value as an exhibition flower	0 6
SNOWDON. Very large beautifully formed flowers of the purest white, a splendid variety for exhibition	0 6
SNOWSTORM. A magnificent pure white, dwarf and sturdy in growth, and a continuous bloomer	0 6
SWEET BRIAR. One of the most beautiful varieties of recent introduction. The flowers are large and borne well above the foliage. The colour is an exquisite soft bright pink	0 9
THE IMP. Dark maroon crimson, almost black, quite distinct. It is of good Cactus form and quite remarkable with regard to its colour	0 6
THOMAS PARKIN. Pale terra-cotta, long narrow incurved florets; splendid variety	0 6
WILLIAM MARSHALL. Immense flowers of the most perfect form. Rich orange, bright yellow in the centre	0 6

6 for 3s. 6d. ; per doz. 6s. ; per 100 40s.
6 for 2s. 6d. ; per doz. 4s. 6d. ; per 100 30s.

SPECIAL OFFER

We offer eighteen grand Exhibition Cactus-flowered Dahlias as named below, 10s. Carriage Free.

CORAL	†INDOMITABLE	NEW YORK	SNOWDON
CHARLES H. CURTIS	J. B. RIDING	†RED ADMIRAL	*†SWEET BRIAR
*†DOROTHY	*†JOHANNESBURG	†REV. T. W. JAMIESON	†THE IMP
†GOLDEN WAVE	*†MRS. DOUGLAS FLEMING	†SAXONIA	†WILLIAM MARSHALL
*†H. L. BROUSSON	*MRS. STEVENS		

Twelve Superb Varieties, marked (†) 6s. 6d.   Six Very Choice Sorts, marked (*) 4s.

FINE NEW CACTUS DAHLIAS.

No 1
F.W. FELLOWES
No 2
MR HOGHTON
No 3
MRS H RANDLE

1

2

3

Daniels Bros Ltd Norwich

DANIELS·BROS·L^{TD}
NORWICH

SHOW·DAHLIA
M^{rs}N Halls

POMPONE·CACTUS·DAHLIAS

Bride

Mignon

POMPONE·DAHLIAS

Cheerfulness

PEONY·FLOWERED·DAHLIA

South Pole

DAHLIAS—SHOW AND FANCY.

The following list includes the finest varieties. Strong plants from single pots in May.

S denotes Show, F Fancy. All in the following list 6d. each.

BUTTERCUP (S). Yellow tinged with red, very fine.
COLONIST (S). Chocolate and fawn, very distinct
COMEDIAN (F). Orange ground, flaked crimson and tipped with white.
DIADEM (S). Deep crimson, fine and constant.
DR. KEYNES (S). A pretty rich buff, having a reddish tint.
DUCHESS OF YORK. Lemon edged with pink ; fine flower.
DUKE OF FIFE (S). Fine rich cardinal, large.
FLORENCE TRANTER (S). Blush white, distinctly edged rosy purple.
GOLDFINDER (S). Yellow, tipped with red.
GRACCHUS. Bright orange buff ; a splendid flower.
HARRY KEITH (S). Rosy purple, very fine and constant.
LOTTIE ECKFORD (F). White, beautifully striped with purple.

MATTHEW CAMPBELL (F). Buff or apricot, beautifully striped.
MAUD FELLOWS (S). French white, tinted and shaded with purple.
MONT BLANC (S). Pure white ; large full flower, of exceptional beauty.
MRS. GLADSTONE (S). Delicate blush, with white centre.
MRS. N. HALLS (F). Bright scarlet, tipped with white.
MRS. SAUNDERS (F). Yellow tipped with white. Fine.
MRS. STANCOMBE (S). Canary yellow, tipped with fawn.
MURIEL (S). Clear yellow, a splendid flower.
PENELOPE. Fawn shaded amber, large flower.
TOM JONES. Yellow ground edged with rose.
WARRIOR (S). Intense scarlet, grand colour ; fine form.
WILLIAM POWELL (S). Primrose yellow ; splendid form.

Our own selection of popular and beautiful varieties, per doz. 4s. 6d. ; six for 2s. 6d.

POMPONE DAHLIAS.

A brilliant and charming class of a neat compact habit of growth, with beautifully formed perfectly double miniature flowers, which are produced in profusion throughout the Summer and Autumn. Our list given below includes all the most distinct and beautiful varieties.

	each—s. d.		each—s. d.
ADRIENNE. Crimson scarlet, small beautifully shaped flowers	0 6	**MERCURY.** Reddish salmon, heavily tipped with white	0 6
BACCHUS. Bright scarlet. One of the best	0 6	**NELLY BROMHEAD.** Soft rosy lilac, base of petals white	0 6
CHEERFULNESS. Old gold, tipped scarlet crimson	0 6	**NERISSA.** Soft rose, tinted with silver ; good centre and outline	0 6
CYRIL. Bright crimson, very fine	0 6	**PINK BEAUTY** (new). Delicate blush, distinct and beautiful	1 0
DAISY. Amber and salmon, a neat and charming flower	0 6	**QUEEN OF WHITES.** Pure white, good dwarf habit	0 6
DARKEST OF ALL. Very dark maroon crimson	0 6	**SOVEREIGN.** Beautiful bright golden yellow	0 6
DOUGLAS. Rich deep maroon, shaded crimson	0 6	**SUNNY DAYBREAK.** Pale apricot, edged with rosy red	0 6
ELEGANT. Primrose, prettily tipped with lake	0 6	**THE DUKE.** The colour is deep velvety crimson ; habit very dwarf	0 6
GANYMEDE. Amber or fawn tinted lilac, novel and distinct	0 6	**TOMMY KEITH.** Cardinal red, tipped with white	0 6
GLOW (new). Beautiful coral red, splendid form	1 0	**WHITE ASTER.** Pure white, quilled flower of the most free-	
LORNA DOONE. Rosy purple, dark purple tip	0 6	flowering habit ; an extremely useful variety for cutting	0 6

Very good varieties, our selection   6 for 2s. 6d. ; per doz. 4s. 6d.

DAHLIAS—Pompone Cactus.

These charming diminutive varieties are very desirable. In habit of growth they resemble the ordinary Pompones. The small cactus-shaped blooms are very pretty and exceedingly useful for cut flowers.

	each—s. d.		each—s. d.
ALWYN (new). Indian yellow, shaded salmon, free	0 9	**NAIN.** Deep orange, of true cactus form, free flowering and good	0 6
ARGUS. Rich crimson-lake, shaded scarlet, very free flowering	0 6	**PEACE.** A free-flowering, erect-growing creamy white	0 6
CORONATION. Crimson scarlet, very fine ; splendid for cutting	0 6	**PEGGY** (new). A neat star-shaped flower of small size but good	
GRACIE. Yellow tipped with pale pink ; a lovely little flower	0 6	depth and of a rich deep plum colour. Quite distinct	1 0
LITTLE DOLLY. Clear mauve-pink. A true Pompone Cactus	0 6	**SOVEREIGN.** Rich golden yellow, very free	0 9
MARTHA (new). Orange red, madder red at tips of florets	1 0	**THE BRIDE.** Small, perfectly-formed pure white flowers 3 for 2s.	0 9

Six Choice Varieties, our selection   ..   .. 2s. 6d.

SINGLE-FLOWERED DAHLIAS.

The Single-flowered Dahlias are charming as cut flowers, and splendidly effective when well staged for exhibition. They commence blooming about the end of July, and are resplendent with a profusion of their lovely flowers till killed by the frost in Autumn.

Customer's selection from the following choice sorts, per doz. 4s. 6d., or 6 for 2s. 6d.

Betty, Brilliant, Columbine, Demon, Donna Casilda, Duchess of Westminster, Flora, Formosa, Hilda, Lady Bountiful, Leslie Seale, Miss Roberts, Mrs. J. Hicks, Princess of Wales, Puck, Sunrise, Wm. Parrott.

DECORATIVE DAHLIAS.

	each—s. d.		each—s. d.
DELICE. A most beautiful variety for garden decoration. The plants grow about 3 feet high and produce quite a profusion of lovely medium-sized double flowers of the most charming bright rosy-pink colour. This is a splendid variety for cutting 3 for 2s.	0 9	**LOVELINESS.** A lovely shade of deep soft pink. The flowers are semi-double and splendid for cutting	0 9
		POPPYLAND. Brilliant orange-scarlet. The plant grows only about 3 feet high, and is a profuse bloomer and very showy	0 6

NEW PÆONY-FLOWERED DAHLIAS.

A remarkably fine and distinct new class, growing four to five feet in height, and producing enormous beautifully coloured semi-double flowers, which at a short distance resemble huge Pæonies. Massed in large beds or in groups on the shrubbery border, they are splendidly effective.

	each—s. d.		each—s. d.
ADMIRATION. Buff ground flushed with rosy carmine	0 6	**LIBERTY** (new). Bright scarlet, very large flowers	0 9
DR. K. W. VAN GORKOM. White shaded rose ; fine	0 6	**QUEEN ALEXANDRA.** Sulphur shading to white at tips	0 9
DUKE HENRY. Rosy cerise, large splendidly formed flowers	0 6	**SOLFATERRE.** Soft rose. Distinct and beautiful	0 6
GERMANIA. Brilliant crimson scarlet, very showy ; four feet	0 6	**SNOW WHITE.** Pure white, the blooms are of moderate size with	
GLORY OF BAARN. Bright pink, enormous flowers ; very fine	0 6	pointed cactus-like petals. A charming variety for cut flowers	0 9
HOLMAN HUNT (new). Deep scarlet, large, splendidly formed	0 9	**SOUTH POLE.** Pure white, large rounded petals	0 9
KAISERIN A. VICTORIA. Yellow shading to white, very fine	0 6	**THE GEISHA.** Orange-red and yellow ; very fine	0 6
KING LEOPOLD. Canary yellow. A fine variety	0 6	**SIX BEAUTIFUL VARIETIES**, our selection, including Snow White	2 6
LANDSEER. Rich deep scarlet ; very fine	0 9		

CHRYSANTHEMUMS—JAPANESE.

The following list includes the finest of the varieties exhibited at the great London and other shows during the past Autumn. All ready for sending out in March and April, in strong healthy plants from single pots. Carriage free at prices quoted.

EXHIBITION CHRYSANTHEMUM.

NEW AND SELECT VARIETIES.

each—s. d.

ALGERNON DAVIS. A really grand yellow Japanese, of the richest golden yellow, and of graceful drooping form ; a splendid door. Award of Merit, Royal Horticultural Society 0 6

ALICE LEMON. Mauve pink, large flowers with reflexing florets. Very pleasing colour 0 6

BEECHAM KEELING. A splendid exhibition flower of enormous size, colour amber shaded cinnamon red 0 6

BESSIE GODFREY. Large beautiful flowers of superb form, colour a beautiful canary yellow deepening towards the centre, the outer petals shaded carmine 0 6

COUNTESS OF GRANARD. Rich yellow shaded bronzy buff, large flowers. Strikingly handsome 1 0

DAILY MAIL (new). A huge and very double flower, with broad flat florets. The colour is a beautiful light apricot yellow and most handsome in appearance. F.C.C. 7 6

DECEMBER GOLD. Rich deep yellow, of splendid size, borne on long stiff stems. A first-class and beautiful variety for late blooming 0 0

DUCHESS OF SUTHERLAND. Richest golden yellow, with extra long curly florets 0 6

EDITH JAMIESON. Creamy white overlaid with rich pink ; very large flower with long drooping petals 0 6

F. S. VALLIS. Pale yellow, immense flowers ; fine for exhibition 0 6

FRANCIS JOLLIFFE. Lovely creamy yellow, long florets delicately edged with pink 0 6

---

each—s. d.

GEORGE HEMMING. A rich and lovely shade of purple amaranth, with reflexing florets ; very fine 0 6

HELENA WILLIAMS. A very fine pale golden yellow, sport from Madame Oberthur 0 6

HIS MAJESTY. Immense flower of the richest velvety crimson. A magnificent variety of splendid habit 1 0

HON. MRS. LOPES. A flower of immense size and great substance. Colour a rich golden yellow, fine 0 6

J. H. SILSBURY. Bright light crimson with shiny yellow reverse, long drooping florets ; a very fine variety 0 6

J. W. MOLYNEUX. Velvety crimson, large flowers with drooping pointed florets. Splendid for exhibition 0 6

KING GEORGE V. Reddish crimson, very fine. An improvement on Master James 1 0

LADY TALBOT. Pale primrose with narrow florets. A deep and splendid flower 0 6

MADAME G. RIVOL. Clear yellow shaded old rose, very fine .. 0 6

MADAME R. OBERTHUR. Pure white, immense flowers, with long drooping petals 0 6

MAGNIFICENT. A grand crimson, with golden reverse ; large and very distinct. A fine show flower 0 6

MARY FARNSWORTH. A magnificent Jap. of huge size and massive appearance. Colour a beautiful golden pink with buff reverse. A superb exhibition flower. A.M., R.H.S. .. 0 9

MASTER DAVID. Very large flower, without the slightest coarseness. The florets are medium to broad, of splendid substance, drooping and pleasingly reflexed ; the colour is a remarkable tone of bright crimson with gold reverse 0 9

MISS A. E. ROOPE. Large handsome blooms of the deepest rich golden yellow, a great improvement in every way on Duchess of Sutherland 1 0

MISS GLADYS HERBERT. A beautiful shade of mauve pink florets of extra length, forming a large and deep flower .. 0 6

MRS. BARKLEY. Beautiful mauve pink, long broad florets .. 0 6

MRS. CHARLES PENFORD. An immense flower. Rich yellow shaded crimson bronze with extra long drooping florets .. 0 6

MRS. DAVID SYME. Pure white. A fine exhibition flower, and one of the best late varieties 0 9

MRS. G. DRABBLE. An immense pure white with massive incurving florets. A fine exhibition flower 0 6

MRS. NORMAN DAVIS. A pure white flower of the Madame Carnot type, of immense size and splendid form. The finest of its class yet raised, and one that will give every satisfaction 0 6

MRS. R. H. B. MARSHAM. Large white, strong and robust grower, outer florets reflexing 0 6

MRS. T. WILLIAMS. A beautiful shade of soft sulphur, with a pretty tinting of pink towards end of florets 0 6

NORFOLK BLUSH. Beautiful blush pink. Large handsome flowers 0 9

POCKETT'S CRIMSON. Deep crimson reflexing florets, large flower, plant dwarf and of good habit 0 6

PURITY. A splendid large white with curly florets of great length, of easy culture and good habit 0 6

QUEENIE CHANDLER. A beautiful flower with reflexing florets. Dwarf habit 0 6

QUEEN MARY. Opens with a shade of pink, but finishes with the purest white. A gigantic flower of the finest exhibition qualities 1 6

REGINALD VALLIS. Light rosy amaranth, immense flower .. 0 6

ROSE POCKET. Old gold shaded salmon. A large and finely formed flower 0 6

SHANKLIN SUNSHINE. Rich golden yellow of the very largest size, broad, deep and of fine build 0 6

SIR F. CRISP. A very distinct and beautiful bloom of large size, colour a real chestnut with gold buff reverse 0 6

W. BEADLE. Violet amaranth striped and shaded crimson, long narrow reflexing florets. Distinct and beautiful .. 0 6

WILLIAM VERT (new). A bright chestnut crimson, reflexing Japanese with thick hard florets, the reverse of petals golden yellow. A magnificent exhibition variety. F.C.C. .. 7 6

Those priced at 6d. each, Customer's Selection, 4s. 6d. per doz. ; 35s. per 100.

CHRYSANTHEMUMS.

EARLY-FLOWERING LARGE-FLOWERED VARIETIES.

A splendid class for Garden Decoration.

This beautiful class commence to bloom about the end of August or early in September, and continue till killed by the frost. They are easily grown and not only produce a fine display in the garden, but are exceedingly useful for cut flowers. For growing fine plants, plant out in May 18 inches or 2 feet apart on well-dug fairly rich soil, and place a good stick to each plant. Stop the shoots once or twice to induce a bushy growth, but do not stop them after the end of June. Water should be given freely in very dry weather.

CHRYSANTHEMUM—ROI DES BLANCS.

SELECT LIST.

each—s. d.

		s.	d.
ALMIRANTE. Red with scarlet shading, a very taking colour; free bloomer, 3 ft. F.C.C., N.C.S.		1	0
BETTY SPARK. Rosy pink, large handsome sprays		0	6
BOULE DE NEIGE. Pure white, large bold flowers		0	6
BRONZE BRIDE. Rosy bronze, large full flowers		0	6
CHAMP D'OR. Deep canary yellow; fine dwarf habit		0	6
CRANFORD WHITE. A very fine white, best disbudded		0	6
CRIMSON MARIE MASSE. Bright crimson; very fine		0	6
DOROTHY ASHLEY. Pink shaded with bronzy salmon. Dwarf, and free blooming, very distinct. F.C.C., N.C.S.		1	0
EDEN. Bright rose, incurving flowers; splendid variety		0	6
ETHEL BLADES. Chestnut scarlet, very bright flowers		0	6
FRAMFIELD EARLY WHITE. Very fine pure white. The best early white yet raised		0	6
FRANKII BRONZE. Dwarf habit, very early, free-blooming		0	6
GOACHER'S CRIMSON. The finest early crimson yet sent out		0	6
GOLDEN GLOW. Fine incurving flowers, rich yellow; splendid		0	6
GOLDEN MADAME DESGRANGE. One of the best		0	6
HOLLICOT WHITE. Pure, glistening white, reflexed blooms, splendid for cutting. F.C.C., N.C.S.		0	9
LESLIE. Rich buttercup yellow. A splendid variety		0	6
LILLIE. Pearly-pink, splendid habit		0	6
LUCIFER. Rich dark crimson, good habit		0	6
MADAME DESGRANGE. White; very useful for outdoors		0	6
MADAME DROUARD. Terra-cotta red with gold points		0	6
MARTIN REED. Pure yellow. A very fine variety		0	6
MRS. A. THOMPSON. Deepest golden yellow, lovely colour		0	6
MRS. BEECH. Bright bronze, fine for cutting		0	6
MRS. J. FIELDING. A bronze sport from Goacher's Crimson		0	6
NINA BLICK. Bright scarlet-red, finishing off with a rich golden bronze; a splendid variety for bunching		0	6
ORANGE PET. Orange shaded red, one of the best		0	6
PERLE CHATILLIONAISE. Creamy white, with rosy peach		0	6
ROI DES BLANCS. Pure white, large flowers, splendid variety		0	6
ROI DES PRECOCES. Rich dark crimson; dwarf		0	6
TAPIS DE NEIGE. Purest snow-white, very free and of stiff upright habit. Fine for cutting		0	6
WELLS' SCARLET. Bright scarlet terra-cotta, very bright		0	6

Strong Plants from single pots in March and April, our selection, 4s. 6d. per doz. ; 6 for 2s. 6d.

From Mr. G. COLLIN, Wattisville.

Sept. 30th.

"I am pleased with the Chrysanthemums I had from you, they are now in full bloom, some being 11½ in. and one 12½ in. across."

INCURVED EXHIBITION VARIETIES.

Strong Plants from single pots in March and April, our selection, 4s. 6d. per doz. ; 6 for 2s. 6d.

each—s. d.

	s.	d.
BONNIE DUNDEE. Orange, shaded rosy bronze	0	6
BUTTERCUP. Clear rich buttercup, yellow without shading; magnificent variety	0	6
CHARLES H. CURTIS. Deep yellow, one of the best	0	6
CLARA WELLS. Rich cream colour; a large true incurved	0	6
EMBLEME POITEVINE. Beautiful canary yellow; large flowers	0	6
ETHEL THORP. Silvery pink, fine for cutting	0	6
LADY ISABEL. Lovely clear, lavender blush, fine	0	6

each—s. d.

	s.	d.
MISS THELMA HARTMAN. Blush pink, splendid variety, similar to Buttercup in form	1	0
MRS. F. JUDSON. Pure white, very fine	0	6
MRS. J. P. BRYCE. Very large beautifully formed flowers of the purest white	0	6
MRS. JAMES HYGATE. Pure white, an immense flower	0	6
ROMANCE. Rich golden yellow	0	6
TOPAZE ORIENTAL. Very large, pale straw yellow; splendid	0	6

SINGLE-FLOWERED CHRYSANTHEMUMS.

These beautiful flowers are now very popular. Their long, wiry flower-stems and graceful Marguerite-like blooms making them of especial value as cut flowers for Table Decoration, and as pot plants for the greenhouse. In pots, ready in March and April. Our Selection, 4/6 per doz.

each—s. d.

	s.	d.
BELLE OF WEYBRIDGE. Bright chestnut crimson, very fine	0	6
CALEDONIA. Beautiful rosy lilac, white ring round the disc	0	6
CROWN JEWEL IMPROVED (new). Rich rosy chestnut	0	6
CAPELLA. Rich golden yellow, with fine clear disc	0	6
EDITH PAGRAM. Lovely deep pink, with white ring round disc	0	6
EDWIN NOTTELL (new). Delicate primrose; a beautiful flower	0	6
ELSIE NEVILLE. Terra-cotta red, beautiful dwarf habit	0	6
FRAMFIELD BEAUTY. Deep rich velvety crimson. Very handsome	0	6

each—s. d.

	s.	d.
J. B. LOWE. Brilliant crimson-scarlet	0	6
KITTY BOURNE. Deep yellow, very fine	0	6
MARY RICHARDSON. Reddish-salmon, a charming colour	0	6
MENSA. Pure white. A fine exhibition flower	0	6
PEGASUS. Pure white; a magnificent variety	0	6
RICHMOND GLORY. Beautiful chestnut red, a very useful variety	0	6
SANDOWN RADIANCE. A splendid variety of fine form, colour a rich chestnut crimson	0	6
SYLVIA SLADE. Beautiful deep rose, white centre	0	9

SINGLE-FLOWERED ZONAL PELARGONIUMS.
NEW AND SELECT VARIETIES.
All Autumn Struck. Strong young plants from single pots.

NEW ZONAL PELARGONIUMS.

	each	s.	d.
BLENHEIM. Brilliant scarlet with white eye, large		0	6
CALEDONIA. Blush pink, very large perfectly formed flowers		0	6
COUNTESS OF JERSEY. Coral salmon, splendid flower		0	6
DANIELS' ORANGE QUEEN. Brilliant orange scarlet; a quite distinct and beautiful variety		1	0
DR. NANSEN. Finest pure white		0	6
FISCAL REFORMER. Colour clear salmon rose, fine habit		1	0
GERTRUDE PEARSON. Pure rose pink, with conspicuous white blotch on two upper petals		0	6
HIS MAJESTY. Colour Royal scarlet with distinct white eye; pips 3 inches across, and trusses sometimes measure 24 inches in circumference		1	0
LADY ROSCOE. Beautiful shade of pink		0	6
LADY WARWICK. Beautiful white with a bright pink edge		0	6
LORD ROSEBERY. A deep rich salmon		0	6
MR. J. A. BELL. White and shrimp pink, very pretty		0	6
SAXONIA. Brilliant scarlet, very large flowers		0	9
SNOWSTORM. A splendid dwarf growing pure white; first-class		0	6
ST. LOUIS. Scarlet crimson, immense flowers		0	9
VIRGINIA. Pure snow white; flowers large		0	6
WARLEY. Orange and white mottled; a superb flower		0	6
WINTER CHEER. Colour bright cerise impregnated with scarlet; a charming Winter blooming variety		1	0

PRICES OF SINGLE ZONAL PELARGONIUMS.

					s.	d.
Twelve in 12 superb varieties, our selection					4s.	6d.
Six in 6 extra fine varieties, our selection					2s.	6d.

A splendid class of beautiful free blooming plants, admirably suited for greenhouse or conservatory decoration, and may be had in bloom nearly all the year round.

DOUBLE-FLOWERED ZONAL PELARGONIUMS.
(A FINE CLASS FOR POT CULTURE.)
SELECT VARIETIES.

	each	s.	d.
CALIFORNIAN GOLD. Brilliant orange scarlet; fine		0	6
JULES LAFORGNE. Fine trusses of very large semi-double purplish crimson flowers with distinct white eye; splendid		0	9
MADAME ROZAIN. A very fine double, pure white; plant dwarf, and free blooming, large flowers		0	6
MISTRAL. Brilliant clear scarlet, large semi-double flowers with conspicuous white eye, very fine showy variety		0	9
PAUL CRAMPEL DOUBLE. Magnificent variety, bearing large trusses of deep scarlet double flowers. Splendid for Greenhouse decoration		1	0
PICOTEE (Fraicheur). Beautiful pure white, the petals delicately edged with deep rosy pink		0	6

	each	s.	d.
RASPAIL IMPROVED. Bright rich scarlet; large flowers		0	6
THE SPEAKER. Of a salmon-cerise colour, leaves beautifully marked, a strong grower and good habit		1	0
TRIOMPHE DE FRANCE. Salmon-red, with creamy edges; splendid variety		0	6
VESUVIUS. Intense vermilion scarlet		0	6
VIOLET DANIELS. A fine variety of immense size. The colour is a beautiful transparent salmony-gold		0	6
WHITE KING OF DENMARK (new). A very fine variety bearing large handsome trusses of pure white double flowers		0	6
CHOICE VARIETIES, our selection, per doz. 4s. 6d., 6 for 2s. 6d.			

DOUBLE-FLOWERED IVY-LEAVED PELARGONIUMS.
A splendid Class for Pots, Hanging Baskets, Vases, &c. They are also charming when planted out of doors in small beds, and are very useful for Cut Flowers.
SELECT VARIETIES.

	each	s.	d.
ACHIEVEMENT. The splendid large double flowers, which are produced in grand trusses, are of a brilliant rosy carmine colour. This is highly recommended as a beautiful variety 3 for 2s.		0	9
COL. BADEN POWELL. Soft blush lilac flowers, produced freely in large trusses; a beautiful variety		0	6
CUVIER. Beautiful rich violet purple, very fine		0	6
HIS MAJESTY THE KING. A lovely shade of dark cerise, large trusses of bloom and very free-flowering		0	9
JAMES T. HAMILTON. A grand new hybrid, ivy-leaved variety, bearing a profusion of large trusses of semi-double flowers of an intense glowing carmine-crimson colour. A.M., R.H.S.		1	0
JEANNE D'ARC. White, suffused with lavender		0	6
LEOPARD. Clear lilac-pink, heavily blotched with crimson all over the upper petals; very distinct		0	6
MILLFIELD GEM. A cross between an Ivy-leaf and Zonal, the flower is blush white with blotches of crimson-shaded with pink. A very distinct and beautiful variety		0	9

	each	s.	d.
MADAME THIBAUT. Brilliant crimson cerise		0	6
PURITY. Splendid pure white, with large full double flowers, by far the best white, and one tint will be found exceedingly useful for cut flowers		0	6
QUEEN OF ROSES. The flowers are very large, 2½ to 3 inches across, perfectly double, of splendid form and substance, and of the most beautiful rosy crimson carmine colour		0	6
RED CROUSSE. Rosy crimson, splendid for hanging baskets		0	9
RYECROFT SCARLET. Very large bloom, the very best of its colour and a very free grower		0	6
RYECROFT SURPRISE. It has a fine bold vigorous upright habit, blooming at nearly every joint. Colour a lovely salmon-pink		0	6
SOUVENIR DE CHARLES TURNER. Splendid variety, large, well-formed flowers of a beautiful deep rose colour, and borne in large trusses		0	6
CHOICE VARIETIES, our selection 6 for 2s. 6d.; per doz. 4s. 6d.			

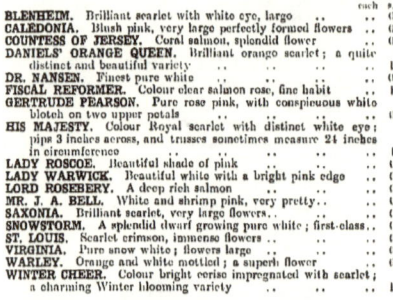

MRS. E. G. HILL.

FUCHSIAS—Select Varieties.

Those marked (*) are double-flowered.

each s. d.

*ALFRED RAMBAUD. Very large double flowers; sepals of a lovely scarlet; and the petals deep violet 0 6

BEAUTY OF EXETER. Immense bright salmon rose blooms, most abundantly produced on a plant of a vigorous habit; most charming variety 0 6

*DUCHESS OF EDINBURGH. A superb variety bearing large well-formed flowers; tube and sepals are of a rich crimson-scarlet; the corolla a creamy white .. 0 6

EARL OF BEACONSFIELD. A splendid hybrid variety, flowers over three inches long, carmine, with deep carmine corolla 0 6

FASCINATION (now). A most charming variety with long white tube and sepals which are broad and prettily recurved; corolla a lovely shade of rose-pink .. 0 9

GOLDEN QUEEN. Beautiful variegated foliage 0 6

*JUPITER. Large, beautiful double flowers; sepals well reflexed, brilliant scarlet; corolla a deep plum violet 0 6

*LA FRANCE. The sepals a bright rich scarlet, the corolla a bright light violet .. 0 6

*MADAME BRUANT. Immense flowers; tube and sepals a rich scarlet, corolla a beautiful lilac-mauve veined with rosy red. The blooms are very double 0 6

MADAME ROZAIN. A truly grand variety, bearing immense flowers of the most elegant form; the tube and sepals a deep rich scarlet crimson colour, the corolla a charming creamy white 0 6

*MAGNIFICENT. A grand variety, bearing immense double flowers. The sepals are well reflexed, of a bright rich crimson colour, the corolla deep violet blue .. 0 6

*MOLESWORTH. Tube and sepals a bright deep carmine-crimson colour; full double white corolla 0 6

*MRS. E. G. HILL. This magnificent Fuchsia is one of the most splendid ever sent out. The plants are short-jointed and sturdy in growth, with beautiful dark green foliage. The flowers are of an immense size, the tube and sepals being of a deep rich scarlet colour, the corolla a beautiful creamy white, veined with pink; grand variety 0 9

MURIEL. Very large finely reflexed flowers, sepals a brilliant scarlet, corolla violet red, very distinct and fine 0 6

*P. RADAELLI. Enormous double corolla of a rich bluish-violet colour, striped and stained with lovely carmine. The tube and sepals are of a rich red, the sepals well recurved 0 6

PRINCESS MAY. A most charming variety. The tube and sepals are of a lovely creamy white, the corolla a brilliant carmine-rose colour 0 6

ROYAL PURPLE. Corolla dark velvety purple, sepals clear crimson scarlet; immense massive flowers 0 9

Twelve choice named varieties, our own selection .. per doz. 3s. 6d. and 4s. 6d.

Six ,, ,, ,, ,, ,, ... 2s. 0d. and 2s. 6d.

HARDY FUCHSIAS.

A fine class of beautiful hardy plants of shrubby growth, very effective in Summer and Autumn, with their numerous scarlet and purple flowers; should have a slight protection the first Winter after planting.

CONICA. Scarlet. Height 2 feet.
EXONIENSIS. Globular-shaped scarlet flowers. Height 2 feet.
GRACILIS. Drooping, graceful habit. Height 3 feet.
MADAME CORNELLISEN. Scarlet with white corolla. Height 3 feet.
RICCARTONI. Very free flowering, forms a dense bush during the Summer. Very hardy, and of the best.
THOMPSONI. A dwarf growing variety about 18 inches high. Very free flowering and handsome.

Strong young plants from single pots, customers' selection, per doz. 5s.; each 6d.

HELIOTROPES.

These are delightful subjects for pots in the greenhouse or for planting out of doors in Summer, their delicious perfume being always welcome. When grown outside they should be planted in a partially shaded position and kept well supplied with water in dry weather. These will grow into fine plants and may be taken up and potted in the Autumn for Winter blooming in the greenhouse. Planted out or grown in large pots in a moderately heated greenhouse, the plants will live for several years and will be almost continually in bloom.

per doz. d.

BOUQUET BLANC. Pure white; very fragrant 3 6
MADAME DE BUSSY. Beautiful blue, with large white eye; deliciously scented 4 0
MADAME ARTHUR GUE. Flowers violet with white centre; free flowering and very fragrant 4 0
QUEEN OF VIOLETS. Dark violet with white eye, very free flowering and of good habit 3 6
WHITE LADY. Deliciously scented 3 6

CALCEOLARIA CLIBRANI (New).

Erect stems freely branched, and bear numerous pale lemon yellow flowers. The habit of the plant, and its floriferous nature, make it a subject of great value for decorative work. 3 feet high. each 9d.; doz. 7s. 6d.

CAMPANULAS.

each s. d.

MAYI. A lovely trailing variety, beautiful lavender blue flowers; a gem for pots .. .. .. 3 for 2s 6d. 1 0
ISOPHYLLA, BLUE. Lilac blue .. .. 3 for 1s. 3d. 0 6
,, ALBA. White; beautiful .. .. 3 for 1s. 3d. 0 6
Beautiful dwarf trailing species, with large salver-shaped flowers; splendid for suspended pots, &c.
PYRAMIDALIS. Blue { Beautiful upright- 3 for 1s. 3d. 0 6
,, ALBA. White { growing vars. 3 for 2s 0d. 0 9

COLEUS.

NEW LARGE-LEAVED HYBRIDS. We offer seedlings, in May, from our splendid strain of large-leaved, brilliantly coloured varieties. Strong young plants from single pots per doz. 2s. 6d.; 6 for 1s. 6d.

MARGUERITES.

DWARF WHITE. Very compact and free-flowering; a gem for pots or window boxes .. .. per doz. 5s.; each 6d.
BOULE DE NEIGE (new). Large, beautiful, white double flowers; a splendid pot plant for the greenhouse per doz. 3s. 6d.; per 100 25s.

MUSK.

HARRISON'S GIANT. Splendid variety of a robust habit of growth, finely scented, fine for pots .. .. per doz. 2s. 6d.; each 4d.

SALVIA.

SPLENDENS IMPROVED. Brilliant scarlet spikes of flowers; magnificent for the greenhouse .. .. .. 3 for 2s.; each 9d.

HARDY PERENNIAL FLOWERING PLANTS.

A PORTION OF AN HERBACEOUS BORDER AT OUR NURSERIES.

We have a fine collection of these popular, interesting, and beautiful plants, which are daily coming more and more into favour with the Gardening Public. All the varieties are perennial, extremely hardy, and many of them produce flowers of the most exquisite beauty, which are very valuable for cutting, whilst the dwarfer-growing sorts are admirably suited for rockeries or edgings. No special soil or position is necessary, as with but very few exceptions, they will thrive almost anywhere, and with a good collection, a charming variety and succession of bloom may be had throughout the Spring and Summer. The plants we offer are all grown in pots, and may be removed at any time or season.

Of many of the more popular border plants such as Pyrethrums, Delphiniums, Asters, etc., we are able to supply extra sized clumps from the open ground, and we shall be glad to send a list of these to anyone wanting to obtain immediate effects.

NEW AND CHOICE HARDY PERENNIAL FLOWERING PLANTS.

ANCHUSA PICOTEE (new). White, edged with blue .. .. each 1s.
ANEMONE SYLVESTRIS FL. PL. Double, snow white .. .. .. each 1s.
„ **PULSATILLA.** Flowers deep rich purple, with long silky hairs. 1ft. 9 ins. each 1s.
***ANTHEMIS AIZOON.** Silvery foliage, with heads of white flowers, close tufted habit. Height 6 inches .. .. each 9d.
ASTILBE. PRINCESS JULIANA. A striking novelty, the spikes about 3 to 3½ ft. high, with a loose and elegant habit; bright crimson, shaded pink, being the darkest colour of Astilbe yet in commerce. 2/6 each
CLEMATIS REPENS. A lovely creamy white creeping variety, with bell-like flowers 2s. ea.
DELPHINIUM, MRS. CREIGHTON. Deep blue, centre rose .. .. .. each 2s.
„ **BELLADONNA SEMI PLENA.** Semi-double form of Belladonna, bright sky blue, flushed rosy mauve like the type, it flowers all through the Summer. Height 3 ft.
.. .. each 1s. 6d.
„ **LAMARTIN.** Dwarf Belladonna type, but with rich deep Prussian blue flowers, of a branching habit, well adapted for massing
.. .. .. per doz. 15s. ; each 1s. 6d.
„ **REV. E. LASCELLES.** This is, without doubt, the finest Delphinium ever sent out, with enormous spikes of dark blue flowers, often 3½ inches across, in the centre of each bloom a tuft of petaloids of the purest white. Height 4 to 5 feet .. .. each 5s.

*DIANTHUS CÆSIUS GRANDIFLORA** (new). A great improvement on " Dianthus Cæsius."
.. .. each 1s.
*EDRAIANTHUS SERPHYLLIFOLIUS.** Tufts of deep green foliage with prostrate stems of large purple flowers .. each 1s. 6d.
GEUM, MRS. BRADSHAW. A novelty of sterling merit, with semi-double flowers, fully 2 in. across, freely produced, on long stems, flowering from June to Oct. each 9d.
GYPSOPHILA PAN. FL. PL. A pure white, double-flowered, of the well-known G. paniculata. Valuable for cutting each 9d.
*IBERIS, LITTLE GEM.** Dwarf compact plant, covered with pure white blossoms from Spring until Autumn, adapted for rockery or front of border. Height 6 inches each 9d.
„ **SNOWFLAKE.** A fine new variety, large heads of pure white flowers very freely produced. Height 1 ft. .. .. each 9d.
*HOUSTONIA SERPHYLLIFOLIA.** A minute species, with bright blue flowers each 9d.
PAPAVER, LOVELINESS. Pale flesh pink, dark blotches. Height 3 feet each 9d.
„ **MRS. J. HARKNESS.** Deep rose pink, shaded apricot with glorious dense blotch, flowers of great size, 8½ inches in diameter on stout stems which require no support
.. .. each 2s.
„ **MRS. PEACOCK.** Delightful sherry salmon, petals are very large and perfect formation, a very conspicuous and beautiful blotch adds greatly to its charm .. .. each 1s. 6d.

*Those marked * are ROCKERY PLANTS.*

PRIMULA BULLEYANA. A fine hardy species from China, with orange scarlet flowers ; a wonderful shade of colour. A good water-side plant .. .. .. each 1s. 6d.
ROMNEYA COULTERI (Californian Tree Poppy)- Large white Poppy-like flower, glaucous foliage. Height 4 feet .. each 1s. 6d.
*SAXIFRAGE BATHONIENSIS.** Large-flowered, crimson scarlet, the finest yet raised .. .. .. each 9d.
* „ **GUILDFORD SEEDLING.** One of the best of the mossy section, bright crimson flowers. Height 6 inches .. .. each 9d.
* „ **OPPOSITIFOLIA.** Rosy purple flowers. Height 2 inches .. .. each 9d.
* „ **PYRAMIDALIS.** White, large spikes
.. .. each 9d.
SOLIDAGO, GOLDEN WINGS. The best of the Golden Rods, long arching sprays of yellow flowers. Height 6 feet .. .. each 9d.
TRITOMA, MARIE BIRKIN (new). Most beautiful free-flowering variety, dwarf and compact habit, deep orange scarlet flowers. Continual bloom from June till November. 12 to 18 inches in height each 1s.
TROLLIUS, LEMON QUEEN. Medium sized, lemon coloured flowers. 5 feet each 1s.
VERBASCUM.
„ **DENSIFLORUM.** Flowers of a golden bronzy tint. Height 4 feet .. each 9d.
„ **MISS WILLMOTT.** Very tall, bearing large spikes of white flowers over 2½ inches in diameter, of noble appearance .. each 1s.

SELECT LIST.

ACHILLÆA PTARMICA, THE PEARL. Large double, pure white flowers; fine for cutting. Height 2 feet .. per doz. 6s. ; each 6d.
ANCHUSA ITALICA, DROPMORE VARIETY. The finest blue flowering plant in existence. 1ft. about 4 feet per doz. 7s. 6d. ; each 9d.
„ **OPAL.** A sky-blue variety of the above. Height 3 feet .. .. each 9d.

ANEMONE ALPINA SULPHUREA. 2 feet high, with large pale yellow flowers each 1s.
„ **COUP D'ARGENT.** Beautiful white flowers. Height 18 inches
.. .. .. per doz. 5s. ; each 6d.
„ **JAPONICA ALBA.** One of the very best Autumn-blooming plants
.. .. .. per doz. 5s. ; each 6d.

ANEMONE LADY ARDILAUN. Fine, pure white
.. .. .. per doz. 5s. ; each 6d.
„ **ROSEA.** Rose .. „ 6d.
„ **RUBRA.** Rosy red .. „ each 6d.
„ **WHIRLWIND.** Flower white, with more than one row of petals doz. 5s. ; each 6d.
„ **SYLVESTRIS PLENA.** Double, snow-white flowers ; a most beautiful variety each 1s.

Hardy Perennial Flowering Plants *(continued).*

ASTER, BEAUTY OF COLWALL.

ANTHEMIS TINCTORIA DANIELSII. Height 3—4 ft., bearing a profusion of bright golden yellow flowers. per doz. 4s. 6d. ; each 6d.
  ,,   **PALLIDA.** Beautiful pale primrose yellow flowers. per doz. 4s. 6d. ; each 6d.
ANTHERICUM LILIASTRUM MAJOR. Very fine ; pure white. per doz. 5s. ; each 6d.
  ,,   **(St. Bruno's Lily).** Fragrant white flowers ..   .. per doz. 5s. ; each 6d.
AQUILEGIA CŒRULEA (Rocky Mountain Columbine). Large pale blue flowers with white corolla ..   per doz. 5s. ; each 6d
  ,,   **CHRYSANTHA.** Golden yellow flowers with long spurs   per doz. 5s. ; each 6d
ARMERIA GRANDIFLORA Grass-like foliage with large heads of bright rose-coloured flowers. Height 1 foot   each 6d.
  ,,   **PLANTAGINEA ROSEA.** Large heads of rose-coloured flowers per doz. 5s. ; each 6d.
ARTEMESIA LACTIFLORA (new). A lovely hardy plant of recent introduction, producing elegant branching panicles of fragrant white flowers, superb in every way. Height 4 feet.   each 9d.
ASPERULA LONGIFLORA. Small white flowers, very pretty ..   .. each 6d.

ASTERS

MICHAELMAS DAISIES.
Beautiful Autumn bloomers.

ASTER BEAUTY OF COLWALL. The first and only double-flowered Michaelmas Daisy in cultivation. A pleasing shade of lavender. Height four feet   -..   each 9d.
  ,,   **BESSARABICUS.** Purplish-blue, very large. Height two feet   each 6d.
  ,,   **CLIMAX (new).** The largest in cultivation, flowers a clear light blue, with bright golden centre ..   .. each 9d.
  ,,   **CRENATA.** Dark blue, large flowers, about 2½ feet   each 6d.
  ,,   **CREVIS.** Light blue. Height three feet. Splendid for borders ..   .. each 6d.
  ,,   **DUMOSUS.** Rosy blush, very compact. Height 1½ feet   each 6d.
  ,,   **ELSIE PERRY.** Rose pink, very pretty. Height two feet   each 6d.
  ,,   **ESME.** Large pure white flowers, good habit. Height two feet   each 6d.
  ,,   **FELTHAM BLUE (new).** Clear dark-blue, large flower with bright yellow centre. Grand variety. Height four feet   each 9d.

ASTER HYBRIDUS NANUS. Rosy pink. 15 inches   — .. each 6d.
  ,,   **MADAME SOYNEUCE.** Bright clear rose-colour. Ht. 1½ ft. doz. 5s. ; each 6d.
  ,,   **MARGARET.** Rosy blush. A superb variety. Height 4½ feet .. each 6d.
  ,,   **MULTIFLORUS.** Handsome spikes of miniature pure white flowers ; very pretty. Height 4 feet .. per doz. 5s. ; each 6d.
  ,,   **NOVÆA ANGLIÆ.** Large bluish-purple. Blooms in October per doz. 5s. ; each 6d.
  ,,   **ANGLIÆ ELEGANS.** Lilac. Height 4 feet   each 6d.
  ,,   **BELGEII DENSUS.** Blue. Height about 2 feet   each 6d.
  ,,   **PERRY'S FAVOURITE.** A beautiful red-flowered variety of A. amellus .. each 1s.
  ,,   **ST. BRIGID.** Lovely soft rose. Height 4 feet   each 6d.
  ,,   **ST. PATRICK.** Soft silvery grey, large, loose and wavy. Height 4 feet each 6d.
  ,,   **SENSATION.** White, golden centre, branching habit. Height 2½—3 ft. each 6d.
  ,,   **SNOWDON.** Most charming, about 4 feet in height, lovely bracts of almost pure white flowers   each 6d.
  ,,   **THE PEARL.** Blush white, a superb variety. Height 3 ft. .. each 6d.
  ,,   **TOP SAWYER.** Clear blue, large flowers. Height 5 feet per doz. 5s. ; each 6d.
  ,,   **TRIUMPH.** Very dark pink. Height 5 feet   — .. each 6d.
  ,,   **VENUS.** Pale lavender, flushed with pink flowering from top to base. Height 2½ feet   each 6d.
  ,,   **VIMINEUS PERFECTUS.** White, pink centre, charming variety. Ht. 3 ft. ea. 9d. Ground plants of some of these varieties per doz. 6s. 6d. ; each 9d.

Our Selection, 4s. 6d., 6s., 9s. per dozen

CAMPANULA GRANDIFLORA ALBA. Pure white, very fine for rockeries doz. 5s. ; ea.6d.
  ,,   **MARIESII.** Very large beautiful dark blue flowers ; splendid dwarf growing varieties   ..   .. each 6d.
  ,,   **MOERHEIMI.** Long spikes of semi-double pure white flowers per doz. 6d.
  ,,   **PERSICIFOLIA ALBA GRANDIFLORA.** A fine upright growing variety, with large pure white flowers per doz. 5s. ; each 6d.
  ,,   **CORONATA ALBA.** A most beautiful variety, growing about 3 feet high, and throwing up lovely panicles of pure white flowers. Charming as a cut flower each 1s.
  ,,   **PYRAMIDALIS (The Chimney Campanula).** Long spikes of blue salver-like flowers per doz. 5s. ; each 6d.
  ,,   **ALBA.** A white flowering form of the preceding ; a fine pot plant .. each 6d.
CENTAUREA MACROCEPHALA. A fine ornamental plant, with massive foliage and large rich golden flowers doz. 5s. ; ea. 6d.
  ,,   **DEALBATA.** Rosy purple flowers with fern-like foliage   ..   each 6d.
  ,,   **GLASTIFOLIA.** Tall with silvery foliage, yellow heads ..   .. each 6d.
CHRYSANTHEMUM MAXIMUM. Pure white flowers. Fine -.. per doz. 5s. ; each 6d.
  ,,   **LI HUNG CHANG.** Magnificent blooms, five inches across .. each 9d.
  ,,   **MRS. C. LOWTHIAN BELL.** A magnificent early-flowering dwarf variety, producing enormous pure white flowers. Awarded a First Class Certificate, R.H.S. per doz. 7s. 6d. ; each 9d.
  ,,   **KING EDWARD VII.** One of the finest varieties, about 3 feet high, with large, beautiful, white flowers ; erect stems per doz. 5s. ; each 6d.
  ,,   **LATIFOLIUM.** Pure white, invaluable for Autumn decoration per doz. 5s. ; each 6d.
  ,,   **FILIFERUM.** Of free, vigorous habit, with large flowers   ..   each 6d.

CHRYSANTHEMUM PERFECTION. Snow-white flowers per doz. 5s. ; each 6d.
COREOPSIS GRANDIFLORA. Flowers 2½ to 3 inches across, bright golden yellow per doz. 5s. ; each 6d.

DELPHINIUMS.
Single and Double-flowered.

DELPHINIUM BELLADONNA. Lovely sky-blue, one of the finest in cultivation per doz. 10s. 6d. ; each 9d.
  ,,   **GRANDIFLORUM.** Stronger stems and larger flowers than the above ; a striking acquisition per doz. 21s. ; each 2s.
  ,,   **CAPRI. The** best sky-blue single Delphinium in commerce each 1s. 6d.
  ,,   **CLARIBEL.** Rich peacock blue, hardy and useful   ..   each 1s.
  ,,   **K. TH. CARON.** Bright gentian blue, with white centre ; quite distinct each 1s. 6d.
  ,,   **LIZE VAN VEEN.** Remarkable for the immense size of the single flowers, which are a blue colour .. each 1s. 6d.
  ,,   **MR. J. S. BRUNTON.** Flowers are of the finest sky-blue, in the style of Belladonna ; produces an immense quantity of long, graceful spikes   ..   each 1s. 6d.
  ,,   **PERSIMMON.** Azure blue, with sulphur centre, bold spikes, extra fine. Height 3 feet   each 2s. 6d.
  ,,   **USTANE.** Light blue, inner petals rosy mauve   — .. each 1s.
OUR OWN SELECTION OF SORTS. each 9d., 1s., and 1s. 6d. per doz. 7s. 6d., 10s. 6d., and 15s.
DIELYTRA SPECTABILIS. Lovely bending sprays of deep rose-coloured flowers ea. 6d.
DICTAMNUS FRAXINELLA (Burning Bush). This remarkable plant is one of the most singularly interesting herbaceous perennials in existence ..   ..   each 6d.
  ,,   **ALBA.** A fac-simile of the preceding, but with pure white flowers ; very showy   ..   .. each 6d.
DODECATHEON JEFFREYANUM. Large umbels of Cyclamen-like blossoms, rose coloured .. per doz. 7s. 6d. ; each 6d.
  ,,   **MEADIA (The American Cowslip).** Very pretty heads of lilac and crimson each 6d.

DELPHINIUM.

Hardy Perennial Flowering Plants (*continued*)

ANCHUSA OPAL.

DORONICUM, HARPUR CREWE. A magnificent variety, bearing yellow flowers
       per doz. 5s. ; each 6d.
DRACOCEPHALUM VIRGINICUM. Erect stems, 2½ feet high, with numerous bright pink flowers .. per doz. 5s. ; each 6d.
  „   **ALBUM.** Fac-simile of preceding, with white flowers per doz. 5s. ; each 6d.
EREMURUS HIMALAICUS. A magnificent hardy plant throwing up grand spikes of white flowers six or eight feet in height ; splendidly effective when planted in groups
       each 2s. 6d. and 5s.
  „   **BUNGEII.** Beautiful variety, growing only about 3 feet high, with spikes of bright yellow flowers each 5s. and 7s. 6d.
  „   **ROBUSTUS.** Huge spikes of bright peach-coloured flowers, eight to ten feet high, with three to four feet of bloom, sweetly scented. Beautifully striking
       each 2s. 6d., 3s. 6d., and 5s.
ERIGERON SPECIOSUM SUPERBUM. Lavender-blue flowers. per doz. 5s ; each 6d.
ERYNGIUM OLIVERIANUM. A plant of handsome flowers, of a lovely amethystine blue   per doz. 5s. 6d. ; each 6d.
  „   **PLANUM.** Numerous small blue heads. Height three feet. July to September 6d.
FUCHSIAS. Perfectly hardy Fuchsias are very interesting, they delight in well-drained land in sunny positions
       per doz. 5s. ; each 6d.
FUNKIAS. A beautiful genus of handsome foliage plants, exceedingly attractive either for pot culture or for planting in the open
       per doz. 5s. ; each 6d.
GAILLARDIAS, CHOICE MIXED SEEDLINGS
       per doz. 4s. 6d. ; 6 for 2s. 6d.
GALEGA OFFICINALIS. Numerous lilac flowers on branching stems. Height four feet
       per doz. 5s. ; each 6d.
  „   **ALBA.** Similar to preceding, with white flowers   per doz. 5s. ; each 6d.
GEUM HELDREICHII. Rich orange-coloured flowers   .. per doz. 7s. 6d. ; each 9d.
  „   **SUPERBA.** Similar to the preceding but deeper colour .. .. each 6d.
  „   **COCCINEUM PLENUM.** Bright scarlet flowers   .. per doz. 5s. ; each 6d.

GEUM MRS. BRADSHAW. A novelty of sterling merit, with semi-double flowers, fully 2 in. across, freely produced, on long stems, flowering from June to Oct. .. each 1s.
GYPSOPHILA PANICULATA. A fine border plant, valuable for cutting .. each 6d.
  „   **FL. PL.** A pure white, double-flowered, of the well-known G. paniculata. Valuable for cutting, one of the best recent introductions   ..   .. each 9d.
  „   **REPENS MONSTROSA.** A fine variety for cutting, flowers pure white, and nearly double size of type .. doz. 6s. ; each 9d.
HELENIUM AUTUMNALE. .. .. each 9d.
  „   **GRANDICEPHALUM STRIATUM.** Large deep orange flowers, irregularly striped and blotched with crimson ; very erect robust habit   .. per doz. 5s. ; each 6d.
  „   **CUPREUM.** A sterling novelty of recent introduction, flowering from June onwards; deep coppery-crimson flowers, often striped with yellow, splendid for cutting. Height three feet .. each 6d.
  „   **PUMILUM.** Beautiful Autumn-blooming plant, eighteen inches high, bearing a profusion of bright yellow flowers .. each 6d.
  „   **MAGNIFICUM.** This forms immense heads of soft yellow flowers, two to three inches across. In flower through Summer until late Autumn .. each 6d.
  „   **RIVERTON GEM (new).** Brilliant terracotta red. A continuous bloomer from Aug. to end of Oct. 3—4 ft. each 1s. 6d.
  „   **BOLANDERI.** Pale yellow flowers, with brown discs. Height 2½ feet each 6d.
HELIANTHUS, GOLDEN BOUQUET. Rich golden yellow. Height four feet ; very free flowering   .. .. each 6d.
  „   **LAETIFLORUS.** Semi-double flowers
       per doz. 5s. ; each 6d.
  „   **MISS MELLISH.** Much larger flower than Lætiflorus. Height six feet each 6d.
  „   **RIGIDUS.** One of the best. Rich golden yellow flowers with a black disc each 6d.
  „   **SOLEIL D'OR.** A fine variety, with deep orange-yellow double flowers
       per doz. 5s. ; each 6d.
  „   **SPARSIFOLIUS (new).** By far the finest of perennial Sunflowers, bearing very large, bright yellow flowers, with several rows of pointed petals. Ht. 6 to 8 feet. each 1s. 6d.
  „   **TOMENTOSUS.** A most distinct and characteristic plant, growing about four feet. The flowers are of a rich golden yellow, and three inches across   each 6d.
HELIOPSIS B. LADHAMS. Orange-yellow flowers, medium size, a showy plant, vigorous grower. Ht. 4—5 ft. each 6d.
HELLEBORUS NIGER (Christmas Rose). Fine, pure white, abundant bloomer
  per doz. 10s. 6d. & 15s. ; each 1s. & 1s. 6d.
HEMEROCALLIS (Day Lily). Handsome for clumps on the border
  „   **AURANTIACA.** Large orange-yellow flowers. Height two feet .. each 9d.
  „   **MAJOR.** Flowers large, trumpet shape, of a deep orange colour. Height 3 ft.   ..   ..   .. each 9d.
  „   **FLAVA.** Large umbels of beautiful Lily-like flowers of a bright yellow colour
       per doz. 4s. 6d. ; each 6d.
  „   **FULVA.** Bronzy orange, shading to crimson   .. per doz. 4s. 6d. ; each 6d.
  „   **KWANSO FL. PL.** Broad foliage and rich bronzy yellow flowers. Height four feet   ..   ..   .. each 9d.
  „   **THUNBERGI.** Bright yellow each 6d.
HEPATICAS ANGULOSA. Sky blue ; beautiful
  „   **TRILOBA ALBA.** Single white per doz. 7s. 6d. ; each 9d.
  „   **CÆRULEA.** Single blue per doz. 5s. ; each 6d.

HEUCHERA SANGUINEA GRANDIFLORA. Brilliant scarlet ; a gem for cutting
       per doz. 5s. ; each 6d.
  „   **SANGUINEA SPLENDENS.** A bright variety of H. Sanguinea .. each 1s.
  „   **WALKERI.** One of the finest varieties ; flowers large, of an intense rich crimson, produced very freely   .. each 1s.
  „   **MACRANTHA.** Loose panicles of white flowers   ..   .. each 6d.
  „   **EDGE HALL HYBRID.** Large rose-coloured flowers. A very fine variety. Eighteen inches   ..   .. each 9d.
IBERIS SEMPERVIRENS SUPERBA. A fine hardy Candytuft, with pure white flowers ; first class for dry rockeries .. each 9d.
INCARVILLEA DELAVAYI. Height about 2½ feet, with large Allamanda-like flowers of lovely crimson purple colour each 6d. & 9d.
  „   **GRANDIFLORA.** A grand variety of recent introduction, very large, deep rosy-crimson flowers, with pale yellow throat. Very fine   doz. 10s. 6d. ; each 1s.
INULA GLANDULOSA. A fine hardy plant, growing about two feet high, and bearing large single, Helianthus-like yellow flowers
       per doz. 5s. ; each 6d.

IRIS GERMANICA.

We have a fine collection of these beautiful flowers, which may be planted any time from September to March.

IRIS GERMANICA ADONIS. Erect petal blue, drooping petals velvety purple-veined white.
       each 9d.
  „   **ALBA.** White   ..   .. each 6d.
  „   **AUREA.** Golden-yellow .. each 6d.
  „   **BLUE SKY**   ..   .. each 6d.
  „   **DARIUS.** Chrome yellow .. each 6d.
  „   **FLAVESCENS.** Light primrose ea. 6d.
  „   **GRACCHUS.** Pale yellow .. each 6d.
  „   **MAORI KING.** Golden yellow each 1s.
  „   **MME. CHEREAU.** Pale blue each 1s.
  „   **NEGLECTA.** Dark velvety purple, reticulated white   .. each 9d.
  „   **NE PLUS ULTRA.** Chrome yellow, with purplish crimson   .. each 6d.
  „   **PRINCESS OF WALES.** White, very handsome   ..   .. each 6d.

THALICTRUM AQUILEGIÆFOLIUM.

Hardy Perennial Flowering Plants (continued).

PÆONY CANDIDISSIMA.

IRIS GERMANICA PALLIDA DALMATICA (true). A magnificent variety, producing very large beautiful flowers of a lovely pale lavender blue colour. The finest of all the blue varieties per doz. 10s. 6d. ; each 1s.
,, **QUEEN OF MAY.** Rosy lilac, veined yellow, a very fine and distinct form each 1s.
,, **ROWLANDIANA.** Lavender, drooping petals white veined purple each 1s.
,, **VICTORIA.** Erect petal white, blotched purplish blue .. .. each 1s.
,, **PUMILA ATRO CŒRULEA.** Flowers large, with purplish blue .. each 6d.
,, **CŒRULEA.** Flowers large, pale blue, tinged purple .. .. each 6d.
,, **LUTEA MACULATA.** Pale yellow ea. 9d.
,, **PURPUREA.** Large purple flowers, very free .. per doz. 7s. 6d. ; each 1s.
,, **FŒTIDISSIMA.** Bright evergreen foliage, large seed pods with bright red seeds ea. 6d.
,, **OCHROLEUCA MAGNIFICA.** A noble species, with large white and yellow flowers. Three to four feet .. Clumps, each 1s.
,, **AUREA.** Yellow variety of the preceding .. .. each 1s.
,, **STYLOSA.** A lovely Winter-flowering species, having beautiful light-blue flowers, with yellow blotches, produced in January ; as it blooms so early, should be protected or planted in a warm, sheltered spot ; near the sea it does well .. each 6d.
,, **KÆMPFERI.** Large, splendidly coloured flowers of grand effect. A warm, moist situation is the best. These are an important group of early Iris, quite distinct from any other, of strong, vigorous growth, stems stout and branching. Choice mixed. each 6d. ; per doz. 4s. 6d.
Splendid named sorts 9s., 12s., and 18s. doz.
LATHYRUS LATIFOLIUS, WHITE PEARL. A superb well-known Everlasting Pea. With very large pure white flowers double the size of those of the old variety each 1s.
,, **ALBUS (The White Everlasting Pea).** Useful hardy climber. Height 6 feet, June to September .. doz. 8s ; each 9d
LITHOSPERUM PROSTRATUM. Blue each 9d.
,, **"Heavenly Blue"** .. each 1s. 6d.
LUPINUS ARBOREUS (The Tree Lupin). Yellow. Height five feet .. each 6d.

LUPINUS ARBOREUS SNOW QUEEN. Pure white. Ht. 5 ft. per doz. 7s. 6d. ; each 9d.
,, **POLYPHYLLUS MOERHEIMI.** A grand variety, with stately spikes of rose and white flowers, good for cutting and fine for borders .. .. each 1s.
,, ,, Blue .. .. .. 6d.
,, ,, **ALBUS.** White .. .. 6d.
,, ,, **ROSEUS.** A charming variety of the perennial Lupin, perfectly hardy, flowers of a soft rose-pink colour, which darken with age and are produced in great profusion per doz. 7s. 6d. ; each 9d.
LYCHNIS CHALCEDONICA. Height about three feet. Brilliant scarlet, very showy
 per doz. 5s. ; each 6d.
,, **DIOICA RUBRA PLENA.** Heads of double rosy crimson flowers ; very pretty each 6d.
,, **VISCARIA SPLENDENS PLENA.** A distinct variety ; large double, brilliant rose-coloured flowers per doz. 5s. ; each 6d.
MORINA LONGIFOLIA. Rosettes of deep green spiny foliage and stout spikes, three feet high, of rose-coloured flowers each 6d.
MYOSOTIS DISSITIFLORA. Large blue flowers. Ht. six inches. per 100 12s. ; per doz. 2s. 6d.
,, **ROYAL BLUE.** Dense tufts, with sky blue flowers .. per doz. 2s. 6d.
,, **SEMPERFLORENS.** Perpetual flowering Forget-me-not, sky-blue flowers ; requires a damp situation per doz. 4s. 6d.
ŒNOTHERA ACAULIS VERA. A beautiful dwarf-growing species, with large white flowers .. per doz. 5s. ; each 6d.
,, **MACROCARPA.** A trailing mass of foliage covered with large soft yellow flowers .. per doz. 5s. ; each 6d.
,, **FRUTICOSA MAJOR.** Height two feet, with deep golden yellow flowers ; a first class hardy plant per doz. 5s. ; each 6d.
OREOCOME CANDOLLEI. White flowers, with handsome, graceful foliage. Height five feet .. .. .. each 9d.
PAMPAS GRASS. Beautiful white plumes each 1s. 6d. and 2s. 6d.
PHYSALIS FRANCHETTI (Winter Cherry). A new giant species, growing 1½ to 2 feet high, very showy .. per doz. 5s. ; each 6d.
PINK PROGRESS (new). Rosy mauve, very large flowers and strongly scented ; useful for pot culture .. per doz. 7s. 6d. ; each 9d.
POTENTILLA ATRO-SANGUINEA. Dark crimson .. .. .. each 6d.
PRIMULA COCKBURNIANA. A beautiful Chinese species with orange-coloured flowers. Height 9 inches .. .. each 1s.

PÆONIES.

Well-known magnificent hardy border plants, producing immense blooms of the most charming colours. Many of the varieties are deliciously scented ; will thrive in almost any soil or situation, but to be planted well should be planted in an open position and where they are not likely to be disturbed for a few years. We have a fine collection of these.
PÆONIES, DOUBLE. 24 of the best varieties per doz. 6s.
,, **Unnamed Varieties** .. .. per doz. 6s.
,, **SINGLE.** Choice sorts per doz. 10s 6d ; each 1s
PAPAVER NUDICAULE (Iceland Poppies). Most beautiful hardy flowers. Height 1 ft.
,, ,, **Bright pale yellow** doz. 4s. ; each 6d.
,, ,, **ALBUM.** Pure white doz. 4s. ; each 6d.
,, ,, **MINIATUM.** Brilliant orange scarlet per doz. 4s. ; each 6d.
,, **ORIENTALE. BLUSH QUEEN.** Blush pink, deep purple blotches .. each 1s.
,, **BRACTEATUM.** Deep blood crimson and black blotch .. .. each 6d.
,, **MAHONEY.** Very dark crimson ea. 1s.

PAPAVER ORIENTALE. (Iceland Poppies).
MRS. MARSH. Crimson scarlet, white blotch .. .. .. each 1s.
,, **MRS. PERRY.** A peculiar shade of orange chrome. Height five feet each 1s.
,, **PRINCE OF ORANGE.** Orange scarlet each 9d.
,, **SALMON QUEEN.** Lovely salmon scarlet .. .. .. each 9d.
,, **SILVER QUEEN.** Lovely silvery white with a very faint blush hue .. each 9d.

PERENNIAL PHLOXES

Magnificent large-flowered varieties, blooming from July to October. Our collection includes many of the finest of recent introduction.

PHLOXES. Splendid varieties with names, our selection. per doz. 6s. ; per 100, 40s.
,, **COQUELICOT.** The brightest of scarlet with purple eye .. each 9d.
,, **ETNA.** Brilliant scarlet, very fine each 1s.
,, **EUGENIE-DANZANVILLERS.** Soft lilac, white centre .. per doz. 5s. ; each 6d.
,, **GRUPPEN KONINGEN.** Lovely pale rose with carmine eye, very large flowers each 1s. 6d.
,, **IRIS.** Violet blue, very fine .. each 6d.
,, **LE MADHI.** Rich violet blue each 1s.
,, **TAPIS BLANC.** Pure white, only one foot high .. .. .. each 1s.
PHLOXES IN POTS, excepting those priced per doz. 5s. ; each 6d.
Some varieties from ground per doz. 6s. 6d. ; each 9d.
POLEMONIUM CŒRULEUM VARIEGATUM. A variegated form of Jacob's Ladder. Height two feet .. .. each 1s.
PYRETHRUMS, DOUBLE-FLOWERED. Strong plants, choice named, our selection, including the finest sorts per doz. 4s. 6d. & 6s.
SINGLE-FLOWERED. In brilliant varieties to name .. .. per doz. 4s. 6d.
RUDBECKIA LACINIATA FL. PL. (Golden Glow). Large double golden yellow flowers per doz. 5s. ; each 6d.
,, **LÆVIGATA.** Large yellow flowers, produced late in Autumn. Height 4—5 ft. each 6d.
,, **NEWMANII.** Flowers golden yellow with black centres per doz. 5s. ; each 6d.

PERENNIAL PHLOX.

Hardy Perennial Flowering Plants *(continued)*.

RUDBECKIA MAXIMA. The flowers are a deep golden yellow with black centres each 9d.
,, **PURPUREA.** Height two feet; large purplish flowers with black centres; very striking .. each 9d.; each 6d.
SCABIOSA CAUCASICA. Large, handsome, pale lilac blue flowers per doz. 5s.; each 6d.
,, ,, **ALBA.** A pure white variety of the beautiful Scabiosa Caucasica each 9d.
SEDUM TELEPHINUM. Pink. Height 1½ feet each 6d.
,, **SPECTABILE.** Rosy head, fine heads each 6d.
SENECIO PULCHER. Purplish crimson with yellow centre. 3 ft. high doz. 5s.; each 6d.
SIDALCEA. Rosy Gem. This is a distinct and pleasing plant, producing long, graceful spikes of bright rosy flowers. 4 ft. each 6d.
SOLIDAGO ALTISSIMA. A fine showy plant about 4½ feet high, with large panicles of deep golden yellow flowers each 6d.
SPIRÆA ARUNCUS. A handsome stately-growing border plant, from three to five feet high, with magnificent plumes of creamy white flowers .. each 9d.
,, ,, **KNEIFFI.** The most graceful of this class; large plumes of white flowers with finely divided foliage .. each 1s.

SPIRÆA ASTILBOIDES. A beautiful species, about two feet high, producing dense plumes of feathery white flowers; grows in pots or borders per doz. 5s.; each 6d.
,, **FILIPENDULA FL. PL.** Corymbs of double white flowers and pretty foliage per doz. 5s.; each 6d.
STOKESIA CYANEA. Lavender-blue flowers, three inches across. Height 2 ft. each 9d.
THALICTRUM ADIANTIFOLIUM (The Maiden-hair Thalictrum). A beautiful plant rivalling Maiden-hair Fern in delicacy of foliage, and quite hardy doz. 7s. 6d.; each 9d.
,, **AQUILEGIÆFOLIUM.** Large plume-like flowers .. .. .. each 6d.
,, **DELAVAYI.** Attractive rose-coloured drooping flowers, and pretty glaucous green foliage. Height two feet .. each 1s.
TRITOMA CORALLINA. Brilliant scarlet, dwarf .. .. .. each 9d.
,, **GRANDUS.** Scarlet and yellow. Height 4 ft. .. .. .. each 9d.
,, **TUCKII.** Bright red, changing to yellow each 1s.
,, **UVARIA GRANDIFLORA.** One of the grandest of the group; large brilliant spikes of orange-red flowers .. each 6d.

TROLLIUS. Foliage and stems dark, flowers bright orange .. .. .. each 6d.
,, **EUROPÆUS (Potten's variety).** Splendid variety; flowers nearly double the size of the old "Europæus".. .. each 9d.
,, **ORANGE GLOBE.** Very large, deep orange flowers; strong grower and free bloomer .. .. .. each 9d.
TROPÆOLUM SPECIOSUM. Producing a blaze of scarlet flowers in late Summer and Autumn; it grows rapidly .. each 9d.
,, **TUBEROSUM.** Showy scarlet and yellow flowers, does well on poor soil .. each 6d.
VERBASCUM PANNOSUM. Tall spikes of bright yellow flowers, large woolly leaves. Height 5 ft. .. .. each 6d.
,, **CALEDONIA.** Grand spike of sulphur, shaded lake flowers. Four feet each 9d.
WALLFLOWERS—Strong, transplanted.
Blood Red .. per doz. 9d.; per 100 5s.
Cloth of Gold .. ,, 9d.; ,, 5s.
Double German
Golden Monarch .. 1s.; ,, 7s. 6d.
Vulcan .. .. ,, 9d.; ,, 5s
BROMPTON STOCKS, Mixed
per 100 10s. 6d.; per doz. 1s. 6d.

DANIELS' SPECIAL COLLECTIONS OF HARDY FLOWERING PLANTS.

We have much pleasure in recommending the following collections, which contain a very choice selection of the above, specially arranged for a brilliant and varied display of colour and a long continuance of bloom in the open garden.

COLLECTION A. 100 in 50 fine varieties, our selection **25s. 0d.**	**COLLECTION C.** 50 in 25 fine varieties, our selection **15s. 0d.**
COLLECTION B. 50 in 50 fine varieties, our selection **17s. 0d.**	**COLLECTION D.** 25 in 25 fine varieties, our selection **8s. 6d.**

Our own selection, per doz. 4s. 6d., 6s., and 9s.   All strong established plants from single pots, carriage Free.

PLANTS SUITABLE FOR ROCKWORK.

ALYSSUM SAXATILE COMPACTA. Yellow, dwarf .. per doz. 3s.; each 4d.
,, **FL. FL.** Golden yellow doz. 5s.; ea. 6d
ARABIS ALBIDA. Pure white, very floriferous
,, **ALPINA FL. PL.** Pure white per doz. 4s.; each 6d.
,, **VARIEGATA.** A capital edging plant. Height six inches. Suitable for rockwork .. per doz. 5s.; each 6d.
ARENARIA BALEARICA. White flowers per doz. 5s.; each 6d.
,, **PURPURESCENS.** Forming dense growths and sheets of purple flowers. Height 3 inches .. .. per doz. 5s.; each 6d.
ARNEBIA ECHIOIDES (Prophet Plant). ea. 1s.
ASTER ALPINUS. Blue, six inches each 6d.
AUBRIETIA DR. MULES. Rich purple, profuse bloomer .. per doz. 5s.; each 6d.
,, **FIRE KING.** Crimson, distinct and grand .. .. per doz. 5s.; each 6d.
,, **HENDERSONII.** Dark violet purple per doz. 5s.; each 6d.
,, **LEICHTLINII.** Rich crimson, very profuse .. .. per doz. 5s.; each 6d.
,, **PERKINSII.** Rich purple flowers with large white eye .. .. each 9d.
AURICULAS, ALPINE. Choice Seedlings. Self-coloured and laced .. per doz. 3s. 6d.
CAMPANULA CARPATICA. Beautiful sky blue per doz. 5s.; each 6d.
,, **ALBA.** .. per doz. 5s.; each 6d.
,, **TURBINATA.** Very free-flowering per doz. 7s. 6d.; each 9d.
,, **PUSILLA** syn. *Pumilla*. Pale blue, dwarf habit, very profuse. 3 inches .. each 6d.
CHEIRANTHUS ALPINUS. Dwarf species, flowers lemon yellow .. doz. 6d.; each 6d.
CYCLAMEN COUM, Red doz. 5s.; each 6d.
CYPRIPEDIUM SPECTABILE. The hardy lady slipper orchid each 2s. 6d. and 3s. 6d.

DAPHNE CNEORUM. Deliciously scented per doz. 18s.; each 1s. 6d.
DIANTHUS CÆSIUS. Glaucous green foliage, rosy pink flowers. Height 9 in. each 6d.
,, **GRANITICUS.** Tufts of dark spring foliage and myriads of rosy flowers on wiry stems, lasting in bloom for several months; very rare. Height 9 inches .. each 6d.
DRABA AIZOON. Yellow, very neat each 6d.
EPIMEDIUM NIVEUM. White flowers ea. 9d.
EPILOBIUM OBCORDATUM. Rosy crimson, fine for rockwork. Ht. 6 inches each 1s.
ERINUS ALPINUS. Bright rosy purple flowers. Height 4 inches .. .. each 6d.
,, **CARMINEUS.** Flowers of a rich carmine, rose colour. Height 4 inches .. each 6d.
GENTIANA ACAULIS. Intense blue per doz. 5s.; each 6d.
GERANIUM SANGUINEUM, (Crane's Bill). Trailing habit .. per doz. 5s.; each 6d.
GYPSOPHILA PROSTRATA ROSEA. A charming variety, producing an abundance of delicate pink flowers .. .. each 6d.
HELIANTHEMUM (Sun Roses). In beautiful variety of colours .. .. each 6d.
HEPATICA ANGULOSA. Sky blue, beautiful per doz. 7s.; each 9d.
,, **TRILOBA ALBA.** Single white per doz. 7s. 6d.; each 9d.
,, ,, **CŒRULEA.** Single blue per doz. 5s.; each 6d.
,, ,, **RUBRA.** Single red per doz. 7s. 6d.; each 9d.
IBERIS SAXATILIS. White, very free each 6d.
IRIS PUMILA. Beautiful dwarf-growing varieties, only six or eight inches high, very early. Choice named sorts per doz. 5s.; each 6d.
NIEREMBERGIA RIVULARIS (The Cup Flower). Thick carpet of foliage covered during Summer with large creamy-white flowers. Height 3 inches .. per doz. 5s.; each 6d.

ONONIS ROTUNDIFOLIA. A neat shrubby bush, bearing bright rose, pea-shaped flowers. Height 1½ feet .. each 6d.
ONOSMA TAURICA. *(Golden Drop).* Very sweet .. .. .. each 1s. 3d.
PHLOX SUBULATA. All the best sorts, distinct .. .. .. each 6d.
POLYGALA CHAMÆBUXUS. White, compact silvery 6 in. high .. .. each 1s. 6d.
SAXIFRAGA AIZOON. White, compact silvery rosettes .. per doz. 5s.; each 6d.
,, **CERATOPHYLLA.** White flowers on dark green foliage per doz. 5s.; each 6d.
,, **GUILDFORD SEEDLING.** One of the best of the mossy section, with bright crimson flowers; height 6 inches. each 6d.
,, **LINGULATA** White .. each 6d.
,, **MUSCOIDES ATROPURPUREA.** Cushions of red flowers .. per doz. 5s.; each 6d.
,, **OPPOSITIFOLIA ROSEA** each 6d.
SEDUM ACRE. Dense green, yellow each 6d.
,, **ALBA.** White .. .. .. 6d.
,, **KAMTSCHATICUM,** Yellow .. 9d.
TIARELLA CORDIFOLIA (Foam Flower). Feathery white flowers, height 1 ft. ea. 6d.
TUNICA SAXIFRAGA FL. PL. A pretty rock plant with pink double flowers, a neat little Alpine, lasting in flower from June till Autumn .. .. .. each 1s.
VERBENA VENOSA. The hardiest of Verbenas, deep violet flowers; height one foot each 6d.
VERONICA PROSTRATA. Deep blue, one of the best .. .. per doz. 5s.; each 6d.
,, **REPENS.** Compact tufts with blue flowers .. .. per doz. 5s.; each 6d.
VIOLAS. All the best sorts for bedding and rock planting per doz. 6d.; 100, 12s.
VIOLA GRACILIS. A lovely species with violet flowers .. per doz. 3s.; each 6d.
,, **CORNUTA "G. WERNING."** Deep blue flowers .. per doz. 3s.; each 6d.

Our own Selection, per doz. 4s. 6d. and 6s.; per 100, 21s. and 30s.

CARNATIONS—Perpetual, Border, &c.

The Perpetual or Tree Carnations form a beautiful free-flowering class for Winter and early Spring blooming under glass. They are invaluable as cut flowers for Bouquets, Button-holes, &c. Will thrive in any moderately heated greenhouse. The plants we offer are all growing in five-inch pots and are in bud and bloom.

Perpetual Carnations.

Strong plants in 5-inch pots, our own selection from the following list. Per doz. 15s. and 18s.
Young plants in 3-inch pots, ready in March, per doz. 6s.

	each s. d.	per doz. s. d.
AFTERGLOW. Rosy cerise, large and shapely flowers	1 6	16 6
BEACON. Light orange scarlet, very sweet	1 6	16 6
BLACK CHIEF. Deep velvety crimson, sweetly scented	1 6	16 6
BRITANNIA. Crimson scarlet, one of the best reds ..	1 6	16 6
CAROLA. Very dark crimson, large and sweet ..	1 6	—
ENCHANTRESS. Soft pink shade, perfect form ..	1 6	16 6
FORTUNA. Pale chrome yellow, strong and free ..	1 6	16 6
HARLOWARDEN. Very rich crimson, and sweetly scented	1 6	16 6
LADY BOUNTIFUL. Glistening white, very good ..	1 6	16 6
MAY DAY (new). A delightful flesh pink	2 6	—
MRS. C. W. WARD. Rose cerise shade of pink ..	2 0	—
MRS. H. BURNETT. Salmon pink, rich clove fragrance	1 6	16 6
MRS. T. W. LAWSON. The famous cerise pink ..	1 6	16 6
ROSE PINK ENCHANTRESS. Lovely shade of pink ..	1 6	16 6
SCARLET GLOW. The best of all scarlets	2 0	—
WANOKA. Crimson, very free and good	1 6	—
WHITE ENCHANTRESS. One of the best	1 6	—
WHITE PERFECTION. A pure white, blooms very early	1 6	16 6
WINSOR. Silvery pink, strong, free and easy grower	1 6	16 6

Malmaison Varieties.

In 3-inch pots, 1s. each, 10s. 6d. doz. Our Selections, 9s. per doz.
In 5-inch pots, 1s. 6d. each, 16s. 6d. doz.

BLUSH WHITE. Very large and full.
DUCHESS OF WESTMINSTER. Deep rose-pink with salmon shades.
LADY GRIMSTON. A pinkish white marked rose, the flowers a good size.
MAGGIE HODGESON. Darkest of all Malmaisons.
NAUTILUS. Most charming flowers of a delicate flesh colour.
NELL GWYNNE. The finest pure white, strong grower, and good size.
PRIME MINISTER. Brilliant scarlet.
SOULT. Deep salmon, very fine.
YALLER GAL.

BORDER CARNATIONS AND PICOTEES.

	each—s. d.
ALICE CONNEGRAVE. Large, white, broad, smooth edged petals	0 6
CASSANDRA. A lovely delicate flesh colour	1 0
CECILIA. Large clear yellow of splendid form	1 0
CICERO. Salmon pink, good	0 9
COSMOS. Pink suffused heliotrope	0 9
DORA. Salmon pink, a very useful flower	0 6
DOREEN. White, marked clear heliotrope; one of the finest borders raised	1 0
DUCHESS OF FIFE. A delicate rosy pink, with fine flowers	0 6
FIREFLAME. Large, well-formed scarlet flowers ..	0 9
FRANCIS SAMUELSON. A very pleasing shade of apricot	0 9
FRANCIS PRIOR. Pure white with bluish purple edge ..	1 0
FRIAR TUCK. Dark crimson	0 9
GLEE MAIDEN. Yellow ground, beautifully margined and slightly marked with clear rose	1 0
GOLDFINCH. Yellow, large well-shaped flower ..	1 0
GRAHAM WHITE. Very dark crimson, strongly scented, very good	1 0
HEARNE. Carmine rose, robust growth	0 9
HELMSMAN. Pure white; very fine	1 0
HERCULES. Rich crimson, a splendid variety of good form	1 0
HEROINE. Good white, smooth edged petals ..	0 9
HOMER. A lovely delicate pink colour	0 9
LADY GREENALL. Rosy red, edged soft blush, extra fine	1 0
LADY HINDLIP. Brilliant crimson scarlet of perfect form	0 9
LORD ROBERTS. Clear yellow, very large flowers, strong grower and very free flowering	1 0
MISS CHANNELL. Heavy purple edged Picotee ..	0 9
MISS REEVES. Apricot, shaded crimson	0 9
MRS. CARRINGTON. Good dark crimson, medium sized flower ..	1 0

	each—s. d.
MRS. CHAS. DANIELS. Deep rosy pink, very sweet scented and of fine form	0 6
MRS. CUTBUSH. Bright scarlet	0 9
MRS. ELIZABETH SHIFFNER. Rich orange self, a most handsome variety	1 0
MRS. F. BRAZIER. Buff-yellow, striped rose pink ..	1 0
MRS. NICHOLSON. Deep rose pink; very fragrant ..	0 9
MRS. REYNOLDS HOLE. Salmon apricot; a fine variety ..	0 9
MRS. ROBERT MORTON. Apricot, well-shaped flowers ..	1 0
MYRTLE ROSE. Salmon red	1 0
NEDDA. White with bright salmon-red flowers ..	0 6
NONI. Salmon pink	0 9
NORA. Pale yellow ground edged crimson ..	0 9
NORICUM. White, very free flowering	0 9
OLD CRIMSON. The true old clove-scented variety, very dark crimson; deliciously scented	0 6
PINK BEAUTY. Salmon pink, very good	0 9
RABY CASTLE. Soft salmon pink, beautifully fringed petals ..	0 6
ROSALIE RIEFFEL. A remarkable fine Picotee of extraordinary size, the colour pure white with deep bright bluish margin ..	0 9
ROSIA. Deep scarlet, fine flower	1 0
ROY MORRIS. This is without doubt the brightest and largest scarlet border Carnation in commerce	1 0
RONY BUCHANAN. The best of the terra-cotta colours, petals well formed	1 0
SNOW ELF. Pure white, erect habit	0 9
STEPHANIE. White, finely edged with crimson purple ..	0 9
STROMBOLI. A dark silvery crimson, nearly black ..	1 0
TRIPOLI. Rich crimson	0 9
TROJAN. Pure white; an exquisite flower, good habit ..	1 0

Choice varieties, our own selection to name, per doz. 6s. and 9s.   25 for 17s. 6d.   Selected Border Carnations unnamed: all good double flowers in fine variety, strong plants, 6 for 2s. 6d.; per doz. 4s. 6d.

GREENHOUSE AND STOVE PLANTS.

ACACIA DRUMMONDII .. each 2s. 6d.
  „ **ARMATA** .. .. each 1s. 6d.
ADIANTUM CUNEATUM (Maiden-hair Fern)
    each 6d., 1s., and 2s. 6d.
  „ **FARLEYENSE.** Very fine variety
    each 1s. 6d., 2s. 6d., and 3s. 6d.
ALLAMANDA HENDERSONII. Beautiful stove
  plant .. .. each 2s. 6d. and 3s. 6d.
  „ **WILLIAMSII.** Very fine variety, flowers
  rich yellow, very free each 3s. 6d. and 5s.
ARALIA ELEGANTISSIMA .. each 5s.
  „ **GRACILLIMA.** A pretty variety, with
  finely cut leaves .. .. each 5s.
  „ **SIEBOLDII** .. each 1s. to 2s. 6d.
  „ **VARIEGATA.** Beautiful plant
    each 2s. 6d. and 3s. 6d.
  „ **VEITCHII.** Very graceful .. each 5s.

ARAUCARIA EXCELSA.

ARAUCARIA EXCELSA. A fine plant for the
conservatory .. each 2s. 6d. to 3s.
ASPARAGUS PLUMOSUS NANUS
    each 1s. 6d. and 2s. 6d.
  „ **SPRENGERI** each 1s. 6d. and 2s. 6d.
  „ **TENUISSIMUS** .. each 2s. 6d.
ASPIDISTRA LURIDA each 2s. 6d. and 3s. 6d.
  „ **VARIEGATA.** A very beautiful and
  distinct plant, with handsomely variegated
  foliage .. .. each 3s. 6d. and 5s.
AZALEA INDICA. We offer a choice collection,
  finest varieties, all in good healthy flowering
  plants, varying in height from about ten
  inches to sixteen inches from the pots.
  Our own selection
    per doz. 24s., 30s., 42s. ;
    each 2s. 6d., 3s. 6d. and 5s.
BEGONIA GLOIRE DE LORRAINE. A charm-
  ing Winter bloomer, bearing a profusion of
  bright pink flowers .. .. each 1s. 6d.
BEGONIAS, REX VARIETIES. Beautiful
  foliaged plants .. each 1s. 6d. and 2s. 0d.
BOUGAINVILLEA GLABRA SANDERIANA.
  The splendid new high-coloured variety
    each 1s. 6d. and 2s. 6d.
  „ **MAUD CHETTLEBOROUGH.** The largest
  and brightest flowers each 1s. 6d. to 3s. 6d.
CALADIUMS. The most beautiful varieties
    each 2s. 6d. and 3s. 6d.
CAMELLIA JAPONICA. Height of plants from
  pots varies from about a foot to eighteen
  inches. Our own selection ; in variety
    each 2s. 6d. and 3s. 6d.
CANNAS. Crozy's new dwarf varieties
    per doz. 6s., 9s. and 12s.
CAREX MARGINATA GRACILIS each 1s. 6d.
CHOISYA TERNATA .. .. each 1s. 6d.

CHOROZEMA LOWII .. each 2s. 6d.
CLERODENDRON BALFOURII. Useful climber
    each 1s. 6d. and 2s. 6d.
  „ **FALLAX.** Lovely bright red panicles of
  flowers, strong broad dark foliage ; very
  effective and useful .. each 1s. 6d.
COBÆA SCANDENS VARIEGATA. Useful
  greenhouse climber each 1s. 6d. and 2s. 6d.
COLEUS. In 8 most striking varieties, from
  cuttings, in 4½ in.pots ea. 9d.; per doz. 7s. 6d.
COPROSMA BAUERIANA VARIEGATA.
  Beautiful greenhouse plant with variegated
  foliage .. .. each 1s. 6d. and 2s. 6d.
CROTONS. A fine collection of choice sorts in
  nice young plants each 2s. 6d. and 3s. 6d.
CYPERUS ALTERNIFOLIUS .. each 1s.
DAPHNE INDICA ALBA. Pure white,
  deliciously scented variety
    each 2s. 6d. and 3s. 6d.
  „ **RUBRA.** Very sweet
    each 2s. 6d. and 3s. 6d.
DRACÆNA AUSTRALIS. Fine for furnishing
    each 1s. 6d. and 2s. 6d.
  „ **BRUANTII.** Excellent for rooms
    each 2s. 6d.
  „ **VARIEGATA** .. each 3s. 6d.
  „ **GODSEFFIANA.** Green foliage spotted
  with creamy white ; very distinct ea. 1s. 6d.
  „ **GRACILIS.** Very useful for decorative
  purposes .. each 2s. 6d. to 3s. 6d.
  „ **DOUCETTII.** A very beautiful variegated
  form of D. Australis. Graceful dark leaves
  with very distinct white stripe ; does well in
  a room .. .. each 5s. and 10s. 6d.
  „ **TERMINALIS.** Well-known and useful
  variety .. .. each 2s. to 3s. 6d.
ECCREMOCARPUS SCABER .. each 1s.
EUCALYPTUS CITRIODORA. Deliciously
  scented .. .. each 1s. and 1s. 6d.
EULALIA GRACILLIMA. One of the most
  elegant grasses, splendid pot plant each 1s.
  „ **ZEBRINA.** Very handsome .. each 1s.
EURYA LATIFOLIA VARIEGATA. Handsome
  decorative plant, with golden variegated
  foliage .. each 2s. 6d., 3s. 6d. and 5s.
FERNS, GREENHOUSE. A fine selection of the
  most useful and ornamental
    per doz. 6s., 9s., 12s. and 18s.
FICUS ELASTICA (India-rubber Plant)
    each 1s. 6d. and 2s. 6d.
  „ **VARIEGATA.** Beautifully varie-
  gated with yellow each 2s. 6d., 3s. 6d. and 5s.
GARDENIA INTERMEDIA. Well-known stove
  plants, pure white double flowers, deliciously
  scented .. .. each 2s. 6d. to 3s. 6d.
GENISTA FRAGRANS .. .. each 1s. 6d.
GERBERA SEEDLINGS. A beautiful plant for
  cool greenhouse, in colours varying orange,
  red, and pink .. .. each 1s. 6d.
GLOXINIAS. In beautiful variety
    strong plants, per doz. 9s. and 12s.
  „ **SEEDLINGS.** Very choice strain, ready
  in May .. .. per doz. 9s. 6d.
GREVILLEA ROBUSTA each 1s. and 1s. 6d.
HOYA CARNOSA. A charming stove climbing
  plant, producing wax-like flowers
    each 1s. 6d. and 2s.
HYDRANGEA, MADAME MOUILLÉRE. A
  very fine pure white variety for Easter
    each 2s.
LAPAGERIA ALBA. Lovely pure-white, wax-
  like flowers ; beautiful each 5s. and 7s. 6d.
  „ **ROSEA SUPERBA.** Beautiful climber for
  the cool greenhouse
    each 2s. 6d., 3s. 6d. and 5s.
MARGUERITE. BOULE DE REIGE. A fine
  Winter flow ring variety, flowers double, of
  pure glistening white ; an excellent variety
    each 1s. 6d.
MYRTLES (Myrtus). Broad and narrow leafed,
  nice young plants each 1s. to 1s. 6d.

OLEANDER (Nerium). Well-known Greenhouse Shrub, requiring plenty of moisture
  until after flowering. Flowers on well-
  ripened wood. Pink and White
    each 1s. 6d. and 2s. 6d.
PALMS. A nice assortment of choice plants
  suitable for the dinner-table and general
  decorative purposes, including :—Areca
  sapida, Cocos Weddelliana, Corypha
  Australis, Kentia Belmoreana, Kentia
  Canterburyana, Kentia Fosteriana, Latania
  Borbonica, etc. each 2s. 6d. to 21s.
PANDANUS VEITCHII VARIEGATUS
    each 2s. 6d. and 3s. 6d.
  „ **UTILIS** (The Screw Pine). each 2s. 6d.
PASSIFLORA PRINCEPS. Lovely stove
  climber, with large scarlet flowers
    each 2s. 6d. and 3s. 6d.
PLUMBAGO CAPENSIS. Blue .. each 1s.
  „ **ALBA** .. .. each 1s.
POINSETTIAS. Large scarlet flowers or bracts ;
  valuable for Winter decoration
    each 1s., 1s. 6d. and 2s. 6d.
PRIMULA OBCONICA GRANDIFLORA. A fine
  variety, with handsomely fringed flowers
    each 6d. and 1s.
RHODODENDRONS. All the best sorts for
  Greenhouses .. .. each 3s. 6d. to 5s.
SMILAX (Medeola asparagoides). Strong plants
    each 1s. and 1s. 6d.
SOLANUM JASMINOIDES. A greenhouse
  climber, beautiful white flowers each 1s. 6d.
STEPHANOTIS FLORIBUNDA
    each 2s. 6d. 3s. 6d., and 5s.
STREPTOCARPUS. White, and hybrids
    each 1s. and 1s. 6d.

DRACÆNA BRUANTII.

SWAINSONIA GALEGIFOLIA ALBA. Lovely
  clusters of pure white Pea-like flowers ;
  splendid for pillar or wall in the cool greenhouse .. .. each 1s. to 2s. 6d.
  „ **SPLENDENS.** Lovely bright carmine
  flowers .. each 1s. 6d. and 2s. 6d.
TACSONIA EXONIENSIS. A fine variety
    each 1s. 6d. and 2s. 6d.
  „ **VAN VOLXEMII.** Brilliant climber for
  the greenhouse each 1s. 6d. and 2s. 6d.
TECOMA JASMINOIDES. Valuable greenhouse
  climber .. .. each 1s. 6d.
GREENHOUSE PLANTS, in choice variety, our
  selection, per doz. 18s., 24s., 30s. and 40s.

MISCELLANEOUS BEDDING PLANTS.
READY FOR SENDING OUT IN MAY.

BEDDING GERANIUMS.
Autumn-struck good healthy plants from single pots.

This magnificent class of bedding plants is as popular as ever, and may fairly be considered as indispensable for garden decoration. The superb varieties, "King Edward VII." "Scarlet King," and "Paul Crampel," are especially recommended for their splendid effectiveness in the garden.

	per doz.	per 100
	s. d.	s. d.
KING EDWARD VII. (new). Deep crimson, very dwarf	4 0	—
SCARLET KING (new). Brilliant deep scarlet	3 6	24 0
PAUL CRAMPEL. Deep scarlet, very striking	3 6	24 0
HENRY JACOBY. Dark crimson, very fine	3 6	24 0
MASTER CHRISTINE. Beautiful clear pink	3 6	24 0
MRS. C. LOWESLY. Bright salmon-rose	3 6	24 0
VESUVIUS. Brilliant scarlet	3 0	21 0
QUEEN OF THE BELGIANS. Pure white, beautiful	3 6	24 0
CRYSTAL PALACE GEM. Beautiful	3 6	24 0
GOLDEN TRICOLOR. LADY CULLUM	4 0	30 0
,, MRS. HENRY COX. Splendid; gold		
crimson foliage	4 0	30 0
VERONA. Golden foliage, pink flowers, beautiful variety	4 0	
SILVER TRICOLOR. LASS O'GOWRIE. Charming variety	4 6	
,, MRS. JOHN CLUTTON. Very handsome	4 6	
SILVER-LEAVED. FLOWER OF SPRING. Very free	3 6	24 0
,, ,, MRS. MAPPIN. White flowers	4 0	30 0
,, PRINCE SILVERWINGS. Dark flowers	3 6	24 0
BRONZE-LEAVED. BLACK DOUGLAS. Scarlet blooms	4 0	30 0

From Mrs. M. MARTIN, Cock.

"The Mixed Single and Double Geraniums I have had from you two or three times were very good."

MISCELLANEOUS.
All strong young plants from single pots.

	per doz.	per 100
	s. d.	s. d.
BEGONIAS, FIBROUS-ROOTED, SEMPERFLORENS		
ROSEA. Rose, very pretty, dwarf-growing variety	2 6	17 6
,, VERNON COMPACTA. Bright red flowers, dark foliage	2 6	17 6
,, TUBEROUS-ROOTED. From single pots.		
Single-flowered, in beautiful variety	4 6	30 0
Double-flowered, selected, mixed	6 0	42 0
CANNAS. Fine varieties, mixed, strong plants	4 6	30 0
CANTERBURY BELLS. Mixed, strong plants	2 6	17 6
,, Mixed, from open ground	1 6	10 6
CALCEOLARIA, GOLDEN GEM. A fine bedder	3 0	21 0
CENTAUREA CANDIDISSIMA. Silvery white foliage	3 0	21 0
DAHLIAS, CACTUS-FLOWERED. Choice named sorts		
4s. 6d. and	6 0	—
,, POMPONE. Fine named sorts 3s. 6d. and	4 6	—
,, SINGLE-FLOWERED. Our Selection	4 6	—
,, NEW PÆONY-FLOWERED. Six beautiful varieties. Our Selection, including Snow White	2 6	—
FOXGLOVES	1 6	10 6
HELIOTROPES. Choice named sorts for bedding	3 0	21 0
HOLLYHOCKS. Choice mixed Seedlings	3 6	—
,, In six choice colours; separate	4 6	—
LOBELIAS, KING OF THE BLUES. Dark blue	1 6	10 6
,, TRIUMPH. Dark blue with white eye	2 6	17 6
,, WHITE PERFECTION. Fine white	2 6	17 6
MARGUERITES. White, from single pots	3 0	21 0
PELARGONIUMS. Ivy-leaved, beautiful varieties, named	4 6	—
PENTSTEMONS. Beautiful free-flowering plants, throwing up handsome spikes of bloom from July till late Autumn. Height about 18 inches.		
Choice named varieties from our fine collection, 3 6.		
SALVIA, "PRIDE OF ZURICH." Brilliant scarlet	4 0	30 0
SWEET WILLIAMS.	1 0	7 6
VERBENAS. Brilliant scarlet, pink, white, blue or purple	3 6	24 0
,, In distinct colours from cuttings, mixed	3 0	21 0

DOUBLE DAISIES.

LARGE CRIMSON, double	per 100, 16s. ; per doz. 2s. 6d.	
LARGE WHITE, double	per 100, 16s. ; per doz. 2s. 6d.	
LARGE PINK, double	per 100, 12s. ; per doz. 2s. 6d.	

MYOSOTIS. (FORGET-ME-NOTS.)
Well-known beautiful flowers, indispensable for Spring gardening; tufts from open ground.

PALUSTRIS SEMPERFLORENS. Sky blue flowers per doz. 4s. 6d.

DISSITIFLORA. Beautiful variety, bright blue per 100, 12s. ; per doz. 2s. 6d.

ROYAL BLUE. Deep blue, long sprays per 100, 12s. ; per doz. 2s. 6d.

OUR GUINEA HAMPER
OF CHOICE BEDDING PLANTS.

We annually sell large numbers of these Collections, which contain the very liberal assortment named below. As, however, provision must be made for supplying in accordance with the list given, we shall be glad if our customers will kindly send in their orders as early as convenient.

30 Geraniums, assorted	6 Chrysanthemums
12 Verbenas, assorted	6 Dahlias, named
12 Calceolarias, yellow	6 Fuchsias, named
24 Pyrethrum, Golden Feather	6 Phloxes, choice perennial
18 Lobelias, dark blue	6 Heliotropes
12 Petunias, mixed	4 Pentstemons
12 Pansies or Violas	12 Hardy Flowering Plants

Half the above quantity 11s. 6d. ; double quantity 40s.

No Charge for Hampers or Packing. Ready for delivery in May. Orders executed in same rotation as received.

We do not pay the Carriage of these Collections.

MISCELLANEOUS SPRING-FLOWERING PLANTS.
BEDDING VIOLAS.

AMY BARR. Dark pink, with deeply veined white centre.
BULLION. Bright golden yellow, free bloomer.
CRIMSON BEDDER. Bright violet, shading to dark purple.
DUCHESS OF FIFE. Light primrose, distinctly edged blue.
ETHEL BAXTER. Rich crimson purple.
JOHN QUARTON. Light mauve self, beautiful colour for bedding ; highly recommended.
KITTY HAY. Deep yellow self, one of the best bedders.

MARY McLEAN. A lovely blue rayless self, best blue for bedding.
OSBORNE WHITE. Pure white, clear yellow eye.
PRIMROSE DAME. Primrose self, slightly rayed ; first class.
PURPLE KING. Rich dark purple.
ROLPH. Light bluish violet, heavily rayed, useful colour for bedding.
SEA GULL. Pure white, rayless, one of the best bedders.
WM. NEIL. Light lilac, a pleasing effective variety, being quite distinct.

We offer strong plants of the above, per 100, 15s. ; per doz. 2s. 6d. ; each 3d.

PRIMROSES AND POLYANTHUSES.

A beautiful and indispensable class of brilliant Spring-flowering plants, blooming at the same time as Narcissi and many other bulbs ; the single-flowered Hybrid Primroses include the most beautiful shades of crimson, scarlet rose, &c., to pure white.

SINGLE, MIXED HYBRIDS. Very fine and brilliant. Strong Seedlings per 100, 17s. 6d. ; per doz. 2s. 6d.
POLYANTHUS, GOLD-LACED. Fine seedlings .. per doz. 3s.
POLYANTHUS-PRIMROSE. Large-flowered hybrids in splendid mixture per 100, 21s. ; per doz. 3s.

PRIMROSES.—Double, White, Lilac, Yellow .. .. ..

POLYANTHUS-PRIMROSE. Large-flowered yellow and orange shades, very beautiful varieties .. .. per doz. 4s. 6d.
G. F. WILSON'S SINGLE BLUE. A very fine selected strain of the most beautiful dark violet blue flowers ; splendid per doz. 5s. ; each 6d.
PRIMROSE, MISS MASSEY. Dark crimson per doz. 4s. 6d. ; each 6d.
.. .. per doz. 4s. 6d. ; each 6d.

GARDEN PINKS.

	per doz.—s. d.
ASCOT. Soft fleshy pink, with deep carmine centre ; erect habit	3 6
EARLY BLUSH. Blush pink, large double fringed flowers	3 0
ERNEST. Lacing rich ruby red ; large flowers	3 6
ERNEST LADHAMS. Blush, fine claret centre ; extra large	3 0
EURYDICE. Rosy red lacing ; a very fine variety	4 0
GLORIOSA. Pale pink colour, very powerfully scented ; large flower each 9d.	7 6
HER MAJESTY. One of the finest and best White Garden Pinks	3 0

	per doz.—s. d.
MRS. SINKINS. Large pure white flowers ; very fragrant	3 0
OLD DOUBLE WHITE FRINGED. Very sweet	2 6
PADDINGTON. Deep rose, dark centre, edged fringed	3 0
PROGRESS. Rosy mauve, perpetual flowering, also useful for pot culture .. .. each 9d.	7 6
SAM BARLOW. White, with crimson centre ; very free bloomer	3 6
SARAH. Dark velvety red, laced	3 0

Choice named varieties. Our selection, per doz., 3s. ; per 100, 21s.

NYMPHÆA ALBIDA.

HARDY WATER LILIES.

Foremost among the best Aquatics are Nymphæas or Water Lilies, of which there are a number of new varieties of great merit, which are wonderfully free flowering, producing flowers of almost every shade—white, cream, yellow, rose and red—and blooming from May to October. They are quite hardy, and can be successfully grown in tubs sunk in the ground. They may be planted from March to June, and should be planted in shallow baskets in rich loam to give them a start, and sunk overhead in water. A fast-running stream is not satisfactory for them.

	each—s. d.
NYMPHÆA CANDIDISSIMA, VAR. PLENISSIMA (WATER LILY). Very large, double white, extra fine	3 6
" " **ROSEA.** Bright carmine rose, orange stamens, very fragrant ; first-rate variety	3 6
" " **ALBIDA.** Large milky white flowers, tinted with pale pink ; very free	3 6
" " **SULPHUREA GRANDIFLORA.** Large sulphur coloured flowers ; very fine	3 6
" " **SANGUINEA.** Large bright crimson, changing to deep blood red. Centre light orange red ; an exceedingly good variety	3 6
COMMON WHITE WATER LILY. Strong roots	2 6

The above six varieties are all large-flowering and which we consider the best. We have others in stock, names and prices on application.

BOG PLANTS.

Suitable for the margins of water, bogs, damp beds, &c.

	s. d.
ARUNDO DONAX (The Great Reed). A grand ornamental bamboo-like grass. Likes a moist spot	1 0
" " **FOL. VARIEG.** Having beautiful green foliage, striped white. Height 4 feet	1 0
BAMBOOS, in variety. See page 137.	
GUNNERA SCABRA. A most handsome and imposing foliage plant, requiring plenty of room. Strong plants	2 0

MISCELLANEOUS SEEDLING & OTHER PLANTS,
FOR BEDDING, &c.

Well-grown transplanted Seedlings of the following can be supplied during May and June at moderate prices as below—**CARRIAGE PAID.**

NEMESIA.

	per doz.	per 100
	s. d.	s. d.
ASTERS, DANIELS' GIANT OSTRICH PLUME. Mixed } A fine class	0 6	3 6
" " " White } for exhibition	0 6	3 6
" **COMET.** Choicest mixed } Excellent for cut flowers	0 6	3 6
" " Pure white }	0 6	3 6
" **VICTORIA.** Choice mixed } Beautiful for bedding	0 6	3 6
" " Pure white }	0 6	3 6
ANTIRRHINUM, DAPHNE. Rose and white	1 0	6 6
" **AURORA.** Scarlet, white throat	1 0	6 6
" **NIOBE.** Dark crimson, white throat	1 0	6 6
" **BLACK PRINCE.** Dark maroon crimson	1 0	6 6
" **GOLDEN QUEEN.** Pure yellow	1 0	6 6
" **WHITE QUEEN.** White, very fine	1 0	6 6
" **TOM THUMB.** Scarlet } Dwarf-growing, only about	1 0	6 0
" " White } 6 inches.	1 0	6 0
" " Rose } First-class for edgings of	1 0	6 0
" " Yellow } beds or borders.	1 0	6 0
" " Mixed }	1 0	6 0
" Tall Varieties, choice mixed, very fine, height 2 feet	1 0	6 0
CARNATIONS, MARGARET. New large-flowered double, mixed	1 6	10 6
COSMOS. Mixed Seedlings	1 6	10 6
DIANTHUS HEDDEWIGI. Fine mixed, double	1 0	6 0
HELIOTROPE. Large-flowered hybrids, choice mixed	1 6	10 6
KOCHIA TRICOPHYLLA (Summer Cypress), fine decorative plant	1 0	7 6
MYOSOTIS DISSITIFLORA (Seedlings). Beautiful variety, bright blue	1 0	6 0
NEMESIA STRUMOSA GRANDIFLORA. Choice mixed	1 0	7 6
NICOTIANA AFFINIS. Long white tubular flowers, sweet scented	1 0	7 6
" **SANDERÆ** hybrids, mixed, very showy	1 6	10 6
PANSIES, DANIELS' PRIZE BLOTCHED. Magnificent strain	1 6	10 6
" **BLUE KING.** Bright blue, good bedder	1 0	6 0
PENTSTEMONS. Large-flowered hybrids, choice mixed	1 6	10 6
PETUNIAS. Large-flowered, single, very fine strain	1 6	10 6
" Dwarf bedding, rosy carmine	1 6	10 6
PHLOX DRUMMONDI. Finest sorts, mixed	0 6	3 6
PYRETHRUM, GOLDEN FEATHER. Useful for edging	0 6	3 6
STOCKS, DANIELS' LARGE-FLOWERED TEN-WEEK. Choice mixed	0 6	3 6
" " " White	0 6	3 6
" **BROMPTON**	1 0	7 6
VERBENAS. Large-flowered hybrids, splendid mixed	1 6	10 6
" Red, white and pink, from cuttings	3 0	21 0
ZINNIAS. Large-flowered double, finest mixed	1 0	7 6

SEEDLING PLANTS OF CHOICE FLORISTS' FLOWERS, &c.
READY IN JULY AND AUGUST.

	per doz.	per 100			per doz.	per 100
	s. d.	s. d.			s. d.	s. d.
CALCEOLARIAS. Very choice strain	1 6	10 6	**PRIMULAS, BLUE.** Very fine strain		2 6	—
CARNATIONS. Choicest double ; fine	1 6	10 6	" **CHOICEST MIXED**		1 6	10 6
CINERARIAS. From a grand strain	1 6	10 6	" **STELLATA VARIETIES, MIXED**		1 6	10 6
PRIMULAS, CRIMSON KING	1 6	10 6	" **MALCOIDES.** Beautiful pink		1 6	10 6
" **ALBA MAGNIFICA**	2 6	—	**SCHIZANTHUS WISETONENSIS**		1 6	10 6

VIOLETS—(SWEET-SCENTED).

The plants we offer are strong, well-rooted, and with good flowering crowns. If planted out in May, when flowering is over, in good soil on a shady border, they will make fine clumps for lifting in Autumn, for blooming under glass.

SINGLE-FLOWERED VARIETIES.

	per doz.	each.
	s. d.	s. d.
ASKANIA (new). The finest winter flowering violet ; an improvement on "Princess of Wales," the best of all single varieties	6 0	0 9
CYCLOPS. A very fine variety, with tall handsome foliage. The very large flowers are of a rich violet blue, the centre having fine little white petals	4 0	0 6
CALIFORNIA. Very large beautiful flowers on long stems	4 0	0 6
LA FRANCE. A superb variety. The flowers are of extra-ordinary size, of a beautiful purplish-blue	4 0	0 6
PRINCESS OF WALES. A grand variety, producing very large, beautifully formed, rich violet blue flowers	4 0	0 6
THE CZAR. Blue, large, an almost constant bloomer	3 0	0 4

DOUBLE-FLOWERED VARIETIES.

	per doz.	each.
	s. d.	s. d.
COUNT BRAZZA'S WHITE. Large, double, pure white flowers, deliciously scented	4 6	0 6
DE PARMA. Deliciously fragrant flowers of a delicate pale lavender purple, in great profusion	4 0	0 6
MADEMOISELLE BERTHA BARRON. A fine vigorous compact grower ; flowers of a beautiful indigo blue, deliciously scented	4 0	0 6
MARIE LOUISE. Large double flowers, rich lavender blue	4 0	0 6
MRS. ARTHUR (new). An improved "Marie Louise," the best of all double varieties	4 0	0 6
NEAPOLITAN. Lavender blue, flowers very large and double, profuse bloomer	4 0	0 6

This most important department of our business receives our very careful attention, and the designs we supply may be relied upon as being exceedingly artistic and in the prevailing fashion. To ensure all blooms being freshly gathered, we cultivate large quantities of Flowers especially for this work, and they will consequently travel well, and arrive at their destination in splendid condition.

All designs are most carefully packed in special cases, and our system is such that they will stand a journey of twenty-four hours, if necessary, and arrive quite fresh. It is much the best plan to keep the boxes closed and in a dark cool place until needed, so as to hold the moisture about the flowers, and thus retain their freshness for a longer period.

MEMORIAL WREATHS, CROSSES, ETC.

These are most beautiful and artistic in appearance, being made up of freshly cut flowers. They are composed either of white flowers, or with violets and other coloured blooms, according to the wishes of our customers.

We are continually asked to make up special designs and emblems for Masonic and other funerals, and we shall be most happy to be entrusted with instructions for these special occasions.

Each 5/-; 7/6; 10/6; 12/6; 15/-; 21/-; *31/6; 42/-, and upwards.

WEDDING AND OTHER BOUQUETS.

All orders for Bouquets are made up with the choicest flowers in season, and the important details of artistic arrangement and blending of colours receive most scrupulous attention; we are glad to say we invariably give the highest satisfaction.

It is most important that instructions should be given at the time of ordering, as to whether "Shower" or hand bouquets are desired, also the colours of the dresses which the flowers used in the Bridesmaids' Bouquets are to match.

BRIDES', PURE WHITE FLOWERS. Either with or without "Showers." Each 7/6 to 42/-.

BRIDESMAIDS', WHITE OR DELICATELY TINTED FLOWERS. Each 5/-; 7/6; 10/6; and upwards.

PRESENTATION BOUQUETS FOR BAZAARS, FETES, ETC. Each 7/6; 10/6; 21/-; and upwards.

GENTLEMEN'S BUTTONHOLES. White or coloured flowers. Each 6d, and 1s.; per doz. 5s. and 10s.

LADIES' SPRAYS. Beautifully made up to order, any colour. Each 1s. 6d. and 2s. 6d.

LOOSE CUT FLOWERS AND FERN. For Wedding, Altar Vases, and other decorations in liberal quantity in boxes. Each 2/6; 3/6; 5/-; 7/6; 10/6; 15/-; 21/-; 31/6, and 42/-.

IMPORTANT.

All orders are despatched promptly on receipt, if required, but customers should, if possible, give at least two days' clear notice before the flowers are required, also full particulars for forwarding. Orders from unknown Correspondents must be accompanied by remittance. We would suggest that orders for Wreaths, &c., should be marked URGENT on the Envelope.

TELEGRAPHIC ADDRESS—DANIELS, NORWICH.   TELEPHONES—38 & 39.

NEW CUSTOMERS.

We shall esteem it a favour if, when
sending order, you will kindly state below
THE NAME OF THE NEWSPAPER in which
you saw the advertisement that led you
to write for a Catalogue.

NAME OF ⎱
  PAPER ⎰ .....

Spring 1914. — ORDER SHEET — *Spring 1914.*

Please use this Form when sending an Order to

DANIELS BROS. LIMITED, (Seedsmen by Appointment to H.M. KING GEORGE V., and Nurserymen by Appointment to H.M. QUEEN ALEXANDRA) **NORWICH.**

Name..

Address...............

Post-town.................................County..

Nearest Railway Station }
and distance from same }

☞ •.• In filling up this form it is of the greatest importance to write clearly the Name and Address of the sender. **The Railway Station should always be given.**

Attention to this will save trouble, and prevent unnecessary delay.

For *Terms of Business, &c., see inside front cover of this Catalogue.*

CAUTION.—According to Post Office Regulations, Letters containing coin MUST be registered. The Registration Fee is only 2d., and this ensures a safe delivery.

Date.......................................1914

Please keep a note of the date of this order, and should it become necessary to write us further respecting it, kindly quote such date in subsequent correspondence.

AMOUNT ENCLOSED:

	£	s.	d.
Cheque			
Money Order ...			
Postal Order ...			
Coin or Stamps			
Total			

KITCHEN GARDEN SEEDS, POTATOES, &c.

QUANTITY REQUIRED.	NAMES OF ARTICLES.	PRICE.		QUANTITY REQUIRED.	NAMES OF ARTICLES.	PRICE.	
		s.	d.			s.	d.
	Carried forward, £				Carried forward, £		

☞ **Spaces for Flower Seeds, &c., &c., provided overleaf.**

t.	d.	No.	s.	d.	QUANTITY REQUIRED.		s.	d.
						Brought forward, £		

Carr. for. £   *Total,* £

INDEX.

Flower Seed in Alphabetical Order, see pages 75–108.

Flower Seed in Alphabetical Order, see pages 75–108.

TO GENTLEMEN REQUIRING GARDENERS, &c.

We keep a register of Gardeners seeking situations, and have almost always on our list the names of some first-class men requiring situations as head or under Gardeners, Farm Bailiffs, &c. We shall be happy to hear from any of our customers requiring such, and will at once put them in communication with men we consider suitable. We are always most careful to recommend only men of excellent character and good experience. We make no charge either to Customer or Gardener.

DIEU · ET · MON · DROIT

DANIELS BROS

· LIMITED ·

ILLUSTRATED GUIDE

FOR

Amateur Gardeners

· SPRING 1914 ·

DANIELS BROS L? SEED GROWERS & NURSERYMEN, NORWICH